# PLEDGE OF ASHES

Pledge of Ashes

Copyright © 2018 by Amy Sevan

Amz - Print - ISBN: 9781794102347

Cover Design by Teresa Sarmiento

NYLA Publishing

121 W 27th St., Suite 1201, New York, NY 10001

http://www.nyliterary.com

# PLEDGE OF ASHES

AMY SEVAN

*Valerie,*
*Enjoy the ride!.*

*AS.*

# DEDICATION

*To all those amazing characters, fictional and otherwise, who compelled
me write.
You know who you are.*

# EPIGRAPH

*"Speramus Meliora; Resurget Cineribus"*
*We hope for better things; it will arise from the ashes.*
*~ Detroit City Motto*

# CHAPTER ONE

The smell of burnt oil hung in the air, and rap music blasted from a boombox covered in grit and dust. An ancient Chevy Cavalier hoisted over her head, Sydney Hoven muscled a rusted drain plug. She was sweating under her Carhartt, but as soon as she stopped moving, the October chill would catch up with her. For all the activity going on around her, Syd worked alone. Partly her choice, partly their fear.

Her teeth gritted and bicep straining at the stubborn bolt, she startled when a hand tapped her shoulder.

Scowling, she flipped off the bolt and glanced over. Her ponytail definitely needed an adjustment, but she didn't care enough to fix it. "Yeah?"

Benji, one of the heavy techs, pointed behind him. "Ay, so, we got this 'vette over there. Guy says there's a knocking in the engine, but we can't find it. Thought maybe you could take a look."

Holding up her hands, Syd smiled at him. "Just an oil-change tech."

Benji huffed out a laugh, and his white teeth gleamed. "Never heard a larger load of bullshit, Hoven."

Benji was one of the guys who remembered Syd's father, a

Detroit muscle car legend. Benji was a couple years older than her, maybe pushing thirty, but Syd had been wrenching far longer than he had. Her dad had begun teaching her as soon as she could say the word 'horsepower.'

Still chuckling, Benji added, "You're just an oil-change tech, and I'ma 'bout to go get a pumpkin spice latte." He wagged his eyebrows and flashed his wide smile.

Syd studied him a moment more. "Yeah, sure, I'll take a look." She glared and pointed at the Cavalier. "I'll be back for you."

Benji shook his head. "How long you gonna change oil, Syd, seriously? Damn waste a' talent."

"It's all they had open. Gotta pay the bills, Benj." Syd shrugged.

Benji dropped his voice. "You got other skills."

Syd avoided his gaze and looked ahead, spotting the bright yellow Corvette like a beacon across the service bay. She assessed the performance add-ons, the generation of 'vette, the rumble of the engine. Likely, naturally aspirated. Which meant it wouldn't even almost touch her GTO. Or her dad's car. She smiled. The size-up was automatic.

"Changing oil is fine. It's better than...my other skills," Syd muttered.

Benji glanced at her but said nothing.

The memory flashed. The House of Cards, her previous employer, the lavender room where she gave psychic readings. The forlorn woman sinking into the chair across from her. Syd letting down her mental wall, giving out a *real* reading, instead of the 'you'll find love in the next six to twelve months' bullshit she and Brie had usually peddled. She'd wanted to help, knew she could, and that was her error.

Then the rest of it.

A chill slithered up her spine, and Syd rolled her shoulders.

Benji walked on her left, and he suddenly cut away toward the overcrowded bulletin board. "What the hell, guys?"

Damn. She'd forgotten, but Benji, under the gruff and grease, was actually pretty cool. For some reason she didn't understand, he had a soft spot for her.

He stomped over to the bulletin board and ripped down the newspaper clipping, then the invitation to the Baptist Church next to it. 'Devil worshippers can be saved' was written in red Sharpie. Syd smirked at that. Seriously? Inviting her to church? Like *that* was going to be enough to help her? Her mother had tried that for years. But, hey, maybe the Baptists had some special juice on the Catholics.

"Benj, don't bother," she said, not slowing her walk. "Not worth the effort."

"The hell, Syd." Benji looked around at the other mechanics studiously working and avoiding him, and his eyes blazed as he lifted the papers in the air. "Jus' quit it with this shit."

He ripped up the papers, letting them flutter to the ground and stalked back to her.

"Ignore it." Syd halted and watched him, wondering why he was so upset on her behalf. Every few days of the couple months she'd worked here, some version of this message had been on the bulletin board. She'd become immune. Why hadn't he?

"Nah, Syd, it ain't like that. You helped that family. Don' let anyone tell you different."

Syd shrugged. They could agree to disagree. Finding a missing child was one thing. Locating a body something totally different. She hadn't helped the family bring their little girl home. She'd given them the sick evidence of everything the girl had been through. The mother's shrill voice rang through Syd's mind for the bazillionth time. "*I wish I could still have my hope!*"

That's what Syd had done. Taken their hope and replaced it with horror.

Syd put a hand to her shoulder and massaged the tight rope of muscle leading to her neck. "Thanks, Benj, really. But you don't need to get involved in this. I'll change oil."

She turned around and nearly ran right into Nina, one of the cashiers. A blonde, pixie-cute glitter bubble in human form.

"Syd! I was looking for you!"

Syd managed a half-smile. Syd and Nina had known each other since high school, though they hadn't been friends. An overstep Nina seemed compelled to rectify, despite Syd's lukewarm reception to the requests to go out. In the ten years since she'd graduated, Syd hadn't spoken to anyone from the struggling Catholic high school she'd attended. Her life was vastly different now, punctuated not with a husband, career, or babies, but death, struggle and isolation. The last was by choice; the other two had been the impassive card dealer of life.

"Hey, so we're all going to The Dive tonight, you should come."

Syd glanced to Benj, who held up his hands. "I'm out, Syd. You white girls, you do your thing." He paused and nodded. "Although, you could use a night out."

She narrowed her eyes.

Smiling, he shrugged and sauntered away.

Traitor.

Syd turned back to Nina's smiling face.

Nina clapped with excitement. "What do you say? Come on, it'll be fun. Some of the crew from St. Clarence will be there. They'd love to see you!"

Nina kept up with the list of reasons Syd should come out. Syd filtered it out and stared at Nina, wondering alternately when she would stop to take a breath and why she seemed so excited. It wasn't like Syd had been overly friendly with her. Syd wasn't good at it, the friend thing. It didn't come naturally, though there were plenty of times in her life that having a shoulder to lean on would've come in damn handy.

Syd interrupted the chatter. "Why me?"

Nina blinked, stymied into silence for a moment. "Why *not* you?"

Syd could love the girl for that comment alone. It was a comment of commonality. All the same. No one different because of weird abilities. A vision of herself dancing with a drink in her hand popped in her head. Loud music thudding through her chest.

"Why *wouldn't* you want to come out with us? What do you do in that big old house all by yourself?"

If Nina was embarrassed at the reminder Syd's parents had died in a car crash a few years earlier, it didn't show. Syd had been adopted with no siblings. Then Detroit had heralded the economic crash before the rest of the country, and, despite her efforts, her dad's performance shop had gone the way of so many things in the city: the slow death of starvation. Abandonment. Nina was right; Syd didn't have much left.

"Just say 'yes' this once, and I won't bother you again, for, like, at least a month."

Syd tapped the wrench in her hand and studied the dirty work boots she wore. The reality was her psychic abilities were going nowhere. She controlled them, sure. She could build a life with them in one corner, and good things in the other. Separate. Always separate. She could do it. She had to. Her dad would've wanted that for her. Thinking of him, she smiled faintly and looked up to Nina. "Yeah, I'll go."

As Nina giggled with excitement and jumped up and down, Syd's psychic intuition growled despite the wall she'd built.

Nina's smile faded around the edges. "Damn, forgot the reason I came back here in the first place. Some lady up front wants to see you."

Syd's mental wall strained further, a trickle of intuition leaking through, sending a shiver down her back. Nah, just sweat. Just sweat. She reinforced her wall, and the feeling subsided.

"What does she want with me? No way I screwed up an oil change."

Nina shrugged. "I dunno. Didn't ask. But she asked for you specifically. She's waiting at the cashier's desk."

Syd rolled her shoulders, deposited the wrench with a *thunk*, and grabbed a shop towel, making a half-hearted attempt to get the grease off her hands. She strode up front, pushing into the front half of the dealership. She mostly avoided it, with its polished surfaces, purified air, and people with clean nails.

She leaned a hip against the cashier's reception desk, wiping her hands. "Someone wanted to see me?"

"I did."

Syd swiveled her head around. In the waiting area, a woman in a black trench coat stood up. Everything from her sensible pumps, to the hair pulled into a bun, to the piercing green eyes told Syd she'd never met the woman before.

Yet.

Something about the woman rang too familiar.

Syd crossed her arms over her chest and tamped down on her mental wall. She didn't encourage her psychic abilities. She never had. She'd never needed to. On the rare occasions she used them, they were there. Waiting to be used like an eager puppy. A scary, rabid puppy.

"Can I help you?" Syd asked in a voice that was decidedly unhelpful.

The expression on the woman's face didn't budge. She approached, heels clicking smartly on the ground. She stopped five feet away, her gaze cataloguing Syd.

Syd stayed leaned against the cashier's desk, but her breath stopped. Her mental wall strained. Something about this woman triggered all her abilities.

"What do you want?" Syd's voice was flat, and she gave zero fucks if she came across with none of the appropriate customer-centric attitude the dealership tried to ingrain in her. She wanted back in her service area; she wanted another shot at that stuck bolt.

The woman extended a hand with a business card. "My name is Dr. Blair Byrne."

Syd lifted a brow and accepted the card, glancing down.

"I'm studying gifted individuals."

Aaaaand...we're done.

Syd extended her hand back out. Byrne didn't make a move to retrieve the business card.

"I've upset you." The doctor shifted in her heels.

Syd cleared her throat. "Look, Doctor. You read the article in the paper about the missing girl, I get it. But I've got a good thing going here. I keep my...abilities...under lock and key, we have an agreement. They only come out to play when I say it's okay. And that's not often. I don't want anything more from them."

Dr. Byrne considered her. "You could make the world a better place. *We* could make the world a better place."

Yeah, once upon a time, Syd had thought she could, too. Now? She wasn't so sure the world wanted to be better. But the words of the doctor pulled at her, more than she cared to examine.

Sensing the hesitation, Byrne advanced a step. She reached a hand out but stalled before contact was made with Syd's arm.

"You may have capabilities you've never dreamed. I want to help you." The intelligence in Byrne's eyes was keen, like looking into a razor blade. "I want to understand how it works."

Syd held the business card between her fingers like it had teeth. "And I want a mint '69 Camaro Zl-1 in garnet red. We can't always get what we want," Syd retorted, then felt bad. The doctor was trying to help the world; she was wrenching on a Chevy. On a scale of zero to hero, the doctor was approaching cape status. She was...not.

"Look," Syd sighed, glancing down at the card. "I'm trying to find my life. I'm happy here, wrenching, paying the bills." Or almost paying the bills, she amended to herself. "Whatever capabilities I may have—"

"Lights turning on before you need them to, lost objects appearing—" the doctor cut in, watching Syd closely.

Syd's brow furrowed. "How did you— Actually, it doesn't matter."

Syd thought about the night out with Nina. How would this fit into the party conversation? Hey, you know what I did today? I went some doctor's lab and learned my mind is a freak of nature, cool, amiright?

Nope.

She had precious few people in her life that accepted her now.

If Syd had learned anything, it was that life was only worth the people you could trust. If no one trusted or cared about you? Life was damn empty. Hard fought, but she was finally accumulating people in her life. Brie. Benj. Nina. She wouldn't risk that. Not again.

She pushed the card farther out. "Sorry, Doc. I'm not who you're looking for."

The doctor inclined her head, lips pulled down, eyes averted. "Please. Keep it."

Fine, whatever. Syd slid the card into the pocket of her Carhartt and turned to go.

"Wait, Sydney." There was a plea in Dr. Byrne's voice.

She turned back to meet the doctor's eyes. "It's Syd. Only my mom ever called me Sydney."

Byrne blinked and swallowed, and her outstretched hand lowered. "I'm not the only one." Her voice stalled. She cleared her throat. "Please. Call me if anyone else comes looking for you."

Under her heavy coat, goosebumps rose. Syd's wall slipped. She cocked her head. "Who?"

Byrne shook her head, and her eyes took on a far-off look. "You wouldn't believe me. Just please, call me. I've tried to keep you away from them, but I think they know."

The look in Byrne's eyes...haunted. Syd swallowed.

"Whatever this is, Doc, I'm not a part of it." Trembling, Syd turned away.

She pushed against the steel door, the business card in her pocket weighing her down, slowing her steps.

Back to the safety of a stuck bolt.

# CHAPTER TWO

Detroit came alive under the cover of darkness. Noisy clubbers laughed raucously, ear-deadening bass pounded from cars with twenty-four-inch rims, and thick steam billowed from the sewer grates.

Syd slammed the door of her cab and glanced around. Damn straight she took someone else's ride. Like she'd risk door dings on the GTO? That's a firm *no*. The Dive, looking exactly as the name would imply, leered at her with its crumbling concrete and prison-style windows, the electronic music reverbing through her chest even as she stood outside. Her booted feet seemed content to plant themselves on the broken pavement, but she couldn't stay out here forever. In seconds, the October chill had already worked through her cropped leather jacket.

Feeling the buzz in her back pocket, Syd pulled out her phone. Nina's text was pleading. *Still coming, right? I'm @ the bar.* Syd stared a moment more and put the phone away.

So here she was. Attempting the friend thing. Syd rolled her shoulders.

She closed her eyes and drew her mental wall around her, thick like a shield. If she were the praying type, now would be the time. Instead, she shook out her hands and willed her feet forward. The club's scarred oak door was cold in her grip. She pulled and was assaulted by the beating sounds, alcoholic vapor, and the sensual movement of sex-about-to-happen on the dance floor.

Syd pushed forward, jostling as little as possible, but making slow progress nonetheless. A waitress with a skimpy outfit and bored expression split the crowd, and Syd made use of the trail she left.

A shiver of apprehension traveled through her, and she stalled, losing her path. People brushed at her from all sides, and her breath hitched.

She double-checked the lock on her mind, defied the warning bells in her head. Syd wouldn't stand up Nina for some weird psychic social anxiety. She'd said she'd go out, and she would. Step by step, inch by inch, her intuition, the part of herself she understood least, fought her.

She glanced down at her deep-red polished nails with a bit of grease around the edges that wouldn't come out for anything. Man, she wished she had stayed in the garage with her GTO. The car was a puzzle. Parts had specific places, and when you put them back just right, wonderful things happened. You went fast. Sometimes fast enough to forget.

One more step and the crowd cleared. Nina sat at the bar, leather-clad legs crossed as she laughed. Her friend's attention riveted on the man sitting next to her at the bar. Syd's intuition roared forth, itching inside her skull like locusts, cementing her to the spot.

Catching sight of Syd, Nina's eyes brightened, and she smiled.

Nina waved. "Syd! You actually came."

Syd focused entirely on her breath, pushing her intuition to the back of her head, locked behind the wall she'd worked so hard to build. Deep breath in. Out. The feeling of insects crawling in her head receded. She blinked. She could do this, she could totally do—

"You must be Sydney."

A shiver that had everything to do with sweaty bedsheets and reckless abandon traveled her body. That *voice*. Goosebumps flew down her arms, her cropped leather jacket no protection. She shifted her eyes several inches to the right.

Dark espresso hair, long enough to wave across his forehead. Like a master sculptor had created the work of a lifetime, his angular cheekbones cut a hard line. It fit the symmetry of his stubbled jaw perfectly. Broad shoulders, lean and muscular.

Syd swallowed. Her eyes traveled over him, drinking him in. Sweet Jesus.

His eyes glowed an ice blue in the darkened bar.

He stood, Syd's head tipped back, and she followed those eyes. He was a big man, nearly a foot taller than her five-foot-five. He straightened a leather jacket that would probably cost her an entire month's pay. Gorgeous and loaded. His lips tipped into a devastating smile, as if he knew the direction of her thoughts and liked it.

"Call me Syd," She didn't smile back. He was too...perfect. And her abilities still screamed at her. The din in her head was deafening. "Only my mother called me Sydney."

"I'm definitely not your mother." He extended a hand. "Devon."

The moment broke, hammer-to-glass style. The invitation for skin to skin contact felt like a threat. She was too on edge, her mental wall already straining. It made no sense, but she'd learned to trust it.

She put both hands in her back pockets.

Nina cleared her throat and hopped off the bar stool, standing between them. "Um, Syd has a...a *thing*, about touching strange people."

Devon's laugh erupted from his throat, deep, full, and unconcerned. "Strange?"

"No. *No*. I mean—" Nina's face fell. She glanced over at Syd for backup.

Syd couldn't place ground zero for the feeling, but she was beyond uncomfortable. Something about this man fired everything psychic in her into hyper-vigilance mode. She'd never felt anything like it. Swallowing, she could admit she'd never seen anything like him, either.

"No offense taken. I've been called far worse." Devon reached around to grab a tumbler of amber-colored liquid from the bar.

Because she was actively developing a pretext to ditch him and —let's not lie—avoiding the intensity of his eyes, Syd focused on his tumbler as he reached.

It slid across the bar the last four inches, coming to rest in his hand.

What the hell—

Suddenly Devon's shoulders pulled straight, and he gazed toward the door. "Ladies, excuse me."

Without waiting for any indication of assent, he strode between them. The crowd did a Red Sea imitation, parting for him even before he required it.

Keeping one eye on him, Syd said, "Let's go dance—or whatever we're supposed to do."

"Wha—" Nina breathed, her eyes locked on the direction Devon had gone.

Syd raised an eyebrow. "Starstruck fangirl is not a good look on you."

"Hey!" Nina punched Syd lightly in the shoulder.

Syd glanced at Devon's retreating back. "Maybe we should find a different bar?"

Nina pulled a small compact out of her purse along with some gloss, fluffed her pretty blonde waves. Ignoring her comment completely, Nina spoke to the compact. "Tell me he's not the hottest thing you've ever seen. I can't believe he's here alone. He was totally into you. Forgot all about me as soon as you walked up." Her tone was all light, teasing. "Bitch."

He was mind-bendingly sexy—Syd couldn't argue. Bringing back the memory of Devon made her tingly all over again. "He seems..." She wanted to say dangerous. But the only reasoning she had for her feeling wasn't a reason at all. It was all her intuition, the doorway to her psychic senses. It was easier to lock them away than to learn her limits. Easier and safer.

Nina stopped primping and grinned at Syd. "Hey, I'm not even mad. You need a good night out more than I do. I formally bequeath him to you." She waved her hand with an exaggerated flourish. "Consider it a damn fine 'thank you' for coming out tonight."

Syd glanced back the way Devon had gone. She knew, unequivocally, no one owned that man. That, and she was still dealing with her last one-nighter-turned-pseudo-stalker. "Nah, I don't need another Bryce. Maybe let's just go dance or whatever?"

Nina shook her head. "You've brushed off all my other invites. I've finally got you out of your garage, so chill. Enjoy a drink. I know your life hasn't been easy, I get it, I do. Time to live, Syd. The lay of a lifetime hits on you, and you wanna run for the hills? You don't want him, that's fine. Crazy, but fine. Be my wingman. Don't leave."

Syd studied Nina. That was a surprisingly insightful comment from the human glitter bubble. More, Nina was right. Spot on. Syd was here, what, five minutes and already had an excuse to bail?

She was in a crowded place, with a friend. What's the worst that could happen?

"You know what? You're right." Syd smiled, only mildly forced, and signaled the bartender.

He nodded to her and held up a finger.

"You still seeing Bryce?" Nina popped her lips twice and put the gloss back in her purse.

Syd sighed, dropped onto the bar stool Devon had vacated, and rolled her eyes. "We were never 'seeing' one another."

"That's not what he said." Nina lifted a well-sculpted brow.

Bryce wasn't exactly on the fast track for rocket scientist. But he was persistent, and she had been lonely.

"It was a one-night thing. He can't seem to get that straight."

Nina chuckled. "Isn't that supposed to be the guy's line?"

Syd shrugged, finding her mood lifting. "I may have been accused of being a tomboy once or twice."

"You? No!" Nina fake exclaimed. "With all the cars, and the wrenches... I can't imagine!"

They were laughing as the bartender arrived. Syd ordered a shot of Jager, wanting a little extra help to loosen her too tight conversation muscles. Nina ordered a Cosmo, heavy lime.

Syd tapped her fingers on the bar in time with the heavy beat. Things with Bryce were reaching a pitch she wasn't liking. Not at all. She kept saying no, but he kept right on coming.

The drinks arrived, and Nina sipped her martini while Syd tilted her chin to knock back her shot. The licorice liquor coated her throat, a satisfying burn slithered all the way to her stomach.

The crowd around them began to part. All her internal bells lit up again, rapid fire. Without glancing over, Syd knew exactly who to expect this time.

Devon's voice caressed the air, even in the loud bar, penetrating her ears. "Sorry for the rude departure, ladies, someone arrived... unexpectedly." His raspy voice was still the sound of sex, but there was strain in it.

What could irritate Mr. Perfection?

Instead of ignoring him, this time Syd stared openly. Where was the flaw in that perfection? There had to be a flaw. There had to be—ah, there it was. The set of his jaw, combined with the intensity of his eyes. He looked like a predator sizing up the degree of fight in his prey. Looks like her psychic sense might've had it right. This man was dangerous—but to her safety or her self-respect? Syd shivered but squared her shoulders to him.

Nina wheeled around, instantly back in flirt mode. "Hey." Her smile faltered a bit as Devon didn't bother to make eye contact. His attention was focused one hundred percent. On Syd.

Damn it. Some wingman.

He wasn't alone anymore.

"Lay off it, Dev." This voice wasn't so much Devon's sexy rasp as a deep grumble. Syd's eyes traveled up and to the left of Devon. Sandy blond hair just long enough to tuck behind his ears, eyes reminiscent of the warm waves of the Caribbean Sea. Sunglasses were tucked into the collar of a t-shirt that looked like it had been around the block a time or two. The shirt stretched over impressive pecs and two large biceps, followed by distressed jeans (not because he'd paid too much for them) and scuffed work boots. Not exactly club attire. Not that she was about to point that out to the beautiful, muscled man.

Syd stole a glance over at Nina and would've laughed out loud at the return of her love-struck expression if she hadn't started feeling itchy and uncomfortable again. Glancing back and forth between the two men, Syd assessed their features, the strength of their presence. Had to be—

"Brothers?" Syd asked.

Devon grimaced. "By blood only."

"What other kind is there?" Syd wondered aloud.

Devon's smile was bland. "The kind which inspires mutual respect and affection."

Syd blinked. What a jackass. She'd give anything to have family to bicker with again.

"Ladies." The other man stepped forward and dipped his head in greeting. "I'm Jack. I'll apologize in advance for my brother. He's—"

"—self-absorbed, cynical, mercenary..." Devon quipped with an amused smile.

"I was going to say a dick." Jack scowled.

Devon's smile turned up the wattage. "That, too."

She met Jack's kind eyes, which immediately slid over to Devon.

"This is something of an...unexpected reunion for Devon and I." Jack scanned the bar, his eyes roving over all that went on around them.

What caused the hyperawareness? Habit, maybe? Jack had the stiff presence of military.

Come to think of it—Syd turned her head back and forth, taking in the incongruence. The bar was a packed, throbbing mass of inebriation, except around the four of them. Like an invisible wall separated them from the crowd.

"Feels like centuries." Devon leaned on the bar and hailed the bartender. "Want a drink, J? Maybe something with a pretty little umbrella?"

Jack's lips pulled into a tight line. "I still don't drink."

"Check." Devon made the motion with his finger. "Add that to the boring-as-hell column of your personality."

The barbed banter pinged back and forth, and Syd's skin grew more and more prickly. She nudged Nina and looked meaningfully at the door. Despite the antipathy between the brothers, Nina shook her head and raised her eyebrows, mouthing, "No way."

Bad wingman, maybe, but no way Syd would leave her friend alone with these two. She was stuck. Syd wasn't the best friend to have, but, damn, she wanted to at least give it solid effort.

The bartender sauntered over, wiping his hands on a dishcloth that had seen cleaner days. "What'll you have?"

Devon smiled and pointed. "Hand me the bottle of Gentleman Jack and a couple tumblers."

Without hesitation, the bartender grabbed the bottle of top-shelf whiskey and set it before Devon along with two tumblers.

Tensing, Syd glanced at her friend. Nina adjusted her shirt for maximum cleavage, oblivious.

Jack cleared his throat loudly.

Devon tossed a bored expression over his shoulder and poured three fingers worth of the whiskey. "I'll pay for it, J." Devon withdrew several hundred-dollar bills and pushed them across the bar. "I'm picking up the tab for these ladies, too."

Syd stepped closer to him before she realized it. The words 'the hell you are' froze on her tongue. Being this close to him was electric, her whole body on fire, and she wanted to touch him. Badly. Her hand reached out, inches from his stubbled jaw, and he made no move to stop her. No, he wouldn't stop her, but that wasn't the test.

Reigning in her self-control, she pulled back. Her hand trembled. Devon's lips turned up the slightest degree. His intense eyes searched her face, like he was reassessing her.

Swallowing, she glanced back to Nina, chatting easily with Jack. Jack had one eye on her friend, the other trained on his brother.

Gesturing to the bartender, Devon watched her. She felt caught, ensnared. If she thrashed, she'd only make it harder to escape. His expression dared her: *thrash*. "What do you want, Syd?"

She *wanted* to walk away. That's the lie she told herself, anyway. He knew damn well what she wanted. It was laced in his question, in the way his body leaned toward her. So much more than a simple drink request, but she wasn't taking the bait. "World peace."

Devon laughed, and Syd wanted to wrap herself in the sound. "J and I, we're working on it." He raised the bottle of Gentleman and gestured with it to the bartender. "He won't go anywhere until you tell me what you want to drink."

The bartender made no response to the statement, and continued to stand there, waiting patiently, as if there weren't a line of irritated people calling for his services down the bar.

Nina spoke up from behind Syd. "I'll have some whiskey."

Syd cut her eyes toward her friend. Apparently, the barely-sipped Cosmo was forgotten.

Devon poured two fingers and handed it to Nina. His eyes never left Syd, which was starting to tick her off, but she wouldn't give him the satisfaction of looking away.

Syd finally said, "Shot of Jager."

Cocking an eyebrow, Devon's lips pulled down. "That's the shit you drink?" He jerked his head once, and the bartender turned to fill the order.

She smiled and winked at him. He didn't miss the sarcasm in her action. But instead of standing down, as she'd hoped he would, he smiled back. Dazzling, beautiful, it took her breath away for a moment. It wasn't just the smile; his arrogant mask slipped for a second, and she got a glimpse of what lay behind it.

Nina sipped the whiskey and covered a cough. "So, um, Devon, you want to dance?"

The smile bled from his face, so much that Syd wondered if she'd really seen it. With his blank mask back in place, Devon turned to Nina. Syd fought the urge, barely, to step in front of her friend. Out of the corner of her eye, Syd watched Jack's hands curl into fists at his side.

The moment hung.

Devon smiled, but it wasn't the same one he'd offered to Syd. "Why don't you go find someone else to dance with?" The air charged with electricity, acid dripped over all her nerves.

It was rude, and Syd was about to pop off a cutting response to this asshat—but Nina turned around and headed for the dance floor, leaving Syd behind. Her jaw dropped, and Syd turned to follow Nina, but Jack stepped in front of her. He may as well have been a brick wall, all that muscle and male, but his expression was pained.

From behind her, Devon spoke directly into her ear. "You stay with us." Like he expected compliance. Like he was used to getting it.

Syd faced him, picturing his surprised expression if she decided to use that whiskey bottle as a blunt instrument to the head.

Devon laughed and nodded to Jack. "I *like* her."

Not if you knew what I was thinking, Syd thought.

Devon's gaze shifted and skewered her to the spot. "Precisely because of that." Devon nudged the whiskey bottle toward her. "Go ahead. Give it a try."

She froze, and her mind emptied. She pulled herself up, a distant part of her reptilian brain, the part that prioritized survival above all else, kicked into high gear. It helped that this city was in her blood, and, when pressed, she could turn on Detroit-style survival skills.

Her heartbeat started to keep pace with the house music bumping in the bar. Options for her escape fast-forwarded through her mind.

His electric gaze traveled her body. "Tough girl exteriors always make for the most interesting soft spots." Devon returned the sarcastic wink she'd given him earlier.

Pissed now, Syd pulled her shoulders straight and kept her expression neutral, though her pulse pranced like a deer in flight. She couldn't help her words. "You won't be feeling any of my spots."

Devon took a healthy swallow of whiskey, his hooded eyes all heat. "I'll take that bet."

Once met, like a force of nature, she couldn't look away from his hard, cold eyes. The electricity in the air thickened again, making breathing a full-time job.

A vision of Devon, this man she didn't know and sure as hell didn't *like*, filled her mind to the brim. In her bed, on top of her. *Shit*. In the vision, Jack stood behind them, warm eyes turned hot as he watched. An unintentional moan passed her lips, while thought and speech left her, and her brain played out the vision. She was a passenger and, yeah, a part of her—the starved, isolated part—had absolutely no desire for the ride to stop.

Engulfed, the vision of Devon and Jack shut out any other thoughts. Devon easily supported his large body, arms corded with muscle, moving with the skill and grace of a man who puts his own satisfaction second. Over Devon's shoulder, she watched Jack stalk forward, stripping off his shirt, clearly ready to join the party.

Oh. My. *God*.

This was pure pleasure, unhurried, luxurious. Debilitating in its sensory completeness.

It was a lie.

And it was seriously out of character for her to play out her personal porno upon meeting a couple pretty faces. And bodies. Whatever. *Breathe.*

With focused effort, Syd imagined herself taking the vision, crumpling it up into a wad and throwing it away. All at once, the beat of electronic music and the bar's odor of sweat and alcohol came back, reality punching her hard. She sucked in a breath, her hand coming to her stomach.

Devon's eyes narrowed. Lines, the only imperfection in his face, appeared by his lips as they tightened.

Shaking and unable to help it, Syd stepped up to Jack, her neck craning back. "I'm leaving. You wanna stop me? You're going to have to get physical."

Jack put up his hands. "I wouldn't hurt— Look, can we just talk?"

*Talk?* Seriously? "Not a chance." Syd searched the dance floor, needing to find Nina and get the hell out of here.

Devon leaned against the bar, his tone amused. "White Knight crisis. What happens when your assigned damsel doesn't want to be saved? Do they cover that in Chivalry 101, J?"

Up close and as near to his personal space as Syd could be without crossing into dangerous territory, Jack's body tensed with a barely-heeled rage. "Shut up, Devon. You're making this more difficult. *Ei servient mi engel-wird—*"

Devon snarled from behind her. "Shut the hell up, *bruder.*"

She'd have to be stupid not to take a step back from the expression on Jack's face, but that would put her closer to Devon. And after that fantasy—that qualified as a horrible idea. Syd could sense him, like Devon was inside her head, a piece of her own body she was moving around. An itch she had no idea how to ease. She reinforced her mental wall, bricked it over and slammed it into place. The feeling receded, but now she couldn't sense Devon at all. And of all the weird things happening, Devon was the larger threat. No question.

"Move." Syd drew out the word, meeting Jack's eyes.

He captured the bridge of his nose with his fingers and stepped aside.

Not taking a moment to understand the change of heart, Syd pushed past him, toward the dance floor and Nina. One quick glance back, though, and Syd met Devon's cold eyes. Her body revolted, a tingling traveling bone deep. She needed to get The Dive in her rearview, but first she had to find Nina.

# CHAPTER THREE

D evon smiled as his brother stalked forward. Jack stopped inches from his face. Man, it was fan*tastic* to see getting a rise out of his twin was still Devon's personal gift.

Devon stood and closed the remaining distance between them, so close he could smell mint on his brother's breath. "Step off, J. Or we throw down in the middle of all these humans. You know I've got no problems with that. But maybe you do."

The bar patrons danced and writhed all around, compounding the tension thick between them.

With a growl, Jack pulled away.

Satisfied, Devon sat back down and took a healthy swallow of whiskey.

"Why did you have to be such an ass to her?" Jack demanded, gesturing the way Syd had fled.

"Why'd you have to break out the twin language?" Devon retorted. He drew in a breath, remembering he was the one who needed to do the pissing off. Jack getting under his skin wasn't on tonight's menu. Devon shrugged, forcing his shoulders to relax. "Besides, being an ass is kinda my thing."

"The language was ours, something only between us. I was

reminding you of your promise." Jack rubbed his eyes with his hand.

Devon laughed drily. "Long broken. What does it matter?"

Jack dropped his hand and stared at his brother. "It matters. Will *always* matter."

"Tell you what." Devon set down his drink and spread his hands wide. "Free shot."

"I'm not hitting you." But Jack's tone begged to differ. He wanted to. Of course he did. Violence was a hallmark of their fucked up brotherly love.

"Go ahead, J." Devon smiled wider. "Take the shot. You're wound tighter than a psych ward full of paranoids."

Jack was damn near quivering and then he let it fly, that beefy fist coming full speed ahead.

Devon didn't even blink. The impact snapped his head around. No lying, it took a second for the room-spinning to stop. Getting cold-cocked by a big sonofabitch like his brother was not on his bucket list, but Devon needed Jack off guard. He needed to figure out why the hell his brother was here in the first place. Invited or not, Jack would feel bad about the punch in five minutes or less. It was written somewhere in the White Knight Code of Ethics.

"This may be a personal best, inciting you to violence in under ten minutes." Devon massaged his jaw.

Jack snorted. "You're deliberately goading the woman we're supposed to protect. You deserve it."

"We?" Devon schooled his face back to his default disinterest. "Thought you had vowed never to work with me." Devon folded his arms and exaggerated a pouting face, which pulled at the site of fist-impact. "Ever again."

Jack opened his mouth, but his voice didn't cooperate. He tried again. "The Captain decreed it."

Devon dropped his agitated-child pose and narrowed his eyes. "You and your boy-band buddy Rafael on the outs? Why would he force you to work with me again?"

This made no sense. And it made Devon suspicious.

Jack looked away. "I don't question orders."

Devon chuckled. "Bet you'd rather be shackled and beaten than stuck here with me. I've always told you that dick doesn't give a damn about any of his soldiers. He's in it for himself, nobody else."

"Show some respect." Jack sank onto a barstool, eyes looking out over the crowd.

No doubt his brother was keeping tabs on Syd. She was why they were both here.

Much as Devon hated to admit it, verbally torturing Jack wasn't giving him the satisfaction it normally did. Perhaps he was out of practice at annoying the shit out of his twin. In Devon's defense, it had been one hundred eighty years since they'd seen each other. A long time, no question, but not nearly long enough to forget the bloody circumstances of their last meet. Or everything that had happened after.

Jack's shoulders slumped, and his eyes lacked shine. There had to be something serious in the works, an all-else-fails type of gig.

"So, the Archangel pulled you out of your ridiculously extended bereavement to work with me. Why bother?" Devon thrummed his fingers against the bar. "Protect one human woman? I got this."

They both knew how capable Devon was. And of what he was capable.

Jack cracked his knuckles. "I was told to protect her at any cost."

"Yeah, that didn't answer my question, baby bro. Why would Rafael assign us both?" Talk about overkill. Devon didn't want to consider the fact his boss thought he needed a chaperone. But it would follow. Dev and the Archangel Rafael had—what would Dr. Phil would say? Trust issues.

Jack's jaw clenched tight, his voice monotone. "I don't question orders."

Broken. Record. Damn, his brother was a predictable son of a bitch.

The bartender returned with Syd's shot of chilled Jager.

Devon lifted the Jager with a smile. "Here's to someone trying to kill Syd. Provide us good entertainment and, if we're lucky, bloody carnage." He poured the liquor down his throat and dropped the shot glass back to the bar with a grimace. "God, that shit's disgusting. Gotta teach that woman some better drinking habits."

Jack gripped the bar tight, like he needed the grounding. "We're supposed to protect her, not wish her ill."

That holier-than-thou attitude was nails on a fucking chalkboard. Always had been.

Devon gestured around the bar. "Protect her from what, exactly? You see any hellish creatures that need killing? Maybe the two most qualified soldiers in the Archangel's army need to protect her from a guy copping a feel on the dance floor? It's bullshit, J. Why her, why is she worth protecting?"

Jack's face tightened.

Devon took his time drawing in a breath. "Ah, I see."

Why should it surprise him the Archangel Rafael was playing favorites and keeping secrets? And Jack would always be the favorite. Had to be the whole 'moral code' thing. Devon never could commit to one.

Fine. Devon could play connect-the-dots himself. He'd never met a human able to resist his compulsion like Syd had. Hell, even he'd been pretty into that hot fantasy he'd implanted in Syd's beautiful, stubborn head. Was more than a little disappointed when she'd broken it. Disappointed and surprised. Devon had the ability to see through anyone's eyes. His angelically gifted powers weren't at all like Jack's, all muscle and warrior-skills. But Devon had the art of mind control down like Einstein understood $E=mc^2$.

"You keeping an eye on her?" Jack rested his forearms on the bar, staring straight ahead.

"Not until you tell me what you know."

Jack lifted his head and glared at Devon. "I won't allow you to compromise the mission."

Devon met the gaze, didn't flinch. "Me? I'm fully invested in living life. That means protecting her, which I *will* do, to the best of my considerable abilities." Devon poured more Gentleman Jack and lifted his tumbler, swished the liquid around. "You, on the other hand. If anyone's the weak link here, J, it's you. You've been out of the game a long time."

Jack turned away, but not before irritation and anger cleaved into something Devon had absolutely no desire to see. Some would say it was soul-deep grief. Devon called it weakness.

Devon chuckled. "Why don't you go find Syd? Tell her she now has a pair of super powered babysitters for some unknown reason. Try that. Let me know how it works out for you. If you hadn't noticed, Syd doesn't fit your damsel profile. She's strong."

Syd's face floated through his mind. Her emerald eyes masked something behind them. And since she'd kicked him out of her head, he didn't know what. Curiosity was a novelty for someone like him. Whatever she hid, it would drive Devon toward her until he could solve it. Puzzles needed to be solved. Solved and discarded to move on to more difficult puzzles. It had been a long, long time since he'd come across a puzzle, much less one he couldn't solve.

Jack rubbed at his eyes. "You have a better idea?"

Devon tapped his fingers against the bar. In his mind, he was playing Chopin on his favorite baby grand. "I already pitched it to her."

"What are you talking about?"

"Ménage, bro." Devon shrugged. "Keep her with us, alive, unaware, and very, *very* satisfied."

"What?" Jack breathed, his eyes going wide in shock. "You didn't—"

"Put a fantasy in her head of the three of us? Actually, yeah, I did. Don't worry, I had the starring role." Devon smiled. "She seemed into it for a minute—"

"You are...unbe*liev*able." Jack's face twisted into a disgusted grimace. "It's all a game to you. What happens when a demon shows up?"

Devon chuckled. "You've never fought a demon naked?"

Jack stood. "I'm going to find her."

Unconcerned, Devon gestured with the fifth of whiskey. "Go with God."

———

JACK PUNCHED OPEN the door to the bar's restroom, one hinge crying out at the abuse. The door banged off chipped tile, but the sound was lost to the throbbing bass. Or it would've, had he been any other bar patron. Humans couldn't hear like he could.

Jack massaged his temple and tried to steady the pounding in his chest.

God, Devon hadn't changed a bit in nearly two centuries. Scratch that, Devon was *worse* than he'd ever been. Coming here had been a mistake. Devon oozed egomaniacal, arrogant, reckless—

Pull it together.

Letting his hand drag down his features, Jack heaved out a breath.

He'd done thousands of tasks for the Archangel Rafael over the centuries, been the model after which all other Guardian soldiers were molded. The pressure of leaving, of breaking that mold had been gut-wrenching. Nothing, though, compared to the pain of losing her. *Elaine.*

Devon had one thing right. Jack wouldn't be here at all if Rafael hadn't strong-armed him. For the last ten years, the Archangel had let Jack mourn, seclude himself in the cabin he'd built for her, and bury himself in the grief of her loss.

Let this be a quick one, he prayed. The prayer was more out of habit than from expecting an answer. It had been a long time since God had answered a damn thing Jack had to say. And, yeah, he served faithfully in the Guardian army, but Jack deserved no special treatment. There were far better people than he who went with prayers unanswered.

Gathering his resolve, Jack pulled open the bathroom door and reentered the throbbing mass of half-drunk humans. Scanning the display of flesh, unease crept into the muscles of his shoulders. Syd was nowhere to be seen.

He had to keep her safe, complete this assignment. That's all he had to do. Then he'd never have to see Devon again. Rafael had promised him that, and so much more.

Just this one time.

One last time.

## CHAPTER FOUR

Three steps onto the dance floor, remnants of spilled drinks coated Syd's boots. The jostling of people dancing with abandon made her jumpy, and she looked around to try to anticipate who would knock into her next. Syd didn't go out of her way to be touched, but when her mental wall was in place, she was level; she could fake normal all day long. When she felt in control, yeah, it was fine, but tonight she didn't feel at all in control. Despite the crowding heat of bodies on the dance floor, she shivered in her leather jacket.

The fantasy of Devon and Jack flooded her mind again, and her feet stopped, like she couldn't walk and hold onto that visual simultaneously. Holy hell, what had that been about? Her little excursion with Bryce should've nixed the physical connection urge, at least for a while.

A beefy hand grabbed at her shoulder. The heavy scent of alcohol whiffed past her ear with the words. "Hey, let's dance."

Syd whipped around, afraid it might be Devon or Jack. Night-dark skin with warm brown eyes. Detroit was a divided city, notoriously so, but you'd never know it here. Piercings and body ink seemed to be the glue holding the clientele together, regardless of skin tone.

"I'm looking for my friend, pretty blonde..."

"Nina?"

Syd nodded, not surprised lots of people knew Nina. Nina was gregarious and pixie-cute. Why Nina had gone out of her way to try to befriend her was beyond Syd. But a part of her was grateful, even if the night had already turned disaster-worthy.

He nodded good-naturedly and pointed a finger behind Syd. "Love that girl. She's over there, dancing her ass off." He studied her with interest. "You a friend of hers?"

"Too early to tell," Syd half-yelled over the bass.

She shimmied her way through the dancers and stepped in front of Nina. "Hey, that was too weird, right—"

"Syd! So glad you could make it!" Nina hugged her and pulled back. Her smile faltered. "What's wrong?"

Syd opened her mouth to respond, but all that came out was a confused 'meh.'

"Don't just stand there, girl, dance!" Nina bumped her hips with the guy next to her.

"That guy, Devon, he was not—"

Nina cupped a hand to her ear. "Devon? Who's that?" She glanced around. "I don't know him."

Syd stopped, but the dance floor was all movement, and she became disoriented. Had she imagined the whole thing? Turning, she caught sight of Devon's espresso-dark hair right where she'd left him at the bar and knew she hadn't. But somehow, Nina seemed to not remember meeting Jack and Devon. How the hell was that possible? Answer: it wasn't.

Syd hedged. "Don't you want to leave? Those guys were—" She didn't have the right word.

Nina stopped dancing, and her lips pulled down. "What guys?" She pointed back to the group of four dancing around her. "These guys? They're harmless. Don't you remember them from high school? Zoe and Lucy are here, too."

Syd reached up and grabbed her neck in a moment of frustration.

"Hey, don't worry." Nina's face lit up, and she winked conspiratorially. "If you need to blow off some steam, Bryce said he might show up tonight. Seemed interested when I mentioned you might be here."

Seriously? Did the universe truly hate her *that* much?

Syd gave a weak smile. "Are you cool with these guys? I think...I think I'm going to go home."

"I'm fine." Nina searched Syd's face, and she stopped any pretext of dancing. The fun and party leaked out of her expression, replaced with concern. "Are you okay? This was supposed to finally be our opportunity to hang out."

Syd forced a smile. "Yeah, I'm...just not feeling well." She turned to go, but Nina grabbed her hand. The skin-to-skin contact caused a pulse of heat to travel up Syd's arm. Her mental wall slipped. Flashes of Nina's life pinged through Syd's skull, but before the images could grab hold, she pulled away and reinforced her mental wall.

"Bye, Nina."

Nina had to raise her voice to be heard. "Why do you want to be alone?"

Syd turned to go, even as the question echoed through her head. "I'll see you at the dealership on Monday."

The bar was more crowded since her arrival. Pushing her way out seemed to be the opposite goal of every other patron. Mercifully, the door appeared, and Syd couldn't exit quickly enough.

Taking a deep breath of the freezing air, she scanned Woodward Avenue for an idle cab. Hopes weren't high... She'd probably have to call for one this early in the night—

"Syd?"

Grimacing, she turned, hoping she was wrong. No such luck. Bryce strode up to her, hands shoved into his jeans, shoes polished to a sheen, blond hair bright against the dark of the night. Two of his closest friends, Zach and Adam, flanked him.

"You ain't leaving already, are you?" he asked.

Syd glanced back. "Hey, Bryce."

"You gotta let me buy you a drink." Bryce smiled. Anticipation in his eyes. "Yeah, come on, a drink to good times, hopefully some more good times."

She was so done with one-nighters.

"I'm calling a cab, Bryce. I'm heading home."

"Come on, Syd, stay. Nina said you guys were hanging out here tonight."

Zach leaned in and whispered to Bryce, who smiled wide and clapped Zach on the back. With a leer, Zach and Adam went into The Dive.

She folded her arms over her chest and turned away.

Bryce held up his hands. "Okay, Syd, whatever you want. Zach went in, he's ordering you a shot, and if your cab is here before he gets back, no drink. Otherwise say you'll have a drink with me. Just one."

Syd bristled at Bryce's tone. He was so used to getting what he wanted. His dogged persistence was part of the reason she had grown to like him. And then it became part of the reason he felt okay to pester her continually.

"Fine." She dialed the cab company and hugged her leather jacket tighter. Cab company said ten to fifteen minutes until someone would be there for her. Time ticked by. Slowly.

Zach sauntered out of the bar.

"Here's your shot." Bryce tapped her shoulder.

Reluctantly, she turned. Bryce stood there, his right arm outstretched with a double shot of something red.

She kept her arms by her sides. "What is it?"

Bryce smiled. "A Red-Headed Slut."

She opened her mouth to retort.

Bryce laughed. "Nah. Your hair's more...auburn or some shit. It's got Jager in it. Thought you'd like it." His smile faded. "Drink it, and let's let bygones be bygones."

Syd grabbed the shot from his hand.

"Go on," Bryce encouraged, "drink it."

Syd held the shot glass between her thumb and forefinger. "On one condition."

Bryce folded his arms across his chest. "A guy can't even buy you a drink without conditions?"

Syd extended the shot glass back to him.

He held up his hands in surrender. "What's the condition?"

"We're done. It was a fun night, but there's nothing long-term here."

Bryce chuckled, his eyes traveling her body. "Who ever said anything about long-term? I'm in the market for a fuck buddy, and you make a pretty good one of those."

Syd shook her head, the shot glass still extended back toward him.

Bryce grunted, a contorted mix of acquiescence and anger hiding out in his eyes. "Fine."

Syd ignored the dissension pounding through her brain. She shoved her psychic wall back in place, willed her mind to get on board with the plan. And the plan was titled 'No More Bryce.'

She chugged it. Fruity and thick with the chilled Jager. Not bad, actually.

Bryce smiled. "Atta girl." He took the shot glass from her and threw it against the brick of the bar, smashing it.

She jumped and took a step back.

Bryce hovered and tried to make idle conversation.

Syd watched Woodward for a bright yellow rescue vehicle to appear, keeping Bryce in her periphery. Like every other inhabitant of the city, the cab seemed to be on its own timetable.

Suddenly, Bryce was way too close, his face closing in, like he was going to kiss her.

She shoved him back, pissed. "What part of 'we're done' was unclear to you?"

Bryce's smirk fled his face and deep-seated rage rolled through his eyes. So fast, and then gone, making her wonder if she imagined it. He closed the distance. "You think you're better than me? That it?"

No, not really. She'd thought she needed companionship when she met Bryce. They could talk engine displacement and the pros and cons of super versus turbo charged all day long. She'd mistaken common interest for same wavelength.

She stepped back.

"After tonight, believe me, we're done," Bryce said.

Something...something in his voice. Syd shuddered, due to the cold or his words, she wasn't entirely sure. She took another step back, but the ground felt spongy beneath her. She tripped and caught herself against a lamppost. The ground spun, and her vision darkened to pass-out level. Her head felt too heavy to lift.

"Boy, Syd, looks like you're turning into a lightweight." Bryce wrapped one arm tightly around her waist. It kept her upright.

Oh, shit. Her heart pounded loudly in her ears, faster even than the frantic beat vibrating behind the doors to The Dive. Syd's head fell back against her shoulder, and she tried to open her lips to let out the scream buried deep in her lungs. Nothing happened.

"And hey, there's that cab you wanted. Mind if I share the ride?" Bryce's laugh melted and turned vicious in the dazed fabric of Syd's thoughts. Her lips thickened past speech, her eyelids drooped.

The yellow cab pulled up to the curb.

Another set of arms held her up. Her head lolled, and her vision blurred. Adam? Zach? She wasn't sure.

Damn it, she should've stayed home with the GTO.

# CHAPTER FIVE

Devon ignored the insistent internal knocking in his head. It could only mean one person. Jack. It was a unique feature of their relationship and as irritating as everything else about his brother.

Devon sighed from his position at the bar. The brunette who'd been shamelessly flirting with him tossed her hair back, gave her best *sure thing* smile. Sad the prospect wasn't at all appealing. He studied her clinically, as a sommelier might a common vintage.

The vision of Sydney underneath him flashed in his head, auburn hair fanned out, green eyes daring to meet his—

The knock came again.

"Sorry, sweetheart. Duty calls. *Go away.*" He laced compulsion into those last words, and, without another word, she turned and teetered off in her stilettos.

Inside his mind, he let his brother in and opened communication. As if hearing Jack in real life wasn't annoying enough, he could do without the surround sound in Devon's head.

*She's gone.* Jack's voice sounded concerned.

*Maybe she went home?* Devon suggested.

*I just saw a taxi leave with her and three other men. Did she arrive with them?*

He'd been watching her before she arrived at the bar. She'd arrived alone.

*No.*

Radio silence.

*No sarcastic retort? Feeling ill, Dev?*

*A bit,* he admitted. This couldn't be good. Devon got up from the bar and almost ran right into a woman. Black trench, calculating expression, forty-ish. Out of place in the bar. He moved to step around her. She moved with him.

Annoyed now. He sighed but mentally responded to Jack. *I'll track Syd. Be ready to ride when I find her.*

Jack's tone shifted distinctly into all business. *Copy that. Find her.*

Not a question. Devon was the best tracker Rafael had. Devon thought briefly of the alternative and all the fiery hellish punishment waiting if he didn't. *You know I will.*

Jack's presence in his head receded.

Devon tilted his head down and met the gaze of the woman in front of him. Her pale skin struck a heavy contrast with her dyed black hair. She didn't flinch when she met his eyes. Point for her.

The woman impeding his exit spoke, "Do you work for him?"

Devon's suspicion-o-meter pegged, his eyes narrowed. A quick scan of her mind showed her to be human without any taint of Hell, but he didn't have time to dig further than that. Which meant she wasn't a factor. Syd was the priority. He made a move to leave.

She grabbed his arm. "Leave her alone."

Devon stilled and met her gaze. "Let go of me before I do something you'll regret."

Her hand on his arm didn't budge. Her resolve tipped from impressive to irritating. And he did not have time for this shit.

Problem was, if he moved through space with her attached, she came with. And she was another human liability he did *not* need.

He compelled. Came as natural as his breath. *"Let go of me."*

Her hand sprung open, and her jaw dropped in surprise. "How did you—"

He didn't hear the rest. He willed his body through space, using Syd's mind like a homing device. Let that woman try to rectify what had happened, not like he gave a shit. He had more pressing problems.

Devon focused in with all his power on Syd's location. He'd been in her head recently, so he could pinpoint her easily. She was moving north. She wasn't conscious as evidenced by the darkness he processed trying to get in her head. He was blind as to her circumstance, except for the unconscious part, which didn't exactly bode well.

Rematerializing, he stood in the middle of a five-lane through-way. The light directly above him switched to yellow. The approaching cab slowed for the light. He walked up, put his hands on the hood, and made mental contact with the driver. White-knuckle grip on the wheel, mouth dropped open in surprise, the cabbie stared. Syd sat sandwiched between two men in the back-seat, her head lolled onto the shoulder of the one on her right, and her eyes firmly in the 'off' position. Another man was in the front passenger seat.

He compelled all the passengers to shut up and stay still.

With little effort, Devon penetrated the layer of the driver's conscious thought. *Turn down the street, pull the cab into the alley. Get out of the car and walk away.* Devon stepped out of the way and motioned with an 'after you' gesture.

The cabbie obeyed, running the red light. He turned down the nearest alley, left the driver's side door open, and walked away.

Devon flashed himself into the alley, in front of the cab. He reached out again to Sydney. Inside her head was an abnormally blank space. He couldn't say for certain, but his guess was drugged. That, or beaten unconscious. Either way? Not fucking cool. Failure in his mission meant Rafael could release him from service. And he was not getting taken out by three low-life thugs.

Fist. Open. Repeat. His left hand made the motion, over and over. Fist. Open. Repeat. Once his rage turned cold, Devon released the compulsion on all three men.

The passenger rear door popped open. The blond man who exited had cocky written all over his face. Probably a matching dumbass tattoo somewhere on his body in Chinese characters.

Cocky glanced back to Sydney. "This ain't your business, man."

Fist. Open. Repeat. "You are so wrong about that."

"What's it to you if we wanted to have a little fun?"

"Fun for who?" Devon rolled his head on his shoulders. "Call me old fashioned, but I like my women awake and active participants when I rock their world."

Devon sifted quickly through Cocky's memories... Hold it... *Bryce*. And he confirmed Bryce had indeed drugged Sydney. That, and he was planning all kinds of nasty.

"Take off before my boys get out of the car." Bryce sneered.

Devon smiled like someone had invited him to an amusement park. "Let's speed up the process." He shifted his gaze to the two men still in the car. "*Get out of the car.*"

With a slight glazing over of their eyes, the other two men obeyed. Sydney slumped down and disappeared from Devon's sight. Shit, she needed medical help.

Thrashing on these guys could wait. Briefly. Devon held up a finger. "*Stand there and wait patiently for your beating.*"

Making use of the two-way street, Devon reached out mentally to Jack. *Woodward Avenue and Eason Street. Behind the abandoned restaurant, in the alley. The human men drugged Sydney. I could use your skills, J.*

A moment of silence and Jack replied, *On it. I'm nearly there.*

Devon glanced back again to the cab. *Hurry it up.* Sydney's head was gone entirely from view, and didn't that make him twitchy. *Too bad you can't teleport.*

*Too bad you can't heal,* Jack retorted.

*Touché.* Devon's powers were entirely different from Jack's. And if Devon could do something nifty, chances were good Jack couldn't.

There was a second of pause, then Jack's concerned voice. *Don't kill them.*

Devon didn't justify answering that. Of course they were about to die. There had been only one instruction from the Archangel regarding Sydney: kill anything that threatens her. Probably Rafael had meant supernatural beasties, but humans could do their own brand of damage. Devon had been merely human once, so he was well-versed on the subject.

The three men stood in front of Devon wearing the blank expressions of the compelled.

A pickup truck turned into the alley, headlights outlining the scene. A moment later, the lights cut out and the weak glow from one ancient flood lamp provided the only relief from complete darkness. A door slammed, and Devon watched the massive form of his brother approach.

"Where is she?" Jack's gaze travelled the alley, his jaw clenched tight.

Devon nodded to the cab. Jack could heal that nasty concoction out of her veins. Probably have her up and about in a jiff.

Jack turned, walked over to the cab, and picked Sydney up, cradling her head against his broad chest. She could've been a body filled with air for the effort he needed to put behind it. "Remember what I said about killing them."

Devon waved dismissively. "Sydney still breathing?"

"Thready."

Jack's hands lit up with the power of his healing. That light was something to behold. Humans couldn't see it, but to Devon, Jack's skin looked like sunlight reflecting off the ocean. Everywhere Syd's skin touched Jack, it would tingle and draw out whatever poison the assholes had put in her. Question was, how much of a toll would it take on J? No free lunches applied across the supernatural border.

Devon hated to admit it, he really did, but there was no way

Sydney would die on Jack's watch. Let's hear it for another day on the fine planet Earth.

Devon turned his attention back to the compelled men. The men that had almost ended this assignment before it began. Wouldn't be any fun, though, if they couldn't fight back. He released them from his thrall. The men blinked and looked around. All kinds of 'what the hell' on their faces. Devon smiled lazily from about twenty feet away.

Bryce walked back to the cab and peered in. "What'd you do with Syd, man?"

Devon rolled his shoulders through his leather jacket. "My brother's taking care of her as we speak."

Bryce took a menacing step forward. "Never said we'd share her."

Devon raised his lip. "Never asked."

Bryce took another step. His buddies stepped in behind him. The greasy one on the left pulled a switchblade out of his jacket pocket. The crew cut on the right curled his fist.

"Guess a pretty boy like you always asks for permission before taking what he wants." Bryce sneered.

Devon couldn't help it. He threw his head back and guffawed. "Lemme get this straight. You think I'm pretty? Thanks for that. But polite? We haven't been properly introduced."

Greasy bolted toward Devon, leading with the sharp edge of the switch. Devon side-stepped him, hitting the man's forearm, causing his hand to spring open. Devon caught the blade on the way down. He pushed Greasy's back and used the man's forward momentum to send him hurtling headfirst into the crumbling brick of the restaurant where he dropped to all fours.

As predicted, Bryce roared with anger. "What's your problem, man? She ain't worth it. Worth a ride or two, but she's a psychic fucking train-wreck otherwise."

Psychic? Devon filed the knowledge away. Might explain her ability to resist his compulsion.

"Here. You'll need this." Devon tossed the blade back to Crew Cut.

Devon cast a quick glance back to the pickup.

Syd would be fine.

She had to be.

# CHAPTER SIX

S yd tried to open her eyes. So heavy. They were so heavy.

A deep voice rumbled through the fog in her head, vibrating all the way through her chest. "Easy, Syd. It'll take another minute."

She focused on trying to breathe, not panic, and, yeah, open her *eyes*. Every moment they felt a bit lighter. She was certain she had finally cracked them, but all her vision reported was darkness.

She moved her lips to speak, but the words were thick and mumbled. "Where am I?"

Her body shifted, not of her own accord, and that deep voice rumbled through her chest again. "Alleyway. Don't worry, though, we'll keep you safe."

Safe? *We?* She didn't feel safe... How did she get here? And possibly more to the point...where exactly was *here*?

Every moment brought more sensation, but clarity was a far cry away. Something warm and hard was behind her and covering her arms. Something cold and metal under her. Raised angry voices nearby.

Her senses adjusted slowly to the darkness.

"If you're feeling ready, you can put your shirt back on."

What!

She glanced down, and saw she only wore her lace cami top. Thank you, Jesus, her jeans were still on. She wanted to shiver, but she felt...warm. How could she feel—

Seated upright, her legs kicked out in a 'v' in front of her. Long, thick-muscled legs in ripped jeans traced the outside of her thighs. She steadied herself and leaned forward. With only a bit of wobble, she looked behind her.

Sweet Jesus.

Brother from the bar...what was his name? Jack. He had his chest—his muscled, *naked* chest—pressed up to her back, his arms draping over her arms. His skin lit from inside, and there was a residue of that glow on her skin wherever he touched her. "You're...glowing."

He startled at her insight. "I'm sorry, Sydney. Healing works best with skin-to-skin contact." That deep voice matched the physique perfectly. Only thing that didn't fit the hardcore badass persona was the softness in his expression. "I'd never—" Mild panic rolled through his eyes. He inched back and grabbed a wad of fabric. "Here's your shirt and jacket."

She scooted forward and turned back to Jack. The light in the alley was dim, but she could swear—

"Are you blushing?" And yay for her, the words weren't thick with slobber.

Jack cleared his throat and pulled his white T-shirt over his head, covering that magnificent chest. With a grace she didn't expect from such a large man, he swung his leg over her head and leaped down in one fluid movement.

Another thought jumped the ranks for precedence. "What do you mean...healing?"

He walked around the bed of what Syd now realized was an old Chevy pickup. "It's my gift," he said simply.

His tone, matched with the easiness with which he met her eyes all pointed in the direction of truth. But touch didn't heal...

did it? And how did all that contact not cause her psychic senses to short-circuit?

So many questions. How did she get here, and why did she feel like her head had just had an intimate meeting with a mallet? Last thing she remembered...

Red-Headed Slut.

"He drugged you." Jack held his hand out.

Oh God. She did a quick body check. It seemed her head was the only thing that hurt, but could she be sure? "Did he—" Syd breathed.

"I don't think so." Jack averted his eyes. "I'm so sorry. We never should've left you alone."

Not like she was their responsibility. "Where is Bryce?" she asked tightly.

Jack glanced back down the alley. "Devon is handling it."

Syd swallowed. "Bryce has his friends, too, Devon will be outnumbered—"

Jack chuckled with no humor. "It's not Devon you should be worried about."

As if on cue, the angry voices rose up, closer than Syd had originally thought.

"Sydney, I'm sorry, but I need to—"

"Just Syd." She shivered.

"Syd." Jack nodded with that incongruent softness in his gaze. "I need to go to Devon, but I won't leave you here alone. I'll keep you safe."

Looking at him, she could believe it—all that muscle and strength, but it was his eyes that sold it. Syd held Jack's gaze, fighting with her fear of being left by herself, and her fear of what was waiting in the alley. The last thing in the world she wanted was to go closer. She was bone-tired, straight-up freaked out, and she had no clue what had happened while she had been passed out. But what if Jack left her and didn't come back? She had no idea where she was. It was late, dark.

She gripped his proffered hand. With nearly no effort on her part, she was set gently on the ground. Good thing, too, as her legs had a lot in common with a poorly-formed Jell-O shot.

Jack squeezed her hand in reassurance. "I can't say this will be easy, but I can promise we're the good guys."

Syd blurted, "You'll take me home?"

Jack's smile grew, transforming his serious expression into the grin of a friend. "Yeah, Syd, I'll take you home. I just need to make sure—"

A cry tore through the darkened sky.

Syd's head whipped in the direction from which the scream had come. Jack scooped her up and ran. One flood lamp dimly lit the garbage-strewn alley. Chain link with child-sized holes traced the edge of the crumbling concrete. Jack set her down, making sure she didn't stumble, but his focus was all forward.

Devon stood in the middle of the alley, arms idle at his sides, a devilish grin on his face. "Syd, you're a lioness, up and about already. Impressive."

Syd didn't respond. Couldn't. She took in the scene in front of her.

Zach struggled to his feet, using the wall of the restaurant as a crutch. Adam lay face-down across the hood of the cab, moaning but unmoving. Bryce faced them ten feet away, standing stock still, blood dripping from his nose, and cradling his left arm.

"You've made your point, Dev. We're done here." Jack used the tone a parent would take to placate a tantrum-bound toddler.

Devon's smile faded. "Let's give our lioness the option. It was her life they almost took, after all."

I would've died without them? The thought tasted bitter on her tongue, complementing the pounding in her head.

Devon's penetrating gaze shifted to her.

Not gonna lie, she fidgeted under the intensity.

"Want me to kill him?" Devon asked. Like he'd just asked her preference of draft or bottle.

Kill him? *Kill* him? Syd's breathing huffed up, double time.

Devon closed the remaining distance between them.

It took every ounce of courage in her to hold her ground. Something told her a show of weakness in front of this man was her worst option.

"It's fair you understand what they were going to do to you before you make your decision." Devon studied her.

"Dev, don't," Jack bit out.

Ignoring him, Devon walked over to Zach, moaning against the restaurant. *"Tell her what you were going to do."*

There was that electricity in the air again, her psychic sense pounding behind the constructed wall in her mind.

Zach's eyes glazed over. Grabbing a fistful of his hair, Devon dragged him to a standing position. Supporting the majority of his weight, Devon sent words laced with some kind of—God, what—*power*. Her mind tripped over itself to get out of there, but Syd's legs may as well have been concrete.

*"Tell her."* Even without the power rippled through the sentence, Devon's voice demanded compliance.

Zach swallowed, and Devon's firm grip on his hair kept the wobbling man on two legs. "Bryce was... We was...gonna have some fun. Stupid bitch couldn't take a joke. So, we was gonna get serious. He said she liked it rough."

Silence wrapped itself in the fibers of the darkness surrounding them, making it thicker, harder to breath. Syd's shoulders tightened, muscles straining all the way up her neck. Other than that, though, she was numb, fingers to toes.

"Now you can make a fully informed decision about Bryce," Devon said, matter-of-fact.

Bryce was trouble, but would he really do that?

A groan caught her attention. Bryce stumbled, caught himself against the brick wall, his right hand bracing him, blood trickled down a flap of skin hanging off his forehead. He held his left arm gingerly against his body.

Devon had beaten the *shit* out of him.

"Is it true?" She switched off her emotional fuse panel. Reality could become too much, and Syd had learned how to deal.

There was such an enveloping comfort in the void.

Bryce glanced up and groaned again, seemed to remember her presence. "Dumb bitch. Tell me I wouldn'ta been doing you a favor." He spit blood and laughed. "Not like anybody'd care. Not sure people like you deserve to live."

People like her?

Syd became very aware of her breathing, the anger overtaking her fear. There was no other sound in the alley, just the pounding of hot blood through her veins. She was here and, yes, alive. Living through another personal tragedy. This one, though, was like practicing for Hell by sunbathing in the Bahamas. Bryce had a way to go if he thought he could break her.

She had survived before, and she would survive this, too.

*Brooding over troubles increases them.* Her dad's voice came back, as it so often did. His soothing tone, so matter of fact, the way he'd read *Aesop's Fables* to her as child. Nothing could go wrong when he was around. Remembering him, his presence, gave her strength.

Jack's hand on her shoulder brought her mind back to the alley, to the cold and the pain.

Syd had enough. She sprinted over to Bryce without a further thought and landed a solid kick between his legs. He dropped with a squeal that echoed through the alley.

She tightened her hand into a fist and coldcocked Bryce's jaw. His one working arm flew up to shield his battered face, but that was the extent of his exertion. He slumped to the ground, and Syd was on top of him in an instant, raining punch after punch on his face and neck.

He began to choke.

Didn't slow her down.

Suddenly, she was airborne, still swinging. In the air and kicking in a frustrated rage.

"That's enough, Syd." Jack held her with his hands on her waist, his arms fully extended to avoid any of the shotgun ferocity she spewed. She was at least two feet off the ground.

His hands lit up where they made contact with her skin, and she bellowed, "I'm not hurt."

Quietly, Jack muttered, "I'm not so sure about that. This will help calm you." Jack set her down, his hands still on her shoulders.

Syd pushed away from him, forced her lungs to slow down. "I'm fine."

Jack's warm eyes assessed her, as if he was rearranging some thoughts in his head. He nodded slowly.

She turned away from Jack, and Devon came back into her line of sight. He still held Zach by the hair. Jack stiffened against her back.

"Bryce was all yours. This one, though—" Devon snapped Zach's neck with one smooth motion. *Crack, crunch.* The expression on Devon's face didn't change. Zach's only noted surprise and froze. Then Devon dropped Zach's body to the ground like a heavy bag rocked permanently from its chain.

Oh shit, oh shit...oh *shit.*

Huddled on the dirty concrete, Bryce screamed, "You can't just kill us!"

Devon gestured to the dead body at his feet. "Sure, I can. But I've left the decision of your pathetic life to Syd."

Syd swallowed. No way. Life or death was not her decision to make.

"I'm taking her home, Dev. She's been through enough tonight." Jack raked a hand through his hair. "Come with me. Please."

Syd wasn't a fan of that plan. Jack taking her home, maybe. But Devon? Despite her body's gut-level reaction to him... He wasn't just dangerous—he was freaking homicidal. She took a step back, however Jack grabbed her hand, halting her movement. Meeting his gaze, he shook his head.

Ignoring Jack, Devon walked toward her. "Can I take your silence as your concurrence? You want me to kill him?"

Bryce deserved it. He really did. But guilt was already her unwelcome roomie for headspace. Another death would only cramp the space further. Her nose filled with the acrid stench of her parents' burning bodies. She pushed the thought away and reminded herself it wasn't her fault. Most days she even believed it.

Jack stepped out from behind her, his deep voice cutting through the air. "Careful, Devon. She's mine to protect. And I will protect her from everyone, even you."

What the hell were they talking about? She wasn't *theirs*. And it kind of pissed her off.

With an amused chuckle, Devon put up his hands, surrender-style. "Got me there, J. But you know as well as I do, I wouldn't harm her. I enjoy my life too much."

Jack's face stayed stony. "And you know as well as I do, we have different ideas of harm."

From behind Jack's back, Adam silently rushed toward Jack, knife drawn.

Syd screamed, "Jack, watch out!"

Adam let the knife fly.

If Jack moved, the knife would be coming straight for her. Before she could retreat, Jack grabbed her and covered her body with his. Jack grunted but barely reacted when the force of the weapon sliced into him. In the shelter of his chest, the sleeve of his white T-shirt turned crimson. He reached behind with his left arm, pulled the knife free and gripped it.

Eyes wide, Syd stumbled back from Jack's protective custody.

Adam let out a battle cry like a crazed crack-head on a mission, continuing his charge, maybe thinking he stood a chance now Jack was wounded.

Jack faced his attacker. "Don't," he spoke softly.

Adam didn't slow. When Adam was in range, quicker than Syd could follow, Jack delivered a stunning uppercut with his injured arm.

Adam flew backward almost ten feet in the air. His body hit the green dumpster near the chain link and did a wet noodle when it landed on the pile of trash. Adam didn't move. Syd was no expert on deadly force, but she was pretty sure she'd just witnessed it.

Jack huffed once, whether from the pain or the exertion, Syd couldn't tell. She noticed the crimson stain had made no further progress on his shirt. She hoped he could heal himself as well as he had healed her.

"Two down." Devon lounged against the brick and examined his fingernails, looking as comfortable as she imagined he would in a five-star hotel. "That was for punching me in the bar, prick."

Syd's jaw dropped. "You let that guy stab him—because Jack *punched* you?"

Devon looked amused at her indignation. "I didn't *let* him stab Jack. I *compelled* him to. Big difference."

Syd leaned back, stunned. "What do you mean 'compelled'?"

Jack snarled. "He means he's a treacherous bastard who should've been put down a long time ago."

All righty, then.

So, yeah, who was going to protect her from *them*?

# CHAPTER SEVEN

Devon gazed impassively at Syd, standing so close to Jack, and tapped his imaginary watch. "Clock's ticking. I'm sure eventually even the Detroit cops will find two dead bodies. Shall I make it three?" He gestured to Bryce, sprawled on the ground, moaning.

Syd had given a few nice punches. The poor bastard was down for the count. Devon smiled, but Syd wasn't sharing his happy-happy joy-joy.

"You aren't serious," Syd whispered, shivering into Jack's embrace.

Goading people was basically Devon's favorite pastime, but this was different. Bryce was an impediment to the mission. An easily remedied impediment, at that. Devon rolled his shoulders. Seeing Syd in Jack's arms annoyed him.

"Come on, let's take you home." Jack tried to nudge her, but Syd remained rooted and staring at Bryce's inert form.

The blank stare snapped, and Syd pegged Devon with her gaze. "Don't kill him."

Seriously? Looks like his little lioness had found her courage.

Devon crossed his arms across his pecs, the leather jacket creaking. "Why not?"

He waited to hear her reasoning. No doubt it would be something every other human, Jack, the Archangel always told him: because it's the right thing to do. Except...who knew what was right, what was truly *good*? There was only the side he was on and the side of their enemy.

Keeping the Pledge in place was all that mattered. The Guardian Army fought to keep humans safe from Hell's Legion. Rafael had tasked him with keeping Sydney safe, no reason why, no explanation. To Devon, a reason was inconsequential anyway. Casualties were a given in war. Far as he was concerned, that was a license to kill anything that threatened her. Especially Syd's dickhead would-be rapist.

"Because...I asked you to." Syd still held his gaze, the words measured. "You wanted me to decide. I decided. Respect the decision."

Devon turned away from Bryce and walked right up to his auburn-haired ward. He didn't try to compel her, though the urge was there. He wasn't used to asking for anything—he simply took what he wanted. His gaze locked down to hers, emerald eyes bright with intelligence and shiny with a touch of fear. Fearing him was very smart.

He waited for her to flinch, look away.

She didn't.

He hadn't really planned on heeding her wish. In his head, Bryce was a corpse in the rearview.

Studying her, there was a strength to her delicate features he couldn't help but respect. He loved a good puzzle, anything to keep his mind occupied and pass the decades. And Syd definitely qualified as a puzzle. How could she kick him out of her head? Why was she so important to the Archangel?

He leaned down a bit closer, until his lips were level with hers. She made no move, not forward, not away. Didn't even breathe. Plenty of men didn't have those kind of stones. Whatever else he had planned, Rafael should definitely recruit her for the army. Maybe that was the plot, maybe not. Rafael had a hard-on for her; that was certain. Why else send his two best soldiers to protect her?

Devon let a smile pull across his features. He drew back to his full height.

"Fair enough. He'll live to rape another day."

Syd sagged, her knees giving out.

Maybe not as tough as she seemed to be, then. Devon resisted the urge to reach out to support her. No need, though. Jack's White Knight gene kicked in, and he had her supported before her knees met concrete.

Without looking back, Devon laced his words with compulsion. *"Leave now, Bryce."*

Bryce scrambled to obey, his injuries slowing him. Before he even got vertical, a gust of cold blew through the alleyway. The temperature dropped by about twenty degrees and turned the chilly night frigid.

Bryce shrieked.

Devon straightened his spine and turned. Air temp drops like that indicated a supernatural nasty in the vicinity. Question was, what? He searched the night.

Behind him, Jack whispered, "Elemental."

What Devon had in mercenary cold-bloodedness, Jack had in pure warrior-instinct. Half a second later, Devon pinpointed it. The elemental was a roiling shadow closing in on Bryce. Devon let his gaze slide to Jack. Save the recently-spared asshole, or protect his ward? Devon wouldn't kill Bryce, but he sure as shit wouldn't stop something else from doing the deed.

"I'll get it. Stay with Syd." Then Jack was gone.

Well played, baby bro.

# CHAPTER EIGHT

"What's an elemental?" Syd whispered. She didn't need to be told that she didn't want to meet one, well, in a dark alley. But there it was, and here *she* was. Though she didn't know Jack or Devon at all, they seemed invested in keeping her breathing. Good thing, too. Fear clawed itself into her gut and spread out, extending to every hair on her head, her entire body going rigid.

The thing rose, stretching, gaining height, and Syd swore it looked right at her. Her shoulders crawled with the evil emanating from it.

Leave. You have to leave. Now.

But her body froze in place. It was the instinct of a prey animal, knowing, as soon as she moved, a deadly chase would ensue.

Devon's voice suddenly echoed in her head. *Jack will take care of it. I won't leave you.*

Her hand flew to her temple. His voice in her head pushed like an invasion of the most personal kind. Without conscious thought, Syd reinforced her mental wall. The space in her head cleared, Devon gone as if he had never been there. She had a second to take a refreshing deep breath, and then a vise-like grip closed around her arm. Devon's strong fingers held her fast. Electric energy coursed through her, crippling in its force.

"What did you just do?" Devon's hand on her arm tightened.

Her fear shifted from the thing in front of her to the man who'd already killed once tonight.

God, he was intense. Syd's gaze met his; she was lost inside those ice-cold, unsettling eyes. Whatever pithy insult she had been about to lob back became a worthless jumble of words. Instead, she struggled, in vain, to get her arm back under her own control.

"Let me go," she said, oh-so-tired of being manhandled.

Even with her abilities shut down, Devon was a force, his presence undeniably masculine and powerful. Psychic or not, he was still a big, dangerous man holding her against her will in a dark alley. Things were looking up. *Shit.*

Devon held her fast, not budging an inch.

The single operating lightbulb in her head illuminated; he was trying to intimidate her, use that imposing presence to get his way. He'd already said more than once he wouldn't hurt her. He was bluffing.

She increased her struggle against his grip. Not because she thought she could get free—because she needed him to know she wasn't willing to concede the fight.

"Answer the question. What. Did. You. Do?" His gaze bored into hers.

"Let me go, and maybe I'll give up that info." A little bitchy, yeah. But he deserved it.

His grip loosened, and his gaze narrowed. He stepped forward, forcing her back. That, or make full frontal contact. She stumbled back, but he gave no ground. His body inched along with hers, albeit much more gracefully. She fought the urge to stop, to allow the contact, to feel the electricity of his touch again.

Finally, her back hit the brick wall of the restaurant, her lungs emptied out with the force.

"You'll give it up." He inched his face closer to hers and smiled, two shades from cruel.

"Fuck you." She threw the insult hard and fast, a well-aimed jab.

His smile lightened several degrees, and, with surprising gentleness, he pushed a strand of hair back from her face. "Glad to see we're on the same page."

Completely off kilter, her mouth opened for another retort, but he spun around first, using his body as a shield from whatever creature was in the alley with them.

She peeked around Devon and saw Jack tracking the elemental. The shadow hadn't moved but roiled in place. Syd strained to see in the same general direction as her recently acquired protectors, and her mind tried to process what she was seeing. In the light of the single flood lamp, a hazy, black shadow churned disjointedly. It watched her, wanted her. More, the only thing preventing it from attacking her was Jack advancing and Devon standing like a concrete barricade in front of her.

Jack's form blurred past Bryce, and an inhuman scream erupted from the elemental. Jack grunted, his arms slashing through the air in a violent dance, choreographed to kill.

The shadow split, and both halves began to evaporate into a dirty gray smoke.

Devon turned and winked at her. "Cake."

"Dev!" Jack shouted.

Devon whipped around, his arm coming back to corral her.

Syd peered around Devon's big form, seeing nothing but darkness. The air temp dropped further, making Syd's teeth chatter. Devon stared ahead in Jack's direction.

"Where's Bryce?" Devon called.

"Gone," Jack said grimly. "It took Bryce and both of the bodies."

"The elemental?" Devon asked.

Jack paused. "Something else."

The presence snaked through her consciousness. *Demon.* The word rang through Syd's mind, echoing from a deep place inside her, the same place her dark premonitions lived. Her last premonition had been particularly vicious, and she felt it take a step closer to culmination. *Blood like acid, burning my face, my hands—demon.*

The scream built in her chest.

"Syd?" Devon's raspy voice rose, only barely cutting through the din of her internal breakdown.

*Burning, burning, burning...*

Make it stop, make it stop, makeitstop. It hurt so bad. Skin melting—

"She's losing it, J."

*Sleep.* The command whispered through her mind, like ice water in the desert. She let it inside, accepted it with grace and relief.

Then there was only darkness and release.

# CHAPTER NINE

J ack glanced over to the passenger seat of his Silverado. The door was locked, but something like that wasn't a hindrance to Devon. Where a moment ago it had been an empty seat, now Devon lounged, examining his fingernails. The truck was parked street-side, in front of Syd's Tudor mansion.

It wasn't the best idea, having Devon take a passed-out and vulnerable woman to her bedroom alone. But Jack couldn't accomplish the task without breaking and entering. Devon only had to pick her up and move through space.

"She okay?" Jack asked hesitantly.

Devon's lips twisted. "Is that some veiled inquiry as to whether or not I'm a rapist?"

"You don't exactly have to beg for it, and your pride would never allow that, so no. It's not." God, there was so much history, so many things that could be said between them. Jack needed to get right with everyone, especially now. Dealing with Devon was going to be the biggest test of his resolve.

Devon slouched down in the gray cloth seat. "She's fine. I tucked her beddy-bye and poofed. She seems stable. Probably the passing out was just a culmination of all tonight's shit."

Jack snorted. "So maybe murdering someone in front of her wasn't the best play."

Devon shrugged, a noncommittal lift and fall of his broad shoulders. "Whatever. She's in it now. No helping that. Speaking of...we didn't get to the main event. What'd Rafael tell you?"

Jack hoped like hell his poker face had improved since the last time he and Devon had verbally sparred. "Not much."

Jack could feel Devon studying him in the darkened truck. He met his twin's gaze with no hesitation, no flinch or balk.

"I don't believe you." Devon's voice had dropped.

Jack laughed with no humor. "So what else is new?"

Devon let the silence hang between them for a moment longer before shifting topics, thank God.

"So, an elemental. I haven't seen one in decades. You?"

Jack shook his head. He hadn't seen anything in the ten years since Elaine had died. He hadn't fought at all. Hadn't had the drive or the emotional integrity to perform the work. He wasn't sure he had it now.

"Any idea who or what the other nasty was?" Devon rapped his fingers against the door panel, tapping out an upbeat tempo.

Jack considered the question. It was a good one. Hell's creatures loved to fight, so to have one hang back, evaluate, and ultimately decide not to engage? Made his skin crawl. "No."

"That makes things a bit more interesting."

Jack frowned. "If, by interesting, you mean dangerous and a threat to our mission?"

"Yes." Devon smiled.

Jack looked away. His battle-lust used to serve him. There had been a time when he'd've been as excited as Devon about the possibility of a challenge. There wasn't much, in all their centuries, that had truly put either of them to the test.

Devon kept tapping his fingers in a melody Jack thought might've been Mozart. "Any theories about Syd? Why Rainbow Bright is so hardcore for her?"

Jack sighed. "It is ridiculously disrespectful to refer to an Archangel that way."

Devon's white teeth gleamed in the dark. "I know."

Rafael told him plenty, though Jack was certain the Archangel hadn't told him everything. It was blatantly clear that this assignment, protecting Syd, was of the utmost importance to Rafael. The Archangel hadn't given him any other option and made it clear Devon was to know as little as possible. Safer that way. For Syd. For the mission.

Jack settled for something he could tell Devon. "She saw my healing light."

Devon whipped his head around, his eyebrows rose. "Really?"

Jack nodded.

Devon cleared his throat.

Jack folded his arms across his chest. "What?"

Devon pushed out an audible breath and rubbed his hand over his mouth.

Jack pressed his lips closed. Devon wouldn't be forced to disclose anything and arguing would only decrease the chance his brother would divulge. He waited. He'd always been more patient than his brother. Hell, there were puppies with more patience than Devon.

Finally, Devon spoke. "She kicked me out of her head."

Jack's mouth dropped open. Seeing his healing light was one thing, but— "Has that ever happened to you before?"

Devon threw a sardonic grimace at Jack. "Maybe I'm past my prime. Things like that happen when you get old." Devon rolled his eyes. "No, prick, that's never happened to me before. Not with anything human, not with any...anything." Devon paused. "I didn't try to get back in her head. Didn't want you pissed if I broke her."

Jack cut his gaze to his brother. "Thanks for that. You're a real pal."

Devon could be glib all he wanted, but the disclosure of weakness was heady coming from someone as powerful as Devon.

Maybe his brother had changed. Maybe, maybe they could bury the past between them.

"Devon, I want you to know, I'm sorry for—"

Devon jerked his head back and forth and held up hand. "Stop. You don't get to—"

"—the way everything went down."

Devon met his brother's gaze, and Jack saw the rage building. Yeah, but it was Devon's hands that had always been his tell. Right now, there was no more Mozart. His fists were opening and closing, the prologue to violence. "This isn't a game, J. We're not going to sing *Kumbayah* and run through fields of flowers. Me 'n you? We're done. Rafael wants us working together, I have no choice. But I don't have to make it easy on you, you self-righteous bastard."

Jack tried to keep his breathing steady, keep his own anger under lock and key. Maybe he was self-righteous, but at least he didn't have the kind of blood on his conscience Devon did. The anger surged forth. Why the hell was he playing submissive to Devon anyway? He wasn't in the wrong here.

*Because you don't want your only remaining family hating you after you're gone.*

The thought had the stamp of truth, and it stalled out further conversation. What could he say? His relationship with his twin wasn't merely damaged; it had been worked over atomic-bomb style. He wasn't even sure pieces remained to be put back together.

Devon gripped the car door handle.

Damn it, this wasn't how the conversation was supposed to have gone. Jack tentatively touched Devon's jacket sleeve.

Devon went completely rigid, and his voice was deadly serious. "You sure as fuck don't have permission to lay a hand on me."

Jack's grip tightened. "Don't screw around with her, Dev. Last thing Syd needs—"

The door clicked open, and Devon shrugged roughly out of Jack's fingers.

"Oh, I get it. Last thing Syd needs is trash like me trying to get in her pants."

Dev pushed himself out the door, slammed it, and pulled his move-through-space trick.

Jack didn't even need time to consider. No question where Devon had gone.

Right back to Syd's bedroom.

## CHAPTER TEN

Syd awoke with a gasp, eyes flying open. She was in her four-poster bed, encased in her burgundy bedding, late morning sun leaking through the bay window. A vision of the premonition that haunted her dreams last night came up for air with her. *A coin, weird rune markings on it. Hers.* One of two premonitions haunting her for weeks. The second one...the one where blood was on her tongue, burning and choking her...that one floated in the dark water of her thoughts, but she pushed it down further.

The least of her worries as reality came into clearer focus. Devon sat ten feet away, languidly folded on her worn leather recliner, the one she insisted on having in her room to read. Back-dropped by the portrait of a stalking lion, he looked at ease as if it were his own chair, his own home. On his lap, Devon set down the hardcover he'd been reading. Her copy of *Aesop's Fables*. The book her dad had read to her each night when she was a child.

Syd tried to steady her heart, hammering like a techno beat in her chest. Her mouth formed words, but no sound came, and her lips smacked with dryness. She tried to grab the glass of water on her nightstand, realizing belatedly her hand was sleep numb. The half-full container tumbled, spilling the contents onto the plush nude carpet.

Devon unfolded himself from the chair, rocked up, and crossed the short distance between them. For one crazy second, Syd was sure he was about to climb into the bed with her. She froze, fear and anticipation competing in a bloody battle. In the seconds it took for him to close the gap, thoughts pinged like out-of-control bouncy balls through her head, too wild for her to grab any at all.

Devon's cocky smile played like a strip tease across his face. He grabbed the glass, sauntered away, and she could hear water running in her bathroom. He reappeared, glass full, set it on her nightstand, and dropped back into the recliner. "Morning, Lioness. Nice digs."

Yeah, Palmer Woods was top-notch in the Motor City. Tudors with three stories, servant stairs, the lasting construction of the 1920's. An elegant, wounding reminder of the wealth the decaying city used to enjoy. Detroit's best times were long ago.

Her bedroom was her place of solace, a refuge from a world that didn't understand her. Devon's presence in this, her personal space, stabbed like a violation.

Syd drew herself up in the bed. Her thoughts slowed despite her pounding heart. She glanced down and noted though she was still clothed in her bar attire from last night, her boots were off. She had no memory of getting home. Nothing past...the drugging, the snap of Zach's neck, the—her mind stuttered over the word—*demon*.

Her Glock was in her nightstand, loaded, provided Devon hadn't taken it. If he made a move toward her, it would be close, but she may be able to get to the gun before he got to the bed.

"I wouldn't try it." Devon stretched his long arms out, placed them behind his head. "In case you forgot, your life got a helluva lot more complicated as of last night. Big bad-ass monsters chasing you, two badder-ass bodyguards following you around."

Syd's mind flashed back again, delved into the previous hours.

What had that thing in the alley been? Had it been real? She had been drugged, after all...

"I hate listening to people rationalize." Devon rocked easily in the recliner.

...And Devon could read minds.

She had done something to stop him.

"Yes, do tell. I'm really curious myself."

The heart-pounding picked up steam. He was inside her head. Right now. Listening to her thoughts, her private....

Panic kicked in her most basic reaction. She visualized her brick wall, the one she used to shut down her abilities, and she fortified it, made it the Great Goddamn Wall of Sydney.

Devon applauded, and her head snapped up. In the leather recliner, he relaxed, Hollywood-spa comfortable, with one leg kicked over the arm.

"Bravo. Way to make a man feel inadequate."

Enough. As quick as she could manage, she opened the night-stand, withdrew the semi-auto, and stood. She whipped around to face him, gun pointed at him stiff-armed.

Devon lounged in the chair, irritatingly unconcerned she had a firearm.

"It would be really bad form to shoot your bodyguard." A note of impatience in the sudden staccato of his raspy voice.

"You need to leave," Syd said, as evenly as her pounding heart would allow.

Devon continued as if she hadn't spoken, "Not to mention stupid. If last night is any indication of what's on its way to get you, you're going to need all the protection you can get."

Syd gritted her teeth. The feeling of that thing...demon...in the alley worked its way into her consciousness, cold as a subzero night. Her arm developed a tremor. She brought her other hand up to steady her shooting arm. "I can take care of myself. Have been for a while now."

Devon cocked his head to one side. "Really?" He leisurely drew his leg off the arm of the chair, placed his elbows on his knees.

"Yeah, real—" Syd's retort fell off. Her brain tried to process what her vision was reporting to her. Devon was gone. As in, thin air, Houdini, disappeared. Gone.

Fast as the flap of a hummingbird's wings and strong as steel bands, arms gripped her from behind, pulling her ass down on the bed. Electricity pulsed through her. In the next gasp, the gun was pointed at the ground.

Devon's soft chuckle whispered over her skin like a lover's caress. His hot breath carried the sharp tang of whiskey, and he had her effectively immobilized. She had no idea how he had done it. One second, he had sat ten feet away, then like a magician's sleight of hand, he gripped her from behind. Her arms were at her sides, the loaded gun hanging loosely from her left hand, a potential bomb.

Her surroundings melted into background noise, and the hardness of the male body behind her demanded all her concentration. An orchestra of texture and scent. He was so much taller than she, her head barely touched the top of his chest, his long legs pushed alongside her thighs. She detected expensive cologne, a soothing mixture of ocean and deep woods.

One strong arm wrapped around her, while the other hand gripped her weapon hand. Everywhere his skin touched hers, she tingled. Syd tried not to give into the sensation symphony. Her breathing sped, and his grip tightened.

"You're not fighting very hard," Devon murmured, his words penetrating her, going straight to her gut, heating her insides.

She double-checked the wall in her mind. Strongly in place. For a lot of really good reasons, she didn't think he should know what was in her head at the moment. His promise to keep her safe only mildly counteracted his murderous actions. He unsettled her mind, but her body wanted him. A man like Devon would only use that knowledge to his advantage. And he had enough of those already.

"You smell good." Syd tried to make her voice level, to hide the toxic cocktail of her emotions as much as she could to throw him off-guard.

"Yeah, so, the proper reaction to being held against your will is to panic, not sniff your captor." Devon's voice rumbled against her ear and held the faintest twinge of amusement.

His body pulled back. She used the advantage, however small, to attempt to elbow him. Nothing but air met her strike. Still, the pressing weight at her back disappeared. She fell against the bed with the force of the blow and saw Devon back in the reading chair in front of her. As if he had never been behind her at all. Her mind raced, trying to figure out which part was the illusion.

Spirits existed—she'd seen plenty when her wall wasn't in place. But that was the extent of her paranormal beliefs. Monsters, angels, and demons...she'd never had any reason to believe in that shit. Until last night. Until now.

Reality was screwing with her. Again.

"What the hell are you?" Her right hand braced against the nightstand, her gun a forgotten postscript in her left. Whatever weapon she needed against him, it wasn't made of lead.

A large form appeared in her doorway, and a deep voice answered her question. "I told you last night, Syd, we're the good guys."

Syd blinked. Jack ducked his tall form under her doorway, his expression somber, his eyes soft.

"You are in my house. Uninvited." She kept her voice hard, but her emotions continued to churn. "Since when is breaking and entering in the good guy playbook?"

Jack clasped his hands in front of his body. "We are soldiers in an army under the command of the Archangel Rafael. He's tasked us with your protection." Jack had stopped moving, like maybe he was afraid he'd spook her. "You have to trust us."

Devon winked.

Archangel? Seriously? "'Try before you trust,'" Syd retorted.

"Just read that one," Devon said, picking up *Aesop's Fables*. "Lion and the Eagle, right?"

Syd made a split-second decision. These guys had protected her last night, from monsters, human and otherwise. They probably wouldn't hurt her; they'd said as much. And Devon was fucking around with one of her most prized possessions, second only to the GTO and her dad's car. She jumped off the bed and marched up to him.

"Give the book." She held out her hand.

"Why?" Devon's smile held a hint of mischief, a dash of daring.

"My dad read them to me." Every night, a new fable until she had them memorized. She almost smiled at the memory. And Devon was screwing with it. The dick.

He made no move to hand over the aged volume. Clearly, he didn't think she'd do it. Clearly, they weren't well acquainted.

Syd's hand snaked out, snatching the book out of his hands, and clutched it to her chest. He offered no resistance, and the smile spread over his features erasing the derision and replacing it with pure amusement.

His pose was all languid possibility, and he *tsk*ed. "Careful, I'm beginning to like you."

Why did that sound like a threat?

Jack cleared his throat. "Syd, we'll give you privacy. Take your time, get freshened up. We'll be downstairs, and when you're ready, we can talk, explain. Our only purpose in life right now is your protection. It's daylight, so you're relatively safe, but we won't be far."

*Relatively* safe?

"Unless you want me to stay in the vicinity." Devon paused, and his lips twitched. "I like being in your vicinity." He stretched out the word until she was sure it was the dirtiest word in the dictionary.

*Sweet Jesus.* Syd glanced from one brother to the other.

"If you want, I can cook breakfast after you get ready," Jack offered, shooting a pointed glare at his brother.

Devon rolled his eyes. "J's a real domestic goddess."

A vision of Jack in a pink frilly apron tugged her lips into an amused grimace. Syd stared blankly at the two men in front her. "You're really brothers?"

"Twins, actually." Devon scowled as if the admission pained him.

Syd raised an eyebrow to Jack. "I'm guessing you wouldn't've healed me to poison me again."

"Breakfast it is." Jack turned to leave the room, but he waited to close the door until Devon did the same. The sound of heavy footsteps receded down the servant stairs.

Absently, she wondered if Jack could actually cook.

What had happened to her life in the last twenty-four hours?

# CHAPTER ELEVEN

---

Syd picked up her toothbrush, loaded it with minty goodness, and began to scrub her morning breath to oblivion. She jumped in the shower after pulling her long hair into a messy bun. Soaped and rinsed in under five. Wrapping a towel around her body, she braced her hands on the vanity.

She caught the vision of herself in the gilded mirror above the marble vanity. Took her a minute, but she figured out the problem.

There should be something in her face, some emotion, some tell. Something to indicate she'd totally lost her mind. Right? The only other alternative was, what? She would walk downstairs and face two ridiculously gorgeous men who would explain why an Archangel thought she needed protection. Really? Insanity seemed a much likelier scenario. Occam's razor and all that.

Or had her mother been right all along? Fearing her abilities, begging her child to lock them away. A montage of psychiatrists in brightly colored offices flowed through her mind. A litany of prescriptions and a sick feeling in her gut, a disconnected, foggy feeling in her head. Until her father had decided no more. It was the only thing her parents had argued about. Naturally, she had caused the friction in their marriage.

She pulled on jeans and an emerald-green sweater.

From the next room, her cell phone began to belt out Stevie Wonder's *Superstition*. Syd followed the sound to her closet, where someone (maybe Devon?) had hung her leather jacket. Only one person had been assigned that ringtone and ignoring Brie's call was never good. It could mean she'd show up at the house.

Syd answered, breathless, on the fourth ring. "Yeah?"

A pause, then Brie's booming, melodic voice. "Baby girl? What's wrong?"

Brie's brother had been a fixture at Street Wise Performance, her dad's shop, and Brie had been a close family-friend ever since. Syd groaned internally and wished Brie's default wasn't concern for her.

Game-face time. "Nothing. Just got out of the shower."

"You have a good time with Nina last night?"

Syd had figured telling Brie she was going out would make the woman happy, make her think Syd was trying. And with Jack and Devon downstairs, she had bigger issues than a nosy would-be chaperone.

"I left early."

Brie *hmph*ed. "You need more friends."

"I'm working on it." Syd scowled. "What I need is for you to let me be. You're not my boss anymore, remember?"

"Um-hum. Then why you got back taxes owed? You know you can come back to work at the House anytime."

Syd steeled her voice and began to pace. "I can't do that." Brie owned the psychic parlor where Syd used to work, the House of Cards, on the east side. The very *last* thing Syd needed was an excuse to cozy up to her abilities. "Besides, how do you know that?"

"Public record, baby girl." Brie's sigh came through loud. "Your daddy be turnin' in his grave, he know how you—"

Syd blew up. "What? How bad I screwed everything up? How I lost his shop?"

"Nah." Brie's voice toned down several notches, softened.

"How isolated you keep yourself. People wanna help you, you know."

"I'm helping myself. I'm fine."

"Girl, you stubborn to the marrow. And normally I find that a positive quality in an individual." Road noise cut into the conversation.

Suspicion rose in Syd. "Where are you?"

Brie laughed. "Almost to your house. You and me, we're overdue for a serious conversation."

Syd's argument froze on her tongue. "We can talk on the phone."

"Don't wanna see my hoop-dee in your hoity-toity neigh-borhood?"

A favorite joke of Brie's. Palmer Woods was about as exclusive as it got in Motown, old homes built in the heyday of a once-great city. Brie could fit four of her run-down bungalows on Syd's main floor.

"You know that's not it. I just, I mean, I can't—" Syd groped in the blankness of her thoughts for something, anything. Arguing with Brie was a losing proposition on most days, but with her mental housekeeping in shambles, Syd didn't stand a chance.

There are two gorgeous men in my house first thing in the morning, and you're definitely going to draw the wrong conclusion. But she couldn't say that, could she?

"So, it's settled." The sound of a turn signal rung loudly in Syd's ear, and she peeled the phone away from her face.

The fighter in her wasn't ready to concede. "No. It's just—"

"See you in 'bout a minute."

The phone went dead. Syd stared at it.

"Jack?" She flew out of her bedroom and raced down the hall. "Devon?"

She rushed down the servant stairs and collided with Jack, who gripped her shoulders in his massive hands. He moved so quickly that she hadn't seen him. He scanned the area behind her, and his hands came up fisted, ready to fight. Devon came around the corner a second later, a handgun in his left hand.

*Jesus H.*

When no immediate danger presented itself, Devon cocked his head, one eyebrow raised. "Testing the emergency response system?"

Syd breathed heavily, but it wasn't from physical exertion. "You have to hide."

Jack's attention snapped down to her. "Beg pardon?"

Syd waved her hands frantically in the air. "Brie will be here any second."

Devon's eyebrow arched further. "That requires our disappear-ance—why exactly?"

Jack folded his arms across his wide chest. "Who's Brie?"

"She's—" Syd groaned. "My former boss. My friend. My personal pain-in-the-ass."

Syd would *never* hear the end of it if she had two—*two*—men in her home first thing in the morning. Most especially two who looked like...that. As a matter of course, Brie's mind tended to skim gutter level. Claimed life was more interesting down there.

Plus, Brie crowbarred herself into Syd's love life. She had despised Bryce. And, now, because Brie had been precisely right about him, she would be way too interested in the men in her life from now on.

If Brie didn't hit on them, which was equally probable.

"You can't tell her about what happened last night. It's not safe for her to know." Jack's face twisted in a grimace. "I'm sorry, and I hate you having to keep things from your friend, but it would be kinder for her to not worry."

"And safer." Devon tucked the gun in his jeans, his button down covering the bulge.

It made sense. Problem was, where Syd was concerned, Brie tended to be the human lie-detector.

"Yeah, I get that. But my poker face doesn't work with her."

Syd tapped her foot on the steps. "Can't you guys not be here? The house is plenty big. It'd be so much easier."

Jack shook his head, showed his polite smile. "After last night, there is no way you're answering your door alone. Any time. Any day. Any reason. Hell's creatures are tricky, and shape-shifting isn't out of the question. You may think it's Brie, but we'll know for sure."

Dear God. She hadn't even thought about that.

Devon smiled, enjoying her when she was so obviously off-kilter. "And, also, your best bet to rid yourself of any hell beast is always decap or burn." He shrugged. "You should probably be aware."

Decap or burn? What the hell world had she entered where that was casual conversation? Shaking her head of the visual, Syd frowned.

If she were any of Brie's other friends, taking two men home for a little rough-and-tumble after a tough day might be believable. But Syd didn't do stuff like that, which would increase Brie's need to know what the hell the men were doing in her home. Vicious-circle material.

Devon cocked his eyebrow. "I have an idea."

Jack shook his head. "Not the ménage idea again."

Umm...*ménage*? As in ménage à trois? What the—

Devon shrugged, undeterred. "I'll compel her to forget. I can make her believe anything you want."

Jack's hand gripped the banister, and Syd worried about the ability of the beautiful woodwork to hold up.

"You wanna screw with her friend's head? *Knowing* it won't be right afterward?"

"Compelling her?" Syd questioned.

"Devon can not only read people's minds, he can also control them, make them believe whatever he wants," Jack said. "They aren't right after."

Didn't sound good. Not at all.

"No way I would cause her harm." Syd shook her head. Brie

was many things, maybe the closest thing left Syd had to family. Someone who knew her and didn't shirk away.

She heard the distinct click of the gun's hammer being pulled back. Syd looked around Jack. Devon's face oozed menace, and he gripped the gun in front of him.

"Jack should probably keep his mouth shut. Especially when he has no clue what the hell he's talking about." Devon's raspy voice was too soft.

"I've seen it, Dev." Jack turned on the stairs slowly. "Don't make me disarm you in front of her. And cleaning up a gunshot will take a whole lot more explaining."

Silence, a three-way standoff, and the tension wouldn't give.

Syd broke the uneasy quiet with a grunt and passed them both on her way down the stairs. At the bottom step, she reconsidered and turned back. Both sets of blues had tracked her, and she couldn't help but shiver under the scrutiny.

She ticked off her demands on her fingers. "No compelling her, no telling her I almost died last night—either time." She moved into the kitchen and threw the final retort over her shoulder. "And be nice."

What choice did she have? She couldn't forcefully remove the two big hunks of testosterone from her house.

The doorbell gonged.

Syd shook off her agitation, walked into the great room, continued under the bridge, and passed into the foyer. The doorbell gonged impatiently again.

Her hand on the knob, Syd stalled out, her gaze falling to the hardwood floor. What exactly would she say to Brie? And could she lie convincingly enough to satisfy her inconveniently intuitive friend?

Syd's gaze came back up. Brie was standing on the other side of the smoked-glass panel next to the door, hands on her ample hips. The glass was too distorted to see it, but Syd would put a Benjamin on Brie having her lips pressed into a pucker of irritation.

To drive home the fact, Brie shouted from the other side,

"What the hell you waitin' for? The Easter Bunny? Open the damn door."

Yeah, so. Not a demon. Not in the horror-movie sense of the word, anyway.

With dread, Syd clicked open the deadlock and swung the solid wood door wide.

Brie tapped her stiletto knee-high boot in a staccato beat. Her arms folded under her abundant bosom made to look all the more impressive by the shelf of her arms. Perhaps most impressive was the filmy material which somehow held all the bounty inside, albeit with a nice amount of décolletage showing. Her bedazzled belt, as wide as Syd's hand, could've fit around Syd twice, and held up skintight denim that more closely resembled spandex. It would be nice to think Brie had dressed up to come over, but Syd knew better. This was casual wear.

Syd tried to smile, but her facial muscles seemed to be on strike.

"Baby girl?" Brie looked her up and down, stepped through the threshold. "Ain't you happy to see Mama Bear?"

Mama Bear was an extremely apt nickname Brie had donned for herself after Syd's parents died. Though Syd had been an adult when tragedy struck, Brie had adopted Syd. Forcibly.

*Pull it together.*

Syd smiled. Eighty percent more believable this time. "Of course. Like I said, I'm tired."

"What happened last night, why'd you leave—" Brie stared past Syd.

Without turning to confirm, Syd knew what held Brie's attention. Few things in this world shut Brie's mouth, but beautiful men did the trick every time, however briefly.

Not to mention, Syd realized with a start, she could *feel* Devon. When he'd walked in, there was a disturbance in the air, like all the electrons had a fit of the giggles.

Brie reached out, put a hand on Syd's shoulder and turned her in the direction of the great room.

The left side of Devon's mouth twitched in amusement, and cocky confidence fueled his stride toward them. "Hey." Devon's voice was at its best, top-shelf whiskey with the right amount of burn. Refined as it might be, enjoyed in copious amounts, it would still fuck you right up.

Syd cleared her throat.

"Introduce us, Lioness."

At the endearment, Brie's head whipped around, her face full of *you got serious explaining to do*.

Devon wanted to be an ass? Fine, she'd use that to her advantage. Brie wanted her to have *friends*, right?

Smiling, she walked up to Devon and grabbed his right arm with both her hands, laced her fingers around his elbow, leaned in. A spark flew between them at the touch, Syd's knees morphed into pudding. His skin was warm, even through the button-down he wore. "Brie, this is Devon. You owe him a big 'thank you.'"

Devon's lips parted slightly, and he looked down at her. Was he uncomfortable? She couldn't imagine why.

Syd ignored him with effort and turned to Brie. Man, if she had a camera. The look on Brie's face was convoluted—part awe, a pinch of confusion, heavy dash of jealousy. Syd reveled in the moment. Two people who were seldom left without comment stared blankly at her.

She smiled up to Devon. "Bryce tried to mess with me last night. Devon and his brother stopped it. That's why I left early."

Brie took in one whoosh of air, and the magical silence was a thing of history. "What do you mean, Bryce... He...*what*? I always hated that mother—"

Syd held up her hand. "Like I said, Devon and his brother took care of it. S'all good. No harm, no foul." No reason to mention she had been drugged and nearly brutalized. Then she'd have to explain the healing and yeah, no.

Syd cut her gaze back up to Devon, and he was back to the faint hint of a joke in his features. Certainly quick on the uptake, that one.

Brie's hands fisted at her sides. "I'm gonna kill him. I'ma straight-up make him wish his bitch of a momma didn't push him into this miserable—"

Devon unwound his arm from Syd's and strode up to Brie. Syd froze, praying Devon had taken her seriously when she had told him not to mess around in Brie's head. Realistically, though, how could she stop him? Jump on his back and scream for Brie to run? Given his performance with Bryce and Zach last night...

She had no choice. She had to trust him to respect her wishes. And he had, hadn't he? Bryce hadn't died. Syd shivered, remembering maybe some hell beast was torturing Bryce even as they stood here, pretending it was just another day.

Brie was tall for a woman, but, even in four-inch stilettos, she was shorter than Devon. Was it Syd's imagination, or did Brie's hand tremble a little? Her friend's expression was rapt, her neck craned to stare at Devon.

"I offered to kill him." Devon shrugged, his back to Syd. "She said no."

Vehemence in his voice. Like maybe he had taken it personally Bryce had screwed with her. But why? He had known her less than twenty-four hours.

"Weak stomach, that girl has." Brie shook her head. The rage in her expression simmered to a dying fire of anger, her mouth puckered.

Devon chuckled. "Brie, I think you and I will get along famously."

Out of words, Syd walked up, embraced her friend. She lingered there, grateful to be encircled by the familiar and the safe. Her wall firmly in place, the hug was comfort.

Brie tucked her lips in close to her ear. "Girl, I need *all* the details."

Syd ducked her head into Brie's shoulder to hide her smirk. Some things didn't change. Thank God. Reluctantly, she pulled away. "Jack's in the living room."

Brie's brow creased in confusion.

Devon smiled blandly. "My brother."

Brie's eyelashes fluttered. She sucked in a deep breath, then led the way.

Syd cast one glance back to Devon, who brought up the rear of their procession ten feet back.

He winked. "Well played."

Syd stopped in the great room. Jack lounged in the loveseat, normally meant for two. In this case, though, it was seating for one —maybe an additional half. Jack's right leg made a square where it rested on top of his left knee. He held a tall glass of orange juice, and the kindness in his eyes was sincere.

They entered the room and Jack rose, managing to make all that muscle look agile in the process. He set the glass down on a coaster, wiped the condensation from the glass on his worn jeans, bent toward Brie, and extended his hand.

"Jack." He widened his smile. "Pleased to meet you."

Brie took a moment, her gaze sliding over to Syd. "You punkin' me?"

Jack's smile faded around the corners of his mouth, and he pulled his hand back. He adjusted the shades resting on his head, using them to hold the thick sandy blond hair out of his face.

"I'm sorry?" Jack's voice held a note of hesitation.

He really had no idea why Brie was thrown. The man had no concept of how he looked to mere mortal women.

Brie's shrewd gaze slid to Jack then back to Devon, who leaned casually against the wide door frame, his feet crossed at the ankle.

Syd shrugged and felt mildly vindicated. This was bound to happen, just as she had warned them. Brie was straight up Detroit OG, and by necessity her instincts had grown as sharp as any thug's tongue.

Devon uncrossed his feet, pushed off the jamb and strode into the room. "Brie, it's like she told you. We helped her, she didn't feel safe, and she invited us back with her."

"You? A bodyguard? Ain't *GQ* missing some models?" Brie

pursed her lips. "You look like you never seen the wrong end of a punch to the face."

Devon lifted an eyebrow and glanced at Jack. "'Tis more blessed to give than to receive.'"

Brie continued. "An' furthermore—why you still here? Full light out now. She's fine."

Devon nodded, his mischievous smile returning. "That she is, but we just woke up. Had a lot of *activity* last night." He let his gaze meet Syd's.

Brie followed that smoldering look. Double whammy. She strongly considered telling Brie everything right then, but the demon's cold presence flooded her memory, and the guys were right. To keep Brie safe was to keep her out of this. Whatever *this* was.

Jack spoke up, breaking the tension. "Brie, I was just about to cook breakfast. You want any?"

"He cooks." Brie's hands went to prayer position. "Heaven above, he cooks."

Jack smiled and looked around, like he didn't quite get the joke.

Brie turned to Syd, winked conspiratorially, and replied to Jack. "Wouldn't feel right, you cooking all alone. Plus, guarantee I got recipes you never seen before."

Syd tried to keep the grimace off her face. Brie's gaze followed Jack around the room like a cat anticipating the first bite of mouse. Poor Jack. He didn't stand a chance.

Jack gestured to Brie, indicating she should lead the way. Brie smiled coquettishly and exaggerated the swing of her already impressive hips toward the kitchen.

Once they were out of sight, Syd turned to Devon. Devon's attention had already been fixed on her.

"You sure my brother's safe with her?" Devon broke the silence with a lifted brow.

Syd shook her head. "Does Jack like overbearing black women with hearts of gold and spines of steel?"

"I wouldn't know his type." Devon shrugged and began to stroll around the great room. "Jack's never let me meet any of his wives." His smile turned devious. "At least, not with his permission. And not for very long."

Syd's forehead creased in confusion. She wasn't sure what was more bizarre—a twin not allowed to meet his brother's wife, or the plural form of the word. "You guys Mormon or something?"

"I'm agnostic, myself." Devon chuckled. "No, only one wife at a time. Jack's too much of a prude for anything else." Devon picked up a family picture. "But when you live as long as we do, you tend to accumulate things like wives."

Syd's knees gave a little. She couldn't help the words. "How long exactly?"

Devon set the picture down and flashed a wicked grin. "Until something manages to knock us off. In our case, eight hundred years and counting."

*No fucking way.* "You're old. Really...*old.*"

Devon dragged his finger along the armoire next to the bay window. "Most other Guardian soldiers don't make it two centuries before some hellspawn rips their heads from their shoulders. J and I, we were the first recruits. Oldest, most powerful. Which is why you should be counting your lucky little stars we're here together. It's an event unprecedented in recent centuries."

Syd swallowed her sarcastic retort. Barely. Or not. "How did I draw the short straw?"

Devon smiled his light-up-the-room smile. "No idea. Jack knows, but he's not sharing intel. I'm just a tool Rafael pulls out when he needs heavy lifting." Devon chuckled with no humor.

Syd frowned. It was the first thing bordering self-deprecation she'd heard Devon say. It seemed incongruent with the cocky demeanor he wore as comfortably as his leather jacket.

Smells of frying bacon drifted from the kitchen. Syd's stomach grumbled, and she peeked around the corner. In the spacious kitchen, Brie had her shoulder pressed to Jack's elbow.

Syd cleared her throat. "How long 'til food's ready?"

Jack looked up quickly, deer-in-the-headlights, cheeks flushed.

"Ah, half hour, maybe? Brie's pretty insistent about showing me her quiche recipe."

Brie looked at Syd, and her grin could only be described as shit-eating.

Syd coughed to cover her chuckle. Brie wanted a shot at Jack? Far be it from her to judge or interfere. Jack was a big boy. In every sense of the word. "Her quiche is amazing. I'll be in the garage."

Jack's expression turned serious. He glanced to Devon, who had followed Syd into the kitchen.

"Yessir." Devon saluted.

Syd rolled her eyes. A babysitter in the garage? Really? She grabbed her keys and walked down the hallway, not stopping to confirm Devon was behind her, but feeling his presence all the same.

Syd hit the light in the garage for the first of the four bays and walked down the three steps to the epoxied floor. Light gleamed off the GTO. The electric blue car, with its twenty-inch rims sparkling shiny enough to make a jeweler nod appreciatively, made no secret of the fact it was highly modified. The aggressive hood scoop, roll cage, and window sticker, which read 'NOS,' all testified to the fact.

The second bay was empty, her Typhoon was in the third bay, and the fourth bay was occupied by her dad's prized possession. A black cover fit perfectly from grill to spoiler, a huge Chevy bowtie embroidered over the windshield.

A low whistle came from behind her.

She turned, hands on her hips. Devon stood in the doorway with an appreciative, lustful expression. He took the stairs slowly, his gaze fixed on the Goat. "Serious muscle. Yours?"

"Yup." She walked over to her toolbox and opened the first drawer, revealing a row of well used wrenches, aligned by size. Men always assumed her driving skills were subpar, or that she'd freak at the first sign of grease under her nails. Deep-red polish hid that nicely, thank you very much. Hey, she was still a girl. A woman wouldn't drive something like the Goat, and certainly not drive it well. Or so they thought. Usually, she'd stomp all over their pride in the quarter mile. Then she'd talk shit.

"That's a lot of car to handle," Devon said.

She glanced up at Devon with a wry expression. "I'm sure if I had a penis, it would improve my driving tremendously."

Devon laughed. "If you had a penis, you wouldn't have all those pretty curves. And *that* would be a pity."

The compliment was blatantly suggestive, as usual, with the riptide of sexual tension. Her first instinct was to blush and turn away...

"That's just your default, isn't it?"

Devon lifted an eyebrow.

Syd gestured toward him. "All the cockiness and come-ons. It oozes out of you like sweat off a normal person. But you don't mean it, do you? You probably don't even find me attractive, it's just your way of keeping control."

Devon pushed his lips tight and cocked his head. "Are you calling my bluff? Not a wise choice."

Syd cleared her throat and turned away, strode to her toolbox. "It's effective, I'll give you that. You wear the sexy-stud mask like a second skin. But you can cut the crap with me. I'd rather be alone than be with someone wearing a mask all the time." As the words echoed in her mind, bile gurgled in her stomach. Hypocrite much? But she didn't have a choice. She didn't have a mask—she had a wall. And the wall was there for her protection.

She walked over to the driver's side, popped the hood. She couldn't stop herself from keeping him in her line of sight. To say she didn't trust Devon was as solid a bet as you'd never see a Toyota in her garage.

Devon's expression dissipated from sexily playful to neutral. He walked over to the radio, flipped it on. Currently, the station was on WJLB, hip-hop, and Devon left it there, cranking the volume. She watched him a moment more, but he acted like she wasn't even there. He rifled through her toolbox—she was pretty sure to irritate her—but she didn't take the bait.

Whatever. Two could play that game.

Lifting the hood, she started work on the Goat, checking fluids. In a few weeks, her baby would be stored for winter hibernation. She needed to make some adjustments to the fuel map. The nitrous system was running a bit rich. Keeping the cars in good working order was priority one. She couldn't let them go. Money was tighter than tight, sure, but she'd let the house go before the cars. Of course, that meant the cars wouldn't have a home, either—maybe she should take Brie up on the offer to work at the House. She could do it on the weekends, evenings. A vision of the looted House flew into her mind, and she discarded the idea immediately. The house, the cars, she treasured them, but she loved Brie more. No matter how big a pain in the ass she could be. Brie and her family had known Syd's parents, had been friends for a very long time.

A couple songs played through and periodically she stole a glance to her pensive-faced bodyguard as she worked.

Finally, he came back to her, inspecting over her shoulder as she worked. Very aware of where his body was, the heat and electricity coming off him, she inched away.

She wasn't good at silence and gestured to the GTO. "My dad and I... We built it. Back when he had the performance shop." The memory tugged her lips up. Her dad had taught her everything she knew by the time she went to college. She'd loved to wrench, and he'd promised her a way to earn a share of ownership in the shop, but she had to get a degree first. That was the deal, and he wouldn't budge. So, she'd stayed local at the University of Detroit-Mercy, the private Jesuit university only a few miles from home. She worked with her dad on the weekends. Probably the only mechanic in the world with a bachelor's in Psychology and a minor in Religious Studies, a concession to her mother. The other minor in Women and Gender Studies, she'd done for herself.

Devon walked along the driver's side, peering in the cockpit. "Don't think my truck could keep up."

Interest piqued, Syd looked up. "Truck?"

Devon shrugged. "I picked it up, short notice, when I was told to come to Detroit. It's still at The Dive."

"Maybe." Syd raised an eyebrow, thinking of the neighborhood. "*Maybe* it's still at The Dive."

Devon met her eyes, the ice-blue instantly penetrated her. "It's there."

Oh, yeah. For a minute she forgot who she was talking to. It had almost been a normal conversation...with a super-powered soldier of an Archangel. The chill of the garage caught up with her, and she shivered despite the sweat wrenching had generated running down her back.

Absently brushing back her hair, she slammed the hood, wiped down and replaced all her tools, and turned off the radio.

She was up the first step back into the house, when Devon grabbed her arm. She glanced back, nearly in alarm, but it wasn't bad news written across his features. His lips were tight, brow drawn down.

He let go abruptly.

Heart picking up its pace, she waited.

"You've got some grease—" He licked his finger, rubbed a spot above her temple.

His touch tingled. She raised her hand to check, but his hand lingered. For a moment, their fingers brushed, electricity traveling in the wake of contact.

Pulling away, he brushed his hand across her cheek, his fingers trailing heat over her skin. "For the record, I don't find you attractive."

Syd yanked at her hand, but he caught it, kept it. She glared daggers at him.

He smiled, with none of the normal sarcastic undertones. "Nothing so mundane as attractive. You're strong, smart, your mind is a total mystery. And you're gorgeous."

Tauntingly sexy Devon was knee-weakening, but sincere Devon was undeniable.

He was so close now.

Her lips parted, anticipating, wanting.

He leaned closer—

The door to the house opened, and Syd froze, whipping her head around. Framed in the doorway, Jack's lips tightened. His gaze fixed on his brother.

"Breakfast is ready." Jack's voice was cold, even.

Blinking, Syd caught her breath. What the hell had she been doing? Pushing past the gravitational pull of testosterone, Syd entered the house and smelled Brie's glorious quiche.

Glancing down, she wondered when her hands had started to shake.

# CHAPTER TWELVE

After breakfast, Syd and Brie washed a copious number of dishes. Brie's arms were elbow deep in the sudsy water, and she shook her head. "Used to think your luck was pretty damn terrible. Now I think you was just saving it up for these two beef-steaks. You got a strong preference? They were yours first, I know." Brie stopped scrubbing and stared at Syd. "Unless you wanted both, which would be damn selfish, you ask me—"

"You do know they're brothers, right?" Syd kept her eyes on her drying towel. "I don't have designs on either one." But the memory of Devon's face coming closer betrayed her.

She shook the vision free. "Nothing happened, Brie. They helped me last night, that's all."

A flash of the previous night—Bryce's attack, the temperature-dropping elemental, the demon. Syd focused on drying the dish in her hands to keep the shaking to a minimum.

Brie's expression was pure disbelief. "Mother Teresa woulda had a hard time keeping chaste with those boys. And you ain't a nun."

Syd finished drying the platter that had served as Jack's plate.

Boy could eat. Syd kept silent; Brie would carry the conversation for both of them.

"Jack... He seems so *nice*. Bet he'd be a real gentleman in the sack, bet he'd—"

"Stop." Syd held out her hand for another wet dish. Brie handed one over, unfocused on the task in front of her, as evidenced by the soap still on the plate. Syd ran it quickly under the water.

"Devon, though," Brie began and stopped. "Damn."

Syd shivered. She couldn't help it. Just saying the man's name started her body trembling. It wasn't all hormones, either. Nope, it was largely 'scared as shit.' One tender moment in a garage didn't change who he was, of what he was capable.

Brie took notice and pursed her lips. "I dunno, baby. That one, he seems like he could send a girl's heart straight through a meat grinder. And don't think he'd particularly care, neither." Brie clucked her tongue. "Hell, the poor girl probably ask for more."

Syd shook her head and gestured for another plate. "Not interested. Sure, he's hot in every physical way, but—"

Brie placed a wet, soapy hand on her forearm. "*Every* physical way? You get the full monte, I need details, like *now*."

Syd laughed. "No, I haven't seen—"

Devon's raspy voice flowed through the kitchen, somehow made the large room seem small. "What is it, exactly, you'd like to see, Lioness?"

Syd whipped around, dripping frying pan in hand, and froze. A mask, she reminded herself. The sexiest mask in the world, but a façade nonetheless. She drew a breath and continued drying. "I'd love to see a Barbados sunset."

An amused grin on his face, Devon strolled into the kitchen and leaned on the black marble of the kitchen island. "That could be arranged. You in a bikini..."

Stiffly, Jack walked in behind Devon. "Lay off, Dev."

Breakfast discussion had been pulling teeth. Jack and Devon

hadn't said a word to each other. Even Brie had had a hard time carrying the conversation.

Syd turned back to dry the final plate Brie handed over. Brie wiped her hands and stretched back, pushing the thin material of her shirt to capacity. Not exactly subtle, that one.

"I got to get to the House." Brie stole a glance at the two men. "Rest up, baby girl. Last night was rough on you." Brie leaned close and gave Syd a hug. In her ear, Brie whispered, "And hopefully tonight will be even rougher."

Sweet Jesus. Syd cleared her throat and returned the hug.

Pointing a finger at her, Brie lifted a brow. "Sydney Hoven, you need help, you call me. You need a job, you call me."

"I'm good, Brie. Everything's fine," Syd said. Too bad the expressions of all three occupants of the room seemed to see right through her words.

Brie sashayed toward the door, paused, and patted Jack on the ass before continuing her exit. "Don' worry, Jackpot, I'll be back real soon."

Jack's face reddened, and he put his hand in his back pocket, coming out with a slip of paper. He unfolded it.

Syd knew without asking what was on it. Brie's number.

Devon laughed. "The White Knight has an admirer. I'll be damned."

"Lesser men have wilted under Brie's attentions," Syd said, matter of fact.

With one last 'bye, baby girl,' the front door slammed.

Jack set the slip of paper on the island carefully, like maybe it might bite. "We need to talk."

Minutes later, Syd sat on the loveseat in the great room. With Jack and Devon seated on opposite ends of the couch across her, Syd felt like she was prepping to get grounded.

Jack clasped his hands in his lap, his forearms rested on his knees. "I want to give you whatever answers I can about how this is going to play out."

Finally, a chance at some answers. Where the hell did she start? "Why are you protecting me?"

At the same time, Jack and Devon replied.

"No idea," Devon said.

"I can't say," Jack said.

The brothers exchanged a glance.

Syd cocked her head to Jack. "By 'you can't say,' you mean you don't know?"

Jack's shook his head. "I'm sorry, Syd, but much of what we're tasked with could mean releasing Hell on Earth. If my Archangel commands me to not repeat it, I don't."

Syd nodded and averted her gaze. When he put it that way—

"Bullshit, J." Devon slouched back in the couch, crossed his arms. "Why not give her a bit of clarity now? It would be a mercy to her. I can make her forget after this is all over. You and Rafael know that."

Syd didn't like the sound of that.

Jack was silent.

"I see." Devon's lips tightened. "It's not only her you're hiding shit from. Or is it the old refrain of 'Devon's powers can't be controlled'?"

Jack leaned back and crossed his arms across his impressive pecs, mirroring Devon.

Devon smiled, but it was feral. "You have no idea how much control I have, brother."

Syd no longer felt like she was sitting between two parents prepping to discipline her. Nope. More like she was the only thing standing between two tigers stalking around, measuring each other up.

Ignoring his brother, Jack watched her. "I would tell you if I could."

Somehow it seemed like he wasn't speaking to her.

Devon stayed silent. It was more foreboding than any of his usual cutting commentary. Finally, he said, "You can't keep a secret from me, J."

"You can't read my mind." Jack glanced over as if to confirm.

"True." Devon shrugged. "Won't have to. Keep your damn secrets while you can."

"If you can't read his mind—" Syd questioned.

"Back before we turned into Guardian soldiers, we could practically finish each other's sentences." Devon shrugged. "It's a twin thing."

Syd imagined time and overloaded emotional baggage changed that, sure, but not entirely.

Jack looked away.

"What are you 'authorized' to tell me?" Syd deflected.

Jack uncrossed his arms and ran a hand through his sandy locks. "The Archangel Rafael has been tasked with keeping humans safe from Hell's creatures, in all their forms. When the Crusades ended, there was a Pledge struck between the Archangels and the Satans."

At Syd's questioning expression, Devon clarified, "Satans are basically Archangels that chose *the dark side*."

Syd cleared her throat. "More than one?"

"Lucifer isn't the only kid on the block. Sammael, Sariel...and plenty more," Devon said.

Jack stood, began to pace, and continued. "The Pledge has three main covenants. One, the great Satans are forbidden from coming to earth. Two, no more Archangels would come to earth, either. Three, Rafael himself was forbidden from interceding directly on earth. He's on this plane, but, forbidden from fighting, he keeps the Pledge. We know it was a punishment of some kind for him, but little more than that.

"Rafael's role is to make sure both sides abide the rules. If any of those tenants are broken, peace is lost and there is nothing preventing Hell from ascending and declaring war with the angels again, with Earth as the battlefield."

Devon rose and stretched. "Wasn't too long before loopholes were found. Satans began sending lesser demons in their stead, causing all sorts of problems. So, Rafael got creative, too. He found a way to gift angelic essence, power, into human beings—so he wasn't *technically* fighting. Don't really know how it works, exactly, but he draws the power from somewhere else. Maybe the Pledge itself, maybe not. He doesn't tell us jack. Rafael created an army of us. The Guardian Army. Rafael pressed pause on our mortality, gave power that manifests differently for each of us, and gave humans a fighting chance against Hell's creatures."

"Like elementals." Syd's gaze had gone soft, and she stared into the beige Berber carpet but saw only the dark alleyway.

"Like elementals," Devon agreed. "And whatever else was out there last night."

Syd looked up, found herself caught in Devon's gaze.

"It was a demon." Syd whispered.

Devon's eyes narrowed. "How do you know that?"

Syd shrugged. "I just do."

"Maybe." Jack adjusted the shades resting on his head. "It was something old. Powerful. It was gone by the time I dispatched the elemental. Whatever took Bryce and his friends, I'm not sure I've seen anything like it."

Devon nodded and grimaced. "As a matter of policy, I try to disagree with Jack whenever possible, but on this, he's right. It was able to cloak itself well. I didn't have long enough to figure it out. Whatever it is, I'm sure we'll see it again. And happily dismember it."

Jack didn't look so convinced. "Always too cocky for comfort, Dev."

Syd interjected. "But you *can* beat it, right?"

Jack and Devon looked at her, blue eyes warming and chilling her in turn.

"We will. Or we'll die, and then you'll die." Devon shrugged.

Jack pulled on his reassuring smile. "I have to report to Rafael. He needs to know about last night. I'll do my best to be back before dusk." He glanced out the large picture window.

Syd followed his gaze. In true October a la Detroit, the day was dull, puffy gray clouds blocking out any appearance of the sun. The trees were all burnished gold and red. Something dark and something beautiful. Detroit in a nutshell.

Devon pulled out his phone and earbuds from his pocket. He popped them in and lay down on the couch. Syd would've raised hell about his boots on her couch, but his legs were long enough they came nowhere near the leather. Everything in the house was a reminder, a shrine, and something to be protected. She'd lost her father's performance shop business. She would fight like hell to not lose the house, the cars, the physical manifestation of his memory.

"Syd, a moment, please, before I go." Jack motioned for her to follow.

Jack grabbed a hoodie as beat up as the rest of his clothes from the front closet. He pulled on his shades, camouflaging those warm blues. "Devon *will* protect you, Syd. He's got a ruthless side to him—" Jack looked away. "He's also very practical. If he disobeys the orders from his Captain, Rafael can remove him from service."

Syd's tilted her head. "Remove him from service?"

"Return him to his purely mortal state."

Syd frowned. "Is being human so bad?"

Jack paused. "After all this time, our mortal state isn't flesh. It's dust."

Oh.

Jack stood there, his huge body halfway between her and the door, lingering. "He'll protect you with his very life, because that's exactly what's at stake for us, and for you."

"If he'll protect me, why don't you want to leave? Are you worried he'll hurt me, or—" She didn't want to finish the sentence. *Bryce was... We was...gonna have some fun.* The words whipped through her memory and lodged heavy in her gut.

"No." Jack took another step toward the door and paused. "But he wouldn't have to, Syd. He knows how to get what he wants, and he uses women like Kleenex. One-time use, if you get my meaning."

Syd stole a glance back to the beautiful man lying across her couch. Devon's eyes were closed, hands clasped on his chest, the white cord hung from his earbuds, draped over his broad frame. He looked relaxed, and yet, even at rest, his body exuded strength and dangerous sexuality. He didn't need to compel with his mind; he was compulsion made flesh.

Jack looked away. "I know what I saw in the garage, Syd. That's why I don't want to leave." Jack raised the shades to rest on top of his head. "Don't let him get to you. You're better than that."

Hell, she'd recently sworn off one-night-stands. And apparently that's all Devon had in mind. She mentally grounded herself.

Don't let Devon seduce her? She wouldn't.

Soberly, she nodded to Jack.

# CHAPTER THIRTEEN

J ack located the nearest cemetery to summon his Archangel Captain. He drove his pickup truck, because unlike Devon, he had no teleportation powers.

Truth be told, it would've been handier and more expedient to have Devon meet Rafael. But that was an impossibility, due to the rift the size of the Grand Canyon between the two. And the fact that one hundred and eighty years prior Rafael had vowed to see Devon dead if he ever dared show himself before the Archangel again. Miracles clearly existed, because Devon still breathing and in the employ of the Guardian Army was one, for sure.

Luckily, the Palmer Woods sub backed up to cemetery, so there wasn't far to go. Jack drove his truck through the opened wrought iron gates and parked.

Momentum stalled out.

Jack turned off the ignition and leaned back in the worn cloth seat. Shoulders slumped, he let the memory of his last time in a cemetery overtake him. Elaine's funeral.

Though it was ten years ago, the memory was crisp as an autumn apple, but the bite was all bitter. She'd looked too still, too waxy, with none of the intelligent wit or summery smile that had been her best features. She wore a simple gray dress, and her fingers clasped the pungent marigolds she'd favored in life. And he'd been lost. Completely adrift. He'd allowed himself the fantasy of forever, bought into the idea God would reward him for his centuries of service by not separating him from her, his touchstone, his reason for fighting. And certainly not after only a few decades together, not so damn soon.

Jack opened his eyes, startled to find the itch of drying tears on his cheek and the sun nearly set. All the other cars had left the cemetery lot. He was alone.

Angry at his lapse and his weakness, he surged out the truck door, boots pounding the concrete. His steps turned to a lope, then a full out sprint, trees whirring past him. Alone in the back of the cemetery now, in a clump of trees, he grunted out pure despair and gripped the trunk of the oak that had the misfortune of being closest to him. His hands didn't make a full circle around. He gripped tighter, his fingers indenting the bark. The tree gave beneath his fingertips. He let his forehead thunk against the tree, but his grip stayed tight, pressing further, now second knuckle deep into the tough wood.

Physical exertion calmed him, always had, and he took a cleansing breath. In the back of the cemetery, tombstones the only witness to his loss of control, he gathered his voice.

"Archangel Rafael, I summon thee, your faithful soldier!" Jack sank to his knees and dropped his head.

Waited.

Warmth spread across his sagged shoulders, like maybe the sun had pulled a fast one, and Jack opened his eyes. Rafael, his Archangel Captain, the one who had taken his humanity and replaced it with a piece of angelic light, stood tall before him.

"Rise, soldier." Power poured off the Archangel, saturating the ground and flowing outward. Rafael dressed as he always did. Perfectly tailored charcoal suit, matched precisely to the gray of his eyes, and long raven hair loose and flowing. His black dress shoes shone, even in the fading of the October twilight. He glanced at the oak which looked like maybe a grizzly had taken a swipe. "Bad news, is it?"

Jack stood. His height, matched by so few, equaled the Archangel in front of him. Jack showed his deference by not meeting Rafael's gaze directly, staring steadily at his shoulder. He waited for an invitation to speak. His last meeting with Rafael had been rife with tension, and given the terms of their tenuous agreement, Jack did not want to offend the higher being in front of him.

"My friend, surely the formality can stand aside. What do you have to tell me?" Rafael stood still, hands put in his pockets. The stance was casual, but nothing about the being in front of him was casual. Rafael was power, undiluted. Jack only knew the Archangel had been a great warrior, but the tenets of the Pledge prevented him from fighting. So why wear a suit, Jack had always wondered. Perhaps it was a deliberate choice.

Jack gathered his thoughts with a breath and pushed both out. "The Fallen know about Sydney."

The warmth of Rafael's light chilled. "Continue."

"We fought an elemental."

"Not so difficult." Rafael motioned with his hand. "I'll assume that isn't the cause for concern."

Jack began to pace, the need for physical exertion already rising in his body again. "The elemental wasn't alone. There was something...else."

Rafael withdrew the coin he carried with him, the oversized silver disk was the token of his power, the physical manifestation of the Pledge, a warning to all the Fallen. He flipped it in the air, caught it deftly, over and over. "I would've thought by now you've faced all that Hell is able to send to this abysmal plane."

A shudder ran through Jack's shoulders. "As would I. But there is at least one thing I haven't fought. Whatever watched us in the alley last night."

Rafael caught the coin, held it up to spark off the fading light. "The Pledge is intact. There are no fallen Archangels on this realm."

Hearing Rafael say the words made Jack feel marginally better. His shoulders relaxed. "I still don't know what it was."

"Did you get an idea of its power, physical form, anything?" Rafael asked.

Jack rubbed his forehead in frustration. "It was able to cloak itself well. I...no. Syd keeps telling us it was a demon."

Rafael raised a brow but said nothing for a moment. Then he made a low noise, almost a growl. "And Devon? Was he able to determine the nature of the beast, so to speak?"

At the sound of his brother's name, Jack's anger flared. *If I agree to this, my soldier, you will work with Devon to achieve the task.* Jack couldn't believe Rafael had made working side by side with Devon a condition of their agreement. As Rafael had vowed to kill Devon on sight, so had Jack vowed to never work with his brother again. Despite the difference in their station, Jack counted Rafael his closest friend, and asking him to betray a vow was tantamount to treason between them.

Rafael had made Jack break his vow, but he had promised it was the only way to get back to Elaine.

Jack swallowed and shook his head. "No."

"Your anger is as awe-inducing as everything else about you, my soldier." Rafael's voice had deepened, cut through the emotional feedback. "I haven't forgotten our agreement. Best you stay focused on the task. Use your brother's considerable skills while you may."

Jack scowled, though the Archangel was correct on every point. Having Devon around was a tremendous asset. Devon was powerful, cunning, and dangerous in equal parts. If only Jack could keep his brother dedicated to the mission. The mission, not the woman or causing undue trouble.

Thinking of the scene he'd disrupted in the garage, Jack spoke. "Why would you assign *him* to protect a beautiful woman of all things?" Jack regretted the words immediately. They reeked of insubordination. And he was nothing if not dutiful and obedient.

Stunned, Rafael cocked his head at the question.

Jack held up a hand. "I'm sorry, it's not my place. But Devon is already *distracting* her."

"Then dissuade her. Teach her to fear him," Rafael said firmly. "Distract her in return."

Jack rubbed at his temple. "She watched him kill. If that doesn't frighten her—I've tried to warn Syd, Rafael, but I can see the way he looks at her. And she's already drawn to him. I don't know what else to do."

Rafael laughed, and the sound rang through the large trees. He raised an eyebrow. "Perhaps you've overlooked an obvious tact?"

Jack searched through the options. He had spoken to her succinctly, respectfully, told Syd of Devon's ruthlessness, how he uses women. She'd seen his mercilessness herself—

"I was referring to you, my soldier," Rafael said wryly. "You two are brothers. I think you forget that sometimes, Jack."

Jack's cheeks flamed, he took a step back, and planted himself on a felled tree. "I will protect her, Rafael. I will guard her with my very life and soul, you know that. I will not—"

Rafael held up a hand, perfectly manicured. "Treacherous suggestion, I apologize. But however you do it, Sydney must stay alive. We both know attachment to Devon is dangerous. If there is something powerful tracking her, then we need to move ahead more quickly."

Jack rose from his seated position. "Move ahead with what?"

Rafael met his eyes. "You know I am banished here. You know I am forbidden from fighting."

Jack was silent but nodded.

Rafael's power thrummed around him. "You know those things, but do you *understand*? Do you understand what it is to be created for one purpose...and to be denied it? To be surrounded with the violence that lives in your soul, to watch that which you want, just within your reach? To be denied it for centuries."

Jack swallowed, memory bringing the feeling of Elaine's breath on his neck, her full lips on his own, her soft body protected in the shelter of his. The ache in his chest clenched tight, and his breath hitched. "I do."

Rafael's lit skin grew brighter. "It's why you made the deal. You know I will do whatever I must to make this torture end, as will you. We understand each other."

Jack understood, but still— "How does Syd have anything to do with it?"

"My brothers were arrogant. They underestimated my resolve." Rafael bared his teeth.

Jack swallowed.

Rafael straightened a cuff of his suit. "I'm working with a human. A doctor. She's helping me identify humans who might help me end my banishment."

Jack studied the ground, his thoughts circling in his head, growing faster. What did that mean? Rafael wouldn't take kindly if Jack asked more questions, not unless they were framed appropriately.

"How could a human help end your banishment?" Jack asked, his voice soft and, he hoped, deferential.

As if the Archangel hadn't heard him, Rafael continued. "I have some preparations to make. Bring Sydney to me."

Rafael moved forward, more a glide than a walk, and held a business card out to Jack. Slowly, Jack extended his hand and accepted it. On the back side, an address was scrawled.

"Bring her there tomorrow. I'll be ready." Rafael's face was hard, cheekbones cut from granite. "Do not fail me in this, Jack. Keep her alive."

The Archangel disappeared.

Jack was alone again in the cold twilight. He walked back to his truck and tried to bring to mind a picture of Elaine. It wouldn't come.

Alone now, Jack got back into his truck, not just with his grief, but also a growing contingent of hesitation for the deal he had struck.

Wasn't it devils who made deals?

# CHAPTER FOURTEEN

Unsure exactly what protocol demanded, Syd grabbed the latest issue of GM High Tech Performance and folded herself into her dad's recliner.

Eyes closed, hands laced behind his head, Devon barely moved a muscle. His breath pushed out deep and even; she faintly heard the music playing in his earbuds. Nothing she recognized or could place.

Saturday afternoon slipped away. Minutes turned to hours. She thought briefly of Monday morning. Did Jack and Devon plan on following her around at the dealership? That would not go over well with management. Maybe the better question was, should she go back to her job? Was it safe?

The magazine she'd grabbed, though one she looked forward to reading, had a hard time competing with the inert figure across from her. Yes, he was dangerous. Ruthless according to his own brother. He was also the most beautiful man she'd ever seen, with the most incredible powers she could imagine. And a murderer. Let's not forget *that*.

She glanced up and noted the sky had darkened. She rotated in the chair and stared at the front door. Jack had to come back soon. Night fell quick this late in the year.

Her internal field of vision flashed back to the fantasy she'd had of Devon at The Dive. This time, though, it was only the two of them. Raised above her, his hips pressed heavy to hers below her burgundy sheet. "Don't worry, I'm right here." He dropped his head and kissed the sensitive spot on her neck, feather-light. She arched into the sensation.

No. No. She rallied. *Not real.*

Fighting the breathtaking vision with every ounce of self-control she possessed, she whipped around in the recliner. Her wall visualized, she fortified it with steel girders.

Devon had sat up, his hands intertwined behind his head, the earbuds hanging on his chest, long legs kicked out and crossed at the ankle. A smile laced with challenge played across his lips. "Whatcha thinking about?" Devon arched an eyebrow.

"You...you put...thoughts...in my head."

He shrugged, unapologetic. "No one kicks me out." His gaze drifted off, deep in thought. "The fact that you can makes me want to push. Jack won't tell me why you rate protection, but it's got to have something to do with your ability to do...whatever the hell you just did."

"I put up my wall."

Devon's expression turned curious. "A mental wall doesn't get built that world-class without a lot of effort going into the construction."

Was this another mind game? Try to get her to open up, soften?

His intent gaze filled with something like respect. "I'm probably the one person on the planet who can appreciate your handiwork. You must've been building it for a long time. Better question is why you'd need to build a wall that impenetrable. Trying to keep others out, or your powers in, I wonder."

His face stayed curious, interested. Patient as someone who had centuries to wait.

In this moment, she could almost forget what he was. Such a sweet seduction to forgetting, starting over.

She shook her head. She wasn't ready to divulge. Not to him.

"What were you listening to?" Awkwardly obvious topic change, sure, but whatever.

Without a word, Devon stood, stretching his long body with an exaggerated groan. He closed the distance between them and knelt in front of her.

He took the right earbud and placed it in her ear, the left one he placed in his. It required them to be close. Way too close. Syd held her breath, her heart pausing.

No way she could be this close to him and focus. She turned her head, lowered her eyes.

A sweet melody rolled through her, a woman's voice, feather light and ethereal, caressed the lyrics. *Trust me...*

A beat picked up, the woman whispered in melody about the force of gravity being no match for her love. It was delicate, but there was a note in the undercarriage of the woman's voice that was all strength. Hauntingly lovely. Not Syd's usual tunes, but beautiful.

Syd swallowed and turned her head to find Devon watching her.

Through the music, Devon asked, "What do you think?"

"It's beautiful," Syd said quietly. "Not what I expected you to be listening to."

Devon's lips tipped up to his devastating smile. "Oh? What should angelic soldiers listen to?"

Syd considered. "Choir music, maybe? Gospel?"

Devon cringed and stood, taking the earbuds and beautiful music with him. "I have eclectic taste, yeah, but I do have lines."

Syd gestured to the phone. "I've never heard her before."

"You wouldn't. This is a demo. I need to decide if I want to sign her."

"Sign her?"

"Turns out demon fighting isn't full time, and music is the only thing in this world worth dedicating myself to."

Syd tried to hide her surprise but expected she failed. "Music?"

Devon said nothing more and turned away, dropping back onto the couch.

Syd's mouth was open before she could close it. "I built my wall to...protect myself."

Devon raised his eyebrow. "From what?"

Syd adjusted herself in the recliner, suddenly uncomfortable. "When I was four, I told my mom that granddad was okay, he wanted her to know that. She laughed and asked wherever I got that idea. I told mom, 'he told me so, last night, in my dream.'"

Syd paused, and Devon waited.

"When I told her, he said he was sorry about using the rope, mom started to shake. And she looked at me with...fear."

"Rope?" Devon questioned.

"I learned later, granddad had hung himself. It was a family secret. There was no way I could've known that. Mom started being more diligent about her rosaries after that. I ended up in a lot of psychiatrists' offices, Catholic school with a side of extra church." Syd shrugged. "So, yeah, the wall is for my protection."

Devon nodded slowly, his expression thoughtful. "From people."

"And what they would say about me, how they would look at me." Syd's eyes hardened, stone that was the external manifestation of her mind's wall. "For a long time, I believed if I was normal, I wouldn't be in this situation. I would still have—" Syd didn't even want to say it but couldn't help the words. "My parents wouldn't be dead."

He knelt down and held out his hand, an offering.

She'd seen plenty of expressions on Devon's face, all of them compelling. But softness? She'd never seen it. It was breathtaking, this incredible man offering his strength to her. Her control weakened, but quick on its heels her resolve kicked into overdrive. She didn't need his strength. She had her own. Hard-won.

His raspy voice was as soft as his eyes. "How could your parents' deaths be your fault?"

Syd drew a deep breath and stared at his hand. Her voice came out hard. "It's not. It's the fault of the damn universe. But it was a long road to come to terms with that."

The admission she'd given him was more intimate than any kiss. More disconcerting, it had the feeling of relief, too.

Even Brie didn't know Syd had ever blamed herself for her parents' accident.

His hand still outstretched, his voice held wonder. "You are a puzzle, Lioness. I thought I might've begun to figure you out, but turns out there's more pieces I haven't even seen."

Was that a compliment? She stared at his hand. So strong, so steady.

If she took his hand—

She rose from the recliner and faced the window.

Why had she opened up? Why to him, of all people? Was he in her head? A quick interior glance around, and she was alone. Enough of this.

He came to stand behind her. She moved away, an inverted dance.

She crossed her arms. "I'm done talking. You're going to have to compel me—"

Devon pressed his lips tight. "I don't want to compel you."

Devon glanced down. Without the intensity of his eyes on her, he looked torn, like maybe he hadn't expected the words to tumble out.

It was the chink in his armor she needed to see. The fault in his mask.

Syd swallowed, but the words escaped anyway. "The first premonition I had about my parents' deaths, I was five." Her mother's voice drilled into her... *You don't talk about those things, Sydney. Good little girls don't tell such horrible lies.* Her breathing sped up. Bile gurgled up in the pit of her stomach, threatening to make an emergency evac.

Devon sank back down into the couch across from her. He dropped his forearms to his knees and leaned forward. His face showed only earnestness, reflecting the need in her own. There was something in his intense expression, deep-seated acceptance— too hard to look at, like staring at the sun. Like she could say anything at all and it wouldn't offend, scare, or drive him away.

When had the air gotten so damn thick?

She crossed the room and walked into the foyer, to the main stairway. She halted at the first step up. The wide steps seemed to go on forever. Syd changed course and grabbed the brass knob of her front door.

He didn't follow.

She thought about telling Devon but decided against it. She wanted to be alone, and, with her emotions bare to the punishing elements, his intensity was the last thing she could withstand. Quietly, she grabbed her Carhartt from the front closet and slipped out, the gentle click of the door closing behind her the only betrayal of her intention.

Syd tucked her hands into the pockets of the jacket, sat down, and huddled on the porch, and let the chill of October-crisp air work itself into her body. Her fingers closed around something in her pocket. Pulling it out, it was a moment before it registered.

Dr. Byrne's card.

Syd stared at it. The doctor's words came back to her. *"You wouldn't believe me. Just please, call me. I've tried to keep you away from them, but I think they know."*

Did Byrne know about all this? Had she tried to warn Syd away? Better question: warn her away from whom? Odds were, all the supernatural shit going down was exactly what Byrne tried to warn her away from.

Her cell was in her hand and dialing before she thought more. Second ring and the doctor's clear voice picked up.

"Byrne."

Syd hesitated.

"Sydney?"

Syd didn't even bother correcting her. "How did you know?"

"You're home."

It wasn't a question, not really.

Fear wove its way through Byrne's voice. "Are you safe?"

"I'm fine— I—" Syd's head snapped up as a car door slammed on a silver Beemer parked across the street.

Byrne strode toward her.

Syd stood from her position on the porch. The wrought iron gate was unlocked, the electronics were busted, and Syd usually only padlocked it at night.

What the hell... Byrne had been casing her freaking house?

Striding fast, Syd met Byrne midway down the driveway.

"What're you doing at my house?" Syd jammed her hands in her pockets, her voice hard.

Byrne glanced up to the house. "Is anyone else here with you?" Byrne studied her, cataloging everything.

Syd wasn't sure what she wanted to tell Byrne, if anything. Did Byrne think she could protect Syd from Devon? Magic show gone bad, with Byrne starring as the impaled assistant if the doctor thought so.

Now Syd tried to figure out why she'd called Byrne in the first place. What was she hoping to achieve? And how creepy was it that the doctor had been waiting in front of her damn house?

"I called you because I wanted answers. You're asking your own questions, and that's not the way this works." Syd folded her arms across her chest.

Byrne opened her mouth to speak and instead smiled and shook her head.

"Something funny here?"

Byrne nodded. "You just remind me of someone."

"Awesome. So anyway. Why're you at my house?"

Byrne's expression turned shrewd. "Fine. Truth. I've been commissioned on a research project. It's been my field of study my entire life, the intersection of quantum physics and molecular biology. My benefactor is looking for people like you. People with psychic abilities."

Syd stiffened, and the chilled wind whipped across her face. "I'm not—"

Byrne held up a hand. "Don't bother. I know, even if you don't want to admit it, what you can do. What I don't know is how much more you're capable of, or for that matter, how you control it so well. That's what we are trying to learn. There have been... setbacks in our experimentation. My benefactor is pushing hard, and it's not ready. I'm willing to do many things, a great number of them morally objectionable. But there are lines even I won't cross." Byrne met Syd's eyes. She held out a hand. "I'm here to warn you."

Syd cocked her head. "Why?"

Byrne lowered her eyes. "It's not your concern and not something I'm willing to discuss. Just, please, listen to me."

"You've given me no reason to listen to you. Just cloaked statements of my being in danger. Who's gonna hurt me?"

Byrne sighed. "I don't understand it...not really." Byrne looked up. "Have you...have you seen things you can't explain?"

Syd swallowed. She thought of Devon and Jack. Mind control and healing bodies—

Things she couldn't explain? All. Damn. Day. She nodded.

Byrne nodded in return. "Then you understand I'm not lying. I don't understand what he wants or why—"

"He, who?"

Lost in her own thought loop, Byrne did not reply. "There have been things...I cannot explain." Byrne raised her eyes, brilliant green, and met Syd's. "I am a scientist. Understanding how things happen is the purpose of my existence. But lately—"

"Hello, ladies." Devon's raspy voice cut through the air. He appeared directly behind Byrne. His body was relaxed, hands in his leather jacket pocket.

Byrne jumped like her body had gotten hit with way too many

volts. She stumbled back several steps. Her hand went to her trench pocket, and Devon *tsk*ed.

"I wouldn't."

Byrne swallowed and pushed her breath out through her mouth. "At The Dive—I saw you..."

Devon smiled.

"You disappeared into thin air."

His smile widened. "Guilty as charged."

"How did you do it?" Byrne had recovered, her voice hard.

"That's above your paygrade, sweetheart." Devon's tone was dismissive, but the doctor wasn't ready to concede.

Syd kept both Devon and the doctor in her sight. Her abilities pushed hard against the constraints she'd built.

The doc's green eyes were sharp. "Has he altered you? Did he succeed, finally?"

Devon stilled and took a step closer. "He, who?"

Byrne sidestepped, putting her within arm's distance to Syd. "Come with me, *please.*"

Byrne gripped Syd's hand, bare skin to bare skin.

Her abilities, already working hard to break free of her wall, snapped to attention at the contact. A shudder ran up Syd's spine. Current reality faded away.

*A white lab, scientific instruments gleaming in rows, a blonde woman restrained on a steel table, unconscious. She was bleeding—*

Syd snapped out of the vision violently, stumbling back. She put a hand to her belly, choked down stomach acid and fear. What the hell had that been? Syd prayed for the spinning to stop. She raised her head to make eye contact with Dr. Byrne, then over to Devon.

He wasn't smiling anymore.

He stepped in front of Syd, his body a shield.

"Touch Syd again and I'll make you use that Glock to put a bullet in your brain."

Byrne started to shake, her hand still in her pocket. She took a step back, one heel landing on a pebble of broken concrete. Her ankle twisted, but she righted herself. She looked to Syd. Pleading. Imploring.

The vision of the bleeding woman still fresh in her mind, Syd looked away.

Byrne turned and ran back to her car as fast as her heels would allow.

# CHAPTER FIFTEEN

With a gentle hand on her back, Devon guided Syd back into the house. He wanted to be pissed. Had every right to be, but she seemed so rattled, her knees shook as they walked up the sidewalk. He hugged her closer, but said nothing, just enjoyed the electric sensation of touching her. She pulled out of his grip the second they were back in the warmth of the house.

Devon recognized the doctor as the woman who had approached him at The Dive. Whoever that doctor was, she was entirely human, with enough intricate scientific notations floating around her head to make Stephen Hawking nod in appreciation. But who did she work for? Devon's priority had been keeping Syd safe, and he'd muddled around in her head for a minute, trying to figure it out. Could it be the demon they'd met the other night? There had been no clear image in her mind, more like a deliberately blank space. And the doctor's mind was strong. Way stronger than the average human, but nothing like Syd. He could've broken her, sure, but getting Syd out had been priority uno.

He glanced at Syd, lost in her own thoughts. Her breathing was uneven. Her eyes darted around, like she was trying to fit a million-piece puzzle together.

Still. A human woman seemed an unlikely tact for Hell to try in their quest for Syd's destruction. But Bryce was human, Devon reminded himself, and he had intentions bad enough for honorary induction into Lucifer's army. If the Doctor Bitch showed up again, he'd take a little more time to sift through her thoughts. He had no problem making good on his threat.

Syd was still trembling.

Devon's jaw tensed.

Byrne would be eating her own bullets.

Syd settled on the couch, while he dropped into the recliner across from her.

"Aren't you going to yell at me?" Syd rubbed her hands together inside her sweater.

Devon laced his hands behind his head and studied her, his thoughts returning to his implanted fantasy. "I can think of more satisfying activities."

Syd shook her head, eyes narrowing. "I told you, you don't have to play games with me."

"What games?" Devon murmured absently, his eyes following her lips as they moved.

Syd gestured to him. "All the flirting, compliments. All of it. Just to—" She stopped mid-sentence and looked away.

Intent now, Devon cocked his head and leaned forward in the recliner. "Just to what?"

"Nothing." Syd met his gaze. "Whatever your motives, I need to tell you I'm grateful. For..." She chuckled. "I can't really believe these words are the God's honest, but—thank you for saving my life last night. Twice."

Devon pushed back and waved absently. Words actually deserted him. God, he sucked at gracious acceptance of gratitude. But then again, he'd had so little practice.

The doorbell gonged, and the moment broke.

If that was the doctor, coming back for round two... Devon's anger peaked. He flashed himself back to the front door, ready to inspire crazy Doctor Bitch with a serious change of heart. A survival habit eight hundred years in the making had him mind-scanning the other side of the door before throwing it open.

Good. Damn. Call. "Shit."

This time, it wasn't anything human waiting on the porch.

Maybe he'd get his wish for violence after all. The prospect got him a bit excited, truth be told. Nothing beat a little fisticuffs.

"Syd, stay within my sight." If shit got critical, he could grab her and teleport to safety.

Devon swung open the door, all deadly intent on the creatures in front of him.

"I'll admit, I didn't think it would be this easy." The demon laughed.

Devon took stock and frowned internally. Not just a demon. Vampires? He hadn't seen a vamp in at least a century, and then it was a rogue or two. Now? He could sense six individual presences on Syd's porch, an unprecedented number. Vamps were typically easy to kill because they were loners, but there was something different about these.

The demon was the one to worry about, no question. An ugly, big fucker, dressed from shoulder to boot in a flowing black robe. Hard to get a read on the musculature underneath, but he had Devon by a few inches. Fingers capped by inch-long, pointed talons. His skin was mottled gray, a few scraggly hairs draped greasily across his pointed skull, and it surged with a demonic energy that made Devon gag.

Jack needed to get back ASAP. Devon sent a quick message via the tracks of their mental railroad. Short, quick, to the point. *We have company. Get your ass back here.* Jack would either get the message or not, but Devon needed all the focus he could get.

Devon stole a quick glance back. Syd stood at the foot of the main stairs. She got a gander at what had come calling, her eyes had that Cheerio look to them, and her hands shook violently.

Syd was scared of him. Which was healthy fear. But she was light years past fear and well into terror territory. He needed to calm her down.

"Lioness, let me introduce you. Vampires, meet Syd. Syd, meet the vampires." Devon gave his most sarcastic smile to the horde on the porch.

The entire troop on her porch hissed in unison. Fangs reaching a full inch below their bottom lip, and were pretty damn pointy. He certainly didn't remember those fangs being so...fangy. His suspicion-o-meter spiked toward full charge. Something was off.

"I wouldn't call them that." The demon's voice sounded like the air pushed out over sandpaper before it hit the ears.

Devon didn't like his vibes, not one bit. Add to that the fact he didn't know exactly what he was dealing with...some demon way up the food chain. With all the subspecies out there, it gave him no information about how to *fight* it.

Syd's weight started to give, and her hand on the bannister kept her standing, barely.

It wasn't even fully dark yet.

Devon sent his power over the distance, searching for Jack. *Serious demon on Syd's doorstep with six vamps. Could really use you right about now, baby bro.*

Jack's internal curse came through loud and clear. *ETA under two.*

*You really should learn to teleport.* Devon severed the contact.

Supernatural beings were controllable by Dev to various degrees, but it wasn't as easy as controlling humans. Plus, it was his ace in the hole. They never seemed to suspect it.

"What? Is there some better, more hip term I should be using?" Devon pulled the gun from the small of his back, let it hang loosely at his side. "Sparkles, maybe?"

Clearly keeping up with pop culture wasn't on the demon's to-do. The demon shook his head. "Vampire is the name humans gave them." He spoke the word 'human' like an aristocrat would say 'peasant.'

"And let me guess, they hate humans," Devon murmured.

"That, and I have made them so much more." The demon's lips pulled back like theatre curtains to reveal the freak show. Not only did this guy have the fangs of the vamps, but each tooth was a mini dagger.

"I'm hoping your orthodontist gets hazard pay," Dev muttered. "You have a name?"

"My name would do you no good. You've not heard of me." The demon ran his hand down the exterior of Syd's house idly, his fingernail talons scraping into the brick like it was cardboard, mortar dust floating down in his wake. "He keeps me close."

"I'll play this game." Devon extended his mental reach out to the vamps on the porch. He let them feel his attempt to breach their minds. It worked, and they focused their attention on him, hissing and staring hard.

"He, who?" Devon smiled, but all the emotion behind it was cold adrenaline.

The demon smiled back. Pleasant, save for all the crazy sharp teeth. "I am Malik, lieutenant and chief scientist of Hell's Most High."

Devon drew himself up, his breath coming a tad too fast. Fuck. This was a lieutenant of Lucifer? Maybe all the cockier-than-thou was warranted.

Syd picked this moment to speak from behind Devon, whispering, "The Devil?"

Malik inclined his head slowly and looked past Devon to Syd. "The Dawnbringer seeks you to *save* your life, dearest. The Archangel Rafael is the one who would end it."

Devon used his peripheral to get a bead on Syd's expression. Looked like maybe a paper bag would come in handy. She'd moved further away. Damn it.

"Give me the girl, human." The demon sounded almost jovial, like there was no contest here.

Devon put half pressure on the trigger. Best case scenario, Jack showed up and took on the vamps, leaving Devon to concentrate on the demon.

"The Butcher, where is he? I rather wanted to test him against my creations." The demon gestured to the vamps behind him. "It was impressive, watching him destroy the elemental."

Devon's brow creased in confusion then rose as comprehension made a smile crack across his face. "Nicknaming is kinda my thing. Doesn't work so well for you. And anyway, Jack went out for pizza. If you want to come back in an hour or so, I'm sure he'll be back."

The demon snarled, making his ugly, twisted features that much harder to look at. "And the Archangel left *you* with her, the one human who might end his banishment?"

Devon's mind worked. This is what this mission was about? Ending Rafael's banishment? What could Syd possibly have to do with that? "Rafael chose me to protect her. You don't want to find out why, hellspawn."

Malik hissed, joviality gone, and the demon breached the threshold.

Devon prepared himself for a full-on assault, one hand on his gun, the other fisted.

"Pitiful Archangel. Did he not think we had been following his work these long years?" Malik smiled his cutting-edge grin, seemingly in no particular hurry. "Rafael should've accepted the permanence of his banishment. Just punishment for his treason."

*Whatever, asshole.* Devon drew the gun, Malik five feet away. Fired four times, as quick as the bullets could fly. The sound exploded through the two-story foyer, echoing, bits of plaster flying around and adding to the assault.

From behind him, Syd screamed, and stumbled further up the stairs.

*Damn it.*

"Stay with me," Devon yelled. No telling if there were others breaching the house from different angles.

Glancing through the opened front door, Devon saw Jack slice through one of the vamps.

Thank you, bro. Devon thought it, but didn't send it to Jack. Didn't want to distract him. Even though it'd been centuries since they'd fought together, they were twins and totally in sync in this battle. Jack would handle the vamps. Devon had the demon—and wasn't that a turn-on.

The four gunshots had only opened holes in the bastard-demon's tunic. A black sludge-like substance leaked out, stinking. The wounds closed within seconds. No discernible difference in Malik's forward momentum or his irritating psycho smile. The demon closed the gap to two feet.

Time to switch tactics.

Devon threw his hands out and sent his telekinesis forward like a freight train.

Malik stumbled all the way back to the doorway, slamming into the wood frame. Devon continued the assault, Malik's knife-like claws dug into the doorframe, trying to gain purchase. The demon's face twisted into a determined, evil snarl.

Devon risked a quick glance backward and didn't see Syd. Damn it, why couldn't she stay where she was told?

If bullets didn't even slow the demon down, then Devon needed a decap. How convenient, the Franken-vamps were armed with blades. Devon tried to locate one of the weapons with his peripheral vision. Jack had taken care of at least two. A sword lay forgotten near the door.

Question was, could Devon split his concentration and keep the demon still?

He strained and took a slow step toward the door, closer to the demon, closer to the sword. The demon lashed out, one clawed hand coming perilously near his face.

Devon rifled through his options. Using his ability to compel Malik was always a possibility. But getting sucked into a demonic mind was a true risk, especially one on a first-name basis with Lucifer.

Devon's telekinetic push seemed to be at least holding Malik in place. He had to risk it. He diverted a portion of his power to draw the sword to him.

*God* damn *it.*

Malik's smile grew larger, exposing more of the razor-sharp

teeth, and he stood upright, the telekinesis no longer enough to hold him. "At least make it a challenge for me," he bellowed.

I'll give him a fucking challenge.

Gathering every bit of internal strength he could, Devon launched a full psychic battering on his rival. Sending the power with the conviction of the innocent, Devon willed himself past the barrier of Malik's skull and into the twisted brain of the demon.

No fake-out this time. Malik's forward momentum stumbled. Devon punched the thought like a hammer through the demon's temple.

"*To. Your. Knees.*" Devon shouted his command inside the demon's mind in a voice strained with effort.

Malik faltered further. The demon's leg shook with the effort of denying Devon's compulsion.

The demon was losing, but it was a close race. And Devon still had no sword.

Devon's lips curled back into a ferocious grin.

The demon rallied a moment, lifted his head, and roared his denial of Devon's command.

Devon threw out his left hand and willed the power in Malik's mind to obey. *Obey.*

Once more, with feeling.

"*To your knees!*" Devon screamed it this time, his voice giving out on the last word, but the power inside his mind sustained the command. The mind of the demon was dark, swirling, and pushing the compulsion through it felt like herding damn cats.

Malik's left knee bent, shaking violently, and hit the floor. The demon's clawed left hand punched the wood floor next. His chest collapsed onto his bent knee, heaving.

Jack's blood-splattered face appeared in the threshold. He stole a quick glance at Devon and Malik.

Devon's strength wavered, the glory of victory premature. Malik's hand dug into the hard wood, creaking under the assault. Malik ratcheted his gaze to Devon's, spearing through Devon with palpable rage.

Malik's left foot lifted up on tip-toes. The surge of power, which had allowed Devon this minor triumph, faded. Quickly. Being inside the mind of a demon was taking its toll. The roiling black matter of his mind was nothing like Devon had ever seen, even inside the most depraved human beings or hellspawn.

Devon's trembling hand stretched out toward the demon, but his gaze flicked up toward his brother for only a second. He simply couldn't spare the concentration, not again.

"Think you could...finish him off...with your handy...dandy sword?" Devon gritted out. His body pressed forward toward the immobilized demon, every ounce of his power straining.

Malik raised his gaunt face, scarred with centuries of pure hate. His whole body seized with effort.

A blood-blackened sword in the air.

"You will die begging!" Malik swore, deep voice booming off the walls.

The demon fought the compulsion with berserker ferocity. Agony like claws kneading his brain tore through Devon.

"This is not possible! You cannot command me!" Malik screamed. The demon's left hand began to lift off the ground.

Two more seconds and Devon was done. His mental stamina began to concede the fight. *No, not yet. Not yet.*

One more second.

Jack started his downswing.

The demon was gone.

Like a plug had been resealed, the drain on his mental abilities reset. Devon fell forward, the sudden snap of his power back into his own head caused nauseating vertigo. He didn't have the strength to stop the fall or teleport himself to safety. Perhaps the 'one more second' had been a convincing lie. For the first time in his immortal existence, Devon was sure being dead would feel better than how he felt right now.

Jack's sword finished the swing, sliced through and implanted itself in the hardwood less than a foot from Devon's head, now thunked firmly against the ground.

"Find Syd." Devon moaned from his prone position on the floor. "—Still in—house."

Jack ran past Devon, and the ground thundered—it was the perfect painful accompaniment to the pounding in his oatmeal-like brain. Every part of his body throbbed.

The sword wobbled, forgotten. Molasses-thick drips of black-ness desecrated the hardwood and splattered Devon's hair.

Through the pain, Devon's heart seized in his chest, suddenly not at all sure where Syd had gone, or if there'd been others in the house. Syd had to be okay.

She had to be.

# CHAPTER SIXTEEN

In the secret compartment behind her closet, Syd clutched her Glock. Her house was old, and the builder had a thing for secret spaces. Her parents were not the original owners, so the hidey-holes were found largely by accident. This was the only one Syd had found on her own and had kept from her adopted family. Whenever she had been bullied by the kids at school or a premonition had pounded on her mind's door, she came here.

Now, she was hiding, yeah, 'cause she didn't want to die, but she had her gun 'cause she'd fight before she died.

Heavy footsteps approached.

Syd's body tensed, scooting back and pointing the gun toward the door.

The person—God, she hoped it was an actual person, not a *thing*—stood in front of her closet door.

"Syd?" Jack asked briskly. "I know you're in there. I can hear your heart beating."

All righty. She never figured her heartbeat would be listed in the 'con' column. She let the air whoosh out of her lungs.

"I can also smell your gun. Please don't shoot me when you

open the door." Jack's voice was low but strained. "I have to make sure you're in one piece."

Syd triggered the release of the secret panel from inside.

The old wood door sprung open, and Syd shimmied out.

Fists clenched, Jack's eyes flitted around the room. His face and shirt were spattered with what could've been engine oil. Didn't smell like oil—more like rotten eggs.

He stared at the gun in her hand and made a 'gimme' gesture. "How 'bout I handle the firearm until you catch your breath?"

Probably, yeah, that ranked as a good idea. With trembling hands, she offered it, butt-first to him. He shoved it in his jeans and offered her a hand up. Grateful, she took it.

"Where's Devon?" she asked.

Jack's attention snapped back to her, and, if she wasn't mistaken, she thought his expression the picture of derision. "Lying on his ass in the foyer."

"Is he hurt?"

"Of course he's hurt. Crazy S.O.B. attempted to mindfuck one of Lucifer's lieutenants."

Before she considered the vast absurdity of leaving her one remaining bodyguard behind, Syd tore down the hall, heading to the servant stairs. A breeze whirred past her. She ran straight into Jack and bounced off his torso like a rubber ball battling a wall of brick.

"You can't outrun me, and you're not leaving my sight. Not from now on." Jack took a step toward her and had her gun in his hand before she even processed his movement. "Perhaps you understand a bit better the gravity of the situation."

"How can you leave your brother injured down there?" Syd deflected. "I thought you were the honorable one."

Jack sucked in a breath, as if her words had made actual impact. "You are the priority. He and I are expendable."

Syd coughed out a curse. "What kind of an a-hole do you take your orders from?"

"Already told you." Jack smiled, as if the thought amused him.

"An Archangel. A very powerful warrior." The smile turned off. "Don't worry about Devon, he doesn't need your help."

"Of course I'm worried." Syd folded her arms across her chest but stood her ground. "I have a thing about worrying about people who save my freaking life."

Jack mirrored her pose and crossed his arms across his chest. She was the picture of a petulant child; he looked like the Hoover Dam.

Syd didn't understand the animosity between the brothers, especially given they fought for the same cause. "Devon is a good guy, too, right?"

Jack's icy expression began to melt. He laughed. "He's my brother, I've accepted him for what he is. And that is a sociopath."

Jack closed the distance between them in a heartbeat. He was so huge that tilting his head all the way down still left a gap of more than half a foot in between her face and his. Encompassed by all that muscle and strength, she was damn glad he was on her team.

"Devon is as dangerous as that demon. More. He has the sanction of Heaven behind him. Did you already forget you watched him murder once? His conscience is warped, so much it barely qualifies for the name. He fights for the good guys, Syd, but he's not...good, not anymore."

Syd shivered, wrapped her arms around herself, and stared at the carpet. She didn't say it, but her mind couldn't stop the thought. He killed *for* me.

"I can't dismiss someone who was willing to lay down their life for mine so easily. Whatever the motive."

Sighing, Jack ran a hand through his hair, demon blood desecrating the sandy blond and offered her the gun back. "I'm only telling you this because you don't need to add his bullshit to your extensive and growing list of problems. He will protect you as long as he must to save himself and not a second longer."

Syd held his stare, unable to look away.

Devon had been inside her head. Now Jack saw right through her.

She tucked the gun in her jeans. She hurried out from behind him, down the stairs, through the kitchen and to the main foyer. She had no illusions Jack wasn't right behind her.

As promised, Devon lay sprawled motionless ten feet from the door.

Syd ran across the foyer to Devon. The stink of the black, gelatinous blood concentrated here, the site of the...battle? Sweet Jesus. White plaster dusted the dark hardwood, a sword stuck in the floor, several others scattered about. The door was open to the cold night, and Syd could see the outlines of several bodies on her porch. The wood doorframe was splintered.

She stopped abruptly, unsure what to do. She set the Glock on the decorative table across from the front door.

Jack strode from behind her and nudged the door closed with his boot. "I'll take care of it. Vamps ash easily." But his expression didn't match the confidence of his voice.

Devon lay completely still.

Her breath caught in her throat. She dropped to her knees, hands hovering over his back. Unsure.

"Please don't touch me, unless you've got your mental fortress built." Devon's voice, for the first time since she had met him, didn't cause that sexual stir inside her. It sounded as if a stabbing pain lanced through him at the words. He curled into a fetal position, groaning the whole way.

"I—I don't have to touch you." Syd threw a glance behind her to Jack. "Jack told me you were hurt." She took a moment and made sure her wall was forged to perfection.

"Not hurt—dying." Devon struggled to push out the words.

Syd's voice hitched in, her hand moved to cover her mouth.

Jack heaved out a breath and took two strides to Devon, nudged him in the ass with his boot. "Get up, drama queen. You know damn well you're not dying."

Devon's inert body swayed with the motion. Unresponsive.

Syd's outrage was palpable. She tried to swat away Jack's boot away but may as well have tried to move a Mack truck with her pinkie.

"Can't you heal him, like you did me?" Syd asked, sitting back on her haunches.

At this, Devon rolled over on his other side, gingerly, and leaned his head across his outstretched arm. "Dr. Phil would say it would be therapeutic to help."

Jack supported himself against the foyer wall, ten feet away, arms crossed over his massive pecs. "To quote you, I 'sure as fuck don't have permission to lay a hand on you.'"

Painstakingly, Devon pushed himself up onto bent knees. The process was slow and hard to watch. "You're enjoying this, aren't you?"

Jack's eyebrows shot up. "*Enjoying* this? We were ambushed; Syd could've easily died. This mission was almost over before it began."

Jack's words tore through her, and she put a hand to her stomach.

Devon's progression was agony. Syd stopped herself twice from reaching out to take his arm.

"Why don't you want my help?" She clasped her hands behind her in an effort to stop herself from bracing him. He stumbled uncertainly toward the wall to support himself.

Devon turned his head to watch her. The ice in his eyes had returned full force. He could've been on the other side of the world given the distance in them.

"My mental shielding is for shit right now. Last thing I need is to hear every single irritating human thought that crosses your mind."

Syd recoiled.

Devon pushed out a labored breath. He turned away to focus on Jack, effectively dismissing her.

Jack's face tightened into a scowl.

Syd stomped over to the stairs, planting her butt firmly onto the old wood, and shot Devon a *fuck you, too* look. Apparently even after almost dying under his protection and caring what happened to him, she didn't rate civility.

"Listen, baby bro. You're free to hate the hell out of me, but I'm a liability at the moment. If more of those vamps show up with that damn demon, we're toast. I formally give you permission to touch me." Devon smiled with effort. "Briefly."

The silence grew to an uncomfortable decibel. Syd raised her head to watch the brothers.

"You don't deserve it." Jack pushed off the wall, cracked his knuckles.

Devon sighed, and his body sagged against the wall. "I'm aware of that. The fact remains—"

"You are not fit to serve the Guardians."

Putting on his arrogant mask, Devon lifted his face to gaze at the ceiling. "Let it all out, J. God knows you've waited plenty of decades to have this scolding practiced to perfection."

Jack cracked his thick knuckles again. When he spoke, his cadence was slow, like he wanted every word heard clearly. "You are anathema to everything I stand for. You place your needs above all around you. You treat humans, Guardians, everyone, like trash beneath your boots. You *disgust* me—"

The vehemence in Jack's voice coated the air. What could Devon have possibly done to deserve the verbal lashing when it was clear the brothers had, at one point, been extremely close? Syd was so itchy in her own skin, she couldn't hold her tongue another second. Not her best skill on a good day, and right now she found the effort of stopping nearly impossible.

"You're supposed to protect me, right?" Syd's voice rang out in the two-story foyer.

Both men turned to her. *Damn*, but that was intense. She drew up her courage like a suit of armor.

"Heal him." Syd gestured to Devon. "Whatever family-drama bullshit you two have going isn't helping. It's about the mission, right?" Syd's hands dropped between her knees on the stairs. "I'm the mission, so stow your damn baggage."

Jack rubbed his face in his hands, gritted his teeth. When his hands came away from his face, his expression's hard lines had disappeared.

"Syd, I'm sorry. You're right." Jack marched over to Devon. One hand's length away from touching his brother, he stalled. Then, sighing, it seemed he made his decision.

Not bothering with the buttons, Jack ripped Devon's shirt and put his hand directly over Devon's heart.

Several minutes ticked off. Progressively, color returned to Devon's face, and he began to depend on the wall less and less. But she couldn't see the healing light as she had in the alley.

Then it dawned on her. She had shut down her abilities at Devon's request. She closed her eyes, began to take the mental wall down, brick by brick. After several more seconds, Syd reopened her eyes.

"It's so pretty." Syd padded across the room to get a better look.

Jack's hand splayed against Devon's chest, but the rest of his body turned toward her, away from his brother. "The light?"

She nodded.

He didn't seem too surprised and withdrew his hand. The light began to fade.

Devon sagged, took two deep breaths, and stood tall. Stretched his arms high overhead.

Jack walked back to the wall, leaned heavily against it. "She's special, Dev. Important."

Syd cleared her throat. "*She* is right here."

Devon shuffled a couple of steps into the middle of the foyer and stopped, maybe to test his sea legs. "How could we forget? You're the reason we're both in a bad way at the moment. Pretty little you."

Syd wanted to chuck something at Devon's recently healed head. "I didn't ask for any of this."

Jack pressed two fingers to his forehead. "The healing will give you energy, Dev, but probably your mental abilities are still drained. I can't do anything about that."

Syd reigned in her overall irritation. To Jack, she said, "Are you okay?"

Jack nodded, but his shoulders were slumped. "Healing takes its toll. I just need to refuel, rest a bit."

Devon massaged his temple. "Then we can't risk going anywhere 'til dawn." He swiveled his head to give Syd his trademark smile, all seduction and invitation. "Slumber party, anyone?" The innuendo was there. Blatant. But the gesture seemed automatic, like brushing your teeth at night.

Syd stole a glance at Jack, to find him already staring at her with a 'resist-the-temptation' look.

"Maybe you should, um, take a shower? Get the stinky demon blood off?" Syd suggested.

Devon smiled and was about to speak, but she cut him off. "Alone. You should take a shower alone."

His smile ghosted away. Devon studied her a moment more, glancing at Jack, then he strode off.

Pushing out a breath, Syd turned to the hall leading to the kitchen.

"Does refuel mean eat?" she called over her shoulder.

"It does. And I'm starving," he said, peeling off his blood-blackened t-shirt and wiping the demon blood from his face.

---

WELL INTO THE NIGHT, Jack sat at her island counter, the heaping plates before him standing no chance against his appetite. Jack needed fuel commensurate with the size of his muscles. Seriously, who eats three freaking boxes of mac 'n cheese—as an appetizer?

"I'm sorry, Syd. I'll reimburse you for the food, but healing sucks energy out of me like nothing else." Jack wiped his mouth with a napkin, set his now empty third platter of food to the side, and pulled the last plate in front of him. Heaped with peanut butter and jelly sandwiches, it was all she had left.

"You saved my life at least...I'm starting to lose count how many times. I'm sorry PB&J is the best I can do." Syd struggled to keep up cleaning the used dishes he produced.

"I'm non-discriminatory when it comes to food. 'Sides, PB&J is a favorite of mine." Jack smiled.

As seductive a smile as Devon had, Jack's was all boy-next-door. Without guile. She could picture enjoying a game at Comerica Park with him, a beer and hot dog, cheering for the Tigers. Come to think of it, aside from the demon-fighting, Jack seemed like perfect guy-friend material. Sure, he was pretty to look at—fine, way more than pretty—but his manner plainly said 'unavailable.'

Syd blinked at the thought and pushed out a breath that suddenly felt heavy in her lungs.

Syd turned to the kitchen door when she felt Devon approach. He didn't bother looking at Jack or her, but sat down at the breakfast nook bench across the room. He produced his phone from his jean pocket and plugged himself into the ear-buds. After kicking his long legs out, his eyes drifted closed.

His obvious avoidance of her was a slap in the face after all they had been through. Maybe Jack was right, and he had no use for her except sexual gratification or prolonging his own life. Syd could hear the faint echo of the music Devon listened to. The beautiful breakfast nook was in an alcove set off from the kitchen and surrounded by exterior facing windows. It had never looked so dull.

Devon's face looked the picture of relaxation with his head leaned back. It was hard to see anything else about him when his eyes were open, they were so arresting. Now, she took time to study him—the sculpted planes of his cheeks, the almond curve to his closed eyes. Devon's dark chocolate hair looked black, the dampness of the shower he had taken evident. He had changed the shirt Jack had ripped open for a black button down. His jeans hugged strong thighs, and his boots had been freshly polished.

"Syd?" Jack broke into her full body inspection.

Her head whipped over, and she cleared her throat. "Sorry. What?"

"I said: I'm not sure if this is a comfort to you or not, but most likely the attack is over for tonight," Jack spoke between peanut-butter-filled bites.

"'For tonight,' how reassuring." Syd rubbed her face.

Jack grasped Syd's hand, his calloused skin hot. She immediately returned the gesture, marveling at the size difference between them. Her hand damn near disappeared in his. Syd wanted to trust in Jack. Everything in his demeanor suggested honor, a person on whom you could rely, but her trust had never been easy to give. Her eyes slid over to Devon.

To distract herself, she shifted and studied Jack. His hair was longish, two shades too dark to call true blond. Long enough to ignore, but short enough to not get in his way as he fought. He was as much a work of living sculpture as Devon, and he certainly seemed like the more stable of the two. But in his own way, he was just as emotionally closed-off as Devon. She wondered why.

Nodding in Devon's direction, she leaned over the kitchen island and whispered to Jack, seated on the opposite side. "Are you sure he'll be okay?"

"My brother is as resilient as a cockroach. We couldn't get rid of him if we tried," Jack said.

"But—"

Jack shook his head. "He's listening to music. It's what he's always done to relax. Sometimes I think music is his only joy. He's recharging Syd, honest, that's all." Jack released her hand. "You shouldn't worry so much about him. He'll use it to his advantage."

Such obvious antipathy between the brothers. Why? But she knew asking about it directly was probably a no-go.

"All righty, no more Devon talk." Syd took the last plate, now empty, and returned it to the sink. She flipped up the faucet handle. Water began a steady flow. "Were you hurt in the fight?"

"One of the vamps sank a sword into my shoulder." His voice

was one-hundred percent casual.

The remark, given so off-handedly, made Syd stop.

Jack took it as a given he could be hurt. He would heal and persist, only to be hurt again. What effect did that kind of an existence have on a person?

The dish dropped to the bottom of the sink, a knife clattered into the water, and Syd nearly pulled a duck-and-cover. PTSD, anyone?

Her head dropped, and she braced wet hands on the sink.

A memory of the kitchen flooded with casserole dishes blinked across her vision. Well-meaning neighbors, coworkers of her mother and dad whispering condolences and rubbing slow circles on her back. She had hated the mourning process, because, really, it hadn't been for her. All the comfort food, comfort words...it had been for them.

She'd known the moment of her parents' death was coming, and she had had plenty of time to get accustomed to the idea. She'd mourned them while they were still alive. Get hurt, move on. She pushed the faucet off, left the dirty dish there, and turned to face Jack. She had a survivor's appreciation for his strength.

Devon finally roused, standing and stretching. He pulled off the earbuds, one at a time. He could have been alone in the room for all the attention he gave Syd or Jack.

Jack tensed. The brothers had nothing to distract each other and pressure thickened the air. Jack strained a smile in Syd's direction.

"Excuse me, Syd. I've got to clean myself up." Jack walked through the kitchen door and into the great room before she had time to process his lithe movement.

"You guys really dislike being in the same room when there's nothing to kill." Syd began putting away the silverware. Hoped Devon wouldn't continue to ignore her.

A pause.

"Not me, so much. That's all J."

"Why?" She bit her lip, hating her perpetual disconnect

between brain and mouth. A man like Devon wasn't pushed for anything. Least of all to disclose personal intel.

"Ask him. His version is much more colorful."

"You tell me." She turned back toward the alcove, leaned over onto the granite of the island.

Devon shrugged as if disinterested in the topic. "He disagrees with many decisions I've made over the centuries. One in particular."

"One decision can cause so much angst?" Syd questioned.

He looked at her, his brow lifted. "When it results in the death of a couple dozen people, yeah, it can."

She held his gaze. Waited. When it seemed as if he wouldn't answer, she said softly, "Tell me what you did."

Devon's lips came up in a twisted impression of a smile. "So convinced I'm redeemable, are you? That there was a reason, not just a whim."

Syd licked her lips, realizing they'd gone dry. She nodded.

"I'm past that, Syd. Redemption doesn't interest me." His smile, his mask, fell, and his expression turned intensely intimate. "Second thought, I'll tell you what I did. If you tell me why you thought your parents' deaths were your fault."

Syd wrapped her arms around her waist. This was where their game of emotional chicken came to a screeching halt. The premonition always found her as a child, and she'd learned to stop talking about it. After a while, it had only been her dad who would come and comfort the sobbing child in the middle of the night. Each time the premonition paid a visit, the images and smells of burning grew more intense and visceral. She had begged and pleaded. Prayed every night. Promised to be so good, if only they would never, ever ride in a car together.

By the time she was twenty, she'd grown hard to it. She'd stopped pleading. She'd been angry. At them. The world. Most of all herself.

Syd came back to herself.

Devon's ice-blue gaze penetrated her constricted chest, her

sealed-off heart.

She couldn't say the words aloud. Her lips would not form the sounds. If she hadn't been placed in their home, would the premonition have come, would it have been true? No. She had been a curse on Joanna and Ari Hoven from the moment they adopted her at two days old.

Through the blackness of her thoughts, Devon's voice cut like fine steel. "It was a hundred and eighty years ago. A nasty demon infestation in a small village. The demons had surrendered, but I made them kill each other instead. Almost all the humans, too."

*Sweet Jesus.* Syd's gut clenched. "Why?"

Devon's fatalistic look turned thoughtful. "You know, you're the first person to ever ask."

"So there was a reason?" She leaned toward him, simultaneously rapt and repelled. His confession allowed her a brief reprieve from her own twisted memories. God help her, but she was relieved for the gruesome distraction.

Devon laughed and walked closer. "Evil exists, Syd. It's why we fight. It's why I kill and sleep like a baby afterward."

"That doesn't answer anything."

Devon held her eyes. "A reason won't make murder any better. Just ask Jack."

The kitchen island stood between them, and Syd couldn't decide if that was a good thing or not. Jack's words rang in her mind, causing a swirl of unrest—*you're better than that.*

Still, her gut told her there was more to Devon and more to the story he'd just told. It didn't have the crystal ring of truth. There was more, she decided. Way more. Devon's mask was so strong, like her wall was strong. It had to be, to hold everything inside.

Syd shivered and stared into her backyard, willing the sun rise. She wanted this night over for a whole laundry list of reasons. Jack was on point. Every inch of her skin wanted to make contact with Devon in a bad way.

Her mind was a different matter entirely.

For Syd, sex was a means to an end, not the deep intimate

connection her happily matched acquaintances spoke of. Nope, in her life, itch equaled scratch. And Bryce? He pursued her relentlessly for several weeks before she agreed to go on a date. He hadn't been interested in a real relationship, and she had known it. It had been so long that the itch had grown to poison ivy levels. The extent of their moving discussions had revolved around quarter-mile times and engine displacement. At the time, it suited her fine. But her body's itch had definitely led her level head astray. She had nearly become another missing person on the milk carton for the error.

She turned away from Devon, back to the sink. The way her thoughts were headed, she did not need to catch his intense stare.

Bryce—now Devon. Boy, she could pick trouble in a double-blind test every time. All for the sake of a romp in the sheets. Comparing her experience in Bryce's bed with what it would be like to be in Devon's, though, had to be like practicing for skydiving by bouncing on a trampoline.

Stop.

Stop right there.

She reached for the last plate to wash, hand trembling. The sensory seduction of Devon pressed against her back moved like wildfire through her body. His scent had blocked out anything else. Devon had already shown her how he used his body as a weapon with devastating effect. Sex as a means to an end. Fucked up, but she understood the sentiment implicitly.

Had he ever truly connected with anyone?

"Someone has her thinking cap turned up all the way," Devon said. "That wall is becoming inconvenient."

Her reverie splintered and fell around her. She swallowed and was damn glad she wasn't facing him.

"Wonder if it's me or the White Knight who's caught your interest."

God, she was glad he didn't know what she was thinking. She dried her hands and drew a deep breath. Gathering her courage, she faced him and shrugged.

He leaned forward on the bar stool, brushing his damp hair back. "Here's a timesaver for you: Jack's still pining away for his dead wife. And I'm not exactly take-home-to-mom material. If all you need is a good fuck, I'm your guy. Need something killed, I'm your guy. That's all I have to offer. So whatever Jack told you about me, I won't argue with any of it."

Not can't, she noted. Won't.

She moved away from the island to lean against the kitchen counter. "I'll draw my own conclusions."

His lips twitched. "I'm getting that vibe loud and clear."

Silence. The thick-with-unspoken-emotional-crap kind.

"What were you listening to?" Syd asked. "More demos?"

"More of the same," Devon said. "Her name is Carina Bettencourt."

"She's amazingly talented," Syd said, thinking of the music and the moment when they had shared earbuds.

Devon, the music business mogul. Yeah, he would look incredible in a suit and tie. But she couldn't see him collaborating with other people. All his sarcastic remarks were well designed arrows to keep people at bay.

Devon slapped a hand down on the counter, jarring her out of her thoughts. "As fun as this all is, I'm going outside to make a lap around the perimeter, make sure our happy home remains a Hell-free zone 'til dawn."

"Jack thinks the attack is over for the night," Syd said tentatively. "Are you sure you're up to it?"

Devon didn't respond or wait for her permission. He strolled toward the door to the garage. He walked without an apparent care, without evidence of the trauma of the night. But she knew better.

"Be careful," Syd whispered.

His stride faltered, and then he was gone.

She couldn't say why that was significant, only unequivocally that it was.

# CHAPTER SEVENTEEN

Stepping into Syd's opulent first-floor study, Jack took in the mahogany cabinets, the ornate coved ceiling, the shelves filled with hardcovers, and the small fireplace. He closed the solid wood door, rounded across the top. The leather chair that sat behind the executive desk had been used well, its material cracked in some places. He ran a finger down the cabinetry, admiring the craftsmanship. It looked like something he would've built himself, back in the '20s.

He sat down at the desk and withdrew his cell. Jack dialed L.A., thankful for the time difference. Gerry probably wasn't up, and her cell phone was most likely turned off. It didn't matter; he needed to check in. Too much time not hearing from him always made her worry, and it had been months since they'd actually spoken.

Gerry was his late wife's sister and as smart as they came. Her intuition was a true boon to the work of The Grace Foundation, which Jack had started in honor of Elaine—Grace being her middle name—and the way she had walked in this flawed world. Jack hoped from Elaine's post in Heaven she looked down favorably on the legacy he and Gerry had built.

Gerry was the brains, but Jack funded and operated in the background, trying to keep a low profile. It didn't do to draw attention to the fact he didn't age. He was a nameless volunteer, and Gerry had free reign to run things as she saw fit. Jack had unquestioning trust in her judgment and her compassionate ability.

She'd left him a message last week that he hadn't yet returned. He could face a dozen demons and not have to work up the courage it took to dial Gerry's number. So, calling when he knew she wouldn't answer was a total copout, but at least he wouldn't continue to worry her.

You're going to leave her soon, Jack reminded himself and swallowed. He'd make sure someone, one of the other Guardians he trusted, told her what had happened...after. The thought caused a thick knot to tighten around all the fuel in his stomach.

As predicted, the cell dumped over to voicemail.

"You've reached The Grace Foundation, touching lives and adding grace where we find need. This is Geraldine Mitchell, Executive Director. Please leave a message."

Jack took a deep breath. If he had hopes of avoiding actual talking, he needed to be convincing.

"Hey, Ger. I'm off unexpectedly on a little side trip, in Detroit." He cleared his throat. "Army business. It's going to take a bit longer than I thought. Don't worry if you don't hear from me. While I'm here, I'll look into potential locations for expansion of TGF. I'll do my best to keep up on emails and such. Text me if you need something, and I'll try to accommodate."

He consciously tried to lift his voice at the end of the message. "Bye."

Pulling the phone from his ear, Jack hit the END button and slipped the thin case into the back pocket of his jeans. Made him feel like shit, lying to her.

Since Elaine's death, the bond between them grew thicker than a skyscraper's concrete foundation. Gerry was the one person who Jack trusted with his truest secrets: who he was, how he came to be that way, and why Elaine's death had affected him so profoundly.

Because of that shared knowledge, Gerry worried constantly about him, though they seldom saw each other. Less and less, actually. Not because of her, though. The absurdity of a nearly sixty-year-old human woman looking over him was guilt-inducing. His death would be a hard blow for her to bear, but at least he wouldn't continue to cause her anxiety.

In a very different way from Elaine, he had come to think of Gerry as the last remnant of his connection to humanity.

When he had realized that, he stopped visiting her altogether.

He couldn't bear to watch her age.

Above him, he could hear the gentle creak of wood as Syd moved around in her bedroom. He thought of everything that had happened to his auburn-haired ward so far. He thought of the rough way he'd treated her, with regard to his brother. Too harsh.

Jack rubbed his hand over his face. Syd needed more information about what was happening, but Rafael had forbidden it. His mind ping-ponged between these two facts.

Before he considered it too closely, he strode out of the study, using Syd's movements like a beacon.

# CHAPTER EIGHTEEN

S yd flipped on her bedroom light. Forget tired—she was ready to roll over and play dead. Of course, she was really thankful at the moment for the useful evolutionary trick of adrenaline, but its effect was temporary, and now she was paying the price. Her mind chugged through thoughts like mud. Lifting her arms to brush her teeth required energy she wasn't sure she had.

Was this her life now? Demon fights and beautiful bodyguards?

A soft knock on her door had her head whipping around.

Jack clasped his fingers together. He stood there, a serious and resigned look on his face. "I owe you an apology."

Syd walked over, opened her dresser. "Um, what for? Saving my life a ridiculous number of times?"

"No." Jack came forward two steps, leaned on the heavy doorframe. His hair slipped out from behind his ear, and he brushed it back absently. "About what I said earlier. About Dev. And you."

Syd turned to face him. "Was it untrue?"

Jack shook his head, pulled his closed lips back into a thin line.

"Then why apologize?" Syd opened the top drawer on the left.

"It was harsh and unkind."

At this Syd stopped and looked back to him. Jack was not the stereotype of a man you'd expect to use words like 'unkind' and have a regretful expression to match. Add to that his voice, so deep —it was a rare picture. The kind that made you want to gather the man in your arms and reassure him. Yeah, maybe, if her arms would go all the way around his shoulders.

"Apology accepted." Syd chuckled. "Besides, that doesn't even rank in the top one hundred of *unkind* things ever said to me."

Jack shook his head, clearly not ready to cut himself a break. "It doesn't suit me to be that way. It's just—"

Syd waited, watching Jack shift his weight from hip to hip against the door jamb.

"Devon brings out the worst in me."

Syd's chuckle faded. "That's family for you. At least—" Syd cleared her throat. "At least you have him."

Jack dropped his eyes and said nothing further.

"Why work together?" Syd glanced at him. "I mean, if it's too much—"

"We weren't given a choice."

"By the Archangel?" Syd closed the drawer and shifted one over to her favorite T-shirts. Her bed was seriously calling her name.

At the prolonged silence, she stopped and turned again. Jack stared at her, hand up and scratching at his head.

"What?" Syd looked down, examined herself for some obvious faux pas.

Jack shook his head. "You're taking all this with ease, asking the important questions. Feeding me."

"I did meet a demon tonight. That changes a girl's perspective." Syd smiled, this time there was only forced amusement. "You have no idea what kind of a freakshow my life has been. Apparently, I'm just getting to the main event. Besides, either all this is true—i.e. evil death monsters coming to get me—or I'm completely balls-out insane."

Jack snorted. "Well, yeah, I guess I get your logic."

"Tell me one thing."

Jack nodded. His expression was open. "If it's within my power, I'll answer truthfully."

"Why me?" Syd needed to know. Jack hadn't wanted to tell her before, but surely, now, with the fight, she deserved to know, didn't she? It was her damn life they were talking about.

"Syd, nothing's changed, Rafael still doesn't want—" Jack gestured to the recliner in the room. "May I?"

She drew a breath, tried to force down her irritation. She was tired and cranky, but she had an idea getting into a screaming match with Jack wouldn't help her cause. Following his lead, she left the dresser and moved across the room to sit on her bed. They sat across from one another. Jack lifted his gaze to the ceiling, brought one hand to cover his mouth.

"Devon and I were chosen once." Jack closed his eyes. His deep voice softened to a whisper. "We were only kids, by today's standards. Fourteen-years old, subject to a family curse. Dev and I—we were part of a prophecy that said we could break our family's curse."

Jack paused, his hands balled into fists. "The prophecy said we could save our family."

She stared at him, and she saw the crystalline depths of the Caribbean in his eyes.

"How?" Syd asked gently.

Jack rubbed his temple. "It's complicated. But we were human once, then Rafael made us Guardian soldiers, infused with angelic power. We must obey him—or we die. So, when you ask me, 'why me,' I have no idea how to answer. I've been asking myself the same question for over eight-hundred years."

Jack rose and headed for the door. "I'll be downstairs keeping watch." At the last second, he paused, but his face pointed toward the hallway. "Rest, Syd. It doesn't matter at this point why you were chosen. You were, and everything hinges on how well we protect you."

# CHAPTER NINETEEN

D evon prowled the grounds of Syd's estate with practiced ease. He didn't bother shielding himself from human sight. One, he didn't have the energy to spare. And two, who cared? He was weakened, not dead.

Jack had been right about one thing—his healing was nifty and gave Devon's muscles the ability to move freely, but his mind wasn't recovered at all. Currently he was about as useful as a steak on a vegetarian's plate. Cabin-fever edgy. Between Jack's heavy-coated honor-and-duty B.S. and Syd's constant attention, his skin itched under all the scrutiny.

*Be careful.*

Syd's words echoed through his mind. He tried to think of the last time someone had said those words to him, knowing he was indeed putting his life on the line.

A disquieting blank space greeted the internal question.

Jack? Nah—he'd washed his hands of Devon long ago.

Rafael, oh Bright-Lighted One? Please.

Stephen handled his business affairs, but they were nowhere near buddy-buddy status.

There was no one else. Nobody. And yet, Syd had said it herself, no compelling. She wanted him to *be careful*.

Why? Maybe she was polite. Maybe she figured two body-guards were better than one. Maybe...maybe she actually enjoyed his company.

Quieting his mind, Devon halted, realizing the last ten dark-ness-filled steps he had taken were without conscious thought. Dumbass.

The odds of Malik returning? As drained as he was, Devon had been in the demon's head fighting the battle. He had drained Malik, too. The million-dollar question: how much? Stupid enough to fill the Pacific with tears of regret if he was wrong. So walking in a daze? Not a good choice.

He centered himself on his task, crouched down, and let his fingers drift across the cold, crunchy grass. Glancing up at the waxing moon, he drew in the cold night air. A light flicked on in the second story. Syd's bedroom.

*Be careful.*

His mind slipped back to the moments before the demon showed up, watching Syd listen to the demo. The best of music had a way of baring your soul, and in those moments, he *saw* her. She had drifted off, let the music take her way, just for a moment. Syd's soul was true and battle-tested strong.

On impulse, he took his phone from his back pocket and dialed his studio in Paris. It was early in the morning there, no one would yet be in.

The studio voicemail kicked on, and he didn't bother to announce himself. "Stephen, sign Carina Bettencourt. Don't care how much." And he hung up.

Glancing up, Devon watched the light snuff out in Syd's bedroom. Jack's presence receded, moving down the stairs and across the house to the only bedroom on the main floor. No way he would sleep. Jack's ability to go without shut-eye would impress a Navy SEAL, and, since Devon hadn't bothered to check in with him, Jack would no doubt be on guard until dawn for any additional attacks. He would stay close, but, gentleman he was, Jack wouldn't come near Syd's bedroom. Luckily, Devon wasn't similarly afflicted.

Standing up, Devon's abused muscles protested only slightly at his prolonged crouch in the frozen grass.

Devon listened. Seconds ticked into minutes. Was she asleep? Unused to practicing delayed gratification, Devon gave one final look around the perimeter of the home. No stirring creatures of any kind. A moment later, he was in Syd's bedroom. When he moved through space it was virtually silent, so the slight creak in the leather of the recliner as he lowered himself was the only sound in the room.

Devon waited a moment, assessed if Syd had noted the noise.

When nothing but steady breathing reached his ears, Devon lounged down in the chair.

He was doing his job. The closer to Syd he was, the better he could protect her. Besides, his mind was so tired and worn that proximity was his ally. His hanging out in her room was not a creeper move, but totally justified. On the up and up. Yeah.

Dawn's good-morning kiss would be here before he knew it. Devon wasn't sure he dared to sleep, but if he didn't, he would only be a liability tomorrow. A fresh wave of exhaustion caressed him, and he glanced over to the bed. Syd's breathing was the steady tick of a metronome. Hypnotic.

God, what he would give to be in her bed.

Actually to sleep. The thought worked its way through his mind, and he reeled. He wanted to gather her in his arms, combine body heat, and sleep for the next two days straight. Usually closeness to women, other than during sex, was something he avoided.

Syd was different. She could quiet her mind, keep him from hearing the constant buzzing thoughts. It was damn near peaceful. And a new experience. On both counts, it was something he'd virtually given up hope of having.

"We can't sleep together." Syd's quiet voice was enough to startle him, but he gave no outward sign.

What, was she reading *his* mind now?

"Your bed looks mighty comfy." Dev drew himself up in the recliner, long fingers curling over the stuffed arms. "Definitely better than this chair."

"Plenty of beds in the house."

He shook his head, and his voice weary. No need to feign it. "How far away do you want me when the demon comes back?"

There was a moment as he hoped she considered it.

"Thank you," she said softly. "Again, I owe you my life."

He cleared his throat and tried to identify his reaction to her words. His chest warmed, and he wanted to smile. So foreign...Was this, maybe, pride in his ability to be of service to someone? His mind tacked on 'someone you care about' before he could stop himself. Honestly, he wasn't sure what churning mess of emotion was riding him. "You're...welcome."

She sighed with exaggeration. "Finally. It was my plan to keep making you uncomfortable thanking you until you acknowledged it."

He could almost feel the smirk on her face. Point for her.

She spoke softly. "Can I trust you to keep your hands to yourself?"

Hell, no. Devon ground his teeth. Usually females were begging him for a taste. Devon was a walking Lust Potion Number Nine. Her request subverted the natural order of things.

At his silence, Syd sighed heavily. "Look, I know I shouldn't be such a prude, but I'm proving a point to your brother."

"J?" As intelligent responses went, it ranked low. But he had nothing better. Cock-blocking motherfu—

"Jack seems to think I can't *not* sleep with you." She coughed. "You know *sleep*, sleep. Not just sleep."

"You mean, have sex. Get horizontal." Devon laughed. "Fuck."

A pause, then: "Um, yeah. That."

Devon could almost feel the heat of her blush. *Wanted* to feel the heat. Why was this beautiful, eccentric woman such a draw to him? Part of it he understood. Part of it didn't make any sense.

But Devon didn't cajole women into intimacy. It was beneath him. He didn't know whether to laugh, cry, or go in search of his impervious brother and try to impale him.

Well played, J.

"So...if I said we would sleep, *only* sleep, you'd share the bed?" Devon spoke softly. No force to the words, no compulsion. Just an honest request.

Her silence was a gift in most circumstances, but Devon cursed it with uncharacteristic powerlessness. Waited for her to make the decision. He didn't want to compel her to get his way. His fingers squeezed down on the recliner arms. What the hell was up with *that*?

Please say yes, he thought.

Syd sighed, like her internal conversation had been a heated one. "I'm trusting you."

Devon stilled in the recliner. Made sure his voice was level, because his thoughts went Tilt-A-Whirl. She deserved a warning. "That's not a good choice," he whispered.

"Are you going to try something?"

So simple to lie. "Most likely."

"Tonight?"

He smiled in the darkness, watching her move under the covers. Definitely squirming. "No, Lioness. Not tonight."

"Promise?" She wasn't ready to leave it at that. Smart girl.

But she wasn't used to dealing with him. She couldn't know oaths were not sacred to him. He'd broken more than he'd ever kept. "Scout's Honor."

"Okay." She pulled the covers tight to her chin. "But only because that demon scared the shit out of me, and you're some-what less scary."

He smiled wide in the darkness as he lifted himself from the chair in one fluid motion. His mental exhaustion drifted to the back of his mind for the first time since the demon battle, and there was damn near a bounce in his step.

Fuck, he *wanted* this. Really had desire for something. Being immortal, becoming jaded was part of the deal, but they never warned you against the boredom—and that was truly killer. So to want this experience with her was as close to a holy sacrament as he was likely to come.

He looked down upon the bed, so close the toe of his boots reached under the frame. Syd was on the other side, kinda hugging the edge of the king-size like maybe she had invited an alligator into bed with her. Didn't bother him. He was simply, yeah, *happy*.

Syd rolled over to watch him. He sat on the bed and began to unzip his boots. The covers had pulled down to her collarbone. One slim white arm shone in the moonlight from the bay window directly across from her.

She gasped. "You don't sleep in the nude, do you?"

Keeping a straight face, Dev stopped taking off the second boot and turned to her. "Is that a problem?"

She began to stutter out a response. Without thinking, Devon reached across the bed to grab her hand above the covers. Electricity traveled his skin, and she trembled in his grip.

"Only kidding. Fighting naked is a bitch. I'll be fully and regretfully clothed."

He squeezed her hand.

"But there is something I should probably tell you." Devon slipped his hand out of hers and went back to the boot.

Her hand dropped back to the lush comforter.

"I never was a Boy Scout."

## CHAPTER TWENTY

Sleep left Syd slowly, like the last savory sip of a warm latte. Her eyes drifted open. She lay on her side, facing the doorway to her room. The recliner across the room was empty. That seemed to be not quite...right.

Her eyes expanded to maximum exposure.

*Holy shit.* Had she— Did she— Was *he*—? She stilled her muscles, tried to keep her breathing normal.

Was Devon in bed with her?

There was the weight of a large hand curled around her hip, and the hair at the back of her neck tickled with an expelled breath. Devon pressed against her back. Asleep. Well, most of his body was asleep, at any rate.

Sweet Jesus.

Jack would go postal. And she didn't want to see that level of pissed-off cross his kind face. It had been the only thing he'd asked of her. For God's sake, he'd *apologized* to her.

Dizzy from images of last night flashing in and out, Syd's mind whirled. Did that count? She and Devon didn't *do* anything. Still— epic fail. Last night, when he had appeared in the room, he had seemed tired, uncharacteristically quiet, borderline forlorn. Yes, he was ruthless. But he had been ruthless in his protection of her, to the detriment of himself. She wanted to give him what little comfort she could.

And he'd promised.

In the cold autumn-morning light, that seemed dangerous and insane.

Devon rustled and grunted out a good morning stretch. "Syd?"

That *voice*. The bright light of morning didn't change the effect he had on her. If anything, the edges of his voice were rougher, sensual sandpaper. Her body tightened, but her mind chilled.

Faced away from him, she swallowed but said nothing.

"I know you're awake. Morning after regrets?"

She looked down at her right hip where his hand rested, where his touch sang through her body even now. Unable to hold her tongue, she said, "You promised you wouldn't try anything."

His hand slid away, to rest on the bedding between them, and he inched his body away. The heat of his hand didn't dissipate, and her heart pounded, desperate desire and common sense duking out a cage match in her head.

Jack's voice ran through her head. *You're better than that.* No, apparently, she wasn't.

She rolled to face him and sucked in a breath.

Devon's hair was sleep tousled, his jawline rough with dark stubble. "If I was trying something, your clothes would be in a heap on the floor. For future reference, that's how you can tell the difference." He looked away. "This wasn't about sex, it was about—"

A knock on her bedroom door.

Syd's eyes went wide.

Beside her, Devon drawled, "Come on in."

Jack appeared in her doorway. He looked ominous with jet black sunglasses covering the normal warmth in his expression. Syd had only seen him concerned or reassuring toward her. Now...his features tightened with grim disappointment; it oozed from every pore. But that was nothing compared to the rage that took over when Jack's gaze fixed on his brother.

"Before you—" was all Devon got out.

Jack flew quicker than Syd could track, and he hauled Devon out of bed by his shirt.

Jack had Devon raised in one hand above his head. Devon didn't fight back.

"Look at her, J." Devon's voice was tightly controlled.

The anger rode him, but Jack glanced at her.

"If she and I had fucked, she wouldn't've had the energy to reclothe. Not to mention...I'm fully dressed, too, asshole."

"You expect me to believe..." Jack swallowed, his Adam's apple bobbing. "The last thing she needs..." He lowered his brother to the ground.

"We've been over this." Devon smoothed his shirt. "The last thing she needs is me screwing around with her, literally or figuratively." Devon pointed his thumb to her. "Ask her. I asked her permission, and she made me promise to be good."

Jack's eyebrows rose skyward, and he rested the sunglasses on top of his head. "She made you promise *to be good?*"

"And he was," Syd managed to croak out. Except for mild snuggling, but she thought she'd leave that out. Syd pulled the covers against her body. The floor vibrated with Jack's footsteps closer to her.

"We have our orders from Rafael." The heavy footfalls stopped in front of her.

Syd looked up to see stolid resolution in Jack's eyes.

"The demon knows where to find us come nightfall. Pack a bag."

---

JACK AND DEVON told her they wouldn't be far. And Syd wanted to pack her duffle alone. She needed the space to take a deep breath.

Was she really leaving with Jack and Devon? The demon clearly knew where she lived, so that was a determining factor. But Jack knew more; he just wasn't disclosing. Discontent caused a shiver.

Syd took stock of the situation. All she could focus on was the current moment. And right now? She felt safe with them—as safe as a girl could feel after being nearly abducted by a demon with his trusty troop of vampire soldiers. Or, was it that particular kind of safe you felt when you became aware that safety was no longer a guarantee?

God, arriving at The Dive two nights ago seemed eons away.

Into her red duffle she packed her favorite overused-abused Pontiac sweatshirt, beaten into softness by sheer hours of wear. She ran her fingers over the hard cover of *Aesop's Fables* on her night stand, the binding well used and faded sea-green. She dropped it into her duffle along with her Glock.

Moving to the vanity, she packed her toothbrush. Picked up her hair brush to stow it, but ran it quickly through her long, tangled hair first. She glanced over the scattered bottles of nail polish all over the vanity. All intense and dark colors to mask the grease that could very well hide out behind her nails after an average day's work.

Thoughts chattered distantly in her head, nowhere near the front of her mind. Her body performed the rest of the pack-a-bag ritual on autopilot.

The giggle started deep in her gut and bubbled through her chest, gaining speed and potency. It filled her throat and escaped her lips. She braced her hands on the vanity in front of her.

Her reflected green eyes were glassy. Somehow that reflection didn't seem to be...her. Someone else, surely, looking like an automaton.

*Perhaps none of this happened. There was no drugging, no demon. No Devon. No Jack. You've finally gone crazy.*

The thought was dishearteningly comforting. *You've known it was coming for a long time.* Seconds ticked by—Syd became aware of the chatter in her head, voices threatening to make themselves heard. Her exhaustion left her vulnerable. She could only stare into the mirror and listen to the voices grow louder.

Her father's voice, cheerfully matter-of-fact and dispensing Aesop's morals. *We had better bear our troubles bravely than try to escape them.*

Her mother's voice, misplaced optimism that religion would be the answer.

Her intuition with its cryptic messages that so seldom made sense.

Jack's voice, so determined that Devon couldn't be trusted.

Devon's beautiful voice...

She took a deep breath, willed the din of all those voices to quiet. Her voice, though. *Her* voice had yet to be heard.

Jack and Devon seemed to believe it an unavoidable conclusion —she was leaving with them. What were her options?

A) Stay—wait for the monsters to come back and kill her. B) Leave with the boys. C) Try to ditch them and make it on her own.

Well, with so many wonderful options to choose from—what's a freaky psychic chick to do?

One thing was certain and disconcerting. Devon and Jack had protected her at every opportunity, at great risk to themselves. The two of them had defeated six vampires and a demon. For her. If they hadn't been here, she wouldn't be having this crisis right now. The decision would've been made for her. Either she'd have been taken to Hell or Malik would have killed her already.

The weirdness blew her mind. How could she possibly be so important? How could her value be so high?

Shouldn't she *know* if she were a queen on the angelic chessboard? And why did she feel like a pawn?

Syd watched her gaze harden with resolve in the mirror. She had made it through worse than this. A demon wanted her? Fine, but that didn't mean she'd be an easy target.

Syd flicked off the vanity light and glanced at the thick burgundy bedding of her king-size. Anything smaller would look silly in a room this spacious. Still, the emptiness of the large bed seemed excessive and sad now. Especially given it had been fully occupied last night.

God help her, but she wondered where Devon was at this moment. Her intuition hummed away, letting her know he wasn't far, though *how* she knew she couldn't say exactly.

It should scare the hell out of her, this connection to him, born of—what—mere days? Alarm was still there, sure, but riding shotgun was some emotion she hesitated to name. And her intuition wasn't happy about it.

Jack wasn't too happy about it, either.

Her mind waged war back and forth. In favor of Devon's ruthlessness. In favor of Jack's honor-bound approach.

Taking one last look at her room, her sanctuary, she walked out into the hall. She would go with them, but she wouldn't let them make all the decisions.

Her life, her choice.

# CHAPTER TWENTY-ONE

J ack heard the click of stilettos approaching.

After last night's demon attack, Syd had been more amenable to the things Jack suggested. Rafael's plan wasn't up for discussion, at any rate. She'd made only one request. Syd had to tell Brie she was leaving.

Jack had agreed, explaining his only caveat: she couldn't tell Brie the truth of why she was leaving. Hopefully she listened better to that request than the one to leave Devon alone.

Now, Brie strode into Syd's great room like she owned it and made a fast track right up to him. Man, Brie made him feel like he needed to put on more clothes. Jack glanced down at his hoodie on the couch next to him. He grabbed it, pulled it over his head, took out the sunglasses perpetually living in the front pocket, and put them on top of his head.

"Hey, Jackpot, you miss me?" Brie gave an exaggerated wink.

He smiled stupidly, completely unsure what to say, and horrified that his cheeks were burning. He glanced over to Devon, leaning against the wall on the other side of the room, arms crossed. If anyone would know...

Jack reached out, pure desperation. *How can I get her to leave me alone?*

*You think I'm going to help you out?* Devon's laugh was purely internal. *On second thought, here's what you do: screw her once. Make it quick and dirty, take away the mystique. Go ahead, do it now, I'll cover for you. What do you need, maybe three minutes?*

Jack gritted his teeth. *You are so vulgar.*

Devon smirked. *Give the lady what she wants, you selfish prude.*

Jack dug his fingers into the arm of the loveseat to stay still. The great room was spacious, but it took all his effort not to fly across the room, snap Devon's head around on his shoulders with a right hook.

Still, Jack couldn't effectively argue the point. By Devon's standards, yeah, he was a prude. So sue him—he found one woman and explored the depths of pleasure thoroughly. One at a time, for periods of months and years. Three-minute quickies had never been his style.

Brie's hand on his arm brought him back, and his muscles tensed under her touch. He used his other hand to draw hers away. "I'm sorry, Brie, I'm spoken for."

Brie chuckled. "Well, what she don' know—"

Jack cast his eyes down. "She's dead, and I'm not ready."

Brie's hand dropped like a stone.

Syd walked into the room then, her steps slow and uncertain. "Brie, can we talk?"

Brie's gaze averted from Jack, and she followed Syd into the kitchen. At the last second, she paused. "I'm sorry, Jackpot. Lucky girl, whoever she was."

Jack let his weight carry him down into the loveseat.

The two women disappeared around the corner and into the kitchen.

With only a second to consider better of it, Jack honed into the kitchen conversation. Simple enough, given the women were making no true effort to be quiet and the fact that his hearing was superhero-sharp. Separated from them by about twenty feet and a wall, he justified the intrusion by telling himself he needed to make sure Syd was safe, that nothing was going on.

Syd was doing her best to guide the conversation, but Brie wasn't having it.

"You honestly expect me to believe you had those two—baby, I don't have words—those two hunks of prime-ass beef steak in your house for *two nights* and nothing happened? And now you're leaving with them? Not one little feel-up, not one little peck—"

"Stop," Syd begged. There was a pause. "No sex or foreplay of any kind, yeah, that's what I'm saying."

Jack let his gaze drift over to his brother. Walking in on Syd and Devon in bed together had been a letdown and a simultaneous shock, coupled by the astonishment of them both being fully clothed. Even still, Jack had had his doubts. Amazing for once it appeared Devon had been telling the truth.

*She made me promise to be good.* Like asking a wolf to please play nice and not rip you to shreds. Jack shook his head at the absurdity. And yet, it appeared Devon had obeyed her request. Why? 'Obey' and 'Devon' were two words that hadn't worked together in the same sentence for a very long time.

"Devon asked me to leave with him." Syd spoke quietly. "For just a few days. Leave and clear my head."

Jack heard no hint of deception in her voice. And the words were truth. Except this wasn't going to be a vacation, was it?

Brie was silent for a heartbeat. "You really think that's the right way to deal? You still got me, just let me in, let me help. Come back to work at the House of Cards with me—"

"No," Syd said vehemently. "You know what happened last time."

Jack leaned forward on the loveseat.

Brie's voice came out low. "That wasn't your fault."

"You were put in danger. By me." Syd groaned. "I'm trying to keep you safe. Don't you see?"

Brie's voice hardened. "You can't believe that. Those were ignorant jackasses. Looking for an excuse."

"They vandalized your shop, because of what I did!"

"What you did? Baby girl, you *helped* find that little girl. Me? I'm just psychic enough not to piss anyone off. You, on the other hand, could get an atheist to scream 'hallelujah.' That family knows what happened to their child because of you."

"But the House—"

Brie made a disgusted noise. "So what? It's already fixed. That's what a woman carries insurance for. I got an 'ignorant jackass' rider on my policy. We been over this."

Syd paused, and when she began talking again, her voice was lower, huskier. "Did you know my dad made me make him a promise, before he died?"

Jack stilled, and the silence from Brie indicated she might've done the same thing.

Syd cleared her throat. "Six years ago, he made me promise to live my life, be happy. I'm trying so hard." Syd pushed out her breath. "I dream of dad all the time, of what he'd say about my life, whether or not he'd be proud of me."

Jack crouched, forearms resting on his thighs, not caring his hair was itching at his temple. There was such profound sadness in Syd's voice, he wondered if that was how he sounded to people when he spoke of Elaine. The difference between them, though they'd both lost someone, was Syd seemed capable of moving on. She was trying.

Jack drew in a breath.

He knew nothing at all about Sydney and the thought ashamed him. He knew where she lived and that she needed protection. He knew she was a tremendously gifted psychic. But he knew nothing about *her*. It changed nothing about the circumstances, but it felt important.

Something to add to his list of failures.

Brie's voice took on a maternal tone. "Baby girl, you got to let yourself feel something beyond the pain."

Brie's words struck like a cathedral bell at close distance. Jack's eyes sheened over with tears, and he dropped his head so Devon wouldn't clue into his emotions.

Syd drew a breath so deep Jack could easily hear. "You're right." Her voice took on a tone of strength. "I'm working on it."

*Oh, the irony.* Jack clasped his hands in his lap. His head hung down further. Weighty sorrow for Syd, for himself—for this God-awful situation that engulfed him. Neither of them had a choice, did they? Lie, Jack's conscience jeered at him. You chose this course; Syd didn't. Unease made him draw in a deep breath.

"Would've thought eavesdropping beneath your sterling character." Devon's sudden intrusion grated, and Jack's hands tensed instinctually into fists.

"Not talking to you." Jack remained concentrated on the women's conversation, but his tears evaporated.

"What are we, like, five?" Devon pressed.

Jack raised his head. Physical exertion rarely exhausted him, but somehow, where Devon was concerned, Jack tired easily. It hadn't always been that way. He looked across the room at his brother, that arrogant sneer on his face.

"What do you know about Syd's history?" Jack leaned back in the loveseat, throwing an arm back, claiming the rest of the seat.

"What makes you think I know anything at all?" Devon sauntered around the room, looking at the two sets of inset bookshelves, dragging a finger along the titles.

"Because you two are getting close."

Devon threw a sardonic look over his shoulder. "A gentleman doesn't kiss and tell."

"Gentleman?" Jack snorted. "Cut the shit. You didn't sleep with her. She would be in there spilling details to her friend. And she's not."

"I appreciate your faith in my sexual prowess." Devon went back to examining the books, pulling out an old King James. "I'd have more to tell you if she wasn't so damned good at kicking me out of her head." He seemed to consider saying something further but turned away instead. "Her parents died in a car accident a few years back."

Jack stilled in the chair. "That's horrible."

"Except to take horrible to new level, she also *knew* that it was going to happen since she was very young. She has true dreams."

Jack's head whipped up. "I haven't met anyone since—" The sentence hung. "You?"

Devon shook his head. "Only Bastian, unlucky bastard. Far as I can tell, it's still the rarest of gifts."

"And most coveted." Jack rubbed his temples. Rafael's interest in Syd was beginning to make an unfortunate amount of sense. "Syd's a Direct Line. Has to be. I haven't seen her do anything like Bastian could, though."

Devon smiled. "That's because she's built an impressive wall in her head. The powers she most likely has are tucked away."

Jack considered.

Devon snapped the Bible closed, nodded. "But the question is why. Why does a Direct Line set off a firework show of 'come get me' to dickhead angels and demons alike?"

Jack ran his hand back through his hair, absently willing it to stay out of his face and pushed his sunglasses up on his head. Rafael had told him why. But Devon wasn't to know; Rafael didn't trust him with the knowledge. Jack knew why, but he had no idea *how*. Only that a Direct Line could be the key to ending Rafael's banishment to earth.

Devon stared at him, probably reading that Jack knew more than he was telling. "There's something else."

Grateful for the topic change, Jack cocked his head. "What?"

"There's a woman, a scientist. She's been sniffing around Syd. Paid a visit just before the demon." Devon's mouth tightened. "She scared the shit out of Syd, so I scared the shit out of her. She warned that someone else wants Syd. Could be our demon."

Unease crept through Jack. A thought slithered through his mind, but he dismissed it.

The women walked back to the great room.

In a habit that refused to die regardless of the passing decades, Jack rose.

# CHAPTER TWENTY-TWO

Syd entered the great room and swiveled her gaze to Devon. Because it furthered her agenda and because she also wanted to keep Brie at arm's length from him, Syd walked over to Devon. She slid an arm around his waist. Energy pulsed between them; Syd's lips opened, and she tried to remain standing. Devon supported her weight, leaning his hip into her, his arm coming around her middle. A very male, very satisfied smile curled his lips.

Devon raised his gaze to Brie across the room. "Should we start packing?"

Brie watched her, Syd noted, and there was a distinct tinge of sadness to Brie's expression.

"You understand how important she is, right?" Brie said evenly, devoid of her normal colorful tone.

"More than you realize." Devon tensed beside Syd, every muscle coiled and ready, and his smile chilled some degrees. "I can keep her safe."

Brie's smile turned shrewd. "But is she safe with you?"

Syd stole a glance up to Devon. His face was his mask, unreadable. It seemed like he wasn't going to respond, and the pressure ratcheted up in the room.

Finally, he said, "I'll do my level best. That's all I can tell you, Brie."

Intensity traveled down from Devon's words to his arm tightening around her waist. "We'll be leaving today, right?" Syd looked up to Devon, then across the room to Jack, who stood several steps from Brie.

"As soon as you're ready," Devon said.

After more assurances and a bear-like hug from Brie, the woman-shaped whirlwind was out the door.

Syd had plopped down on the couch with a sigh of relief when the doorbell gonged.

She made an immediate move to answer the door, given that it was her house, but a giant hand on her arm stalled her movement. Glancing up, she saw Jack's pensive face staring at Devon.

With a solemn face, Devon nodded once, and Jack released her, turning the movement into a gesture. "Ladies first."

Syd let out the breath she'd been holding, trying to keep up with what had happened. Had Devon mentally screened her front door? Seemed likely. And weird. But also convenient, in a demon-avoidance kind of way.

She walked through the great room, crossed the foyer and had a hand on the handle as her visitor rapped smartly twice. Syd unlocked the deadbolt and pulled. Nina stood on her porch, smiling shyly with her hands laced loosely in front of her.

"Hey, is this a good time? 'Cause if not, I could come back later, or—"

"No, I mean, it's not a bad time." Syd smiled and stepped aside.

Nina's gaze shifted further into the house, and her step faltered.

Syd was going to have to get used to this, if she kept hanging out with these two brothers. "Nina, meet Devon."

Nina stepped inside the house, and Syd closed the door behind her. Nina's mouth dropped open, formed a demure, "Hi." She cocked her head. "Have we met before?"

Without skipping a heartbeat, Devon smiled, full wattage, hitting his target with a bull's eye. "Never had the pleasure."

Nina took a step closer to Syd. "Are you okay? You seemed... off...at The Dive the other night."

Syd cleared her throat. "Yeah, I'm good."

"I see that." Nina furtively glanced back to Devon. "Hey, can I ask you something? In private?"

"Of course. Devon can take care of himself for a bit." Syd gestured to her right, to her father's study. She started to walk off, felt the zing of Devon's hand on her shoulder.

"Did you just dismiss me?" Devon's eyebrow raised.

Syd smiled and winked. "Yep, that just happened."

Devon watched her intently. "I'll be in the great room. Not far."

Her smile faded, and she stepped out of his reach. Nina was already in the study, holding her hands and sitting stiffly on the edge of her father's leather chaise.

Shutting the heavy wood door behind her, Syd leaned against it.

Nina pushed out a breath. "You can totally say no. It's fine, I just, I didn't know—"

"What's wrong?" Syd asked immediately, striding across the room to sit next to Nina on the chaise.

"It's my sister. She's gotten mixed up in something. It's bad, Syd." Nina dropped her head in her hands. "It's really bad."

"Why did you come here?"

"You said you did, right? I mean, you, like, really found that missing girl?"

Syd shifted uncomfortably. "What do you need?"

"My sister, she's been snorting every penny she can find." Nina's head dropped. "She stole my grandmother's jewelry. Could you, is it even possible to—"

Nina didn't even want to finish the sentence, but Syd could guess where this was heading.

"You want me to locate the missing stuff?"

Nina's face brightened several degrees. "Could you? I mean, find my grandmother's jewelry? Kenzie isn't right in the head anymore, with the drugs. She's off on another bender and we have no idea what she did with it. My grandmother basically raised me, she didn't have much, but her jewelry was special, she was so proud of it."

Nina raised her right hand, pointing to the diamond solitaire on her ring finger. "This was her wedding ring. Kenzie and I had split custody." Nina sniffed. "It's the only piece left, because I had it when she took everything else."

Syd thought immediately of her father's Impala, how she treated it like the freaking Mona Lisa, how devastated she'd be if someone stole or abused it. "I can try. This stuff is sometimes...unpredictable."

Nina bobbed her head. "Even if it doesn't work, I don't care. Just...thanks for trying, you know? You're the best."

"Um, sure," Syd wiped her hands on her palms, aware that the mention of using her abilities was getting her adrenals activated. She turned sideways, to face Nina on the chaise.

"Can I hold the hand with the ring?" Syd shrugged. "It'll make it easier to...see."

Eagerly, Nina offered the hand. "Of course. Do you, like, light a candle or anything?"

Syd smiled. "Nah." She drew in a deep breath and pushed it out. She never dropped her wall entirely, and now she let her ability peak around the outer edges. Just a bit, just a little.

The air thickened, and when she opened her eyes, her perception of the world had shifted. Colors intensified, everything was sharper, crisper. Cleaner.

She reached forward and took Nina's hand. Syd stared at the ring, letting the way the diamond cut through the spectrum sparkle and mesmerize her. Her wall pulsed a steady stream of energy. She was aware of it, and if she needed it, she could patch it quickly, but she focused on the air. The entire world opened to her.

The breeze shifted as she gazed deeper into the depths of the diamond. She saw a woman. "Did your grandmother live in a duplex and walk with a blue cane?"

Still focused strictly on the diamond, Syd only heard the sharp intake of air from Nina. "Yes," she said softly.

"Your sister..." Syd blinked, confused at image being presented to her. "She's blonde, like you? With a full sleeve on her left arm?"

"Y...yes." Nina's hand was trembling in Syd's grip.

"Your sister is...not the one taking the jewelry."

The image was stark and cruel. Nina's sister had been held at gunpoint by an Asian man and a light-skinned woman. Shaking in his hold, Kenzie directed them to the jewelry with her flat, dry eyes.

Syd released her hold of Nina's hand and rubbed her head, a headache forming behind her eyes. "Kenzie was high, but it looks like she didn't have a choice. She may not be on a bender at all. I think she got in over her head."

Nina's eyes had pooled with unshed tears. "What do you—is she okay?" She wiped her eyes with the palm of her hand, tears wetting the ring.

Syd wanted to be reassuring, but instead she let the truth out. "I don't know."

Nina twisted the ring on her finger. "Forget the jewelry... Could you help me find my sister?"

Syd glanced toward the door, wondering if Jack and Devon were willing to take on a side job.

# CHAPTER TWENTY-THREE

Turnabout being what it was, Jack was the one now prowling around, his powerful limbs itching to do something. His headspace was a mess of sticky emotion. The demon, the Syd situation, and the San Andreas rift between him and Devon all compounded into a swirl of unrest. Minutes ticked away. Rafael had been clear. They needed to leave—

"So, what does Rafael need with a Direct Line?" Devon wondered aloud, sitting in the great room, his arm draped possessively over the back of the couch.

Avoiding the topic was safest. "We should be gone already. No telling when the demon or his creations will return."

Devon waved toward the window. "Strong daylight out. They'd be stupid to attack us now. I don't care what breed of hell beast that demon was, daylight is not his friend." Devon smiled wickedly. "At least they understand we aren't some run of the mill Guardian soldiers. We fucked their shit up."

Jack smiled tightly. "Eloquent, as usual. Did you forget the part where they fucked your shit up, too?"

Twisting his lips to a sneer, Devon murmured, "And yet I'm still here."

Jack stared at his brother, wondering if Devon was replaying the words Jack had spoken in anger last night. God, he hoped not. Though everything he said was true, there was so much more to Devon than what he'd become. He hadn't always been this way, this monstrous way.

Jack continued to stare at his brother, wanting so badly to say what hung between them, but not ready for the ramifications. If he dared to mention how he healed Devon the night before, it would only cause Devon to shuck off the kid gloves. Being reminded of your mortality (even though you might be immortal to a large degree) and your dependence on someone else was likely to send Devon into highly pissed-off territory. Not a place Jack wanted to deal with. Not now. Not when Devon appeared to at least be playing somewhat nice, with Syd around. Maybe there was still hope of true reconciliation.

Time was running out.

The night before they were sworn into Rafael's service flashed unexpectedly in Jack's mind, a nearly forgotten memory. They had been so young, so naïve. But they had been brothers.

"Do you remember the promise you made me, the night before Rafael initiated us?"

Devon stilled on the couch, his bobbing foot ceasing motion, his fingers curling into the plush fabric. He said nothing.

Jack cleared his throat. "You, ah, you had just come out of that ramshackle tent we called a house. I could hear mom crying, still. You had just done your best to comfort her—"

"Where the hell is this going?" Devon interrupted sharply.

Jack dropped into the loveseat directly across from his brother.

He raised a conciliatory hand. "Just hear me out."

Devon's lips pushed together, drawing a harsh line on his handsome face.

"Then you came over to me and starting using our language. I think, because you didn't want anyone overhearing us. Remember, we were so worried that the angels or some monster was eavesdropping? We thought we were so important." Jack chuckled.

Tall, reed-thin, fourteen-year-old twins, scared as hell, and tapped to break their family's curse.

"I didn't want to go through with it. I thought we should just run away," Jack continued.

Devon's voice was low. "I wouldn't let you."

Jack nodded. "And there was no way I'd leave without you."

Sneering, Devon laughed. "Even then I could manipulate you—"

"No," Jack cut in. "You weren't manipulating me. You were *helping* me accept the responsibility. You were doing the right thing. *Biswinte engel-wird.*"

Devon threw up a hand. "That language is dead, J. I'm not your decoder-ring buddy anymore."

Heedless, Jack rushed on. He needed Devon to understand. Time was not on his side here. "You made me promise to always remember that until the day Hell dies, I serve the angels, but my love is always to my brother. *Ei servien my engle-wird bis helledae, verehren*—"

"Stop!" Devon hissed and raised his head, arrogance coating his features.

To Jack, it couldn't be more obvious that arrogance was Devon's armor of choice. "You made me promise, because you knew I needed you. A touchstone. The most important person in my life."

"Times change, though, huh?" Devon turned his face, staring out the window. "So, Rafael needs to protect the Direct Line."

Jack paused, understanding his choice clearly. Push Devon on the promise, made so long ago, as a way to perhaps mend the rift between them, which would nearly guarantee a fight, or drop the subject and get back to the assignment.

Jack rubbed his temples and made his choice. "Maybe she is foretold to have specific knowledge?"

Devon shrugged and worked the arrogant armor out of his expression in an instant, shifting into 'all-work' mode. "It sure would be nice to know. It can only help us."

Devon stood abruptly, looking around. "Do you feel that?"

Jack stood, hands fisted and ready. "Enemy?"

Devon's eyes fixed in the direction where Syd had gone. "No...I think it's Syd. Her power. Shit." He extended an arm and rolled up his sleeve. All the hair stood on end.

Jack wasn't keyed in to power like Devon, but there was a hum in the air. He turned toward the study. "Should we check on her?"

Devon's eyes were filled with unconcerned curiosity. "No."

"But—"

Devon's voice was certain. "She's not in trouble. She's letting her wall down. I've never felt anything like that, not from a human being." Devon shifted his gaze to Jack. "Tell me again you have no idea why Rafael wants her. Lie to me, *bruder*."

Jack turned away this time. Rafael had made it clear—Devon was to know as little as possible. On one level, it made sense. Devon was so clever, and knowledge was power. Rafael approached Devon as a barely friendly foe. If something needed killing, Devon could be trusted. But Rafael had rarely allowed Devon on assignments like this. For good reason. Devon was typically better at bedding damsels than saving them. Sure, Devon would protect her from Hell, but he was a different kind of poison women couldn't help but drink.

So why Rafael had decided they were both required here was a mystery. To Jack it could only mean that whatever Syd's role in this angelic mashup, it was powerful, dangerous stuff.

# CHAPTER TWENTY-FOUR

Clearing her throat, hands resting in her back pockets, Syd walked into the great room. Jack and Devon stood across from each other, looking like they were engaged in a heated debate, or possibly like they were about to launch into a fistfight. She supposed the two weren't mutually exclusive.

Both men shifted attention to her. Jack's expression softened perceptibly, Devon's mask remained in place.

"Your little friend take off?" Devon asked.

"Yeah, she did. Ah, actually—" Syd twirled Nina's grandmother's ring on her middle finger. She'd need it if she was going to track Kenzie's location.

Jack cocked his head.

Devon waved his hand. "Out with it."

"Nina's sister is being held against her will by her dealer on the east side of town. Any chance we could, like, save her or something? Before we go see the angel?"

Jack rose, his expression serious. "Syd, we can't risk your safety, we can't—"

"Sure." Devon cut in and rolled his eyes. "What kind of semi-angelic superheroes would we be if we didn't? You stay here, nice and safe. Give me the address, I'll flash in and grab her, bring her back here. Ten minutes, tops."

"I don't have an address. Just a feeling. But I could guide you there." She'd done something similar with the missing girl. Of course, she had been too late, and she'd only guided the family to a decomposing body. She was nearly certain that Nina's sister, Kenzie, was still alive. For the moment.

Jack sent Devon a scorching look. "The mission, Dev, the mission first."

"Yeah, see, I can never get it straight. Saving the girl seems like the good-guy thing to do, but you're telling me no. Right and wrong get all twisted up in my head. Please explain, J, why saving the innocent life now is the wrong choice, but letting Bryce the asshole live was the right thing?"

Jack threw up his hands. "Fine, whatever. I'm done arguing." He gestured toward the garage. "Let's just get this done."

Devon winked at her. "Ten minutes, tops."

---

SYD NEEDED TO CONCENTRATE, which meant driving was out of the question. Which meant one of the boys needed to drive. Which meant, therefore, they weren't taking the GTO. She trusted no one on Heaven or Earth to drive it, except herself. The Typhoon was torn apart, in the middle of a few performance mods, and the Impala...no friggin' way.

Devon rolled his eyes when Syd made her proclamation.

Syd folded her arms across her chest as the three of them stood in her garage. "Admit it, you're disappointed."

Devon shrugged and gestured to the electric-blue muscle car. "It'd be fun to drive." His smile turned devilish. "But not as fun to drive as some things."

"Flirtation will get you nowhere," Syd said matter-of-factly.

Devon laughed. "When I start flirting, you can re-evaluate your position."

Jack cleared his throat in exasperation. "Can we stop arguing about which piece of metal we're going to take? My pick-up is out front."

"No." Syd and Devon said in unison.

Syd wrinkled her nose. "You clearly haven't washed that thing in months. It's gross. I don't ride in 'gross.'"

"I'm a problem-solver," Devon said. "Be back in no time." Then he disappeared.

Syd shook her head, glancing at Jack. "Can you do that, too?"

Jack snorted. "No. My powers are different, primarily enhanced senses, increased physical strength and stamina, healing. Devon's are about the mind, mostly. Manipulation, compulsion, and the teleportation bit. Which, I'll admit while he's gone, is pretty damn handy."

"Where'd you think he went?"

"Probably to get his Jeep. He left it at The Dive."

And fifteen minutes later, that guess turned out to be truth.

A car horn blared out front, pulled into the drive far enough to be out of the street, but not by much and blocked out by the locked wrought iron gate.

She pushed out the front door, unlocked the wrought iron, and marched up to the black Jeep Cherokee Trackhawk. Hands on her hips, she circled it, appreciation in her eyes. It was one of the few trucks she'd ever consider owning. It was a piece of fucking art. Except, well, she didn't have near six-figures to drop on it.

Turning off the truck, Devon got out of the vehicle and hovered, two steps too close. "You approve?"

She stepped back and held out her hand. "Keys?"

He held them out in front of him by thumb and forefinger. "Say 'please.'"

She grabbed them and shook her head. "Where'd you get this truck?"

"My buyer picked it out. I wanted something fast that could handle Detroit's shitty weather."

"He certainly nailed it. Wait, your buyer?" Syd opened the door.

"Perk to being in the Guardian Army and living for-mostly-ever. Money isn't an issue."

Syd clucked her tongue. "Must be nice."

"Says the girl living in a mansion."

Syd glanced back at the house, thinking how she was barely holding onto it. How the back steps had rotted out. How the wrought iron gate should've been locked with something other than a padlock. That damn property tax bill.

Shaking herself out of the depressing thought, she pushed the red button and engaged the ignition. The truck growled to life. Syd identified the high whine of the pulley in about two seconds flat. "Gotta love the sound of a supercharger. Nice."

Devon shrugged and leaned against the open driver's door. "It's fast."

"Impressive. About a mid to high 11-second quarter-mile." Syd looked to him. "It wouldn't touch the GTO, but it'd be fun to test the theory." She looked around the cockpit and gripped the steering wheel. "I'd own it."

"I get the feeling that's high praise," Devon said.

Syd slipped out of the driver's seat, walked back a few paces to admire the truck. "It is."

Jack strode up to them, his arms crossed across his broad pecs. "We have to get this done." He pulled the phone out of his pocket, checking the time. "We're already pushing it."

Syd spun the ring around her finger, let her wall drop a hair, and said, "Let's do it."

* * *

DEVON DROVE SURPRISINGLY CIVILLY. She rode shotgun with Jack in the backseat behind her.

Devon took the turns as she directed, her eyes closed most of the time. With her wall down, it was hard to see past the presence of the powerful brothers, and she had to flex a bit of her mental muscle. It felt good, actually, to use what she so often neglected. Still, even now, her wall was mostly up, and she was ready to slam it into place at any moment.

Devon touched the edge of her mind once, crisp as an ocean breeze. She opened her eyes immediately. "You're not helping."

He smiled at her, completely unrepentant and with more than a hint of challenge. "There's a part of me that wants to push you so hard, to see if you could really keep me out—"

She shivered but let her eyes bore through his.

"Dev—" Jack's voice was a growl from behind her.

Devon shook his head, and his voice softened. "And the other part of me now realizes why the dickhead Archangel wants you safe."

Jack went silent.

Syd didn't want to delve too deeply into the comment. Later, maybe, when things calmed down.

Kenzie first.

She shut her eyes, let her wall soften again, and took the ring off. It crunched into her palm, the hard edges of the ice digging into her skin.

The image assaulted her, punching the air out of her lungs. "Turn right," she breathed.

Devon took a hard right, her shoulder hitting the door panel. They were heading east, through the rundown houses in Hamtramck, packed so close together, a car wouldn't fit between. Then past Mt. Olivet cemetery, several of the dead whispering to her, beckoning, pleading.

"Faster," she whispered.

Devon obliged, and Syd's head dropped back against the head-rest, her chin pointing heavenward as the images flashed, the smells of old oil thickened.

They were getting closer, her ability pulling her in the direction like psychic GPS.

Close enough now, Syd had a clear view of things. She couldn't hear them talking, not clearly, but she could sense the change in Kenzie. The drugs were wearing off, withdrawal and pain kicking in. Her fear was coming alive, though she was still way out of it.

"Turn left."

It was an abandoned, heavily-graffitied industrial building. The air was thick with the dust being kicked up by the dealer's boots. He was yelling at her, and Kenzie's hands were bound behind her with dirty rope. The chair they had set her in was rusty with padding long deteriorated.

"Left here."

Devon made the turn, tossing her into him, her head resting for a millisecond on his shoulder. She straightened up, and demanded her mind focus on Kenzie.

Almost there.

"Here." Syd opened her eyes and pointed to the building to the left. "She's in there somewhere."

Devon nodded, and Jack gripped her seat as he opened the door. She opened her door and ran straight into Devon as he appeared in front of her. "You think you're going where, exactly?"

She gestured to the building. "I can get you closer."

He pointed to his head. "I'm close enough. Already in their heads. One hostage, one woman and one man." He winked. "Ten minutes, tops."

Then he was gone.

She started to follow. Her abilities rode her, and they knew the task. Jack's hand on her shoulder pulled her to a halt. Abruptly, her abilities focused and shifted onto the large man in front of her. Vibes of all kinds pouring from Jack, she stumbled back, hitting the Jeep with her spine, his hand trailing her, in case she decided to follow Devon.

Grief crashed over her like an ocean wave... God, he was so sad. His wife.

Syd was engulfed in his grief, but the second feeling that rolled off him, such a surprise emotion. The words tumbled from her mouth. "Why do you feel so guilty?"

Jack drew his hand back from her with preternatural speed. "What?"

She rubbed her shoulders through her leather, in defense of the cold and the feelings wafting off Jack. She waved her hand toward him. "Guilt. And grief. It's all over you."

He turned his head away. "Please stay out of my head, Syd."

"I'm sorry— I didn't mean to—" She put her wall back up, every brick. The rebuff was gentle, but her psychic skin had been hurt so many times, it didn't take much to bruise.

Devon appeared before them, holding a passed-out Kenzie in his arms, her head lolling back. "Bet that was under five."

"Is she okay?" Syd rushed over and put her hands on Kenzie's forehead. "Jack?"

Jack came over and removed the burden from Devon, addressing his brother. "Everyone else still alive?"

Devon shrugged. "You didn't specify."

"Dev—" Syd exclaimed.

He waved dismissively. "Calm down, I just did a little creative compulsion. Their drug trade is over. By the way...you interested in the location of the grandmother's jewelry? I might've picked that piece of info out of their drug-addled brains. Pawn shop, south Warren."

Syd smiled at him and glanced back at Jack, who watched the exchange with a funny look on his face.

Jack's skin lit with healing, and Kenzie started to wake. Her head lolled forward and then tilted back, her eyes slitting open. She made eye contact with Jack, and he smiled gently at her. Her eyes grew wide.

Poor thing.

Syd knew exactly how she felt.

Devon tapped his imaginary watch. "Time's wasting, right, J?

Let's get her home, give Nina the pawn shop info, and get on with Plan A. Right?"

Syd opened the back door of the Jeep, and Jack set Kenzie lightly in the seat. "You're going to be okay."

Syd was sliding into passenger seat when Devon dangled the keys in front of her. "Wanna drive?"

A devious smile split her face. Hells yeah.

# CHAPTER TWENTY-FIVE

---

S yd used the paddle shifter to drop to third, causing the Jeep's RPM to spike and the engine to roar.

They'd dropped off Kenzie on Nina's doorstep. To say her friend was speechless was an understatement of the vast variety. Then, as Devon recited the missing items and the address of the pawn shop where they could be found, Nina's eyes filled with tears.

"Thank you," her friend had whispered and hugged her fiercely.

Now they were back to the important business.

"Where exactly are we headed?" Syd asked for the third time. Jack was giving directions but seemed hesitant to give the actual address. And they definitely were on the wrong side of the tracks.

"Not too far from here." Finally, Jack rattled off an address.

A lifelong inhabitant of the city, Syd knew the block. "That's... that's right near the old Packard Plant. It's a really shitty area."

Jack shrugged. "Rafael has an ally there and reinforcements waiting to meet us. He believes the Fallen must know more than he thought, if they have attacked so blatantly."

"Who's this ally you mentioned?" Devon asked.

Jack acted as if he hadn't heard the question, though he'd hear a skip in her heartbeat.

The idea of going into the worst part of the city for help... It didn't make sense to her either. Jack and Devon proved they were willing to fight to keep her safe, but her intuition wasn't fond of the presented plan. She shivered against the chill in the air and in her mind.

"Why bother, J?" Devon casual demeanor tightened. "What can this 'ally' do that we can't?"

Jack swung his gaze to meet his brother's. "I don't question orders."

"But if—" Devon began.

"You want to question Rafael? Ask him yourself."

Silence.

She glanced at both men. They looked much like they had at The Dive, which is to say, ready to brawl. "Why *don't* you ask Rafael, if Jack won't tell you?" Syd asked. Seemed like a simple solution.

Devon was silent.

Jack laughed harshly and pointed to Devon. "Syd, you're looking at the only member of the Guardian Army forbidden contact with his Captain. If he comes before Rafael, his life is forfeit." Jack paused and shook his head. "Why Rafael continues to tolerate you is beyond me."

Devon's held breath exploded in an assault of words. "Tolerate *me?* What about you, J? I've done more for this army in the past ten years than you, playing 'poor me' in your secluded corner of the world. You haven't been heard from in a decade. And why? Your poor *dead* human wife."

Jack's hands tightened into fists, and a snarl roughened his voice. "Do not speak of her."

Devon's lips curled cruelly. "Elaine?"

This was it. Trapped together in a closed vehicle, they were about to pummel each other with the force of the animosity and rage exuding from their pores. Crash and burn was imminent. Even through her mental wall, she could feel the heat of their anger.

Jack turned away, dropped his head in his hands, and took three audible breaths.

"Come on, J, it's just getting interesting," Devon pushed. "You aired the dirty laundry. I'm happy to finish it for you, but Syd already knows about our disagreement."

Jack whipped around. "*Disagreement*? I watched you slaughter dozens of people."

Devon *tsked*. "Let's not exaggerate. It was only twenty-two."

Syd tried to concentrate on driving, but she couldn't help but spare a look between the two men. Warm fuzzies had fled for greener pastures. With no idea of their plan, her confidence in the brothers' ability to set aside centuries of family-drama baggage was not at an all-time high.

One way to get their attention. She floored it, and the Jeep responded beautifully, no lag, just a sharp increase in power, throwing all kinds of G-force their way.

An 'umph' sounded from the backseat as Jack was thrown back. He shouted over the din of the roaring engine, "Is that really necessary?"

Syd smirked. "Nope, but it sure is fun. And you two need to cool the hell off."

Besides, Syd never turned down the opportunity to open up something as mean as this Jeep. It wasn't a race by any stretch, but it gave her a buzz of adrenaline anyway. It demanded her attention. It was the one time in her life Syd felt her focus pinpoint, shutting everything else out completely. Freedom. Going to the track with her dad had been heaven.

She glanced back to Jack, whose knuckles were curiously white where he gripped the seat.

"How in God's name do you still have a license?" he asked through clenched teeth.

Syd laughed. "Cops in this city have better things to do than worry about my driving habits."

The Trackhawk didn't disappoint. Syd took the next turn rated for twenty-five miles per hour from I75 South to 94 East at about double that. Suspension was tight, impressive for a truck. Syd registered Jack's big hand clutching the oh-shit handle, and her smile grew. He was clearly prepared to bail at the first sign of an impending rollover. No need though. She was in complete control of the vehicle; only regret was the fact that it was an automatic. Paddle shifters didn't do it for her. She was a purist at heart. Manuals were so much more fun to drive.

They were in arguably one of the worst neighborhoods Detroit had to offer, taking them past the legendary urban ruins of the old Packard Plant.

Syd turned down the side street, running alongside the abandoned automotive plant which stretched for city block after city block. Devastation as far as the eye could see. Houses succumbing to the despair were directly across from the fossilized dinosaur of American manufacturing. Graffiti and crumbling brick combated the wild overgrowth of weeds and trees. Most of the buildings' orifices were stacked with overflowing trash bags. Syd swerved to avoid a pair of bright sneakers and broken glass in the road. Though the Jeep windows were closed, the stench began to permeate the air.

They passed a fire burning inside the plant, and she heard Jack dialing his phone.

"Don't bother calling," Syd said, her eyes alert and her right foot never letting the truck come to less than a twenty-roll.

Jack spoke slowly, "I'm just going to let them know."

"The fire department won't go into the Packard Plant."

Jack shoved his phone in his pocket. "But—"

"The whole complex is way past condemned, it's too dangerous. There's nothing in there worth saving." Syd shrugged. "The fires go out eventually."

Two minutes later, they arrived at the address Rafael had provided them.

Late afternoon sun peaked from the clouds but did nothing to improve the scenery. The charred porch had collapsed into the broken wood steps leading to the front door of the bungalow. If there weren't homeless in there, there were most certainly rats. Ugh. The homes on either side of their destination were nothing but rubble and a heaping mound of trash.

Detroit, in all her ruinous glory.

"This is it?" Syd had been hoping the Archangel's ally lived in a place that resembled Fort Knox, armed with demon-decimating machine guns for good measure.

The yard mainly consisted of patches of weeds, separated like high school cliques distancing themselves from one another. Shards of glass were more plentiful than blades of grass. Windows were boarded up and decorated with vaguely-insulting graffiti. Weak autumn sunlight filtered in through unintended skylights in the roof.

Ahead of her, Jack surveyed the ramshackle structure before them. Syd followed his gaze down the street. Hard to believe, but it was one of the more habitable structures on the block. Several were the victims of arson. One house had been burned down only partly, as if the weight of completing the crime was too heavy to lift.

"Rafael was clear in his directions. This is the right place." Jack raked a hand through his hair.

"I think I've mentioned this is a stupid plan, right?" Devon slid from the passenger side of the Jeep. He slammed the door and held his hand out to Syd.

Reluctantly, she tossed the key to him.

She scanned the neighborhood again, spotting a house ten lots away littered with children's bright plastic toys.

"This is sad." Devon pocketed the keys.

Syd scowled at him, hands on her hips. "The people here have more heart than you can imagine." She bit her lip and scowled.

Devon's blank look only exacerbated Syd's irritation. The debate was a common one with outsiders. Why do you stay here? Wouldn't it be nice to move somewhere nicer, safer, cleaner...fill in the blank. It was a battle her father had taught her, being a Detroit small-businessman and seeing the city through her worst days:

riots, government corruption, and the death and rebirth of the auto industry. Outsiders didn't get it. There was so much more here. Culture, beauty, strength of the human spirit. It all lived in Motown, ran as deep as the scars of war.

Devon gestured to the house in front of them. "I meant the fact that Rafael's idea of protection is to send you here."

Syd's hands slipped from her hips. Sick of waiting, she took a step forward. Jack's left arm shot out in front of her like a concrete turnstile, and there was no toll she could pay to pass. She looked up at him, and he pointed to the upper right side of the porch.

It took her more than a moment, but she finally noticed the tiny red light and the camera eye that stared openly at them.

Someone *was* here, and they were watching.

Syd's body tensed.

"Dev, stay with Syd. I'm going in first to check things out."

Dev pressed his lips into a thin line. He nodded to Jack and gestured to Syd. "We'll wait."

Syd glanced from one brother back to the other. She walked back to Devon, mirroring his stance of leaning against the truck.

# CHAPTER TWENTY-SIX

L eaning against the truck in a relaxed pose, Devon's mind was hyper-aware. At least half strength. He had hoped for more, but the demon had drained him to dangerously low levels. Probably wouldn't be as good as he was, had it not been for the little slice of heaven that was Syd's bed. And Syd...

He shut down the train of thought. Unproductive. Not to mention he could sense her fear. Which was good. Healthy, even. He'd tried to warn her off him, and then got himself invited into her bed. Selfish bastard. He really was.

He cataloged everything within several hundred feet of them. Most of these dilapidated houses were not occupied. Several were —not legally, he was sure. One home had four young children. Setting aside the immortal-power trump card, his semi-auto was tucked into the inside of his leather jacket. On its face, he and Syd looked textbook stupid white people treading into territory in which they had no business.

Two men wearing the thug uniform loitered on a rickety porch several postage-stamp lots away.

Well, he could remind her how stupid it was to trust him.

Devon called down to the men clouded in a haze of smoke. "Hey, you guys know where the nearest Starbucks is?"

Syd stepped in front of him, incredulous. "What the hell, Devon?"

He shrugged. "Time for my daily dose of Vitamin-V."

*Violence.*

"Stop it," Syd whispered fiercely.

Devon ignored her, smiled, and gave a friendly wave to the men on the porch.

The men shook their heads, turned away. One of the men pulled out his phone and made a call.

Devon didn't delve into his motivations for the provocation. He itched, knowing he was getting closer to Rafael, which could mean his being taken out of service. He fumed, at the demon no-doubt hot on their trail. Like a jonesing tweaker, he fought his body's need to lash out at something. If he did…Syd was too close. And he was *not* safe. Why hadn't she gone with Jack? His brother was stable, noble. Better.

Devon moved toward the men on the nearby porch; this was so much easier. A target for his anger, and a reminder to Syd of who he was.

Syd's hand on his leather jacket wrenched him to a halt. Surprisingly strong. He ripped his arm out of her grip and gave his coldest look over his shoulder. "Stay here."

"The fuck are you doing?" Syd demanded, her arm outstretched toward him, emerald eyes sparking against the drab day.

"What does it look like? Trying to pick a fight." When Devon turned back, the two men had left the porch and swung their arms as they strolled toward the Jeep.

"We don't have enough trouble, you need to make more?" Syd's voice strained, little more than a forced whisper.

"*I'm* trouble, Syd. Haven't you figured that out yet?"

The un-neighborly neighbors approached at Devon's invitation. Syd stepped behind him.

Good, Dev thought. She needed to learn she couldn't dictate his behavior more than anyone else. Which is to say—little to none.

"Man, you need some fancy joe?" The men laughed loudly, clapped hands with deceptively good-natured smiles. "You in the wrong 'hood."

"For real." The second man echoed, hiking up his pants.

"I kinda like the ambiance here." Devon gestured around, echoing their happy-go-lucky routine. Like a fly on the inside of their skulls, he listened into their thoughts. Both had nines and a nice assortment of illegals. The bigger one was already pricing out how much he would get for Dev's Jeep. An insulting low estimate.

"How 'bout you give us the keys to that nice-ass truck."

"That truck?" Devon pointed his thumb back to his Jeep. "Sorry, guys. The lady here really likes that particular truck."

Smiling a mouthful of gold, the bigger man lifted his shirt to reveal the nine Devon already knew he carried. Syd gripped the back of his leather jacket, muttering obscenities at him.

"Or I just take it," the other man suggested. The man's name was Tyler, Devon learned, still in the man's head.

"Tyler." Devon shook his head. "Dr. Phil says you never negotiate by ultimatum."

Suspicion on his features, the man lifted his head. "I know you, bitch?"

Devon laughed. "Nah, but I might know your sister."

The bigger one sniggered. "Man, you didn' jus—"

Tyler swung on him. Devon dodged it easily, and the other man drew his gun.

"Happy now?" Syd whispered from behind him, and her hand on his jacket tightened.

He could end this at any time. He could compel the men to turn around and walk away. So why was he doing this again? Syd's hand on his jacket grounded him.

To prove what? And to whom?

His words to Brie echoed through his mind. He'd told her he'd do his level best to keep Syd safe. Goddamn it.

He flicked his hand in the direction of the men. "*Go away. Leave us alone.*"

On a dime, the men did exactly that.

Sensing movement, Devon pivoted back to see the porch of the house Jack had entered. Syd released the hold on his jacket, giving him a shove, still muttering obscenities. He gave her a solid 'A' on creativity.

Jack reappeared on the porch. Devon had a moment to decide the look on Jack's face was too carefully neutral when someone else stepped onto the porch behind him.

It took Devon only a second to process the disguise of humanity the Archangel wore. "Rafael—" he whispered.

Oh shit.

The Archangel's words rang through his head, from nearly two hundred years ago, but the booming anger wasn't something he'd soon forget: "*If I ever set eyes on you again, Devon, I swear to our God I will kill you where you stand.*"

So—was this it?

He swallowed and drew himself to his full height, shoulders back, and let his arms hang loosely at his sides. He wouldn't go down without a fight. Rafael had to know that.

The Archangel came toward him, and, even disguised, the movement was all grace and resembled floating more than striding. "Stand down, soldier. I am temporarily rescinding my order against you. Your skills are needed more than my wrath. But make no mistake, your continued existence is directly correlated to how well you follow my orders and how well you protect her."

Rafael pointed at Syd, and Devon saw her shudder.

So not only was Syd important enough to assign him and Jack, against Jack's wishes, but she was also pivotal enough to remove his angelic restraining order.

A shiver of memory flowed through Devon's body. The feel of Syd's power. Rafael wanted her bad.

Dev reached out and grabbed Syd's hand. "You know there's no one better to protect her."

Rafael narrowed his eyes.

"So, you're the Archangel." Syd stated quietly, her question aimed at the crazy powerful being in front of them. She shrugged her hand out Devon's grip and took a step toward the angel.

Impressive. Syd had this unassuming way of doing extraordinary things. He didn't really want to admit it, but she had risen in his esteem from something he wanted to some*one* he wanted to protect. And he did not like her so close to Rafael.

Rafael came to stand ten feet away. The air shifted and thickened with contained energy. He might be disguised, but Rafael's power heralded him.

The Archangel gestured to Devon and Jack. "I am. I'm also the one who gifted you these two warriors, to keep your life safe. The Archangel Rafael."

Syd glanced to Devon and whispered, "Am I, like, supposed to bow or something?"

As if the Archangel couldn't hear her. Devon smirked and held his tongue by sheer force of will.

"Some form of deference or gratitude would be appropriate," Rafael said drily.

Syd cleared her throat and bowed a few inches. "Devon and Jack... They've protected me well. Even against the demon—"

"Demon?" Rafael arched an eyebrow.

Devon nodded. "Malik—ever heard of 'im?"

"*Malik?*" Rafael's voice rose, and he swung around to look at Jack.

"Malik." Jack concurred. "A demon with six soldiers. They attacked us last night. After we spoke."

"How do you know it was Malik?"

Devon bristled at the derision in Rafael's tone, swallowed his unhelpful retort. "He introduced himself. I engaged him while J ashed the super vamps he brought along to play."

"If Malik brought them, they were no simple vampires. Did you kill his creatures?"

Jack nodded from the porch. He shifted from foot to foot. "I did, Captain."

"And Malik?"

Devon crossed his arms across his chest. "Once it was me 'n Jack versus the demon, he split."

Silence greeted this explanation. Devon waited three more heartbeats before losing patience and advancing a step. "Earth to Heaven calling? Be happy, your soldiers bested Hell's legion once again." Devon glanced over to Syd, winked. "We saved the girl."

When he finally spoke again, Rafael's tone had dropped several notes, barely above a whisper. "*How* did you engage Malik, Devon?"

Devon rolled his shoulders in a failed effort to release the building tension. "Bullets were a joke, so I tried my telekinesis. That was a no-go. So then I let out the big-dog powers. I—"

"You got into his head?" It was framed as a question, like Rafael wasn't sure.

"Of course I got into his head. It's what I do," Devon snapped, nearly forgetting the shaky ground he was on with the Archangel. "How far up the food chain is he, anyway?"

Rafael paused. "Far enough the Pledge hangs in a precarious balance. As one of Lucifer's few lieutenants, the case could be made that Malik is Fallen, one of the great ones. Lucifer is testing my patience. But the line is not cut so clear and my brother knows it."

Devon was silent, suddenly feeling much better about how he had fared in the battle. "He resisted me like nothing I've ever felt before."

"Were you—" Rafael drew a breath, and his human disguise slipped, angelic light cutting through his skin. "Were you truly able to compel him?"

Standing behind the Archangel, Jack winced against the light.

Devon paused. There was an unfamiliar note of fear in Rafael's voice. But why? He was doing his job, damn it. It wasn't like Rafael didn't understand what Devon was capable of. Rafael was the first one to recognize the skill he had. Rafael had taught him to understand and begin to hone the skill of mind control.

"I did, for about a minute. He fought like a fucking banshee. I can't guarantee the compulsion would've held if Jack hadn't shown up with a sword aimed at Malik's head." Devon hated admitting the defeat, and he wasn't exactly sure what Rafael was looking for. "But I had the bitch on his knees."

Rafael enunciated each word. "So Malik lives?"

Gritting his teeth, Devon pushed the word out with a hiss. "Yes."

"What have I always instructed you?" Rafael's tone grew harsh, and he advanced.

Devon fought the urge to aim his piece at Rainbow Bright. "Never engage a creature of Hell and let it live. Ever." Devon sighed with irritation. "But it wasn't like I had a—"

"Listen carefully, my soldier. Do not, under any circumstances, use your compulsion, unless I deem it necessary."

Devon tried to keep his breathing steady, but his face twisted into a snarl. God, he hated when Rafael told him what to do. Worse, as if his very presence was some kind of atomic bomb waiting to drop. As if sneaking around in someone's head was going to screw them up permanently. Christ, give him *some* credit. Unless, of course, he wanted them screwed up permanently. He'd honed his power to an incredible degree, but had Rafael asked him about it? Nope.

The massacre one-hundred and eighty years ago had altered everything—he never denied it. Everyone assumed he had lost control, or he was a sadistic bastard. Both. He didn't bother to correct them. Devon had had his reasons, but he'd forsaken the support and trust of all the Guardian soldiers for that decision. Ironic, really. Rafael knew what had truly happened, but had the Archangel set the record straight? Fuck no, he didn't. Amazing how fast your 'brother' and 'friends' could turn and think the worst.

Still.

Devon glanced at Jack.

Given the same situation, he'd do it again.

# CHAPTER TWENTY-SEVEN

Archangel. She'd met a. Freaking. Archangel. She glanced at Devon. He was concerned with the angel, his expression alert, suspicious. Pissed.

That wasn't too weird. He and Jack made it clear Devon wasn't on good terms with the Archangel. But if Syd was honest with herself, she wasn't exactly comfortable, either. Not with the angel, the neighborhood, or the secrecy.

"Come inside with me, Sydney." Rafael held out a beckoning hand.

She didn't bother correcting him. Instead, Syd examined him, searching his handsome features for something...an innate goodness her Catholic school education had told her the angel should have. She didn't find it. Instead of goodness, she found a carefully-schooled expression which did nothing to inspire confidence. Jack stood on the ramshackle porch, eyes shielded by his sunglasses despite the gloomy day, his jaw clenched, and his muscled arms hanging loose at his sides.

She didn't want to go inside. Her abilities, locked up tight behind her wall, gave muffled warnings. She couldn't make her feet move forward, and her hesitation was evident.

From his position on the porch, Jack said, "It's not safe in the open, Syd. Trust us."

Syd swallowed, and her mind flashed back to Devon last night. His brutal honesty when she'd said she was trusting him. *That's not a good choice.*

Out of time and options, she moved forward, toward Jack and the angel.

The procession—Jack, Rafael, her, Devon—entered the house. Just past the threshold, her steps stalled out. The house was worse on the interior. The walls had been reduced to an anorexic version of their former selves, and the exposed wood appeared wet, with patches of black. The structure was chilled and damp, all the worse for the cold autumn day. Navigating over missing boards and piles of random trash, she couldn't imagine any self-respecting hobo living here. She couldn't imagine anyone living here. But there was an inhabitant.

The huge bulldog was not on a leash, but she sat patiently in the corner of what had been the living room. One of the dog's ears was jagged. The other ear had been cropped too short. A pink scar where no fur had regrown traced the top side of her skull, about four-inches long. Not an ounce of fat on her, the dog's muscles stood out in stark relief. With a serious face, she surveyed the people on her property. She was nearly all white, though dirty, and the pink skin of her belly showed between her incredibly broad shoulders.

"Who's the pooch?" Devon took a step forward, closer to Syd.

The dog moved from a sitting position to a standing one. Her athletic body poised forward, ready.

Rafael kept walking, but replied, "Minerva."

"*That* dog is named Minerva?" Syd's brow creased. "You call her 'Minnie' or something, right?"

The dog's tail began to wag slowly.

No one answered her, and the procession continued on.

"Well, that's what *I'll* call her," Syd muttered.

They entered what was once the heart of the home. The

kitchen was bare of appliances, and copper plumbing had been stripped from the walls. The sink lay forgotten in the middle of the room, and it crawled with centipede-like creepies.

There was a closed door on the opposite side of the room. Rafael walked over and opened the bi-fold door. It had been a pantry, maybe once. Empty shelves lined each side of the small room. A few forgotten cans were dusty and dirt-covered. Rafael bent at the knees and a pried up a board, exposing a hatch.

The angel positioned himself half-way into the hatch and faced them. "Follow me."

The words were simple, but Syd's heart started to pound.

He climbed down, disappearing completely. A light flipped on, and it shone up through the hole in the flooring.

Jack glanced back, his lips drawn tightly together.

"What's the matter, J? Don't you fit?" Devon's sarcastic voice carried from behind Syd.

With a heavy sigh, Jack followed the angel's lead, though he did have to turn sideways and duck to fit through the opening of the pantry. Instead of navigating the ladder, he dropped neatly down, landing soundlessly.

"Stay up there, Devon," Rafael called from below. "Guard the perimeter and brief the other soldiers. They'll be arriving shortly."

Syd glanced back to Devon. He had taken his gun from his jacket, held it in his hand, and he scowled.

Something in his expression...

"I have no right to ask this, but let down your wall for a second," Devon said, his dark chocolate hair framing his face.

"But then you'd—"

He nodded. "I'd be able to influence you, maybe compel you. Yes. But I won't. I don't know what's going on. And I want to see if you can reach out to me, if you need me. I have a feeling you're powerful enough, but I want to be sure."

Syd glanced down to the basement.

Devon scared her—that hadn't changed. He operated on a completely different level, and the choices that were available to him… She couldn't imagine. Yet there was an authenticity to his tone, to the fact he was asking her, instead of forcing his will on her. Of course, it could be another way for the angels to exert control over her. It could be a ploy, but, regardless of what the brothers said, she needed to trust someone here.

Staring into Devon's pale ice eyes, she made her decision.

She let down the wall partially, felt her ability ripple out like invisible water, seeping through the room. Feelings rushed past her, high speed bullets of emotion threatening to mow her down. Her intuition was not happy to be here, didn't want to follow the angel. She shuddered.

Devon let his head fall back. The muscles of his shoulders moved beneath the thin leather jacket he wore. The tension came off him in pulses of anxiety. Why was *he* nervous? Her heart pounded.

The psychic equivalent of a knock sounded on her mind's door. It wasn't the intrusion Devon's first breaches of her mind had been. It was…polite.

Now or never.

With a deep exhale, she welcomed him inside her mind. *Hi.*

He smiled, and it changed his face from cynical and intense to beautiful and inviting. *Hi.*

He withdrew from her mind and nodded to her. "Now you do it."

"How?"

"Just talk to me." He tapped his temple.

She closed her eyes and pushed the air from her lungs. She sent her mind's eye roving to him. *Devon?*

*You continue to amaze, Lioness.* He winked. *Use this, if you need me. Unless I'm dying, I'll be to you in seconds.*

*Am I safe with Jack and Rafael?* She asked. Of course, she had no reason to believe he'd tell her the truth.

Devon met her eyes. *Jack has a true 'damsel-in-distress' gene, which pairs up nicely with his 'duty-calls' gene.* Devon said nothing about the Archangel.

*Which gene is stronger?* Syd asked.

Devon's lips tightened. *I don't know.*

"Syd, you coming?" Jack called from the basement, his voice hesitant.

Devon nodded, broke the mental contact, and walked away without looking back.

Alone and with scarcely any options, Syd replied, "Yeah."

It took Syd more effort to keep her shielding down than it did to erect it. But if she needed Devon? She wanted to keep the option open. Shielded was her default and going without it felt unnatural. Dangerous times ten. Didn't matter that she had an angelic super-soldier ahead of her. Her vulnerability weighed her down like a lead cloak.

A whimper caught Syd's attention. Minnie trotted up, her panting smile gone, replaced with her nostrils flaring and her tail wagging low.

"I don't think you should come down here, girl," Syd whispered.

Syd stepped into the claustrophobic pantry, trying to hold her breath against the sudden assault of spoiled food smells. Fluorescent lighting illuminated below her, and it did nothing to improve the scenery. Quickly, she maneuvered herself onto the ladder.

She descended, her head on level with the pantry floor. Minnie walked up to the opening, peered cautiously after Syd, her tail now completely tucked, her whimper a reminder to have a care.

Syd took the final four steps down, and her boot met epoxied concrete. She turned. In defiant opposition to the condition of the house above, the basement looked the picture of a scientist's dream lab. Syd shielded her eyes as they adjusted to the stunning amount of sparkling white walls, floor, and machinery. LED lights illuminated the space. How did they have power down here? Her intuition, recently freed at Devon's behest, called out a warning, and goosebumps prickled her skin.

The only thing not pristine and state of the art was an old oak desk to Syd's left, papers in neat stacks covering the working surface. Volumes mostly appearing to be college textbooks filled a rickety bookcase behind the desk. Syd walked over, inspecting the books, almost out of place in the high-tech basement. Running a finger along the spine of a book on the shelf, she noticed that several were authored by the same person. Dr. B. Byrne.

Why did that—wait. Dr. *Blair* Byrne? The woman who'd been stalking her? The woman who'd experimented on some poor blonde girl who'd ended up in a coma?

"What do you have to do with Dr. Byrne?" Syd's voice was shriller than she intended. She whipped around to face Rafael and Jack.

If Rafael was surprised she knew Byrne, it didn't show. "I've been working with the doctor for some time. To identify potentials."

Her intuition screamed at her, but she knew there was no way she could overpower Jack, let alone an Archangel. "Potential what?"

Without answering, Rafael's face turned shrewd. "Imagine my surprise when I found out about you. How the smart little doctor was running her own agenda. How she'd hid you from me."

Syd remembered Byrne, the first time she'd met, in the dealership. *I've tried to keep you away from them, but I think they know.* Syd swallowed. This wasn't good. It was Rafael? The one Byrne had been so afraid of? But Jack and Devon worked for him. What did that mean for her?

Jack shifted behind Rafael. His eyes still hidden behind black sunglasses, his expression gave her no indication of his intent.

"Jack, please. Let's leave. This isn't what I want... Take me home. Please." Syd's voice was level, only the slightest tremor at the end. She considered reaching out to Devon, but that had the feeling of desperation. She wasn't there yet. Jack was good. Jack would help her.

It would all be fine. It would.

Her hammering heart and her caged abilities begged to differ.

Jack made a move toward her, but Rafael held out a hand. Jack stopped.

"You're fine, Syd. We're the good guys, I've told you." Jack's voice was low, his body tense.

Syd licked her lips, put a hand to her belly. "I want to leave. I'm not a prisoner, right?"

"Of course no—" Jack said quickly.

Rafael smiled and nodded to Jack. "You can leave us."

Oh no. No, no. That was magnitudes worse. She did not want to be alone in the antiseptically-clean techno-basement with the angel.

Jack took a step and halted. "Rafael?"

"You have your orders, soldier. Leave." The Archangel's tone brooked no argument.

Syd stared at Jack, betrayal welling up like blood in a bone-deep cut. The vision of comatose girl slammed through her mind again. "This is why you kept me safe? To subject me to torture?"

Jack's face scrunched up in confusion. "Torture?" He looked to Rafael but made no motion to help her.

Syd gritted her teeth. "I'll scream. I'll call Devon with my mind."

"So, you *are* impressively gifted." Rafael's smile split his face into a grin. "Do you really think Devon cares for you? He cares for nothing. Ask his brother." Rafael shrugged. "But if it pleases you, call him. Give me a reason to remove him from service. He'll be dead before he makes one sarcastic remark."

Syd pushed out her breath on a whimper. More death on her shoulders. The weight was unbearable...worse than—whatever they were about to do to her. She hoped. She really did.

With her dwindling last hope, she implored Jack with her eyes.

"Syd," he whispered with plain anguish. "I have to obey, this one last time. Rafael promised me—Elaine."

Jack pushed past her, up the stairs.

She was *really* on her own.

And just like that, duty KO'd the damsel.

# CHAPTER TWENTY-EIGHT

Devon paced the perimeter of the broken and battered house. Like a good little soldier. Like he had been told. He was used to being the one who always knew too much. Not anymore. Now he was a wild animal in a zoo, caged by the secrets and demands of others. Helpless.

He snarled. He couldn't disobey Rafael's command, not if he wanted to keep breathing. All his protective instincts screamed to keep Syd safe. It would be nice to think it was because his life depended on hers, but the dredges of his brain had already wised up. He liked her.

He *liked* her.

He wanted to know what it would be like to spend time with her when survival wasn't an issue. Movie. Popcorn. None of her thoughts seeping into his head when they held hands or some shit. Bantering back and forth with that sharp tongue of hers. Other things with that tongue—

Devon lashed out at the nearest object. His fist flew through the rotted wood of the porch, ripping the skin of his knuckles wide open. Big red drops pooled immediately, flowing down the length of his fingers. He didn't heal anywhere close to the way Jack did, but those knuckles would stop bleeding on their own in a minute or two. And infection was not an issue.

A late-model white Tahoe pulled up to the curb in front of the house. Devon planted his feet shoulder-width apart and took a mental inventory. Three passengers. Two male. One female. All Guardian soldiers. Rafael's reinforcements had arrived.

Devon almost wished it was the damn demon again.

Dutch and Freelander. The woman he didn't know—Rafael, that old misogynist, recruited very few of the female persuasion. Those he did recruit were typically ballsier than most of the men and twice as cunning.

Dev really didn't need to interact with these guys. He'd get himself in deep shit, no doubt, with the murderous thoughts swarming and buzzing around his head like flies on the recently deceased. And his presence usually made the other Guardians itchy as hell, especially Freelander. Dev snarled. Good reason for that, though.

Dutch exited the passenger side of the truck, each step measured. "Hey, Devon."

Like all the soldiers, Dutch enjoyed immortality, taken into service in his early twenties. The kid hadn't changed since the last time Devon had seen him. Under his beaten-up bomber jacket, Dutch wore an 'Optimus Prime for President' T-shirt, two sacred blades, and a wicked good ability with them. He'd crack a lame joke as easy as he'd behead a hell beast. Possibly at the same time.

Freelander stayed inside the truck. No surprise there. Lucky for Free, too. Devon wasn't in the mood to put up with him. Free packed more guns than hands and a nasty anti-Devon vendetta. One day they'd come to blows. Just a matter of time.

"Dutch," Devon nodded. "Take perimeter duty. I'm out."

Dutch's throat moved, and he chuckled uneasily. "You got better places to be?"

Thinking immediately of Syd, Devon clenched his hands to fists. "As a matter of fact, I do."

Too damn bad it was the only place his Archangel Captain didn't want him to be.

Around the forlorn street, twilight fell like a billowing cloak. No sign any of the streetlights would be kicking on, either. Devon walked off, no clear intent on where he was going, just burning off steam. He studied the cracked sidewalk, trying to avoid anything resembling thinking. Shutting down his mind seemed like an excellent plan. It comforted him only minutely that Syd could reach out if she needed him, and he could be to her in seconds.

The bulldog from the house caught up with him and sauntered along at his pace.

"Sure, old girl, you can come. Why the hell not." Dev chuckled at himself as he spoke to the dog, but her eyes caught his, and the laugh died in his throat. He'd never seen that particular brand of canine intelligence before. Unnerved, he picked up his pace.

The gun was in his hand inside his leather coat pocket, but if anyone crossed his path, he would most likely toss them out of his way with his mind for the pure and simple joy of doing it.

He was sick of being told not to use his powers. His powers were what made him lethal, unpredictable. Ten shades darker than dangerous. The weapon of choice.

Marching on with him, Minnie seemed to pick up on his mood, and she quickened her trot.

See? The damn dog knew not to piss him off. Why was that so hard for Jack and Rafael to understand?

Abruptly, the dog cut across the street. Devon swore she looked both ways, too. He stopped and whistled to get her attention. He didn't need to be accused of losing the dog. Minnie stopped and turned around. She wagged, the rear of her muscled body moving in opposition of her tail.

"Come on, girl. Let's go this way." Devon pointed to the street in front of him.

The dog continued to pant, turned back the way she wanted to head and took a few more steps. She stopped again and looked at him.

Okay.

Apparently, she wanted him to follow her.

Devon reached out cautiously to her little doggie mind. He'd never been inside a canine head. No thoughts to be heard. But they saw. They had pictures of steaks and tennis balls and such, probably. Maybe Minnie had a picture to share.

Disoriented, Devon took a moment to center himself in the dog's mind.

*What the...fuck?*

The picture in the dog's mind was similar to the decay of the house, but on a much, much larger scale. Devastation, crumbling concrete, graffiti, and trash as far as the eye could see. In the middle of the ruins was a small room filled with half a dozen people. All unconscious with medical equipment hooked up and supporting life. At first Devon thought they were dead, laid shoulder to shoulder across a span of stainless steel tables. Mostly women, but a couple men interspersed. They weren't dead, but something wasn't right, that was for damn sure.

On edge now, he broke connection with Minnie, her head ducked down and her tail wagging low with trepidation.

"You got my attention, pup. Show me where."

Minnie turned and ran away, her back legs kicking to show the dirt-encrusted pads of her paws.

Drawing in a breath, Devon muttered to himself. "Sad this isn't the weirdest thing I've ever done."

He broke into a run, long legs stretching to keep pace with the dog.

Two blocks later, the overwhelming shadow of the Packard Plant loomed.

Completely awed at the level of devastation, Devon stood alongside the Packard Plant and looked at the decaying series of buildings. Bright graffiti covered the exterior wall in patches, and scraggly trees sprouted from the cracked concrete, weeds and grass so tall they could hide children, but concealed none of the trash. Nature was taking over this place, and only the plant's sheer size allowed man's stamp on the landscape to remain. Even outside the building, the stench of years-old garbage soaked the air.

Minnie navigated the urban ruins like a champ, aware of each of her four paws. She could've been a concert pianist operating from muscle memory, unconscious of each individual movement. She hopped and skipped through the rubble with the level of proficiency suggesting it wasn't her first rodeo. She stood outside the building and looked back at him with a panting smile.

A homeless man, his skin dark with pigment and dirt, limped along the street, pushing a shopping cart some grocery store had long since counted a loss. It was heaped with overflowing plastic bags. His thin wrists gave evidence of his malnourishment, but he wore several coats, one thrown on over the next, hiding most of his thin frame.

Devon turned his head, watching his guide dog out of the corner of his eye. With a breath of asbestos-thick air, Devon let his mind go to work. There were maybe ten people squatting in various parts of the abandoned plant, their resigned existence only darkening the air.

"Yo, man. You got change?" The homeless man was twenty feet away, shuffling toward him.

God, how out of place he must look, in his Italian leather jacket, polished black boots.

Devon swiveled his gaze around and sent his command through the air. *You don't want to come closer.*

The man stopped, leaned on the cart.

Devon began to follow Minnie in the opposite direction.

"Man, you don't wanna go that way. Creepy shit, that way."

Devon stopped and focused on the man. "Like what? I don't scare easy."

The man cackled, and phlegm clogged up the sound. "Don' know, not really. People talk, is all. Tryin' to be a good neighbor."

A quick read into the man's brain showed Devon that was truth. He knew nothing for sure, and though Devon hadn't given him money, the man was still willing to warn him. Perhaps Syd was right about the heart of this city.

Sparing a glance back, Devon saw Minnie waiting, her tail swinging low. Devon walked to the man who used his cart for support. "What do you want the money for?"

The man smiled, revealing only half the number of teeth required to chew a cob of corn.

"Like as not, whiskey."

"Least you didn't say Jager." Devon withdrew his wallet from the interior of the leather jacket. "For the warning and your honesty." He handed the man ten hundred-dollar bills. "*Go get yourself a real bed for the night, something top shelf and a shower for God's sake*. You stink worse than a beheaded demon."

The man looked down, eyes growing wide, and back up again. "You straight, man."

Devon chuckled. "Don't let it get out."

The man mumbled quietly and hobbled away, pushing the cart clumsily over chunks of concrete and random bits of trash.

Minnie whined again, and Devon's attention returned to the task at hand. Glass and concrete crunching underfoot, he followed the dog.

There was evidence of fire damage in several spots they passed. The reek of trash commingled with burned debris, and Devon wished his olfactory sense could take the night off. Repulsive was too kind a word. Minnie decided to enter the forsaken industrial building through a gaping hole in the wall. The maneuver had the feel of routine, and Dev wondered how many times the dog had been here previously, walked this treacherous path. He wondered why she would bother.

Passing from outside to in, the light darkened, and the true nature of the destruction became apparent. He had entered some post-apocalyptic version of reality, after a nuclear blast had had its way with the virgin Earth.

Several near twists of his ankle later, Devon decided using telekinesis to levitate himself a couple inches off the rubble was wise. The ground was unstable in most places, simply disintegrated in others, and thick with trash in the rest. The bright graffiti made a sharp contrast to the wreckage surrounding them. Progress slowed the deeper into the building they went.

Treading cautiously, Devon stopped to watch the dog move dexterously over a large smashed heap of what had once been windows. She leapt, her front paws landed, and her rear end stayed up half a second longer. Her spine twisted, and she landed sideways, unharmed. The dog paused and looked back, wagged twice, and then continued toward a fragmented staircase.

"You can't be serious," Devon huffed.

Minnie began to climb, but her impressive agility didn't save her paw from slipping through a missing stair. She yelped, slid to the base of the stairs, and looked at him.

"Not the twin with healing powers, sorry, pooch." Devon held up his hands, and his boots crunched over cracked concrete. "Christ."

He went to the base of what used to be steps and peered up. Complete flooring up there, hopefully capable of holding their combined weight.

Devon knelt, beckoned the dog to him. "Please don't bite my face off." And when the dog snuggled in close to him, he hefted her substantial weight. She tensed for a second, then became dead weight in his arms.

He and Minnie rematerialized on the second floor. Devon squinted one eye open, and slowly bent his knees with the heavy dog in his arms. A foot and a half off the floor, Minnie struggled to get free, and Devon released his hold. She landed on all four paws and shook herself.

Devon tried not to be offended. "Lotta girls would be happy to be in my arms."

Minnie shook again and trotted off. Toward another staircase.

"Nice." Devon sighed.

The scent in the air had changed. It no longer reeked. No, now he smelled disinfectant.

Without waiting for Minnie, Devon shifted through space again, up to the third floor. People were here, but their minds were strangely silent. Alive...but not quite. He couldn't see anything through their minds, which meant he would be blind going in, if he moved himself to their location. Would not qualify as a wise move.

A door marked with a yellow biohazard triangle loomed ahead. Weird in its completeness, it was an actual room, no broken walls, no missing doors or windows. The walls were clean, no graffiti. Complete and whole in the midst of utter destruction. Completely out of place.

Devon kicked the door, sending it splintering inwards. The door bounced off the interior wall and came back at him. Devon moved forward and held his hand out, catching the door as it prepared to strike back.

Laid out like a ritual sacrifice, four women and two men in hospital gowns lay shoulder to shoulder on an immaculately clean metal table, their arms at their sides, unmoving. Shallow breaths came at irregular intervals, and they were all way too thin.

Devon couldn't tear his gaze away from the scene. What the fuck was this?

Minnie trotted up behind him, her whines quiet. Yes, this was the picture in her head, but why had she brought him here? Minnie walked up to a blonde girl, the most petite of the group, and licked her hand, which had fallen off the table. Devon saw the faintest flicker of a response in the woman's hand, like she wanted to reciprocate and pet the dog.

Devon sent his brain to work, starting with Minnie's friend. Pressing gently, Devon let himself into her head.

Immediately, his brain swam with the effort, and he reached out for the nearest wall to brace himself. Her brain moved too fast for consciousness to take hold and being in her head felt like entering warp drive. Only one image had been crystal-fucking-clear.

The house where he had left Syd. This girl had been there. Whatever had caused her vegetative state had happened there.

*I have to get Syd out.*

He withdrew from the girl's damaged mind and took a steadying breath.

Rafael had some serious questions to answer—

The stink of demon filled his nostrils. Disinfectants or even trash suddenly seemed a fantastic alternative.

Minnie growled and launched herself backward.

Malik stood in the doorway, nearly big as the door Dev kicked in. The demon laughed.

Nowhere to go. Shit. Devon sure as hell wasn't going to teleport back to Syd. Malik could easily reach him, which meant if he teleported, the demon might be hitching a ride. He wasn't willing to risk getting back-up for her safety. Devon spun around, his left arm going immediately for the gun in his jacket.

"You surprised me once, Guardian. Not again." Malik's grin glinted sharp in the darkened building.

The element of surprise was gone, Malik would be expecting an attack in his mind, would be prepared for it. His mind wasn't back to full strength, so Devon didn't have the best chance of doing what full strength and surprise had netted him the night before. Not to mention, no Jack to distract the demon with the threat of beheading.

First things first. Scanning the area with his mind, Dev was nearly sure Malik was alone.

"No lackeys to kill this time?" Devon flexed the fingers of his right hand, wishing he had a big fucking blade.

Malik snarled. "I wanted to see what you really are for myself. I had to be sure."

Of all the things Devon expected a demon to say to him, this wasn't in the top ten. Everyone knew what they were—Rafael's Guardians.

"I know your secret." Malik smiled, his dagger-teeth gleaming.

"Not following." Devon's wariness wasn't being calmed by the conversation; rather it made him itchy to get out of here. Like a claustrophobic in a casket.

"Tell me, does Rafael know, too? Has he betrayed his kind yet again?"

Devon moved through space, appearing ten feet behind Malik outside the small room. The demon blurred. Malik's hand hit his arm, but it flew so fast and hard it felt like a boulder.

Devon flew back, down on the ground. His breath forced out of his lungs.

"Lucifer exterminated your kind long ago. I need to know how it's possible. How can you exist?" Malik wasn't screwing around this time. "Command me, if you can."

Malik blurred again, so fast a sonic boom would be jealous. His claws bit into Devon's thigh, pain searing like a hot iron.

Devon held back a scream by sheer survival instinct. This was going downhill, way too fast. He threw his fist back toward the demon's face, but Malik dodged back.

"Archon." Malik hissed. "That's what you are."

Devon had a fraction of a second to throw the gun in front of him, crack off three shots. Point blank to Malik's face.

# CHAPTER TWENTY-NINE

Alone in the basement, Syd stared at Rafael.

"We're not enemies, Sydney, not if you don't force it. And I sincerely hope you don't."

"To be clear, you're keeping me here, and I do not want to be here. Kidnapping kind of precludes friendship." Syd kept her voice calm. "What do you want with me?"

"You are—hopefully—the key to ending my banishment."

Syd glanced to the stairs. She'd have to pass the Archangel to get to them. "I have no idea what that means."

"How could you? You're human." Such derision in his tone.

Syd swallowed. "What could your banishment have to do with me?"

Rafael shrugged, a noncommittal lift and fall of his broad shoulders. "Perhaps nothing, perhaps everything."

"Very informative," she said, her pissed off getting the better of her.

Rafael's lips turned down, and he pointed a finger at her. "You see, there was a time when that snarky comment would've earned you death at my hand. Humans..." He sneered. "But ever since the Pledge, that cursed day, I have to *protect* you. Your interests, your planet, your vast array of meaningless possessions. My only hope of escape comes in the form of a loophole in my banishment left unwisely by my arrogant brothers. Find a human they said, find a human able to wield such power as to stand successfully against angels and demons alike. Find a human to take your place as Guardian of the Pledge and your banishment will end."

Syd was silent, trying to take in the words, the implication. He couldn't possibly think—

"But you see," Rafael continued, his gray eyes angry, "that is impossible. A human? Able to stand in my place? I thought it a cruel joke of the universe, tempting me with an end to my punishment which could never be. But you humans, you are surprising."

Syd interjected, done with the angelic monologue. "I don't want to lead the Guardian army. That's...completely insane."

"I don't care." Rafael shook his head and pointed at her. "Don't interrupt."

Syd swallowed.

"Your power, it's amazing you kept it hidden all this time. How? Byrne knew about you, but she said nothing, though she'd given up plenty of others to our cause." Rafael's penetrating gray eyes narrowed. "What is it about you that is so special?"

Rafael glided toward the oak desk and leaned a hip. He straightened the cuffs on his charcoal suit and pinned her with his eyes. Power radiated off him in waves. He was making less of an effort to control it. Probably to terrify her further. It was working.

"Tell me about your power."

She said nothing.

His light increased, to the point she squinted and glanced away from him. "We can skip to the main event, if you prefer." Rafael crossed his wrists on his knee and cocked his head.

Shit, keeping the angel talking seemed the path of least discomfort. At least until she came up with a better idea. She drew in a breath. "I wouldn't know. I don't use my power."

"Lie." Rafael smiled. "Try again."

If Syd hadn't spent the past couple days with Jack and Devon, staring at the angel directly would've been a challenge. He was too beautiful, too...everything. Still wasn't easy, but it was manageable.

Irritated, Syd scowled. "I don't use my abilities, not really. I try not to use it. I can see auras and spirits. I have premonitions. Sometimes odd things happen around me." She shrugged.

"Odd things, like what?"

She glanced away, shifted on her feet. "I'll think I need a light on, and it will just turn on. My dad was always losing his keys and I could find them, sort of."

"Sort of?" Rafael questioned.

"I'd concentrate on them, and he'd find them, usually in plain sight."

"You can move objects with your mind?"

Syd shook her head. "No, I don't think—"

"Lie," Rafael repeated softly.

She licked her lips and shifted on her feet. "But almost nothing happens when my wall is up—"

"Wall?"

She tapped her temple. "My wall."

Rafael narrowed his eyes. "You shut down your powers?"

"I tried," she muttered. "Obviously not hard enough."

"Intriguing. Tell me, Sydney. What happens when your wall comes down?"

Syd shivered. "It doesn't. Not ever."

"I'm afraid it's going to have to. If we're to see if you are the one I require."

"No," Syd said flatly and crossed her arms.

"Why is it so hard to accept the truth of who you are?" Rafael asked.

Searching his perfect features, Syd sensed his curiosity. The scrutiny was beyond unnerving.

"And who is that?" Syd kept her arms crossed, hugged into herself.

"If you are able to take my place? You will be a human with

access to incredible power, so much more than you even have now."

"I don't *want* power. I want a family that loves me, I want to talk to friends and have them really understand who I am, not be a sideshow freak. I want—"

Lounging on the oak desk, Rafael laughed harshly. "Do you think that I or the universe in all its infinite glory give a damn what *you* want?"

Syd sucked in a breath. "Fuck you."

Rafael pointed a finger at her, standing to his full height. His head nearly touched the ceiling. "And there again. A human, daring to insult me. It's infuriating. Your wall comes down. Now."

With no warning, light pulsed out from him, the bright basement lightening to surface-of-the-sun levels. She threw her hands up over her face and closed her eyes.

Rafael's power washed over her, a tsunami of light and pulsing, painful energy.

She screamed.

His power sang, beating with angelic fury against her wall. She reinforced it, steel-girders and concrete in her mind. God, it hurt, she sank to her knees, not feeling anything but Rafael's power flow through her into every piece of her mind, beating with no mercy against her.

She held the wall. There was nothing else. Her wall was her defense against the world. It was the key to maintaining her sanity. If it came down—

Like a lightning bolt striking ground, the first crack reverberated through her.

And still Rafael pushed, his power unfathomable and punishing.

The crack widened, her ability soaking through the rift.

She wouldn't be able to hold out much longer. Her wall would fail.

The cry tore through her mind, instinctive. The only option available to her.

*DEVON!*

---

TWO OF HIS three gunshots struck bloody demon gold. Devon had taken out Malik's left eye, part of his cheek was missing, too. Thick, black blood covered Malik's face, and the shoulder of his tunic drenched with the stank-ass stuff. Unfortunately, minus an eye, it seemed to only piss off the demon, who pulled a serrated knife big enough to take down a grizzly from his black robe.

*DEVON!* Psychic pain lanced through him, entered his head, shot down and out his toes, and rendered him motionless for two critical seconds.

*Syd?* He responded to her cry instinctively.

No response. Her call had been of the last-resort variety. Pure desperation.

*I have to get back, I have to—*

Malik's knife struck something vital. Agony tore down Devon's left side, a millisecond delay traveling along after the blade. Before he could surrender to the excruciating pain, Devon kicked up as hard as he could, shoving Malik back five feet, off-balance.

"You are nothing but a human waste of power. Do it, I said, try to make me obey."

Devon fired off two more rounds. *Pop, pop.* Malik took those two in the shoulder, his body dancing with the force of the bullets. Completely deafened by the proximity of the shots, Dev gagged in a breath of air, the stench of demon blood nearly making him choke.

Devon's thoughts went wild. Why does he have such a hard-on for me? Isn't he supposed to be after Syd? And why the hell did he call me an Archon? Whatever that is.

Strength leaked out proportionate to the steadily increasing pool of blood growing beneath him. Devon swung up onto all fours, drawing his concentration to him like a coat of arms. He needed to get the hell out of here.

Malik's hawk-like talons sunk into his shoulder, making the effort to move through space a nonstarter.

Devon screamed; his arms slipped in his own blood and refused to support his bulk any longer. He dropped to his stomach on the ground, blood flowing freely from his left side and his shoulder, impaled with demon claws.

"Now what, Guardian? Out of tricks?" Malik's sandpaper voice grated along Devon's spine, sending a distracting jolt of rage through him. "Try it. Command me, if you dare."

Out of options, Devon focused on the physical contact from the demon and compelled.

*Get off me!*

The demon claws retracted, their tips dragging through flesh as they fought to disobey his command. But the demon still mounted him.

*Get off!*

This was it. He hadn't given Jack his location purposely. Devon didn't want to chance a war of Jack's conscience with convoluted brother-politics in the mix. It was simple. Jack was all that was left to protect Syd.

Malik's weight eased on Devon's back, enough for him to hope. Devon reached back and took the chance. He grabbed Malik's wrist, thick with his own blood, pushing with every bit of strength left to him.

*Turn those claws upon yourself.*

Malik's claws reared up and impaled themselves two knuckles deep into the demon's gut. He screamed, giving Devon a peek inside the crazy bastard's mouth where his cheek had been blown off.

Half-stunned it worked, Devon watched with desperate hope. If he had any opportunity, this was it, while his opponent recovered from a damn serious injury. Malik was injured, but he was still on top of him.

"Lucifer killed all your kind millennia ago." Malik hunched over his bleeding stomach. "You cannot be an Archon. Rafael will die for this!" Malik's spittle flew from his mouth, burning Devon's cheek. The other side of Devon's face pressed into the broken concrete, skin tearing under the force.

In agony and too confused to respond, Devon's only focus was survival. All the enigmatic bullshit could wait 'til later. Assuming 'later' was still a viable option. The demon's hold slackened, and underneath the demon, Devon flipped over. *"Get the fuck off me."*

Throwing the meager energy he had left, Devon gave a telekinetic push, but the demon only stumbled back. Jesus H, that was pathetic.

Praying it was enough, Devon sucked in a breath and crawled the remaining few steps to the room with the unconscious people. Minnie trembled in the corner, her whole body shivering, her mouth closed and serious.

"Come here, girl." Devon gritted his teeth, realizing his words were slurring. "Now." With his forearms, Dev drug his injured body the rest of the way and grabbed the cold clammy hand of the unconscious woman. His legs were worthless, heavy meat dragging behind him.

The dog obeyed, her tail curled so far under belly, the tip nearly hit her chest.

Contact made with both the dog and the woman, Devon closed his eyes, rallying desperately for the needed power to get back to Jack, to Rafael—and for God's sake—to get back to Syd. And hope the injuries he inflicted on the demon would prevent him from following.

The last thing his closed lids reported was a brilliant flash of white.

---

THE ARCHANGEL'S POWER PUSHED, prodded, punished.

The fault in her wall had widened, but Syd's mind held firm long past when her body gave out.

Shuddering, Syd lay in the fetal position on the concrete of the basement. All breath had left her lungs. Her body felt light, like it didn't belong to her.

But her wall had largely held, just that one widening rift.

And Devon had not come.

After everything she'd learned about him, had she really thought he would? Stupid and naïve. Whatever was about to happen, she was on her own. Like always.

Rafael stood over her, his light burning her eyes even behind her closed lids. "Why do you fight me?"

She could only breathe. None of her limbs would move. And she certainly couldn't form coherent sentences. Echoes of Rafael's power traveled her body like painful electric currents.

Distantly, she felt Rafael gather her up from the floor. His body was all heat and strength. Whatever he'd done to her hadn't affected him at all. She'd been nearly destroyed from the inside out. He'd taken a stroll in the park.

But her wall held. It was the only thing she could feel.

His steps were smooth, but her head lolled, and she moaned. Her eyes wouldn't open. She felt herself deposited onto a cool, smooth table. Likely metal. Fear spiked through her, and she tried to open her eyes.

It didn't work. Stuck in the blackness of near unconsciousness, Rafael's words reached her. "I implore you, Sydney. Don't fight me. You couldn't possibly. That you have withstood me so far is testament itself to your strength. I've gone easy on you."

*Easy?* Dread was a living thing inside her, slithering and sliding through her abused body.

She said nothing. She was not capable of it. Only one thought ran through her head. Over and over, like a chugging locomotive heading uphill.

Hold the wall. Hold the wall.

His power beat against her, found the crevice in her wall.

Hold the wall.

The fault widened, and the angel's power worked itself in her mind.

Hold—

The pain was exquisite, and her body began to seize.

A great wrenching tore through her and then she was...

Rafael's mouth moved, though no sound came forth.

Through slit eyes, Syd made out the sound it would've made. *No.*

Wait. How could she see? She glanced around, completely unanchored. She looked down and saw her own body, on the metal table. She observed this from the upper corner of the room, a thing separate from her body.

She gazed at the impossible scene. The Archangel hovering, his body all light, hers broken and seizing still. But she could not feel it.

She wasn't there.

She moved—no, scratch that—was being *pulled* further away from her body.

With desperation, she wrenched forward, attempting to pummel her spirit back into her body.

She bounced off like she had tried to inhabit a brick.

No, no...*no.*

Then she was hurtling fast, far and away from her body. Rafael's cry of anguish echoed, following her like a vicious tailwind.

# CHAPTER THIRTY

Jack paced back and forth in the back bedroom of the dilapidated house. He couldn't face the other Guardian soldiers. Dutch, Free, and the woman soldier, the one he'd never actually worked with, Valentina. He didn't want any of them to see the emotions on his face.

Dropping his head in his hands, Jack prayed. *Please let this be over soon.* He thought he'd been prepared to do anything to end this, to get back to Elaine. The look of betrayal on Syd's face had inspired a serious Doubting-Thomas moment, however.

A loud thud sounded in another area of the house.

"LT!" Dutch's urgent shout came from the living room.

Jack ran at top speed, skidding to a halt. The wreckage of human body in front of him stalled his heart.

Jack sorted through all the blood, gore coating everything. The bulldog, a woman he had never seen—and Devon. All that blood...

With a healer's instinct taking over, Jack dove into the pile of body parts. The dog slunk off, cowering in the corner. Her white coat was stained red, and she was shaking and upset but apparently uninjured.

The woman was unconscious. Jack ran his hand over her and realized that was the extent of her bodily issues.

"Take her away, get her warm and comfortable. She's not hurt." Jack ripped his hoodie and tank off. More physical contact, the better. Plus, there would be no getting these blood stains out.

Valentina appeared. "I'll tend her."

"But, LT, you sure? All that blood can't be from—" Dutch's voice shook. The rest of the sentence died in his mouth.

"It's all Devon," Jack said, his voice hard and his heart pounding a frantic beat.

"How the hell did he get himself back here that injured..."

No time to answer the question. Jack tore the soaked leather jacket from his brother's body. Whatever it was—and Jack would bet its name was Malik—had eviscerated Devon. His brother gushed blood from an eight-inch ragged hole in his side.

"*Bruder*, I promise, you make it through this, and I'll buy you another jacket."

Jack ripped Devon's shirt off, watched for his chest to rise, but nothing happened. Jack's hands quaked, and he prepared for the onslaught of pain that would come with taking part of Devon's injury into himself.

"I'm sorry, but there's no time to make this hurt less."

Jack covered the whole of Devon's side wound with his hands and lit up the room with his healing. Devon's body bowed off the dirty floor, his head thrashed, and he fought weakly to push Jack away.

Dutch knelt to hold Devon's shoulders to the floor and Free stood back, arms crossed.

Jack's concentration slipped for a moment. Failure would mean—

The prayer erupted from his lips subconsciously. "Please...God..."

Jack pushed organs that were never meant to see the light of day back into his brother's body. His gorge rose, but his hands were steady. The pain flowed in through his hands. It radiated up his arms, pounded into his chest and clenched in his gut, where the majority of the damage had been done to Devon. Jack turned his head and gagged, choking back the contents of his stomach.

Exhausted past the point of fighting, Devon went limp from the overload. Jack stayed stoic, his breathing getting harsher. The volume of pain in his body increased to heavy-metal mosh pit levels.

Jack looked up at Free with effort. "Check on Valentina and the woman."

"Don't you want her downstairs?"

Jack shook his head. "We have no idea who she is or why she's with Dev. Until we know something, she stays away from Syd."

With a curt nod, Free went to find Valentina.

"Easy, LT." Jack looked up to Dutch's concerned brown eyes. "Pace yourself, big guy. Dark is here, we have no idea what waits." Dutch swallowed. "If something was able to do this to Devon, we need you in a bad way."

The pain began to overtake Jack, and his head slumped forward, onto his forearm. His gut was a fireball, expanding, pressing against his ribcage. At least Devon had the good fortune to be unconscious for the pain.

"You have to hang on, Dev," Jack whispered, more to himself than anyone else. This was not supposed to happen. Devon was not the one dying today.

From the basement, Rafael let out an anguished cry.

Jack's head whipped up, and he made eye contact with Dutch.

"Dutch, go." Jack did not want to contemplate what was happening downstairs, what could make an Archangel make a sound like that.

"But—"

Valentina appeared in the room, her gaze flicking toward the kitchen.

"Take Valentina. Now, Dutch," Jack snapped through the pain in his gut. His patience and energy wore too thin.

The soldiers' boots slapped hardwood as they ran to their Archangel captain.

With effort, Jack raised his head back up to assess. Devon's chest rose and fell, though the movement wasn't near visible enough for Jack's comfort. Devon's survival was not a guarantee.

Minutes passed, seconds ticking by with agonizing sluggishness.

Jack would have to stop soon. He could heal, and heal well, but there was a price. If he healed Devon as much as possible, that would mean effectively taking himself out of the battle, bare minimum, for a solid day. And they both couldn't be down and out. Not when the battle was clearly ramping up.

But to let his brother die?

"Stop, Jack." Free stood in the doorway to the living room.

Jack ignored the comment. "Is the woman okay?"

Free shrugged. "Not conscious. But she's not dying in the next few minutes."

Jack blew out a breath, refocused on Devon. He pulled his hands away, and they shook slightly. The blood dripped off them, soaking into the dirty floor. The wound started to stitch itself at the edges, and the blood no longer rushed out like a packed theatre under threat of fire. Jack grasped his brother's head.

"Dev?" Jack asked softly.

Devon's head lolled in his hands.

No, not a guarantee.

Jack replaced his hands on the wound, willed the healing into Devon's body. He took two fingers, placed them deep in the wound and closed his eyes.

Sensing a severed intestine, Jack pushed his fingers in a little farther, Devon's muffled grunt his only disapproval. Jack scrunched his face up, feeling drowsy.

Have to fix that bleeder....

There it was, the last one. Jack concentrated on that, sent the light pulsing to fix the gushing leak.

He was nearly finished when his strength seriously waned. He would've slumped down onto his brother's bleeding body if Free hadn't caught his big shoulders.

"Jack, you have to stop. You'll be useless."

Anger giving him fuel, Jack shrugged out of Free's grip and refocused on closing the wound. Skin was a specialty of his. Like he held a needle and thread in his hand, Jack's mind bound the ragged edges of cut skin back together.

Devon moaned. The healing light finally went out, a combination of exhaustion and relief. Jack only hoped it was enough. Even still, Dev was down for the next couple days, easy.

Huffing deeply, his task done as best as he could manage and remain conscious, Jack pushed back from his position on the floor. He braced himself on his hand, elbow locked to lend support. Dazed, he saw the blood dripping from his own nose. The drops plopped down soundlessly, disturbing the dust coating the floor. He stared at them with numb detachment.

"Why you bother with that bastard, I don't get it." Free turned and spat. He walked over and offered a hand to Jack to help him stand.

Jack disregarded the hand, and after two unsuccessful attempts, stood on his own. "If he's a bastard, so am I. Twins, remember?"

Free shook his head with disgust. "You're nothing like him."

"Help me take him downstairs. He needs to be made comfortable in a safe spot, so he can heal."

Free's eyes flashed with defiance, but he walked over to Devon's boots, grabbed both Devon's ankles and lifted.

Clenching his jaw despite the throbbing, burning pain in his own gut, Jack lifted his brother's shoulders. Blood welled around his hand on Devon's shoulder. Devon had been gouged with something sharp there as well. Jack let the healing go back to work, though to a much lesser degree. The less blood Devon lost, the quicker he could be back to his sarcastic demon-fighting best.

The motion began to jar him, and Devon's eyelids flickered.

"Syd...." His dry lips barely moved.

"She's here, Dev. She's safe," Jack tried to soothe, glad to see his brother conscious, if only barely.

"No...she's with Rafael, the doctor..."

Syd's pleading voice came back to him—*help me, Jack*—but he clenched down on the beginnings of guilt. Uneasily, Jack tried to shush Devon. "Worry about healing. We need you."

Devon began to twist, trying to right himself.

"Don't fight us, jackass. I don't need an excuse to drop you." Free hefted Devon's ankles a bit higher.

Jack stared at his soldier, hating the animosity there, but understanding it all the same. The night Rafael had banned Devon from direct contact was the night Alain Freelander went from human to Guardian soldier.

Free had been the only human to survive Devon's massacre.

# CHAPTER THIRTY-ONE

Devon tried to keep still. Hard, because agony coursed through his body, and because Free and Jack carried him about as smooth as sandpaper. He wished like hell he could make the trip on his own. If the wounds didn't kill him, the dependency surely would. His eyes were closed, but he was too stubborn to let unconsciousness take him. Maybe he couldn't move on his own, but he needed to figure out what was happening with Syd.

As gingerly as he could, Jack lifted his brother parallel to the ladder leading down to the basement. Free waited at the bottom to grab onto Devon's dangling ankles.

Bracing himself against the back of the ladder, Jack descended slowly. He balanced himself on the stairs, trying to hold his brother out in front of him. Devon wasn't a small load to carry, and Jack had recently completed the healing Olympics. Jack reached the bottom step and dropped to his knees. Free swore, and Devon bit back a moan of pain when his tailbone met concrete.

Jack shot Free a look. "Get him to the cot."

Movement that way was slow, but Devon didn't say a word in protest. He was lucky to be sucking air, and he knew it. He'd fought plenty of battles, seen plenty of war wounds. He was under no illusions. Jack had straight-up saved his ass from a meet-your-maker moment.

The door to the only room in the basement was closed, and Devon heard muffled voices from behind it. He slitted his eyes, trying to get a bead on what was happening. Where Syd was.

Giving Free a cautious look, Jack motioned for them to lay Devon gently on the cot.

Free obliged immediately, dropping Devon's limp feet a little higher than necessary. Taking an additional several seconds to unburden his load, Jack laid Devon's shoulders on the bare cot, so slowly. Not just because he was being careful. Jack stumbled, left knee hitting the epoxied floor of the basement, and his head drooped low.

Devon had never seen his brother so weak.

Dutch hovered nearby. "How is he?"

"Alive." Jack pushed up off the concrete, weaving where he stood.

"Where is Rafael?"

Dutch pointed at the closed door further into the basement.

"What happened?"

Dutch shook his head. "Dunno. He didn't want me anywhere near her."

Valentina came to stand beside Dutch. "The Captain is with Syd, I only saw a glimpse of her. She appears...unwell."

Devon's heart began to pound, each concussion echoing painfully through his whole body. What the ever-loving fuck was going on? What had Rafael done to Syd?

"Free, go keep an eye with Dutch and Valentina on the perimeter. I need eyes up there."

Devon heard leather creak and knew Free had grabbed a gun from his side holster, turned on his heel, and climbed the ladder to go topside. Dutch would follow Jack's orders. Without question. He didn't know Valentina well enough to say one way or the other, but she followed silently behind Dutch.

Running a hand along Devon's side, Jack knelt beside him and assessed his healing.

"No more, J." Devon pulled back his eyelids further through sheer force of will.

Jack's gaze darted down to his brother. "You shouldn't be conscious."

"And you shouldn't have healed me. The mission, remember?" Devon coughed, and the resultant tightening in his abdomen put his wound through a wood chipper. He hissed against the pain.

Jack ignored the dig. Kneeling on the ground, he seemed to be pretty focused on sucking air himself. What a pair.

"Where's Syd?" Devon croaked out.

Jack glanced back over to the adjacent room, its door closed. His shoulders tightened.

Devon whispered, "What did you do, J?"

Jack's breathing sped. "I...I followed orders, Dev, I had no choice. Rafael promised me—"

"Where is Syd?" Devon repeated. The basement had taken on the hush of a funeral home.

His eyes closed, head leaned back, Jack said nothing. One arm hovered protectively over his abdomen. With the amount of healing he'd already done? Jack had to be in tremendous pain. Close to what Devon himself was feeling.

A huge presence filled the doorway to the room, blocking Devon's sight.

The Archangel Rafael had never looked more human. Angelic light completely absent, Rafael was as subdued as Devon had ever seen him. No, not precisely human—the angel looked vulnerable. He closed the door behind him.

"Soldiers," Rafael spoke absently.

"What happened?" Jack whispered.

Rafael's gaze traveled back to Devon on the cot. "He lives?"

Devon noted Rafael didn't seem at all surprised by his barely-there state.

"For now." Jack pulled himself onto the cot next to his brother, and it dipped precariously low under their combined bulk.

Rafael's cool gray eyes assessed the scenario in front of him, focusing on Jack. "You weakened yourself to a dangerous degree. That was unwise."

The subtext was pretty fucking clear, Devon thought. The Archangel might've said, "He's not worth it."

"He's my brother," Jack said softly. "Syd?"

Rafael reached out a hand, rested it on the shoulder of his favored soldier.

Rafael's presence was enough to make Devon want to back away. Add to that the downer of attitude Rafael was sporting, if Devon could, he'd be high-tailing it. But of course, there was no going anywhere. Devon had used up all his lucky lotto numbers on breathing. Movement was out of the question.

Jack braced, and Devon held his breath. Had it been a figment of his imagination, a hallucination induced by pain? Or had Syd cried out to him, through their mind-link?

"She is not the one," Rafael said, voice deadened.

In Devon's mind, the slate wiped clean, blank. He had to have heard that wrong. All this effort had been...a mistake? They'd made her a target of Hell and destroyed her life, and it was *a mistake*?

"What does that mean?" Jack's throat worked, and his fist clenched. "Have we—I—failed?"

Rafael glanced at Devon, disgust written plainly across his face. Abruptly, his gaze switched to Jack. "I will honor the terms of our agreement."

Agreement?

Jack swallowed and looked around. "But this mission... It's not over."

"It's over." Rafael laughed harshly, lifting his proud face to the ceiling, his expression enraged. "I should've never believed Sammael would allow an end to this punishment."

"Malik is still after Syd..." Jack said. "How can it be over?"

Furious, Rafael's eyes slid over to Devon. "Sydney is no longer the demon's first priority."

The Archangel's scrutiny burned, complementing the scald of his wounds. *Archon, that's what you are.*

"What's an Archon?" Devon wrapped an arm around his side, wincing against the pain.

Rafael smiled, the rage of a moment ago replaced by stark cruelty. "Do you really think I would answer any inquiry you have of me?"

"What can I say, I'm an optimist at heart."

"Your optimism is misplaced, I'm afraid." Rafael's smile turned into a baring of gleaming white teeth. "Especially since your access to unlimited healing is about to depart this plane."

Devon swiveled to look at Jack. His brother's head dropped onto his broad chest. They were only feet apart on the cot, but the distance was growing. "What's he talking about, J?"

Jack was mute, his eyes averted.

Rafael continued, "My soldier made a request of me. An unusual one. In exchange for complying with my wish, ending his bereavement, and undertaking this assignment with you, I agreed to release him from service at its completion."

Devon's jaw dropped. His mouth moved, but it took several tries for his words to make sound. "You can't be serious."

His brother wanted to die?

Jack swallowed thickly and ratcheted his gaze up to Devon. The shame in Jack's expression was a palpable thing. Shame and grief.

Devon's eyes closed. Whether due to pain or trying to avoid his brother, flip a damn coin. "So that's it then. You could put up with the hellish reality of working with me—because he promised you it was over. Fucking coward." Devon spit, more blood than saliva. "You think your dead wife would want that for you?"

Jack sucked in a breath, like he'd taken a perfect punch to the solar plexus.

Devon turned his full attention to the Archangel. "Made

perfect sense, when I thought about it—in the brief seconds of consciousness after Malik disemboweled me. You didn't want me here because you *knew* I wouldn't like what I would see. Dr. Byrne's failed experiments, the lives she's destroyed. That *you've* destroyed." Devon sneered. "Guardian Angel, my ass."

Jack's eyebrows shot up, and he looked from Devon to Rafael.

"What?" Devon asked Jack pointedly. "He didn't let you in on all his plans?"

Rafael hissed, and the façade of his humanity shattered around him. Light sprung forth from all the cracks. "You have no idea, the agony of this punishment my brothers thrust upon me. For eight hundred years, I have been searching for the human able to take my place. I was so sure, so absolutely certain Sydney was that human. And so what! I care not at all about how many humans I've watched be sacrificed to achieve the goal." The angel gripped his hair and let out an anguished cry. "I was so sure."

Devon had never seen the angel this cracked. Both in a figurative sense, and also a literal one. He was splitting at the seams, angelic light belching forth.

Rafael snarled, and his eyes fixed on Devon. "The game is up. Hell has figured out what you are. Thus, I have no more use for you, you who have caused me so much annoyance and anxiety."

Jack threw a hand up to shield his face and stood, weaving, to shelter Devon from the Archangel's wrath.

Damn stupid move.

The light dimmed abruptly. "You *protect* him?"

The hand fell from Jack's eyes, and he looked down at his brother.

"J, don't mess this up for yourself. Him 'n me? This is a long time coming." Devon drew in a labored breath, and his face scrunched up in pain. "I'd say 'see you on the other side,' but I don't think you and I are going to the same place."

Jack swallowed. "I wish things had been different..."

Devon held his brother's gaze and reached a hand out, cupping Jack's cheek. "*Bis helledae, lieve mi bruder.*"

Jack's eyes shone, and his chest heaved with emotion. He covered Devon's hand with his own.

For a moment, the centuries erased, and the pain in Jack's eyes eased, replaced with determination. When certainty flooded his brother's features, Devon didn't need any words to understand the meaning. They were twins with a common language, after all.

Devon dropped his head in assent and steadied himself.

This was going to hurt like a bitch.

Devon braced against the gore-soaked cot, but that probably only made it worse.

Jack enveloped Devon in a bear hug, bare, bloodied chests tight together, Jack's fingers splayed across his back.

The burning was instantaneous, the light too bright.

How the fuck was it possible for healing to *hurt* so much?

*Do not scream, do not scream.*

Devon willed his lips to stay closed, but the sound puffed his cheeks out, escaped.

Past the pain, past the abnormal feeling of skin melting, past muscle and tissue stitching itself back together so fast light would envy the speed, Devon knew unequivocally, he was gonna puke.

"Stop this now, Janek!" Rafael shouted.

Rafael had used Jack's original name—the one their mother had given him. Like a parent using your middle name, Devon knew the shit had gotten deep. Maybe a little deeper than Jack intended.

Jack sagged against Devon, and Devon grew stronger, a complete role reversal. He could hardly believe Jack continued the healing another second, two. Disobedience was like death to Jack. And maybe that's what he figured—he was going to go out, may as well disobey this once. Maybe, for once, he was getting into all that brotherly love shit. Maybe.

"*Bruder.*" Jack whispered in Devon's ear. Devon held his brother up entirely, all Jack's remaining strength now transferred to Devon. "I wish—"

Then Jack was gone. No residue, no nothing. Like a second ago he hadn't been gifting an ungodly amount of strength and healing into his injured brother.

Gone.

Despite all the transferred power, Devon's head swam, and he fell back against the cot. His vision blurred, but not from the pain of the healing.

Staring at his hands, the healing light illuminated Devon but paled like the world's fastest fading glow stick. The burn had penetrated all the way through his body, and the throb of the healing dulled. In its wake, amazingly, there was no more pain. Nothing physical, anyway.

There was no way Jack—given how much effort he had already put into healing Devon—was still standing, wherever he currently was. Hell, Heaven, or somewhere in-between. Devon hoped Jack wasn't suffering for the parting gift. Nonetheless, Devon recited a quick prayer of thanks. Not to any deity, no. To his brother.

His breath ragged, Devon dragged his head up and pegged the dickhead Archangel with his eyes. The only remnant now of his near-death experience was the dried blood covering his body. Physically, he felt amazing, and he hated himself for reveling in it. The sacrifice it had required was too great.

*Get it together, or you'll be joining Jack. Syd's alive and in trouble. She needs you.*

"What'd you do to him?" He willed himself to stand, knew Rafael was going to take this to the next level. Devon touched his side cautiously and was gratified when nothing but smooth flesh and dried blood met his touch. The realization gave him force of purpose. He straightened his legs, bared his teeth, and clenched his fists. Rafael might take him out, but Devon wouldn't make it easy on the bastard.

"Nothing he didn't ask me for." Rafael had become something altogether different now that Jack was gone. His manner resembled Malik's, more demon than heavenly host.

"You don't want to lose both your best soldiers in the same

hour, do you?" Devon gathered his mind's strength. "You should know, Malik as much as threatened your life, too."

"Malik." Rafael's smile chilled Devon. Pure aggression. "Let him come. But you. You're not a soldier, are you, Devon? You're a mercenary. Heartless. Ruthless. Uncontrollable. Just the way I designed you. But your existence is causing me problems at the moment. If I kill you, or Hell ascends to do it, what's the difference? And it would give me such joy."

"We're supposed to help Syd." Devon threw the statement out like a meaty bone, a distraction to the hungry wolf. "You want me to abandon her. Let's be clear. This time, you're playing mercenary."

"She is not the one, Devon. I was so sure." Rafael's shoulders straightened. "The Guardian Army is done here."

Devon's stomach, so recently healed, dropped. He replayed the words, trying to find the fault, the misinterpretation. It couldn't be true; Rafael was fucking with him.

He swallowed. "Fine. Give her to me."

Rafael's ash-gray eyes roiled like an approaching thunderhead.

Devon steeled his will. He wouldn't be bullied. Not now.

The Archangel laughed, the sound turning to a shout. "You want the girl?"

Damn, that really sounded like a trick question.

"I do." Devon sent out a burst of power, searched for Syd. Empty space greeted him on the other side of the metal door, but she was there, he could sense it. Unease ran a sharp current through him. His mind flashed back to the bodies in the Packard Plant.

"She is beyond your help now," Rafael snarled. "I will grant your request, only because I know it will cause you pain. The next time I see you, I will torture you with her memory, and then I will kill you. If Malik has not done so first."

The Archangel moved to the side, waved gallantly to the closed door, as if he hadn't just laid down a stunner of a death threat.

Devon stepped toward the door, but Rafael held out a hand.

"There are no more chances for you. Make whatever peace you can."

Then he was gone.

Devon let out his held breath. He had been reasonably certain Rafael was about to do lasting rearrangement of his facial features. But if Syd was hurt or dead? That was so much worse.

Glancing down at himself, he startled. What a fucking mess. He was shirtless, and blood smeared his entire torso in drying clumps. His jeans were damp with blood and ripped across the thigh where Malik had impaled him with his claws. He pulled his hands up to his face, ran them through his hair which was tangled and blood-encrusted.

Devon squared his shoulders and pushed with his fully restored strength toward Syd. Utterly alone with whatever disaster awaited on the other side of the white, gleaming door.

# CHAPTER THIRTY-TWO

S yd whirled through space, cold reality washed over her, chilling her spirit. Maybe she was dead. Maybe she hadn't survived at all. Maybe she was about to see that legendary white light.

God, if she could, she would never walk into that stupid bar. Not meet Devon with his cutting wit, Jack with his quiet kindness, or Byrne with her mad scientist determination. Certainly not the crazy Archangel.

The thoughts continued to twist Syd about in space, and she could barely make out landscapes. Mountains flashed before her, plains the next moment. Ocean. Syd had no power to stop; rather her spirit drove her forward with a purpose she was not privy to.

Suddenly, as if someone had put a halting finger on a spinning top, Syd stopped moving. Vertigo set in, and she snapped her eyes closed in an attempt to quell the disorienting feeling.

"You shouldn't be here." The voice had a child-like lilt, but the tone was serious.

Syd opened her eyes, letting her spirit see. She stood, weaving, atop a rolling peak, impossibly green, with small lavender flowers carpeting it. Black space surrounded the hill, as far as the eye could see. The feeling she might accidentally slip from the hillside and fall into oblivion panicked Syd, and she pressed her spirit against the blanket of purple flowers. Her knees hit the ground, which felt spongy, not at all as solid as the ground she was used to.

The child voice laughed, the sound a strange combination—admonition and mirth. "You can't fall off when you are Inbetween."

Raising her head, Syd looked at the body belonging to the voice. Light brown ringlets frizzed the head of a slight child in a yellow sundress. Her feet were bare, and she pushed them off the ground in a steady rhythm, swinging in a rickety rocking chair. Her lips spread thin in an amused smile.

Wherever Syd was, it was beautiful, despite the abysmal darkness that surrounded them. She had left her body far behind, but she could feel the cool softness of the blooms underneath her. "Where am I? Is this heaven?" Syd asked, her long-held breath coming forth in a rush.

"Heaven? No." The question turned the girl's lips up further making her look like a cartoon character. "You are Inbetween."

Standing, Syd spun carefully around, taking in her surroundings. "Who are you?"

"Ashira. Ruler and sole inhabitant of the Inbetween."

Syd opened her mouth to speak, but she was cut off.

Ashira cocked her head at an impossible angle. "Sydney Hoven, I presume. The girl all the angels can't stop talking about."

*All the angels?*

Syd tried to process the thoughts, but it felt foreign, impossible. "That can't be—"

Ashira *tsked*. "Oh yes. Rafael's banishment was the talk of the thirteenth century. Everyone knows *that* story. How Sammael taunted him with the possibility of release. If only he could find a human able to absorb his duties, take their weight. Someone strong enough to allow the power of the Pledge to flow through them. Rafael has been searching ever since."

Syd whispered, "Am I...I mean, could I do that?"

Ashira's rocking slowed. "It's not my place to say." Her eyes unfocused, then she smiled impishly. "Your pretty little hybrid is searching for you."

Hybrid? What the hell was she talking about?

The air seethed in this place, like an invisible breath pushed out from the belly of a great beast. Ashira studied her, taking her time. Her lips moved slightly, as if mumbling to herself.

Syd threw up her hands, and spirit mist trailed from them, reminding her she wasn't really here. "So I'm dead, and this is like —what—purgatory?"

Ashira clapped her small hands together in apparent amusement. Her nails were black and pointed.

Syd swallowed.

Ashira shook her head and pulled her legs up under her, crisscrossed. The rocking chair continued to move, though Ashira made no apparent effort to make it do so.

"You aren't dead. You have come to this place uninvited and unwelcome. Great power lives here." Ashira's smiled faded. "You have a decision to make. And you need to do it soon."

"What decision?"

The purple flowers around her darkened, the color bleeding and intensifying.

"If you return, or if you continue on." Ashira's voice took on a note of sadness.

"Continue on?" Syd asked, her heart began to pound.

Ashira smiled, this time it was almost kind. "You understand this. Your fear tells me you understand."

Syd gazed at the plush green carpet of grass that covered the hillside. "My body rejected me. I can't return. There is no choice to be made."

Ashira stood, her legs floating fluid as specters under her long sundress. "Free Will still exists, of course. For now, at least. You can choose."

Syd clenched her jaw. "No, you don't understand. I wanted to get back into my body. That was my choice. I *couldn't*—it wouldn't work."

Ashira drew her sharp black nails through her frizzy hair, catching a finger in a particularly knotted loop. "You have all the tools you need." She tugged harshly on the tangle.

Tools? What tools did Syd have to prepare her for this situation? Shit, her toolbox was in her garage. The thought didn't bring any measure of levity. She stalked back and forth over the same path of grass and flowers on the hillside. Each time she approached the edge she turned back the way she had come.

Syd's mind worked on the problem before her. She came up with...nothing. There was nothing she had that could help her. She was just a human. Alone. Broken.

"This is crap. I don't have *anything*, Ashira. I have no idea what you're talking about."

The tween-girl façade faded for a second, and Syd thought she saw something...some amount of incredible energy seethed under the surface of Ashira's sundress. It was a force, a full spectrum of color moving and flowing through and over the whole hillside. It seemed more concentrated around and through Ashira.

Abruptly the vision faded, and Ashira was a girl in a dress, back to rocking in a chair.

"What was that?" Syd asked, half-frightened and half-intrigued.

Ashira took a deep breath, and when she focused on Syd, there was awe her eyes. "It's the power that lives here. It calls to you."

Ashira's lips curled in distaste. "Soon, your spirit will fade and make your choice for you. Your body will cease to function, and your spirit will be forever severed. Heaven, Hell, the Everafter. True death."

Didn't sound the least bit promising.

Syd tried not to hyperventilate. After all, she was a spirit. There should be some perks.

Ashira stood fluidly and the rocking chair simply disappeared from beneath her. She twirled an especially frizzy ringlet between her pointy black nails.

Ashira traipsed across the distance separating them, skipping as if school had just declared recess.

Each step closer raised Syd's internal hackles a little further. That child-like gesture terrified Syd. She did the only thing she could think. And truly, thought didn't inspire the action. It was an instinct older than fight or flight. Though Devon had requested she take it down, Syd's default was shielded. Had been for so many years.

So many times she had dabbled, lowered the wall a bit, just a bit. But never entirely. Never even close. The prospect was terrifying. The wall kept her sane, kept her whole. Kept her abilities separate.

She dropped it. Without reserve, without restraint.

Immediately, Syd had a feeling like she was filling up her internal gas tank. She hadn't been aware she had been on 'E.' Bone-dry. There was so much room inside her. The spectrum of color came rushing forth, pushing through her spirit. It ran forward, backward and through again. She whipped around with the force, jostling her with unseen power. She could no longer see Ashira, the hillside. All she could see was the spectrum, filling her ears with a sound like a whining electric guitar peeling off riff after riff of incredible, haunting melodies. She could feel it, too, the energy pulsing through her. It was soft, but that was a ruse. Whittled down to its most concentrated core, this was power. Internal, she filled to bursting, but the inflow had not slowed. Not one bit.

It became intense and alarming in an instant.

If she didn't stop soon, she would be no more. The power would simply consume her, override her. She would be lost.

*What happened, how did I do this?*

Her wall.

A wall doesn't get built that world-class without a lot of effort going into the construction, Devon had said.

When things got crazy. When things *always* got crazy. When she tinkered with the goddamn wall. When she tried using the psychic abilities that separated her from everyone else.

But this time, she had dropped it entirely. Could she even

rebuild it? Thinking about the task drained her. It would be a gargantuan effort. But it was that or die.

Drawing all the energy she could muster inside the storm of power, Syd built up one brick. Just one. Slowing the flow of energy felt like trying to hold back a speeding train. Her knees failed, and a paper bag definitely would've come in handy. The effort was intense, like a sustained attempt to hold electricity in her bare hands.

Another brick.

A third.

The flow of whiplash power began to ebb. She put up another brick. God, she had so far to go, so much more to build—

The energy drew back further, and she could almost breathe again. She needed air. Behind the spectrum of light, the hillside wavered into view again. Ashira was nowhere to be seen.

Syd's drudging effort continued. One small brick at a time, the wall now partially reconstructed, but with a juggernaut of power contained and pulsing inside her.

The spectrum didn't seem so overpowering now. This was how she had managed her psychic powers from the time she had become aware of her abilities. The wall was second-nature to her —and, she supposed, it qualified as a tool.

Her gas tank was full way past capacity. The feeling of the energy coursing through her was better than any buzz. Dizzy with power, a terrible clarity overcame her.

Energized and empowered beyond all rational thought, Syd made only one demand of her spirit.

# CHAPTER THIRTY-THREE

Devon was alone with whatever waited on the other side of that metal door. His body shook from Jack's harried healing, and the tremors were only amplified by his fear.

Syd is right here, behind door number one. The thought should've been a pressure release for him, but events had taken a right turn toward Shit City. Plenty of crappy road markers led the way. Syd's condition was TBD. Rafael had demonstrated he could pull the plug on any of his soldiers, at any time.

Rafael, Syd...Jack.

His chest felt like maybe Malik had returned and put that big blade to his chest. Constricted and so hard to breathe. *Jack.* His brother was gone. Devon wanted to rage, but his ever-present anger was silent, an empty space in his mind. He willed it forward, demanded it...required it. How the fuck was he supposed to get through this without his fury?

His forward momentum failed. His legs, though fully healed, gave way. His knees met concrete, and his hands came up to cover his face.

What the hell had his brother been thinking? Asking to be taken out of service? Giving up, all hara-kiri and shit. And now

Devon was on his own. Trying to defeat a demon, save the city, save the girl. Even the Archangel wasn't an ally anymore. The whole freaking world was at stake if the Pledge broke.

Jesus, how fucked up was this—Jack was dead, and he was playing hero.

He wasn't the hero. Jack was.

He choked out one sob. Then his rage welled up inside. Took over. It felt like home, and he screamed. Screamed so loud he was sure Jack could hear him, even if they were separated by realms. "How could you!"

His breath ragged, he let his fist fly into the concrete. The knuckle ripped wide and focused his pain, his grief. He stared at it like it held the secrets to life itself.

Two more uneven breaths.

Violently, Devon shook his head. Like he was flicking off the light switch in the storage room of his mind that held all memories of Jack, Devon shut down his grief. Jack had made his choice; now Devon needed to make his. Hell, focusing on the mission was probably the best way to pay homage to his overbearingly right-eous brother anyway.

He got to his feet slowly, wiping his bloody knuckles against his ruined jeans.

He lifted his face to the ceiling, as he could only imagine the White Knight in heaven. He could see Jack looking down with exasperation, mouthing, "The mission!"

Devon snarled. "You bastard."

Devon jogged to the door. With strange disorientation, he saw his hand shaking, reaching toward the metal knob. Locking down on the fear clamping his chest, he threw open the white steel and braced for the worst.

*Sydney.* His lioness. Unconscious, unmoving she lay on the steel table, long auburn hair fanned out messily around her. She was too pale, her lips parted, dry and cracked. Her right arm had fallen off the table and hung loosely, her fingers cramped toward her palm. A gesture of pain.

Pain he had been unable to prevent.

*Is she safe with you?* Brie's words echoed in his head. He wanted to lash out at something, anything. But if he started, the destruction would be total. He wouldn't stop until the house was leveled. And he didn't have that kind of time.

Left in the helplessness of his failure, Devon could only stare at her starkly beautiful profile. Like the people he had found in the Packard Plant, she was more vegetable than human. His anger sang a song of destruction, the trembling in his extremities accelerating. His breathing rasped and rattled his lungs. Nothing was safe near him. Nothing, least of all her.

The sound of a woman's heels clicked on the metal ladder. Devon reached out with his mind. *The doctor.* The loose patchwork of his control unraveled.

"You don't want to be down here right now." Devon measured his words, not turning around and sure as hell not trusting himself to stay on the law-abiding side of the killing edge. Rafael hadn't lifted his decree to use his compulsion, but in his current state of mind, Devon didn't care. He was dead anyway.

Byrne represented a big part of the reason drying blood tightened his skin and why Syd lay broken on that damn table.

Byrne didn't slow her pace, and the sound of her heels grew louder.

Which fanned the flames burning inside him to wildfire proportions.

*This bitch has a serious death wish.*

A quick read in her head, and he knew she held a gun. Loaded, totally prepared to pull the trigger. "What have you done to her?" The doctor's voice quavered, but there was a steel cord of strength there, too.

Not turning to face her, he said, "For a genius doctor, you are really fucking stupid." The raspy texture of his voice barely hid the violence he contained, a class-six whitewater rapids. All smooth ride on the upside, all treacherous and impassable beneath the surface. One misstep and he would kill her; he didn't think he could help it. He wasn't exactly known for his self-control in the best of situations. At this particular moment? His rage felt more a part of him than his left nut.

"I need to see her." She kept on coming. "I need to see if I can help—"

One more quiet second. The last fateful one, when realization hit: *holy shit, I really did pull the pin from that grenade*—then his anger exploded. A thousand sharp, jagged bits of power all aimed at Dr. Byrne. He slammed into her mind with a viciousness he rarely allowed himself. While he normally slipped past the border of people's minds without causing them to blink, he made sure she understood *exactly* what was coming for her. Mayhem and devastation. Destruction on a cellular level.

The doctor screamed, her hands grasped her head, and she stumbled against the wall. Blood ran from her ears, her nose, ruining the white perfection of her damn coat.

Fuck Rainbow Bright and fuck his decrees. Maybe Jack had it right, after all. Death was starting to look real appealing. If Syd remained as she was—

Stupid, but he had actually begun to hope maybe, yeah, *maybe*, there was more to life on Earth. Once again, death and destruction reigned.

What the hell, that was a party he would crash anytime.

He ripped through Byrne's memories, gathering information and letting her observe him taking all she held dear. His power rode her mind, and he turned from the room where Syd lay and paced back out into the main area of the basement.

He froze Byrne in place. One of those fancy-dancy heels up on tip-toe, the heel suspended in mid-air like she was preparing to do a two-step against the wall.

Devon worked through the thick material of Byrne's thoughts, dense with equations and notations which held no meaning to him. The first important piece of the puzzle clicked into place with horrible clarity. Byrne was just a pawn. In a screwed-up way, Byrne had wanted Syd safe. She wanted Syd kept out of this. Why?

With reckless disregard, Devon pushed further into her mind.

Rafael had engineered the whole deal. Jack and Devon as body-guards, Byrne playing mad scientist. Byrne had helped Rafael locate gifted individuals. Rafael had only required to meet them before she actually did her experimentation. She'd complied because it came with virtual unlimited funding. Except with Syd. Byrne had kept Syd away. For as long as she could.

Whatever had happened to Syd, Rafael was behind it all. She had played a part, but Byrne's intentions were all science. She had some crazy ideas about what the human mind was capable of.

Didn't change the outcome, now did it?

To release the pressure of his rage, Devon stalked over and gripped Byrne's desk with both hands, flipped the solid wood, launching it high, one edge snapping under the assault of hitting concrete. The glass shattered on impact. After that, the only sound was paper fluttering to the ground, then the gentle whirring of machinery in the background. And Byrne dragging in air like there was a Blue-Light Special on $O_2$.

Immobile under Devon's thrall, Byrne held the gun to her side with widened eyes.

The burst of rage released, Devon smiled his cruelest smile and advanced on Byrne, an inch separating his lips from her forehead. He lowered his gaze and locked onto hers with all force of his mind. He put fisted hands on either side of her head against the cold white concrete.

Devon whispered, working to get control back. "If you haven't figured it out yet, you're in way out of your depth, sweetheart."

Byrne swallowed.

"You see, you caught me on a really bad day. I almost died today. My brother just died." His voice broke, and he hated himself, just a bit. "Syd might die, too. It's unacceptable. And you're going to help me fix it."

Byrne continued to meet his eyes. "What did he do to her?"

God, he hadn't truly hated anyone in such a long time. Disinterest and disregard were his normal. But hate—it burned so hot inside him he might've been sitting on the sun. Hate for his Archangel captain.

"Now. Are you going to help me understand all the crazy equations floating around your head? I don't have a degree in quantum biology, but I'm a quick study."

"I have no idea what he did to her— I can't—"

*I'm going to kill her, I'm going to kill her, I'm going to—* Desperately, he tried to remember why he needed to keep her alive — *It's the only chance you have to help Syd.*

Right.

*Put the gun to your head.* Devon sent the command roaring through Byrne's mind with way more force than necessary. *She's only human for God's sake,* a distant and forgotten piece of his rational mind cautioned. *If you rip her apart, Syd might be truly lost.*

Byrne put up an admirable resistance. Nothing like Syd, but it reminded him of her. The thought gripped his heart and squeezed tight.

The gun rose steadily toward its designated position, that vulnerable indentation of flesh.

"What were you trying to do to Syd?" he asked.

Byrne's lips tightened. She said nothing. In her mind, she was actually more intrigued. Intrigued, for God's sake, as she held a gun to her temple at his unspoken command.

She knew he was controlling her mind. Being the single-minded scientist she was, Byrne focused on the possibilities. "How are you doing this?"

Devon applied pressure in her mind, dancing around the imperative to pull the trigger. "I'm not entirely human. Surprise!"

But Byrne ignored the gun at her temple, her gaze widening. "How did he—"

"He, who?" Devon laughed. "Rafael? Your science buddy isn't human, either, much less so than me. He's an Archangel, Byrne. And he's been playing you this whole time."

She blinked rapidly, and her eyes lost focus, like her whole world was doing a massive reorg inside her head. "That's not... It can't be..."

"Possible? Except it is. I can control your body, your mind, not because I'm a science experiment, but because an Archangel gifted me power."

Byrne had totally lost focus on what Devon needed her focused on. Helping Syd. To do that, he needed Byrne to be piss-your-pants scared. She wasn't there yet, but she would be soon. He knew the stages of fear like a sponsor knew the Twelve Steps.

Devon continued to shuffle through her thoughts. Byrne struggled and finally realized she couldn't command her body to move. He wouldn't allow it. This wasn't some conundrum she could solve. He wasn't playing. The fascination dulled, and her more appropriate reaction drew to the forefront. Memories of exactly what losing control meant to her flashed across his consciousness. Being raped at fifteen. The resulting lack of control and pregnancy. Her father's rage and rejection. With seer-like clarity, the memories pinged rapid fire through Devon's mind, and he understood.

Byrne's motivation for all of this was control. To control her environment to the nth degree. The science she surrounded herself with was nothing more than a brilliant shield from emotion. Her mind was such a finely chiseled tool, and she'd worked damn hard to make it so.

Panic built inside Byrne at snowball-downhill pace.

She had delivered the opportunity to force her cooperation with a pretty red bow on top.

His voice was low, intent. "I can hear every thought going through your head. I could tell you to pull the trigger, and you would."

Her stony expression stayed hard, and her chest heaved. One fat drop of blood plopped from her nose.

"Death doesn't scare you, does it?" Devon asked slowly. "But I know what does."

He slid one hand down the wall inch by inch.

Inside her head, the panic continued to build.

"Your mind." He leaned closer, tapping her temple with his finger. "I could take it from you. Just imagine it. You, so smart, stuck in a home somewhere, alive and aware, but unable to communicate. Some minimum wager helping you with every task. Every bodily function. No control."

Panic turned into terror. *No, no. He can't... I...can't.*

"You can't stop me. You can't *control* me. You can only answer my questions. In English." Devon observed her, his own mind cold and intent on the task. Would he really mush her brain for her defiance? Maybe not just that. But for Syd? Yeah. He'd do it. Even as he recognized she was—at best—a surrogate for a certain brightly-lit asshole.

Byrne's thoughts lost focus and turned wild.

Devon's own control was threadbare, and he attempted to temper his compulsion, on the chance Byrne's mind was needed at full capacity to help Syd. But this was getting old.

"How do we fix Syd?"

Devon slammed his hand against the wall behind her, and Byrne flinched. Her knees would've buckled if he had allowed it.

"Sydney was born with a brain mutation that should allow her to tap into an infinite source of energy. But she's not accessing it." Byrne's voice was strangled. "I thought...I thought I could help her do it. I've been working on this for a decade."

In her mind, Devon saw all the people in the Packard Plant. All the doctor's failed experiments.

"I thought we might be close, but—"

"Then what is *that?*" Devon lifted his hand to point to the room where Syd lay.

Byrne winced as if she expected to be struck.

"Sydney was special... I don't *know.*" Byrne's face crumbled, and a solitary tear leaked out.

Devon delved back into her head, needing more.

Like he'd been kicked in the head, he reared back.

The image in Byrne's head... It couldn't possibly be. Devon leaned away from her, needing space in a bad way, but examining the doctor's green eyes, her fair skin. He wondered how he hadn't seen it before.

Byrne's voice was weak. "I failed her."

Devon's rage roared forth from its mild hibernation. He pushed away from the wall, spun around before he struck her. He couldn't stall out the violence, and his left hand fisted and punched the wall. The pain centered him.

He couldn't force the words from his mouth, wasn't sure it was wise. But his brain whispered it anyway. *She's your daughter.*

Syd had been born to Byrne at sixteen and given up for adoption. Christ.

Gathering his conviction, Devon leaned back in. "You're going to fix her." He gestured with his throbbing hand to the room where Syd lay. He released his hold on her body, and the doctor sagged. But only for a second.

She ran into the room, coming up short and gasping when she saw her daughter.

The doctor drew in a breath and got to work. She hooked Syd up to some machines.

The next two minutes passed like centuries.

Devon hovered behind her, arms crossed. His mind jumbled into a mess of emotion. He wanted badly to claw his way out of his own head. His chest heaved out breath after breath, but he couldn't look away from Syd's beautiful face. When he did, it was Jack's face that crowded his vision.

Finally, Byrne stopped moving. She studied the monitor in front of her. She sagged and turned slowly toward him.

"I don't know what he did to her." Byrne's voice rose, desperation creeping in. "She's brain-dead."

Devon's muscles pulled painfully tight, and he pressed his hands into his head. His control threatened to burst—once more, one final time. "Then there is no reason to keep you wasting oxygen. *Grab your gun.*"

Their eyes met. His cold, hers defiantly panicked. Back inside her head, she saw death coming for her. Glancing back to Syd on the table, she obeyed. She didn't even fight it.

Enmeshed in her thoughts, Devon understood. She felt she deserved it. Syd had been her hope. And now it was gone. Thinking of Jack and Syd, Devon could empathize. But it didn't change his resolve.

Byrne was not innocent in all this.

"For Syd, and for all people in the Packard Plant."

At his unspoken command, her finger began to tamp down on the trigger.

Rafael's form crashed into the basement, appearing as a whirlwind whipping around his angelic light. From the depths of the whirlwind, Devon could spot those angry gray eyes.

Trained on Devon.

The whirlwind had faded, and now the Archangel stood, blinding against the white background of the basement. Devon's eyes burned against the assault of light, but he held them open. Insubordinate to his core.

"You defy me. Again." Rafael's voice was low, the cadence and pitch too slow and soft for the words.

And didn't that make Devon all the more edgy. Rafael spitting mad and full of rage was normal S.O.P. But this... Devon was thrown off kilter, yet his hold on Byrne's mind didn't falter. He kept her in place and stationary. His mind's command stayed strong, but her arm muscles were fatiguing, trembling as she held the gun to her head.

It might well be signing his death warrant, but Devon had no intention of releasing her.

Silence enveloped the room. Byrne turned up the volume on her ragged breathing, and the sound filled Devon with agitation. Between Jack's accelerated healing program, Syd's vegetative state, and the mad scientist's bleak prognosis, Devon's nerves jumped like he had just downed a twelve-pack of Red Bull.

"You will release her." Rafael's voice carried a deceptively soft tone, but his entire form shimmered around the edges. Angel for 'highly pissed off.'

Devon let the smile, his best game face, overtake his features, and he compelled Byrne to speak for him. "Or what?" she said, her voice strangled, and her knees shook.

Rafael's gaze flicked briefly to the doctor. Devon's hold on Byrne's mind was most likely the only thing keeping Rainbow Bright from doing something Devon would dislike. Like sending him to Jack's happily-ever-after. So yeah, fuck the hostage-release program.

Not to mention there was the little factoid about them using him to protect Syd, only to play Twister in her brain. Devon's fists clenched.

This time, Devon spoke for himself. "You take one step, and I'll rip her brain apart so fast there won't be enough left to make a bowl of soup. And she seems pretty damn important to your overall plan. You wanna play roulette with her head? You know I won't hesitate. Be sure, Rafael."

Rafael's jaw clenched. Devon could see a tick jumping the hard edge.

"I should've destroyed you the moment I knew what you truly were." Rafael's angelic face twisted into a bestial snarl. "Like all of your kind, you have become too dangerous."

The demon's words steam-rolled through Devon. *Archon—that's what you are.*

If someone didn't explain what the hell an Archon was, and soon, things were gonna get bloody.

# CHAPTER THIRTY-FOUR

*Take me to my body.*

Syd repeated the command over and over as she sped through the ether. And—could she get a hallelujah—it appeared it might actually work. At the very least, she could feel Ashira's presence fading, but her reconstructed wall was straining hard and losing. Power engulfed her, enough that she had to concentrate on keeping herself together.

Her spirit, way over capacity with power, crashed through the atmosphere, plummeting down, and finally through the ground. When the dizziness faded, she recognized the sterility of Byrne's basement all around her.

Her relief at returning was completely smothered by the reality of having her body again. It was all about the physical feelings, none of them good. Pain shot through her temple, pinched and punched down her torso. When the power reached her toes, it rebounded like a speeding car off a brick wall. The fragmented debris of energy flew toward her head again, and she prepared for impact, quite sure she would split apart and combust. There was no way her body could withstand all this power plowing through her.

Syd was more aware of her body than she ever had been. All its bones, connecting tissue, pulsing, working organs. The meat of the thing. But she had learned the secret.

It wasn't her. It wasn't her at all.

No. She was this *power*, electric and immense. The power fueled all that meat to move around. Her wall had always separated her from it, terrifying as it was, but now she knew what happened when the wall was gone.

Still, she had never been more grateful for the body. Meat, yes, but a masterpiece of biological engineering, too.

Her eyes flew open, immediately blinded at the brightness. Her fingers splayed, seeking an anchor. She jack-knifed into a right angle on the metal platform that held her body. Her lungs gulped in a dragging suck of air, the loudest sound she had ever heard. The air crossed her windpipe like broken glass, and she cradled a hand around her throat to soothe it.

Wrapped around her throat, her fingers shook. Tears formed, not from weepy emotion but hardcore pain. God, it *burned*. It wasn't the air, but the incredible power riding her, which caused the pain. She couldn't sustain this, couldn't contain such profound power for long.

The light was too much...and then, a *pop*, and the room pitched into darkness. Instinctively the power riding her had risen to her half-formed command.

Her other hand gripped the metal table, fingers digging into the sharp, stainless edge. The biting pain grounded her, forced her to take another breath. This one degrees more measured, more controlled.

*The wall. Reinforce the wall...* The trip through the ether and back to her body had gone nuclear on the thing that kept the power in check.

Back firmly now into her body, the habit felt like brushing her teeth in the morning. Automatic. The wall sprung up at her command, and her relief was palpable. Her head dropped in reprieve onto her chest, and her eyes squeezed shut. Her body was no longer about to implode. Yay.

*Let's try this again.* She opened her eyes slowly, not trusting the power was indeed locked definitively inside her body. And yep, all her appendages were attached and not bloody stumps blown across the room. Somehow, she had done it. Contained what was surely the force of the universe inside her petite little meat-suit.

Angry, raised voices filtered through the closed metal door. They must be shouting for it to penetrate. That both voices were deeply resonant certainly helped.

Recognition coursed through her, she shuddered, and her recently-won control quivered.

*Devon.*

She spun, her legs swinging off the table. She pushed off and landed solidly on her feet. Standing there, she looked down, half in disbelief she had made it. Made it back into her body, pulsing with contained energy. She held up a hand, examined her fingers with their chipped blood-rose nails, and searched for a flaw, an injury. Evidence of the serious mind-trip she had taken.

Ashira. Had she been real? Had any of it been real?

Her intuition spoke up, chiding. *You know it was.*

Syd put one booted foot in front of the other. Toward the door. Toward those angry voices. The room was small, so it didn't take long. She reached out, had a moment of self-awareness, and watched her hand reach out to take the doorknob. At the scrutiny, her hand shook. *Don't look too close.*

Bearing down on her control, the door swung out. Syd lowered her gaze, avoiding the light emanating from the now-open door. She blinked, trying to process what her vision reported to her. Her hand was outstretched and shaking, but nowhere near the doorknob. She had not touched the door, but it was now open. The power, rising to her command again.

Syd's gaze dragged up, taking in the scene in front of her. Devon stood feet away from Dr. Byrne, his head whipped around, focused on Syd. He had been pointing an accusing finger toward Rafael. That finger now pointed loosely, forgotten as curfew on prom night. He looked like an extra in a B-movie zombie-flick. His bare chest was covered in drying blood, but there was no indication of the horrendous wound that caused it.

Her mind reeled, trying to figure out what was real, what she could trust.

Unable to meet his eyes, Syd's gaze shifted left. Rafael.

She squinted.

The lights in the basement flickered. Syd glanced quickly around, taking in Byrne's papers scattered like a savage animal had been let loose. The desk was upended, and broken glass had skittered across the floor. Her cot appeared wet and covered in blood. The only thing undisturbed was the expensive machinery to Syd's right.

Cot covered in blood...whose blood? As if in a fog, Syd walked slowly over and reached out a hand. A smattering of images flickered across her consciousness, and she flinched. *Devon, recovering from a vicious battle with Malik. He nearly died.* Her chest heaved in protest of the image.

Syd swung her gaze to Devon, confused, because he seemed perfectly fine. How much time had passed in the Inbetween, with Ashira?

How much time had she lost?

Dr. Byrne stood in an unnatural position one foot raised so only the toes touched the concrete, her face frozen in the last fearful expression of some small prey animal.

*She's under thrall.* Compulsion held her in place and was as apparent to Syd as identifying aftermarket accessories on a Chevy. It swirled around, beneath her skin, a whisper binding her as strong as steel bands. Another form of power, Devon's power. Kindred to what she now held inside her.

Syd looked to Devon. "Release her." Syd saw those wisps of his compulsive power over Byrne recede and fade into nothingness as if they had never been there at all. She wasn't sure if she had done it or Devon had.

Devon's face unveiled the emotion behind his pale expression.

*I thought you were gone forever* written all over his face. He took a step toward her. Dr. Byrne, now free, shrank against the wall.

Rafael took a faltering step back, his beautiful face smoothing into a mask.

"Do not go near her, Devon. I will end you, if you try," Rafael's voice boomed out the command.

Devon stopped, his whole body tensed, as if he had made peace with his decision.

He moved toward her.

A beam of light erupted out from the Archangel's hand and shot toward Devon. It reached him in half a heartbeat, and he screamed, dropping to his knees.

"Stop!" Syd heard herself shout, one arm reaching long toward the source of pain, and she was suddenly in front of Devon, facing the Archangel. She had no memory of moving. Had she run, lost time? Seemed borderline irrelevant, as she was where she needed to be. In front of and protecting the man who'd laid his life down for hers more than once.

Rafael widened his stance. "Why do you care what happens to him? I can tell you from experience, his considerable cunning is no match for the pain in the ass he will be in your army."

Confused, Syd tore her gaze away from the Archangel and looked around the room, searching for something that might make sense. Provide context. *My army?*

In response to her unspoken question, the Archangel spoke again, this time with reverence, "You may yet be the one to take my place."

Behind her, Syd sensed Devon rise up off the floor and shift his weight from one foot to the other, his body achingly close to hers. Close enough the electricity snapped between them, a nearly painful pulse. Her body hummed with her own contained energy, begging to be let out of each pore of her skin. Devon's closeness and the Archangel's foreboding words were acting like anti-Xanax.

Devon stepped out from behind her. "Rafael, that's insane."

Rafael's voice drew her gaze up once more. He glowed now, any façade of humanity long gone. "Just one last piece of housekeeping."

Light blew forth from Rafael, aimed with laser-focus toward Devon. He screamed again, his head bowing back. He dropped to his knees with arms flung wide as if preparing for crucifixion.

*The angel cannot hurt you*, her intuition whispered, *not now*.

Syd stepped into the blast of light and stood protectively over Devon.

"Syd, no!" Devon cried.

The light continued its assault at Rafael's bid.

All thoughts shifted from protecting Devon to the burning power filling her soul to the brim. The tenuous hold on her body slipped, and she thought for one paralyzing second she was about to be forced out of her body...again. Her control hunkered down, her psychic wall flying to IMAX 3D in her mind.

The Archangel's force wasn't hurting her. It was filling her past capacity.

*Get it out, get it out of you. It's too much...*

Standing, she turned to the Archangel. Syd did the only thing the vertigo of power would accept. She screamed and threw her hands forward like she was throwing a basketball made of lightning.

The direction of all that light pulled a one-eighty and went back the way it had come. Syd processed the look of startled disbelief on the angel's face before he was thrown back into the wall. Or, the wall he would've hit, if his angelic form hadn't shuddered and gone translucent. He passed through the wall and was gone.

Her breath rushed in and out of her lungs way too fast. She turned back to Devon. "Are you hurt?"

He didn't answer, the shaking in his arms evidence enough of his condition. He wasn't looking at her. Standing, he limped over and ran a hand along the wall the angel had passed through. Devon's hand supported his weight against the concrete.

"What the hell did you do to him? *How* the hell did you do that to him?" Devon's voice was thick with disbelief.

"I don't—know." She blinked several times and stared down at her hands. Her hands had harnessed angelic power and used it against an Archangel. She was suddenly completely unsure if she had made it back into her own body. Her body didn't have any kind of capabilities like *this*. She was a human being—freaky psychic, sure, but human. Wasn't she?

"I can't sense him at all. He's gone." Devon turned to face her, his eyebrows scrunched down. "Did you kill him? *Can* he be killed?"

Her voice was scratchy. "You're asking me? I don't know!" She had no idea what she'd done. At the moment, it was instinct, not some well thought out strategy.

Syd stared up at Devon, willing him to see it was her. Damn it, she needed his help. Perhaps now more than ever. But she saw it clearly. In Devon's eyes there was a shrewdness that was evaluating her threat. To him.

Silence enveloped the basement.

A hiss came from behind Syd. Turning, she realized the doctor stood pressed up against the wall. Her expression was intently fixed on Syd, but her lab coat was askew, and blood darkened the front of it, where it dripped from her nose.

Byrne tried to back up, but with nowhere to go, she stumbled and righted herself against the concrete wall. "Stay away from me." Her wide eyes stayed fixed on Devon. She scooted along the wall, inching toward the escape ladder. Made Syd wonder what exactly he had done to crack that hard-as-granite shell. Probably she didn't want to know.

Syd stared at Byrne, and she could imagine the picture she made. Cracked out, glowing. Pissed. Syd's breathing sped, her power rising in her body.

"Sydney, please—let me help you." Byrne's voice wasn't steady. "These...people... They aren't safe."

"Oh?" Devon sneered. "And you are? What about all the bodies at the Packard Plant? That wasn't Rafael's work. It was yours."

Syd glanced back and forth between them. "Bodies?"

Devon kept his eyes fixed on Byrne. "She's been using people as her lab rats."

Byrne didn't even try to deny it. "That's not the whole truth of it. Besides"—she pegged Devon with her eyes— "are you saying you operate in the realm of ethical? With what you've done to me?" Byrne was getting defiant. That was not going to go well for her.

Devon shifted beside her.

Syd had to make a choice. Byrne had tried to warn her away from Rafael, but she was only human. Based on what Devon had said, maybe wasn't even a *good* human. It wasn't even a close call. Whatever was happening to her now, Byrne wouldn't be able to help. Not in the way Syd needed.

Devon started to advance toward Byrne, but Syd's hand on his arm halted him.

"On my scale of problems, you barely rate." Syd relaxed her fists. "And you're blocking my exit."

Somberly, Byrne backed toward the ladder. She met Syd's eyes once more, then she retreated up the stairs.

When the sound of her heels above them faded sufficiently, Syd spoke. "Why did you do it?" She didn't understand why he was here. Why he had decided to stand against Rafael, after delivering her to the crazed Archangel in the first place?

Devon's face changed from blank emotion to quiet contemplation. "Syd?"

"You set me up."

Devon's eyes flared, lips twisting into a sneer. He took several breaths before replying. "Rafael didn't tell me shit. I had as little a clue as you and, believe me, that burns."

Syd wasn't willing to accept that line quite yet.

Impatient, Devon threw up his hands. "Believe what you want. You see anyone else here volunteering to protect you?"

Syd took a breath and looked around, quieted the anger and evaluated. "Where's Jack?"

Devon flinched, blinked several times in rapid succession before he turned away.

Her pulse sped. "What happened?" She grabbed his shoulder and turned him back to face her. He offered no resistance, and the look on his face terrified her.

He looked bereft.

"Devon...where is Jack?"

Devon gripped his neck and started rubbing, like maybe there was tension that wouldn't give. "Jack did a hell of healing job on me. And then Rafael...released him."

She pictured Jack's warm eyes, his kind smile. Her gut tightened. "Jack's...dead?"

Devon stopped massaging his neck and paused. He was making a choice, Syd could see the thoughts plainly. Grief or his mask.

His eyes hardened into ice.

"He gave up, Syd. He *wanted* out. He made a deal with Rafael to deliver you, so he could be done with the Guardian Army. He ended his life as a fucking coward who would rather hope to be with his dead wife than have immortality, fight the good fight."

Syd blinked. "No," she whispered. "I can't— It's not okay, it's not—"

Devon swallowed thickly and ran a hand over his face, erasing the emotion cracking through his mask in a heartbeat. "Syd?"

Syd broke eye contact with him and looked down at her hands. Amazingly, they were alight with the residue of the angel's power. Rafael's power had flowed through her and sung a choir's chorus of perfect harmony.

She raised her fingertips to examine them, her thoughts drifting to Jack and the impossibility he was gone. It wasn't right, damn it.

Devon swallowed. "What happened to you?"

She looked up at him again. It was crazy, actually. In a different time and place, she would bask in the moment of Devon being completely at a loss when it came to dealing with her. Now? She wished he would smile and proposition her. It would bring a measure of normalcy back.

Syd sighed. "I have no idea. All I know—I want to get the hell out of this basement."

Devon nodded and glanced around. "Malik will attack again. And I don't think we'll be counting on Rafael's assistance this time."

# CHAPTER THIRTY-FIVE

Devon stared at Syd. She strode through the dilapidated house, hips swaying. She had the lead and was met by Minnie at the top of the ladder back to the main level. For all she had been through, her movements were incredibly graceful and fluid. Not like she had been a klutz before, but there was now poise and power behind her stride. The poise he could see; the power he could feel. Like he could sense other Guardians or creatures of Hell. She had it now, in spades.

Whatever had happened while she was unconscious, she wasn't weaker for it. Not unconscious, Devon reminded himself. She had been brain-dead. And now she wasn't. He shook his head to clear the conundrum.

Devon admired the view as she went, a brief distraction from the cataclysmic fucking failure the day had been. After all, taking stock, Devon had nearly been killed today. Would have been, if not for Jack's altruistic use of healing power. Now his brother was dead. A pit opened inside him. He'd never considered it. Jack was a constant. Jack would never die. Jack *could never* die. Devon had seen Jack sustain wounds as bad as he'd had today and heal in under twenty-four hours. Jack was never going to die.

His steps stalled in the dank house, and his head dropped onto his chest. He rubbed the bridge of his nose.

Thousands of memories of his brother warp-sped through his mind. Jack's smile, his goodness, his strength. The way the two of them had fought together—centuries of being completely in sync before the rift had torn them apart. And now there was no mending it. It was done. That was the way it ended for them.

Rage rolled through him. Devon had no idea how, but Rafael would pay for this. Well shit, Rafael would pay for this, sure, provided Syd hadn't already taken care of that problem.

His hands curled into fists, and he resumed his steps through the house.

For the hundredth time in the short span since Jack had been removed from service, Devon asked the question: how? How had his brother been so far in the abyss of despair and not come to him?

And now, well. Jack was dead, and the demon was coming for him. And he had to keep Syd safe.

There would be no more Jack-granted do-overs when it came to Malik. Devon had to figure out a way to destroy that demon, or he would be Guardian-kabobs roasting in a harsh Hell barbeque. And there would most definitely be a next time. The demon had a raging hard-on for him.

*Archon.* Whatever that meant, though it was clear Rafael knew, too. Devon clenched his fists and felt the soft puff of hot air on his legs as the dog followed closely behind him.

The house was dark now, reflecting the night outside. Byrne apparently hadn't had the upstairs wired. He reached out to touch Syd but hesitated. It galled him beyond belief to admit, but he was a bit afraid of her. For Chrissakes, she had blasted Rafael like he was a...a... God, he didn't even know. The *Archangel* Rafael, the one being on the planet for which Devon had a healthy fear.

*Something* had happened in that basement, but what?

She continued walking, and he stopped five feet behind her.

"Syd." Devon's voice held a note of indecision unfamiliar to him.

She stopped, kept her feet planted forward and twisted her torso back to him. "Yeah?"

Devon's body tingled now, and, in the same way skin-to-skin contact had done before, mere eye contact with her ignited him. Her eyes had brightened several degrees, he would swear, since she had entered that basement. Yup, it was more than poise she'd gained. Damn near felt like asking for her help with Malik. Pussy.

"It's full dark, and I can't guarantee there's nothing waiting out there for us now," Devon said. He might as well have said, 'Mommy, I'm afraid of the dark.' Real nice.

Irritated with himself, he continued, "You can't possibly be okay, and that's expected, but I need to know—really—how are you? It'll affect what we do next."

Syd stared at him with her glowing emerald eyes, her expression totally unreadable. "It wasn't Byrne and it wasn't Rafael."

He cocked his head, and his forehead creased in confusion.

Syd gestured to her head. "I let my wall down. Completely. I went...somewhere. I don't know if it was real—" Syd's voice began to break.

"Shhh." Slowly, Devon approached her and gathered her into his arms. She let him but didn't return the embrace. Her power reached to envelop him, and, damn, it felt amazing.

Syd had been spectacularly gifted from the moment they had met. She'd been muting herself and her powers to an incredible extent. Byrne had had nothing to do with it. Well, Devon noted, except in the genetics department. He averted his eyes from Syd's. She had enough problems without adding birth-mom drama to the list.

From the living area, footsteps crunched through the debris. Devon's mind went to work. Dutch and Free. Great. Fantastic.

He released Syd and made sure she was behind him.

"Rafael is gone, his lackeys should do the same," Devon called, voice filled with the menace rolling around his head. Who knew what instructions Rafael had given them?

Dutch came around the corner first, followed by Free, a gun naked in his hand. The hallway wasn't big to begin with; now with four occupants it was damn crowded.

When he met Devon's eyes, Dutch blanched and put his hands up. "Same side, Dev, 'member?"

Devon laughed. "Not even almost."

"Why're you still here, Devon? Rafael said we're done," Free spoke quietly, a hint of his French ancestry swirling in with the words.

At the mention of the Archangel, Syd shuddered behind him.

Devon's anger peaked. "The Archangel wants you to leave Syd here, unprotected, with one of Lucifer's lieutenants in pursuit." He threw up one hand. "And you're cool with it?"

Dutch rubbed his hand against the back of his head, his bomber jacket playing peek-a-boo with one of his sacred blades. "Ah, no offense, but why do you care? When have you *ever* cared?"

Devon grew still. He met Dutch's eyes, let the intensity bleed through and harden them. "I care now."

"Shit," Dutch muttered.

"You...like her," Free said, but it came out as a question.

Coming from Free, the statement sounded very much like a threat to Devon. Free had been waiting a long time to take something of value from Devon. Tit for tat.

Devon needed to change the topic of conversation, like right now. "You should know, no guarantees Rafael is still kicking it. Syd here"—Devon pointed a thumb back to her— "just blasted the asshole through a wall."

Free's face split into a snarl. "Impossible."

Devon shrugged. "If you can't feel the waves of power rolling off her, then you're as stupid as you look. Here's what you need to know, and then you leave." Devon lifted a finger. "Syd is under my protection, Rafael be damned. And"—he lifted another finger and tried to push through, but his voice broke anyway— "Jack is dead."

Dutch pushed out a breath that sounded more like a cry. "That can't—" The Guardian's shoulders slumped, like the light had left his candle. Then he looked up, hopeful. "Devon, you're fucking with us, right? There's no way he..."

Devon sliced his head to the left.

Free was silent, but the grief in his expression bled through his perpetual pissed off. He broke the silence with a curse, spun on his heel, and shouldered his way past Dutch.

Devon's whole body was tight. Seeing the reaction to Jack's loss in the other Guardians cut open his fresh wounds. He felt empty, shredded inside until all that was left was bloody, gaping gashes where his heart should be. He crushed his hands into fists, and he wanted to rage at something.

Dutch stayed a moment longer, head bent, and tears rolled down his cheek. "Jack taught me...everything. He was our center, way more than Rafael ever was. I loved him like a brother. But despite the shit between you, he *was* your brother, man, and I am so sorry." Without waiting for Devon's response, Dutch turned and walked away.

Devon took a minute to gather himself. He couldn't succumb to his grief, couldn't think about Jack a minute longer or he would be lost in a bottle of whiskey within the hour.

And so, he turned back to Syd, reminding himself she was the priority. She hadn't said a word, hadn't inched a muscle. Come to think of it, her eyes weren't really tracking, either. He needed to get her safe. Posthaste.

Minnie's gentle whine pulled his gaze downward. The dog wagged her tail. Seeing she had his attention, Minnie trotted down the hallway, presumably toward the bedroom portion of the abandoned home.

"Déjà vu." Dev looked up at Syd and gestured. "We follow."

Syd nodded weakly. Probably, with the blank look on her face, he could've asked her to start singing "99 Bottles of Beer" and she'd hum. Gently, he took her hand, unable to help the sharp intake of breath at the tremor of power that flowed between them.

He followed Minnie down to the far bedroom. Devon walked through the door with Syd trailing him. The blonde woman Devon had saved from the Packard Plant lay on the floor, unconscious. He almost couldn't believe Rafael would abandon her here. But then again, Rafael had left pretty abruptly, hadn't he?

"How'd you find her?" Syd released his hand.

"Minnie led me to her." Devon's eyebrows scrunched. "You know her?"

Syd shook her head. "No...I had a vision. Byrne experimented on her—"

Devon glanced at Minnie and the blonde woman, then back at Syd. "We need to get her help. Byrne's been keeping them alive, but I don't think she'll be doing that anymore."

Devon scanned the area for enemies and loaded the unconscious woman into his Jeep. He grabbed a spare undershirt from his duffle and put it on. Regrettably, it appeared Minnie was intent upon dusting his black interior with white dog hair. He pointed insistently toward the cargo area in the rear of the Jeep. "You get in my truck, you stay back there. And don't pretend you can't understand me."

He kept one eye on Syd, who quietly watched him. He snapped her door closed, flashed into the truck, and turned the engine over. "Do you want to talk about it?"

Syd shuddered and rolled her head around her neck. "I wasn't sure I was going to get back into my body. It was—"

Devon watched her. He didn't have to be in her head to know Syd didn't have words to describe what had happened. Another time, perhaps, when the shock had faded. He sure as hell wasn't forcing the issue.

He pulled away from the curb, navigated the street, and focused on making sure no demons were waiting. Not a single streetlight illuminated the path away from Byrne's basement.

On their way out of the neighborhood, Devon idled the truck in front of the Packard Plant. He scanned the area of the ruins that held the biohazard-marked door, but he couldn't sense the people who had been there when he was attacked by Malik. They had been moved. By Byrne, Rafael, or Malik, he didn't know. Didn't really care to speculate, either.

"There were others here. Not now," Devon glanced back to the blonde slumped in his backseat, glad he'd at least been able to save her.

He put the truck into gear. Syd guided Devon turn by turn to the nearest hospital, Ford Medical. The best course of action was to drop the woman at a hospital. She was stable now, but only because it was obvious she had been kept alive artificially, as evidenced by the multitude of needle pricks in the crook of her arm. She wouldn't stay that way without intervention.

Avoiding the cameras associated with the emergency entrance, Devon drove around the side of the hospital and found the smoking hangout of several nurses on break.

He glanced at Syd, unnaturally quiet. "I'll be right back." He opened the rear car door and gathered the blonde woman up in his arms. Feeling something in the back pocket of her dirty jeans, he set her down and withdrew a Ziplock baggie with a license and a Michigan State University student ID in it.

The picture was definitely her, cute face smiling brightly and very much alive. Twenty-four years old, blonde hair, brown eyes, not that he had seen her conscious, five-foot-nine. Katie Kall. From Minnesota. Slipping the driver's license into his back pocket, Devon picked her up and walked toward the group of nurses. Probably better if Katie from Minnesota remained anonymous for the time being.

Devon enthralled the three women in their bright-colored scrubs before they had a chance to remark on his blood-encrusted and ragged appearance. *"Take this woman and get her help. You saw her walking, saw her stumble and fall. You went to her, assessed she needed help and brought her inside. You have no other memory of how she arrived, just that she be treated immediately and with care. I was never here."*

Devon laid Katie Kall from Minnesota on the ground, and the nurses crowded around her like benevolent vultures. He walked back to the truck, opened the driver's door, and slipped inside. Devon twisted and looked at the dog. Minnie had her mouth closed, and she watched the nurses intently through the limo-black tinted windows. She wasn't happy about it, Devon could tell, but she let the nurses carry Katie into the hospital and out of sight.

Soon enough, Devon and Syd were back on the road.

Breaking what had become a bed-of-nails type of silence, Syd finally spoke, gazing out the window. "Where are we going?"

Devon glanced over at her. "Cemetery."

Syd chuckled dryly. "A little clichéd, don't you think?"

"A bit." Devon smiled back tentatively. "But we can talk freely there, and demons can't invade it while we claim it as sanctuary. Hallowed ground works as sanctuary to anyone who claims it. I'm going to park the truck at your house, and I'll flash us over to the cemetery. We can stay the night there, return to the house in the morning. There's one just a couple blocks from your house."

Syd lapsed back into silence, but out of the corner of his eye Devon saw her fingers begin to light from within. The hair on his arms rose, but he acted as if he hadn't seen it. Something told him he didn't want to draw more attention to the fact. He guessed Syd wasn't talking because she was waging an interior war with her new power.

God, he wanted inside her head. Just to see what the hell she was thinking. He honestly couldn't begin to fathom. Before whatever happened in the basement, getting her to speak her mind wasn't exactly difficult. Now...she sat next to him like a compliant little doll. It swept another fire of anger through his gut. Byrne and Rafael had created this mess, and now he was left to deal with the aftermath. With Syd despondent and possessing twitchy-weird power. Oh yeah, and one of Lucifer's lieutenants in pursuit.

He drove a few slow laps around the neighborhood, scanning for any nasties.

He wanted to know what she'd been through, but the last thing he was going to do was force her to talk. She'd had enough people forcing her to do all sorts of things lately. He let the uncomfortable silence linger until the tension in the air finally called it quits.

Happened right about the time he pulled into the circle drive of her house.

Devon turned off the truck and reached back to Minnie. "Come here, pooch. I guess you've found a new home."

Minnie wagged hard, her tail hitting her sides, and jumped up into the back seat. Devon drew a deep breath but ignored the breach of their previous cargo-area-only agreement. His right hand rested on Minnie's neck, and he held out his left hand for Syd to take.

He focused on her face, drawn but otherwise blank of emotion and clearly avoiding eye contact with him. He couldn't take it anymore. He really wasn't skilled at giving comfort, but here goes. "Syd—I'm here..."

She finally looked at him, and the emptiness nearly ripped his heart out. "For how long?" She barked out a harsh laugh. "Everyone around me seems to die. My mom, my dad...now Jack. Get out while you still can."

Devon's anger peaked again, fueling his next words. "You don't give me a whole lot of credit. I could've disappeared. Rafael declared this mission over. He gave up on you. I'm here now, with you, because I want to be. And I'm pretty fucking hard to kill."

Today notwithstanding, he added to himself.

"I saw you, Devon. I saw what Malik did to you. Not to mention all the blood." Syd gestured to his torso.

Well, shit. Point for her.

Syd's blank-slate face filled with emotion, drawing a picture of gratitude scarred with pain. She leaned toward him, and he was pretty sure she didn't even realize it. Her lips were so close to his now, looking perfect for the taking. Except...when she got straight in the head, she was going to regret the shit out of coming to him.

Couldn't let it happen. Not like he didn't want to, but he never wanted to take advantage of Syd, of the situation. If she came to his bed—ever—it wasn't going to be because she owed him anything. His pride, and something else he hesitated to name, wouldn't allow it.

She leaned in closer, eyes heavy-lidded.

Not believing his own actions, Devon put his hand out and caught her collar bone. "You don't want to do this. Jack may have been wound tight, but he was right about this. I'm no good for you."

# CHAPTER THIRTY-SIX

Syd drew a deep breath and twisted in her seat. What was she thinking? Trying to kiss Devon? Jack's words rolled through her mind. *You're better than that.*

Had she forgotten? Or had the past two days changed the way she looked at everything...at him? She clamped down hard on the emotions riding her rodeo-style. She'd be lucky to last eight seconds.

*Foolish love brings sorrow.* Or so her dad might've quoted an Aesop moral. Worse, maybe Devon had no interest to begin with. And why would he? She was ten times freakier than she had been hours ago.

She faced forward, so she could see the wrought iron gate of her home, thick chain wrapped tight because she had had no cash to fix the electronics.

Nearly all the nighttime hours had gone by. And sleeping in a cemetery? She stole a furtive glance at Devon. He stared out the windshield, straight-up avoiding her now.

She closed her eyes, not wanting to see anything at all.

"Are you ready?" He quieted his voice, that beautiful voice.

She could only nod in response. His hand, so warm, grasped

hers and gripped tight. The earth shifted, and she had the disorienting feeling she was back on Ashira's hillside. In panic, her eyes snapped open.

The cemetery was black, crowded with light gray tombstones providing reprieve from the dark. Evergreens made up the border in the distance. Devon landed them square in the middle of the cemetery, close to one of the roads which allowed hearses access to the perimeter.

Somehow, she crashed in a heap on the damp ground, while Devon stood tall a few steps away, searching the night sky. Minnie's tail wagged at her, her eyes concerned.

"We're safe, now, right?" Syd stood, brushing bits of earth and pine from her jeans.

Devon nodded, but continued to gaze out in the distance.

"How does this sanctuary thing work, anyway?"

Devon met her gaze then, gave a wry smile with an elegant lift of shoulders. "Damned if I know. I'm not usually the one running."

Syd walked two steps, leaned on the nearest tombstone.

Devon rubbed his hand over his face. He dropped his hand and seemed to consider further disclosure. "Syd—I—"

There was a moment of silence between them. The crisp night air smelled of burning wood nearby. Minnie's quiet whine drew her attention down, and Syd knelt, her hand resting on the dog's neck.

As if dawn had come in the work of a moment instead of hours, the sky brightened to the degree of noon. If noon were shaped like a man.

Rafael stood before Sydney. She was tired, drained of energy. And now scared, too. She wondered how pissed off Archangels could get about being blasted with their own energy. She supposed she was about to find out. Her body stiffened, and she looked back to Devon. He stepped to her side, using his arm as a shield in front of her.

"We claim this place as sanctuary." Devon stepped in front of her.

Disinterested, Rafael glanced at Devon, but settled his gaze on her. "Wise."

The Archangel looked like Syd imagined a Fortune five hundred exec would look, if they glowed from within. He no longer wore the disguise of humanity, and the effect was devastating. Rafael's straight, raven-black hair reached mid-back. The cut of his suit screamed upper crust, and the manner with which he held himself exuded commanding confidence. His hands rested in the pockets of his suit pants, and a small amused smile lit his expression. Relaxed, he seemed perfectly in control of his corner of the world. He stopped one grave away from her and Devon.

"I almost can't believe it," Rafael finally said.

Cautiously, Syd stood, very aware of Devon at her side. Minnie looked pensive at her other side, not panting or wagging. Waiting.

"What do you want?" Syd asked, unable to dull the hard edge of fear in her voice.

Rafael pointed a finger at Devon. "You need to leave."

Devon laughed harshly. "So we can be a target for you? Fat fucking chance."

Rafael swiveled his charcoal gaze to Syd. "I will grant him temporary immunity from harm by me. If he leaves now."

"Why do you need him to leave?" Syd looked back and forth between the men. Latent power surged through the air.

"To talk. Privately."

"To talk," Devon repeated, an eyebrow cocked.

Ignoring Devon, Rafael said in a placating tone, "You seem concerned for him, and this is the best offer you'll get. I won't release him or harm him, if he leaves now."

Rafael was giving her an opportunity to give Devon a get-out-of-jail-free card. She glanced at him. "For how long?"

"Jesus, I can handle him. Been doing it for centuries now," Devon said, irritation sharpening his tone.

Rafael shrugged, all his angelic power focused solely on her. It pulsed against her. "At this point, it doesn't really matter. But for the purpose of our negotiation, I agree not to bring him harm for one week."

"I was thinking, like, years." Syd crossed her arms.

Next to her, Devon's fists clenched, opened, clenched again. This conversation pushed him into third-wheel territory and had to be ticking him off royally, but she didn't care. No way she'd let him be a victim of their acquaintance. Jack had already been removed from service, and she couldn't help but feel it was her fault. Leave it to her to end the life of someone immortal.

"A year, then." Rafael smiled like he hadn't conceded anything of value.

Syd thought back to her words, wondered if there was some angelic loophole she wasn't processing. Finding nothing, she nodded.

Rafael inclined his head. "I so swear under threat of my own peril, for three hundred and sixty-five suns, Devon shall come to no harm by my hand. If he leaves now, I'll bind that promise to you."

Was that the angelic version of a pinkie swear? A bind? She hoped.

She turned to Devon. "He can't hurt me here, you said it yourself. For whatever reason, he wants to talk alone. Let me do this. I'll meet you back at the house."

Devon turned his head away, pushed out an angry breath, and disappeared.

"He left. Now...bind the promise. Whatever that means."

Rafael approached, and Syd backed up. It was instinctive.

"I can't bind the promise if I can't touch you."

Syd shivered. The mere thought of Rafael that close brought back all kinds of bad mojo memories. The pain. Her spirit being ripped from her body.

Rafael said softly, "I thought I'd killed you. I'm glad I didn't."

Ditto on that, dickhead, Syd muttered in her thoughts.

"I can feel something different in you now. Power. Did you let your wall down, Sydney?" Rafael stood where he was, body exuding light and latent power.

"Let's get this bind done. Then we talk."

Rafael nodded. He extended his arm, unbuttoned his cuff and rolled up his sleeve. Script tattooed his forearm, crossing with scarring. He was heavily muscled under the businessman wardrobe. He opened his palm. "Lay your palm across mine. Then we shift our forearms to meet. It locks the bind."

He took a step forward.

She took a step back. The pain of his touch was too close to the surface, scratching like rats at her skin.

"Don't hurt me."

"I've never wanted to hurt you."

"I'm calling bullshit. You nearly destroyed me. A few hours ago."

Rafael shook his head. "I asked you to let down the wall. Remember that, Sydney, I asked first."

Syd huffed out a dry laugh. "We're going to have to agree to disagree."

Rafael's shrug was unconcerned. He extended his palm forward. "The bind won't hurt. You may even...enjoy the sensation."

Syd swallowed. She wanted pleasure from him even less than she wanted pain. "And you won't hurt Devon for a year?"

Rafael studied her, his gray eyes fathomless. "Why do you care for him?"

Her power barely leashed behind her wall, Syd shifted in her boots. "Does it matter?"

Rafael lifted an eyebrow, his palm still extended to her. "To me? Not at all. But the universe has a curious way of getting what she wants. You may be more the answer to my problems than I first anticipated."

Gathering her courage, Syd stalked forward and laid her palm on the angel's. Heat and energy penetrated her immediately. She drew in a sharp breath. Rafael twisted around to make their forearms meet. The intensity increased tenfold. She was cocooned in heat. She moved her body closer to his without thought.

"I am bound to the promise."

The heat and energy flowed inside her skull. Dizziness made her sway, but on its heels was a soothing, deep internal heat. Everything in her relaxed. She sighed.

And then Rafael released her.

Rafael rolled his sleeve down, shook out the wrinkles. "I hope you see that as the olive branch it is."

Olive branch? He couldn't be serious.

"You killed Jack."

The angel let out a *hmmpf*. "If you had the means to reunite with ones you loved, despite the barrier of realms, to what lengths would you go?"

Syd stared. To reunite with her parents? She shuddered. To talk shop with her dad, spend a perfect afternoon in the garage. To feel that safe. She would move mountains.

Syd shook her head and stared at the grass as she spoke to the angel. "What do you want from me?"

Rafael smiled fully and spread his hands wide. "I now have everything I want. A successor to lead my army, an end to this cursed banishment. In short, I have you."

Syd cleared her throat. "You don't *have* me."

Rafael's smile turned to a sneer. "My brothers thought themselves so clever, taunting me with the possibility of escape. Shortsighted and arrogant as usual."

Without preamble, Syd let her thoughts fly like well-aimed daggers from her mouth. "You can't possibly believe I can fight Malik, or anything else for that matter, and live. You are here to protect me, right?"

Rafael held up one finger. "*Was* protecting you." Rafael's smile returned. "You can do this, Sydney. You can take my place and release me, end my banishment. I must find my Lost Ones."

"Lost Ones?"

Rafael narrowed his eyes. "Do you think humans are the only

ones who suffer loss, who ache for their kin? This assignment" — he gestured to her and then swept his hand around the cemetery— "was a punishment for me. My brothers called it treason, I called it the natural order. They devised the most perfect punishment, surely to drive me mad. Me. A warrior held in Heaven's highest regard, told not to fight and, to add to the insult, babysit humans. My brothers thought to deter me."

He laughed, the sound sharp against the night. "They detained me. They have not deterred me."

"Deterred you from what?" Syd shifted, the dampness of the cemetery working through her jeans.

Rafael traced the gravestone nearest to him with the tips of his fingers. His movements were unhurried and curiously self-absorbed. Syd watched him, and it made her twitchy.

He didn't answer the question.

"At first, it seemed an impossibility for a human to take the place of an angel, as equals." Rafael raised his proud face, which caught the moonlight just right, made his skin glow with ethereal light. "Eight-hundred years ago, I would've thought the idea anathema. Now, I never wished for anything more." He stared at her. "You are extraordinary."

Syd paced again, her agitation no longer content to stay internal.

Everyone in her life knew about her abilities, whispered about the fact she was different. The invisible barrier had always divided her from the life she wanted was labeled in big block letters 'Psychic Abilities.' It went without saying her abilities weren't a *good* thing. It flew in the face of her mother's staunch religion, made un-doctored conversation nearly impossible with regular people. And now she had an Archangel telling her what made her different wasn't something that made her less...but made her greater. Beyond ordinary, as she had so badly wanted, and into extraordinary.

Not less. More.

Rafael smiled, slowly exposing each of his white teeth, all

gleaming in the moonlight. "I have been the only one to lead the Guardian army since its inception eight-hundred years ago. The Crusades posed as a cover for the last of the angelic scrimmages on earth. The Pledge marked the end of the Crusades and the end of our war here."

Rafael looked caught up in a distant memory. He blinked, and then focused again on Syd.

"Your job is simple. As Captain of the army, you recruit soldiers as you see fit. You gift them powers as you see fit. You have control over their very existence. You have them kill any of Hell's legion that dares set foot on this plane."

"No way." Syd recoiled. "I can't do that. I don't want that kind of responsibility. I don't even have a pet." Syd glanced down at Minnie, who leaned against her and stared up solemnly. *I don't think I have a pet, anyway.*

Rafael continued as if she had not spoken. "Under no circumstances can you draw first blood."

"What if I'm attacked?" Syd shivered. "What about, I don't know, second blood?"

Rafael raised an eyebrow. "If anyone has the gall to attack the Guardian of the Pledge and first blood is drawn, then you may defend yourself. It would be your choice to declare the Pledge broken or no. But likely, at that point, it won't matter." Rafael grinned. "First blood could well be a decapitation, after all."

Syd had the urge to draw blood, here and now, and her body began to hum in response.

"Lucifer won't take this development kindly, as he most of all sought for my banishment. He'll most likely test the validity of the Pledge once he learns of the succession. Him, or Sammael, but it's nearly a sure thing. You should prepare yourself as best you can." Rafael glanced up, in thought.

"I won't announce my stepping down, to give you as much time as possible." He paused. "I'm not a monster, Sydney. Just driven."

Syd thought of Jack, and her lip curled. "I haven't agreed to anything. You're acting like it's a done deal."

"Accept the role, and I'll grant you a favor, to be fulfilled at your discretion." He smiled, a vicious twist of his full lips. "If I were you, I'd wait to use it until I'm free to fight."

Syd reeled. Too much input. A favor. Lucifer. Lost Ones.

"You're saying I'm supposed to fight the Devil."

"I have no idea what Lucifer is planning these days. I've not spoken to my brothers since my banishment." Rafael spoke with a nonchalance Syd found in no way reassuring. "The reason the Pledge exists at all is because the casualties of our last wars were so high, each side needed a reprieve to avoid extinction. Reproduction for angels is—not easy."

She could only nod blankly. Leaning back against a tombstone, Syd glanced down. James Whitacre, deceased at age forty-three. She'd probably be in the same place as poor Jim soon enough. There was really only one person standing between her and sure death, and it wasn't the angel standing before her.

"Why did you want Devon to leave?"

"You need to know." Rafael looked away, and his face tightened, like he was fighting an internal battle. "Devon is unique, an anomaly, as was Jack. Each in their own way."

The Archangel started to glide around the tombstones. "Through the Prophecy they filled, Devon and Jack were supposed to be the first soldiers of the Guardian Army. No one was more surprised than I when their powers began to manifest."

Supposed to be? Devon had told her they *were* the first. Syd's forehead creased in confusion.

Rafael stopped, and his internal light dimmed. "They matured and grew stronger, and I realized the truth."

Rafael stopped again, and Syd had to bring a hand to her mouth to keep from yelling at him to continue. The Archangel glanced about and reached into his suit pocket, bringing his right hand out. His fist clutched tightly around something.

In a rush, Rafael pushed out the words. "Devon and Jack were born to a human mother, but their sire was most definitely not human."

She couldn't stay silent any longer. "If not human, then what?"

Rafael met her eyes, lips pulled tight. "An angel."

Syd's mind tried to wrap her head around it. Devon...an angel? Jack, she had no problem imagining in the role. But Jack's dead, she reminded herself, and her heart ached.

*Your pretty little hybrid.* Ashira had said it, and now it made sense. She'd been talking about Devon.

"Human-angel hybrid?" Syd asked, petting Minnie, trying to ground herself.

Rafael nodded and scanned the cemetery. "All power they possess comes not from me, but of their own lineage," Rafael said, his voice hushed. "Which is why my Guardian Army has been so effective over the centuries. We have had an immensely unfair advantage in the fight. The only reason we've not been found out is because only an Archangel would question it, and they are forbidden from this plane. Jack and Devon should not exist."

Syd paused her petting of the dog. "What do you mean?"

"All hybrids—Nephilim—were destroyed as abominations long ago. It is a piece of the First Race's history that, were it possible, my brothers would bury."

"Then how do they exist?" Syd asked. "Who's their angel daddy?"

Rafael shrugged. "I have my ideas. But I could not ask, I wouldn't risk piquing curiosity. But, how is it you humans say, don't look a gift horse in the mouth? Jack and Devon are incredible weapons, under the perfect cover of the Guardian Army."

Syd recoiled. "They're people, not weapons."

"If you learn to wield them properly, Sydney, they *are* weapons. Of the most dangerous kind. Devon especially." Rafael shook his head, and his face contorted to an emotion which looked entirely foreign on the Archangel's face.

Rapt, Syd let a small smile through. "Devon frightens you. Why?"

Rafael averted his gaze.

"Is it his mind control?" Syd asked. "Can he compel you?"

Rafael made a low sound in his throat. "Let's hope we never find out. He is an Archon, a being outlawed, even more hated than Nephilim. A being who could will compliance of anyone and subvert Free Will. It is heresy."

Devon...abomination and heretic. No wonder Rafael hated and feared him so much. But not enough to destroy him. Just enough to use him for his own purposes.

Syd processed all the information and shook her head. "That's why you forbid him to be in your presence. He got stronger and you were afraid he'd try to compel you. You don't know if he could."

Politician-style, Rafael neither confirmed nor denied her statement. He deflected. "All Archons were exterminated millennia ago, long before even Nephilim. I have no idea how he exists."

Syd massaged the tight muscle in her neck. What did that mean for her?

"Do you care for him?" Rafael asked, completely swerving the conversation in the direction of oncoming traffic.

Syd started to say something. Stopped. Stuttered. "I— He's protected me when others haven't." She stared pointedly at the Archangel and opened her mouth to send an insult.

Rafael held up a hand, silencing her. "Devon is the way he is..."

Rafael cocked his head and played with the unseen object in his fist. "Devon is the way I made him. I encouraged Devon's ruthlessness at every turn. I beat any hint of clemency from him centuries ago. He and his twin were barely more than children when their family delivered them into my service. Devon has never known any other life. Mercy and compassion do not exist in his soul. By extension, I venture that neither can love exist in such a man. Be wary, Sydney."

Like a projector wheel of home movies, Syd replayed every interaction she'd had with Devon. He'd helped her multiple times. Kept his promises, though small. He had spared Bryce's life at her request. He'd been a gentleman while they slept, had not attempted to compel her when she let him into her head. At

Malik's hands, he'd nearly died for her. Twice. Hell, he'd defied Rafael when it nearly assured his death, just to protect her. Devon had compassion, some degree of humanity—was that even the right word?—to protect her, to stay with her past what duty demanded. Didn't he?

Then her mind fast-rewound to his admission of compelling so many people to kill each other. And the 'all in a day's work' reaction it had evoked from Devon.

"Why would you do that to him?" Syd whispered.

Rafael gripped the object in his hand tighter.

"To ensure his survival. If any creature had returned to Hell with stories of Devon's Archonic abilities, it would not only start a war, Pledge or no, but he would most surely die soon thereafter, as well as untold innocents. Would that outcome be preferable?"

Rafael raised his eyebrow at her and shoved his hand back into his pocket.

"Instead, I insisted he kill every enemy he had contact with, and he complied. Soon enough it was with relish. His soul or his life?" Rafael's face cut a hard edge in the scant moonlight.

Syd's mouth pulled tight. "You only did it because you recognized what assets he and Jack were to your own goals. That's pretty clear."

Rafael's demeanor shifted, and his voice radiated a subtle respect. "He *is* incredible, there is no denying. But his anonymity is destroyed now. Devon fought Malik, and Malik lives. The demon has discovered what Devon is."

Syd waited, as it was apparent the Archangel was considering further disclosure. When it came, it was a mere whisper. "And Devon has no idea."

"You never told him." Syd's eyebrows rose skyward. "You never told him who he is?"

The angel shook his head, braced his left hand on a tombstone, clutching it hard. A fine mist of stone flew forth from his fingers. "Devon and Jack both believe themselves to be Guardian soldiers, humans converted to my service, and under my control. It was safer for everyone if only I knew the secret."

Syd's stomach roiled, and she put her hand on her abdomen. "Bullshit. You used them."

Eight centuries spent under the threat of a lie. And Jack had died believing it.

Rafael released his headstone hostage and walked closer until his polished wingtip shoes were only inches from Syd's own boots. "There is a much larger game here, Sydney."

"Their lives are not a game!" Syd exclaimed, hands on her hips.

Rafael clutched his right hand tightly, raised it to his lips. "Cut your ties with Devon, effective as he is. His secret is destroyed, and Hell's legion will gather to kill him soon, if they haven't already—"

Syd expelled a breath. Her voice rose to shouting volume. "That's why you promised him no harm. You think he'll be dead soon, anyway."

Rafael inclined his head, not denying it. "As soon as you assume my position, they cannot harm you without breaching the Pledge. If you separate yourself from him, you, at least, will be safe. And you will spare the Pledge."

*But Devon will die.*

The measure of Syd's breath increased. Her mind played connect-the-dots, and the image it revealed was gruesome. *If he hadn't protected me, Malik would never know what he is. It will be my fault if Devon dies.* Her mind couldn't conjure a juicy enough curse. Her abilities were throwing another person she cared for right in front of the goddamn bus.

Syd swallowed and cut off her thoughts. "Accepting this position, Captain of the Guardians, will help me defeat Malik?"

"You will have considerably more resources at your behest." Rafael's eyes narrowed. "But Malik is a considerable foe, and you are untested in battle. Not only that, but if you fight him, you will be in breach of the Pledge. It would not be wise to seek him out. You saw how easily he destroyed Devon."

"Devon is not destroyed," Syd corrected quickly.

The Archangel shrugged as if the distinction was inconsequential. "He is as good as dead."

She craned her neck up and finally met the Archangel's gaze.

"Let's see what you're hiding in your hand, angel."

# CHAPTER THIRTY-SEVEN

B ack-dropped by night-darkened tombstones, Rafael stood, his fist closed reverently. He walked toward Syd and opened his hand.

In the Archangel's palm, he held a coin. A jagged metal disk scarred with runes. Syd's intuition came to life, a shouting din inside her head. Too bad the messages were conflicting. She wanted to go closer, claim it. And she wanted to run for her life.

*Mine. This belongs to me.* She stumbled backward.

Syd stared at the disk held in the Archangel's palm, and it began to glow bright green. With no conscious thought driving her forward, Syd understood the nature of her aversion. The disk represented a change in her life so dramatic and course-altering as to be irrefutable and permanent.

This was the moment. *Her* moment of choice. No one had seemed particularly interested in what *she* wanted. But now...yes, now she would choose.

If she took the coin into her hand, she would be altering the fabric of her life, designing an entirely new pattern. A pattern as yet undetermined except to be incredibly dangerous. She'd always held hope for the white-picket deal, if only she could control her abilities enough. She'd be giving that up for certain, if she took the coin.

Syd closed her eyes, drew in a deep breath. Once again, she observed the distinction between her body and *her*. Her body was a stew of unpleasant. Cold, damp toes inside her brown leather boots with silver buckles. Calf muscles tight with the exertion of pacing, her back aching with the need to sit down, to finally rest. Shoulders constricted with tension, and her head dizzy with new, life-altering knowledge. Now she was about to add another burden.

But what *she* was—this power—pulsed steadily, locked away and strong inside her. Ready. She reached out with her mind, her new-found power stirring at the call to use. The power surged around her, wrapped her in a cocoon of warmth. She let her wall down.

Syd's eyes snapped open. The Archangel stood in front of her, arm outstretched, disk in his palm. "What happens if I touch it?"

Rafael glanced at the rune in his palm, a reverent expression. "Inside this disk, millennia of knowledge are contained. If you take it unto your own hand, it becomes yours if you are strong enough to contain it. If not, well—"

Syd picked up the subtext. This wasn't a done deal. There was still a chance the power would consume her, and she would be no more. Ashira's hillside flashed in front of her eyes.

Been there once before. Got the t-shirt. 'I Survived the Inbetween.'

Rafael continued, "You will feel the soldiers at your disposal. Their weakness and strength, their pain. But you will feel also the Pledge, you will sense if any of the great archangels are upon Earth. The coin was fashioned of the blood of my brothers, Gabriel, Lucifer, and Sammael. When I seek to, I feel their presences when I hold it."

Syd shook her head slowly. "All that knowledge and all those people in my head?"

Rafael met her eyes then. "I cannot say, not for certain. We are different, you and I."

Panic ran through her body. Could she do this? The blood-soaked cot ran through her head, and she thought of the terrible injury Devon had suffered keeping her safe. She thought of Brie and what could've happened if the demon had shown up when Brie had been at the house.

More, if what Rafael said was true, once Devon's secret was revealed, it would be all-out war on Earth until he was destroyed. The residual damage to humanity would be unacceptable.

Syd reached out with her left hand, alight as if a flashlight had been held to her skin. She gripped the disk and enclosed it in her own palm. Whether the warmth transferred from Rafael or from the coin itself, she was unsure. She could only stare at it, now lighting her hand with spring-green light, shooting sparks of electric-blue and lilac.

A stinging sensation began at her left shoulder blade. She cried out, seeking help from her Archangel predecessor.

Rapt, Rafael stared at her. His smile was fierce.

The pain shifted from sting to searing burn. She dropped to her knees, head bowing back. Excruciating light erupted from every cell of her body.

She screamed. "Rafael!"

This wasn't going to work; she was consumed. Power tried to push at her skin, force it past the boundaries of what flesh should be able to do. It was ripping her apart. If she was still screaming, she couldn't hear it past the din of power.

For the second time in her life, she let the wall come crashing down.

The power absorbed, burned, soaked into her soul. It was done in moments.

She crumbled to the ground. "Rafael..." Her voice was weak, and her eyes were barely open. Her shoulder continued to sting, but the light faded from her body.

The Archangel was nowhere to be seen.

Another moment and she pushed herself back to a seat, leaning heavily against the concrete reminder of James Whitacre. She tried in vain to grip her left shoulder with her right hand. No matter, another moment and the burning sensation stopped entirely. She huffed out a few more breaths. Her vision snapped back into reality, and she scanned the cemetery, feeling highly exposed in the night sky.

The weirdness was over. She'd made it. Right? Yeah. Or maybe—

Her eyes went sightless, though they remained open. Her hands fumbled on the grass, seeking purchase, something to ground her.

As if she were staring through the windshield of a spacecraft at warp speed, her mind sprinted the distance. First, showing her two men she'd never met, both heavily armed in a mid-market hotel.

A woman of Russian descent playing the piano.

A man in a business suit sitting in front of a computer. Cunning eyes glanced up, as if sensing her.

A lean man sprawled out in bed, body covered in small cuts.

A man covered in intricate tattoos with long blond hair reading from a Bible.

A large man, slumped on a bathroom floor, stitching his arm closed.

A man in a suit, with a strawberry-blond goatee and a crooked nose, sipping espresso.

A dark-skinned man riding a horse at a gallop.

*Flash. Flash. Flash.*

And on and on it went. Her mind touching each one briefly until the features blurred and blended into a Picasso of melded faces and skin tones. Then the warp drive image slid past, and she was, once again, ass-down on the wet cemetery grass.

Her army.

All those people, the majority testosterone-fueled, a few women interspersed. All depending on her. A connection pulled from her to each of them, some by a mere thread, others by yarn, others by steel cable. She guessed these were the powers Rafael had granted. She could feel them tugging gently at her. Softly, she massaged the metaphysical connection, felt it pull taut in response. She looked down into her hand, which had held the coin. She stared, flipped her hand over, searched the grass at her feet. The coin was gone. Her shoulder pulsed where it had burned.

A soft whine came from her right, and Minnie shivered uncontrollably behind a nearby headstone.

Syd reached out. "It's all right, girl. I think...it's all right."

# CHAPTER THIRTY-EIGHT

Devon stepped out of the shower in Syd's house and glanced around. Paranoid much? True the demon was gone for the night, but there were lesser evils out there. He'd needed all the dried blood off his skin in a bad way. *My blood*, he reminded himself.

He could admit in the privacy of his own thoughts he was not relishing the idea of another Malik face-off. Quite possibly because he might be minus his own face at the conclusion. Stopping to do a little soaping action wasn't the safest thing he'd ever done, but he'd needed it. Needed to wipe away the remnants of his last nearly life-ending encounter. Needed the slate wiped clean. Needed to forget Syd's dismissal.

So, when Devon heard a rumbling sound coming from downstairs, his lips immediately pulled back into a snarl. He grabbed his handgun, resting on the toilet next to the shower. Granted, it hadn't been too effective on Malik before, but it had to be better than nothing. He really needed to get a blade. A big, fucking blade.

Hair in his face and dripping, only wearing his jeans, he moved himself through space and down to the doorway of the kitchen. The sound grew louder, and belatedly Devon recognized it. The mechanical whir of the garage door opening, now closing. A second more, and the interior door opened from the garage.

He stood, a sliver of his body visible from the entrance to the great room. The gun was tucked close to his collarbone, ready in case the demon was trying to pull a fast one. A mind scan gave him...Minnie. Minnie and a very powerful presence, but he couldn't sense Syd. Fuck, if it was Rafael—

He stole a quick glance out the window. Only another hour, two max, until dawn.

"Hey."

It was her. But it wasn't.

Devon puffed out a sigh and pivoted around the corner, coming into the kitchen. Slicking his wet hair back out of his face, he lowered the gun and rested it on the black granite island.

Syd's green eyes damn near glowed, her skin looked velvet soft, and the curving lines of her body were all grace. There was an understated strength in her movements. If she was tired, it didn't seem to be a thing of her body. There was something else, too, but he struggled to put his finger on it.

Minnie, however, appeared exhausted. The dog drooped at Syd's side. Another second, and the dog lay down where she stood.

The unnatural silence stretched on. Shifting from foot to foot, Syd clasped her hands behind her back, and averted her eyes. Her momentum stalled out past the threshold.

He was fairly certain he didn't want to hear the answer, but... "What did Rafael say?"

Syd met his gaze, and the amazing green color worked its way to the core of his being, his chest constricting.

"I think...I'm your new boss." Syd rose to lean on the counter, shoulders hunched up.

Immediately, all his muscles went into lockdown mode. He couldn't believe the Archangel would do this, that he would leave *Syd* in charge of an angelic army. Rafael wouldn't place a burden on her Atlas would shudder to hold.

This had to be a misunderstanding. All that talk of honor, doing what was right.

One way to find out for sure.

Devon walked up to her, inches from pressing the length of his body to hers. The force between them demanded attachment, like trying to hold two magnets within kissing distance and not allowing them to touch. His gaze tore along her body, looking for skin. Alas, for an entirely asexual purpose.

"You're gonna have to trust me for a moment."

He gripped her around the waist, almost groaned at the contact with her, and lifted her sweater at the same time he twisted her, baring the black bra strap and her left shoulder. She didn't fight him. No. She was languid in his arms.

He sucked in a breath at the sight of the tattoo, familiar and yet very different from Rafael's. A rune, tattooed on her back, the edges raised more like a scar, about the size of his palm, script running around the perimeter. He pressed his fingers into the writing, some language he didn't speak. The words whipped into a tornado in his head.

*Guardian of the Pledge,* a foreign voice whispered over and over. A warning.

Like she burned, he pushed away, stumbled back behind the island countertop. Placing his palms wide and flat, he dropped his head. Certainly explained the feeling he couldn't exactly place. Syd now felt in his mind like an Archangel, or a higher order demon. Power. He had sensed her power.

"Sonofabitch..." He was mumbling, but his higher reasoning skills had deserted him.

It was true.

Rafael had passed his authority over the Guardian army to Syd.

So, *this* was what an out-of-body experience felt like. Huh. He had always imagined it would be vastly more pleasant than your world being tipped and tossed like some asshole kid shaking a snow globe.

Snarling, Devon whipped his head up and pointed a finger. "Where is Rafael now?"

"He's gone, Dev. He just...left. I—"

Devon pulled himself together and cut off her next sentence. "We'll use the whole army. We'll fix this, we'll run, we'll—"

"You need to leave," she interjected calmly.

He rocked back on his heels. "Syd, you don't understand what you're doing, I'm your best shot at Malik."

She looked away then, as if gathering her resolve. "He'll kill you. He already did once. And Jack's not here to heal you again."

Fuck, that stung. For a multitude of reasons.

"I can take care of myself. I can help you," he said vehemently.

Syd walked over to the island and leaned a hip, her movements finally betraying her weariness. "I can't, Devon," she whispered. "I can't let you die. I owe you that, at least. You have to go."

Jesus, this was gonna be it. No way his pride could take any more of this shit.

"There's something you need to know. About yourself, Rafael told me—" Syd said, the words laced only loosely with control. Wouldn't take much to break it.

*Oh man, here it comes.* He held up a hand, unable to keep his body still. "No thanks, I can fill in the blanks. Believe me. I've heard it all before."

*Unworthy, murderous bastard, sociopath.* Inside Devon's mind, the words were spoken in Rafael's, Jack's, and a host of other voices he had injured throughout his long life.

No way Syd could come up with anything he hadn't heard about a million times before.

"I kill for the good guys, but I'm not *good*." Devon's voice was ice. "Consider the message delivered."

Doing the right thing—what a crock of shit.

Before Syd could utter another word, he moved himself through the ten feet of space that separated them. Appeared right in front of her. And kissed her like his life depended upon it.

She didn't fight it. Not even almost. Her hands came up to

draw him closer, and her mouth pushed out the one word he needed. "*Yes*."

He crushed his lips to hers, captured the back of her neck with his right hand. His fingers gripped her hair, hard, but he couldn't help it. She awakened instincts he didn't know he possessed. Urges that made him actually *want* to go all Jack-style White Knight on her. Protect her, claim her as his. Maybe give someone an opportunity to claim him in return.

This was about as close as he would ever get to expressing it to her.

This was the only chance she was going to give him, and he was going to take advantage of it.

# CHAPTER THIRTY-NINE

Devon had affected her before—little touches, light contact sending her body into a tailspin. Maybe. But now, with his lips devouring everything Syd had to offer, *affect* wasn't the same language they were speaking. Nope. This was body language at its purest. Raw and unrefined. His touch spoke to the power inside her in a language designed only for the two of them.

She tried to remember why she shouldn't. Her hands rose up, and she was unsure in that moment if she would push him away or pull him closer. She reached to trace the strong jawline, grip his wet hair, as he was doing to her. A violent dance, it felt perfect. She gripped him tighter, suddenly afraid this was going to be a one-time event. That her common sense would come back online.

He groaned in response, and his other arm slid around her waist and pulled her flush to his bare chest, so hard.

She had told him to leave. But she didn't want him to leave—he *needed* to leave before Malik killed him.

But before he left, she had to tell him what Rafael said. Devon had protected her from Rafael, from Malik...when his own life was forfeit. He'd more than earned the right to know what he was.

An angel, she marveled. *I'm kissing an angel.*

With more resolve than she had ever gathered before, she released his hair, traced his jaw, rubbed his rough stubble, and when her hands got to his broad shoulders she pushed herself back. She came up from the kiss gasping and completely unbalanced, but knowing what she needed to do. Her lips were wet, bruised. When air hit them, they chilled with the absence of him.

If Malik lived, Hell would rise to kill Devon, the Pledge would be broken, and Malik would be the least of her problems.

Her eyes reopened reluctantly, like waking from the perfect dream. The only thing she could process was those incredible eyes. The heat in them was profound, an enveloping blanket of southern humidity after enduring a northern winter. She halted and found her body moving back in, needing to feel his body again.

"Lioness." He traced the tips of his fingers down her cheek, his voice full of resolve. "You played the boss trump card, believing you're keeping me safe."

She interjected. "Dev, you need to know—"

Shaking his head, he pressed a finger to her lips, silencing her. "You don't want me at your side, you've made that clear. But you can't keep me away."

She turned her head, moving his gentle fingers from her lips. Panic rose inside her. She could send him away from her, but she couldn't make him *do* anything. Damn it, she had to try. "Devon, he'll kill you. Please. You don't understand. I can't—"

"Do what you have to do. I'll do the same," Devon said. Then he was gone.

Tears sprang forth and she brought a shaking hand up to touch her lips. Finally, she whispered exactly what she needed him to know. "You're an angel."

---

AT FIRST, she thought, maybe. Maybe he'd come back. But minutes turned to hours.

Syd's exhaustion was a palpable thing. It pushed down her

eyelids, made all her limbs so heavy. She plodded zombie-like to the family room and anxiously glanced to the windows, all baring her to the night's eye.

*He wasn't coming back.*

That's what she had wanted, right? God, she'd been so drawn to him from the beginning and yet so terrified of him, of what he was capable. He'd used that incredible fierceness to safeguard her life over and over. He still scared her, but now for different reasons. Could the secret of his lineage and abilities bring about an angelic civil war?

Malik had to die. Devon's secret needed to be kept to avoid a celestial war on Earth. If Malik got hold of Devon, Hell would know, *Lucifer* would know what Devon was.

It would make Devon number one on Heaven and Hell's most wanted.

It would make the Pledge meaningless. It would mean war.

She couldn't start a demonic war; she couldn't break the Pledge. So, Devon needed to be as far away from the demon as possible. The safest thing for Earth and humanity was him away from Malik. If she had to confront the demon on her own, so be it.

*You cannot draw first blood.*

She needed the demon to draw blood—not kill or incapacitate her—and then she had to kill him. Assuming he hadn't already told all his demon buddies. Simple.

She swallowed.

Syd didn't have the energy to drag herself up to bed. The first inklings of dawn brightened the bay window, made her feel a tad safer. Tentatively, she let down her wall. She sent a brush of power through the house. It felt natural, like an extension of the abilities she'd had all her life. She could always touch a person and feel their mind; now she could project the sense outward. She sensed no demons. She sensed no one.

Was it safe to stay in her house? She had no idea. Dawn was humming in the distance, nearly arrived. The last time she'd been in this position, she'd had Jack and Devon standing between her and the evil that came.

Their names brought an instant pang of grief. She had gained and lost them both in the space of less than forty-eight hours. How the hell was that possible? Jack was gone; the thought seemed foreign, like it couldn't possibly be true.

And Devon...that kiss. Sweet Jesus.

She steeled her resolve. She should be grateful he left without a fight. Who the hell was she kidding? Devon would try to take on Malik again, and she was helpless to stop him. Unlike Rafael, she wouldn't demand his obedience. She couldn't even if she wanted to. Devon was a force of nature. A stubborn, arrogant, gorgeous force. And Malik would destroy him and ravage humanity along with him.

She had to take the fight to Malik. Before Devon did. And she had to win. Somehow.

She had to defeat Malik. Before he cut Devon's life short. Before the Pledge broke and Hell came knocking on Earth's door. How she was going to accomplish that, she had no freaking idea. These new powers she had—as yet, unexplored and undiscovered —had to be of help.

She grabbed a large throw pillow from the couch Devon had napped on, still smelling of whiskey and deep woods, hugged it to her face and collapsed on the couch. The faintest whiff of him lingered, and her throat constricted. She didn't have his help anymore.

*Figure it out, Lioness.* The voice speaking the words in her head was his.

Ugh.

One hand dropped off the couch and was almost immediately supported by Minnie's velvety coat. Syd absently rubbed the dog, and it brought her a small measure of comfort.

Exhausted beyond reason, sleep knocked softly at her door. She welcomed it in like a long-lost friend.

SYD'S DREAM billowed around her, like a freshly-washed curtain flapping in a perfect sunny afternoon. There were people standing everywhere. Looking at her. Waiting for her. Looking *to* her.

Her left shoulder tingled, and she knew the truth. This was her army seeking leadership.

Hers. Connected, with varying degrees of strength, to each one of them.

Had they come to her, or was she going to them? The dream was unclear. She searched the crowd, looked for Devon. Did not see him. He wasn't part of the army, though, was he? No. He was so much more.

*Own your decision. It was the right one.*

Shaking herself in the fabric of the dream, she marveled at the presence she had. Her premonitions before were always bad, scary, and she knew she was in them. Now she was aware, and part of that awareness told her this wasn't a premonition. This wasn't something about to happen. It was something *happening*. Right now.

She scanned the crowd again, and looked into the distance, seeing a bright purple-flowered hillside, a rocking chair creaking back and forth. No inhabitant in sight.

She brought her gaze back to the crowd in front of her. Normally, all that male attention would not be a thing of security. But this felt right, she felt at home. She felt... She rummaged through her mind, tried to place this feeling.

The nearest she could come was going over to her grandmother's house, being surrounded by comfort food, being surrounded by...family.

Syd went into the mass of people, her arms held out, beckoning, and allowed herself to be enveloped in their warm embrace.

SLOWLY, Syd became aware of random sounds. A pan clacking. The water faucet gurgling. Hot oil crackling in a pan, ready to be used.

She saw nothing and realized the throw pillow was over her eyes. She pushed it off and was immediately sorry. The sun's direct light shown through the two-story windows of the great room. She winced and raised her arm to cover her face. She had slept with her arm hanging off the couch, and her elbow cried out at the sudden use. Minnie was nowhere in sight.

Syd took a moment to process all the sounds, now with a new one to add to the list: off-key humming.

Good news? No demon.

Bad news? Brie was in her kitchen.

*Son of a bit...*

"Mornin,' sunshine," Brie called from the kitchen, her mysterious radar not missing that Syd had awakened.

Syd didn't respond, sat up, and rested her head in her hands.

"Actually, it's not even close to morning. I'm gonna guess that beautiful man treated you right, and you sleepin' it off in the middle of the afternoon."

Syd raised her head from her hands and stared in the direction of the kitchen. Brie ambled out, leading with a glass filled with something thick and vaguely red in color.

"Hangover?" Brie smiled knowingly. "Got just the thing." Brie thrust the glass out to Syd.

"There's no chance you're getting me to drink that shit again." Syd wasn't hungover, but she did feel a rumble developing deep in her gut from the memory of Brie's notorious hangover-be-over concoction.

Brie let out an irritated humph. "Works like a charm."

Syd's lips curled. "What kind of twisted mind puts together tequila, hot sauce, and raw egg in the first place?"

"Suit ya self, baby girl." Brie shrugged, making her generous bosom ripple with the movement. "Please tell me those two hotties will be back soon."

The memory of Devon's kiss tore through her, misfiring all kind of neurons in the all the right places. Syd looked at her knees and clasped her hands in her lap, trying to get a hold of her body.

"I see." Brie's eyes traveled Syd's face. "Lucky bitch."

But Jack wasn't ever coming back, was he? Grief tightened her throat. Syd rose and stretched. "Can we talk about something else please? Like why you're in my house in the first place?"

Brie shrugged, undeterred. "Benj called me when he couldn't get a hold of you. Your manager is spitting mad you didn' show up to work. So I had to check on you. But when I saw the state you in, I figured you needed rest, a little food, a little comfort, maybe a little Mamma Bear."

"Shit." Her job. Wow, going to work felt like something she couldn't contemplate, something that belonged in someone else's life.

Brie shrugged again and turned back to the kitchen. "I tol' Benj you were sick. He gonna cover for you."

In the kitchen, the buzzer went off on the oven, and a delicious aroma floated around the corner, catching Syd's nose and holding it captive. As disgusting as Brie's hangover recipe was, it didn't detract from the glory of her quiche. Syd's mouth began to water. Like an obedient puppy, Syd followed the aroma back to the kitchen. Minnie was already camped out under the breakfast nook. Wise doggie.

"When'd you get a dog, anyway?" Brie asked, disapproval thick in her tone. Brie's mistrust of canines went back to age five when a friend's dog had decorated her skin with his teeth.

Syd sighed. "Long story."

"Can't you keep it outside?" Brie made a shooing gesture toward the back yard.

Minnie whined and looked up to Syd. Syd couldn't help her smile.

"*Her* name is Minnie, and she stays with me."

Minnie wagged and sat on Syd's feet, rubbing her face against Syd's thigh.

Brie went back to working her kitchen magic, but she kept a suspicious eye on the dog.

Two minutes later, Syd sat at the breakfast nook, staring hungrily at a little slice of heaven, Brie's quiche. The crust, secretly seasoned hash browns, filled with a myriad of toppings and baked with doctored eggs. Not caring she would most certainly be burning her mouth, Syd dug in.

"So," Brie began, tapping her fingers against the table. "He leave?"

No question who the 'he' was. Syd nodded, not looking up from her generous plate of food.

"So, whose truck is in your driveway?"

Syd stopped and looked up. Devon had left his truck? No, then —Jack's pickup. Syd blinked as tightness cramped her throat, making swallowing her heaping bite of quiche nearly impossible.

Brie crossed her arms across her impressive chest. "I was thinking maybe you reconsidered. Maybe you took both on your 'vacation.'" Brie air-quoted. "Or, I was hoping to find Mr. Jackpot here at the house, all alone, and give him some company. Or maybe—"

"Stop," Syd said, devoid of her normal color. She stared at the bite of quiche on her fork.

Her emotions toward Jack were mildly complicated. She understood his position, better than she wanted to. He'd wanted to be done, to be reunited with his deceased wife. After eight hundred years of fighting, who could blame him? Not to mention, regardless of anything else, Jack had saved her life from Bryce, from Malik. So, yeah, she didn't blame him, per se, but at this point she could sure as hell use his help. His or Devon's. She had neither.

Dropping her head, Syd held up a hand and put down her fork. "It's not what you think."

Brie's tone quieted. "Baby girl, what the hell is going on? Your face does not equal orgasms of a lifetime. Tell me what really happened, or I keep drawin' my own conclusions."

Syd pushed her plate away and sighed. There was no one left, was there? The Archangel, Jack, Devon. Her family. All gone.

All her fault.

The memory of her recent dream blanketed her mind, being enveloped in...family. How safe, how *pleasant*. How nearly normal. But that family was far away, possibly not even real. Brie was here, now. The only true family she had left.

"Brie, you know I'm not crazy, right?"

Brie's face turned solemn. She nodded.

"I have something I need to tell you."

---

MORE THAN AN HOUR LATER, Syd finished explaining the sequence of events, which culminated in 'the kiss.' Brie had been silent, an event unprecedented in recent years.

"And then he left," Syd finished. The only thing she had left out was the part about Devon's lineage. It would be unforgiveable to tell anyone, save him, first.

The silence continued to accumulate, stacking upward like a tottering game of Jenga. Syd silent. Brie mute, staring.

Syd grew uncomfortable. "Say something. Other than, 'Get me the number for Arkham Asylum.'"

"Knew Jackpot was too good to be a mortal man, looking like that and knowing his way around a kitchen."

Syd cocked an eyebrow. "After everything I just told you, that's what you say to me?"

Brie nodded. "'Cause you ain't gonna like what I have to say next. Your dad—"

Syd stood abruptly.

"Sit your ass down!" Brie yelled with lips pursed and a finger pushed into a bending point on the table.

Syd sank down into the seat.

Brie cleared her throat. "Now. You gonna listen to what I have to say. Something I been trying to tell you for years."

Syd's hands dropped into her lap, and she fought the urge, the need, to get up and *not* hear what was about to be said.

"Your daddy always knew you were something special. Something your momma never understood proper. He knew enough about your visions to know you were right, that one day, he and Joanna would die in a car wreck."

A tear slid down her cheek, but she was too numbed out to wipe it away.

Brie licked her lips. "He knew it tore you up so bad, knew it would be worse...after. Your daddy was a wise man. He made you promise to live your life. Do you know what he made *me* promise?"

Syd lifted her head and shook it slowly.

"He made me promise that I would help you understand your gifts."

Unable to hold her tongue, Syd bit out, "They aren't gifts! Can't you see that?"

Brie clucked her tongue. "I love you, baby girl, but you need to shut your pretty white-girl mouth. Gifts, yes, *gifts*. You think you been given so much, that's *suppos'* to be easy?"

Syd was silent.

"Your abilities are as much a piece of you as...as your smart-ass mouth. You keep fighting them so bad, you'll tear yourself in two. You've always been powerful. That angel didn't do anything other than force you to see that. Stop fighting yourself and look around. You got other things to fight now."

Her breath shook as it left her body. What if...what if there was no distinction, no abilities, there was only—her? What could she accomplish, if she didn't just room with her abilities in her head, but accepted them and became one?

Brie reached out and grabbed Syd's hand.

Syd was so open, so raw, Brie's feelings poured over her in a wash of hope, sadness, and a touch of desperation. The feelings eroded away at the stone block of stubbornness around her heart.

"I believe you, baby. I believe you so special the angels themselves took notice." Brie gave her hand a light squeeze.

Emotion lodged like a painful thickness in her throat. Syd wanted to be coated in the relief that Brie believed her wacked out story, but she was too shaken from the load of emotional baggage Brie had laid at her feet. Her dad had made Brie promise to watch over her, foster her abilities? He had known—accepted, even—he would die?

Needing distance from the conversation, Syd pulled her hand back and began to clear the dishes from the breakfast nook.

Brie said nothing but rose to help clean the kitchen.

Syd couldn't stop thinking about the years of her life, *years*, spent trying so hard to avoid that freaky piece of her, her abilities. If she could've accepted them, moved past the guilt of believing her parents' death was on her hands. If Devon had been right, the universe was clueing her in, not giving her a vote. Was it that easy?

Sadistic bastard, the universe.

Syd bent over, her stomach cramping. Her twenties, the best years of her life, spent alone and awash in guilt. For nothing.

"You okay, baby girl?" Brie placed a damp hand on her back.

Syd breathed heavily and took a step away from the comforting hand. "I gotta get a shower and change of clothes. Then I'm going to fix this. Devon isn't dying on my watch."

Brie pursed her lips. "What you gonna do?"

Syd shrugged. "I have no idea. But Malik will be back, and, as of right now, he's after Devon. Devon is safest far, far away from the demon. I can't risk him dying to protect me, and I can't risk Malik getting hold of Devon."

Brie put a hand on her hip. "So? How we kill a demon?"

All Syd had ever done was add difficulty to Brie's life. And now she had added another layer to the complication cake, complete with mortal-danger frosting.

Syd shook her head. "No 'we,' Brie. This is mine to do. You wanted me to accept my abilities; well, this is what that looks like."

The only thing Syd knew for certain: the demon was going to have to draw first blood, and she needed to survive it.

# CHAPTER FORTY

S yd paced the cemetery, glancing up at the weakening daylight.
Her skin felt tight around her body, power riding her heavily,
pushing inside her, itchy. Absently, she scratched at her shoulder,
where her new angel ink tingled.

If this was going to work, she had to have her wall solidly in
place. The demon couldn't get a whiff of her angelic promotion, or
he wouldn't take the bait. Whatever else was true, the demons
hadn't wanted the Pledge violated, not yet, and she needed the
advantage.

She glanced at her fingers. They trembled, more from cold and
adrenaline than fear. Fear was a luxury she couldn't afford. Later,
when—if—she survived, then fear could have its moment.

Now, how to summon the demon?

Rafael had assumed a lot. He'd assumed Malik had immediately
run off to tell his demon buddies about Devon, but Syd wasn't so
sure. And if he hadn't? It changed the game immensely.

She closed her eyes, and the burn of the angelic rune on her
back rose up. Instead of pushing it down, she let herself fall into
the burning, into the rune. Sinking to her knees, a vision took root

in her mind. She saw herself and Devon, here in this cemetery not so long ago. But she was watching from another's vantage point. The only other person who had been there had been...Rafael.

Shit. She snapped open her eyes. What was that? Seeing through her Archangel predecessor's eyes?

Wincing at the pain in her back, Syd swallowed and turned a three sixty. She was alone, but knowledge coursed through her. She had asked and now she knew how to do it. Kind of.

Gathering her voice, Syd shouted to the deepening twilight. "Malik! One of Lucifer's own, I summon you here, under law of sanctuary." The words were pulled forth from her, from the rune and not her. Some deep knowledge, foreign and slippery in her mind.

Well, Syd thought, if it worked, she would try anything. After all, she needed to play the desperate human for the demon. Which wouldn't be too far from the truth.

Inhaling deeply, Syd visualized her wall and wrapped herself in brick. The itching and the energy drained away, the crashing tide of power drawing back. Audibly, she pushed out the breath and opened her eyes.

The twilight was fading and quiet, the faintest breeze whispering through the large pines.

Also, there was no demon.

Doubt trickled in—

There. Twenty feet away, the air, it folded and created a night-dark space, from which a large, black-booted foot emerged. Another, followed by a thick robe and finally the demon's twisted features. Grinning.

Loudly, Syd called, "I claim this place as sanctuary."

The air snapped and charged. Then it was quiet again.

Malik's strides were long, and, with each closer step, Syd fought her fight-or-flight.

Fight. That's the only option left. To make Jack's sacrifice mean something. To save Devon. To keep the Pledge.

Malik stopped uncomfortably close, five feet away. "The angel has told you some secrets."

*You have no idea.*

Syd folded her arms and attempted to look intimidating. "You have to leave Devon alone."

"The Archon Guardian?" Malik laughed, the sound booming over tombstones, trees, anything in its path. "The blasphemy, the abomination? Oh, when the Dawnbringer learns of the treasure I have brought him, I will be the right hand of Hell. Why would I ever give up the pursuit?"

Syd stared into the demon's eyes. Well, that checked off box number one, didn't it? Malik had it figured out. Malik *knew.* But had he told Lucifer yet?

"You haven't run to tell all of Hell's legion about your big find?" Syd hedged. Hope brimmed, but she pushed it down. It was a distraction, and it was incredibly premature.

Malik's smile disappeared, his lips slashing into a snarl. "Why would I give any of them the opportunity to take my glory? Something of this magnitude requires proof. Would I try to tell Lucifer this treachery without proof? Nay. I may as well place myself upon the rack. I will bring the Archon to Hell myself. Alive preferably, but in pieces would suffice."

Syd swallowed, and her heart began to race. It could work. She could save Devon. She just had to kill Lucifer's Lieutenant to keep Devon's secret.

Lucifer's Lieutenant. Her hope washed away. The task seemed impossible.

Assuming she could do that, first, she had to get the demon to draw her blood. And not die in the process. She swallowed again, her saliva filling her mouth with a bitter taste.

She closed the distance between them, muscles fighting her will with each step. "You. Can't. Have. Him."

Standing his ground, Malik's features filled with amusement. "You summoned me here, little human, to the place where I cannot kill you, to simply goad me?" Malik gestured around. "Rafael is not here. If you were any prize of his, you would be closely guarded. And you are not. That means you have lost all value to them and are of no value to me. But the Archon fought for you, and it is he I want. You will deliver him to me by true night."

Syd's eyes deadened out, and she craned her neck up, holding onto her wall with vibrating effort, the power wanted to rise against the threat. "Like hell I—"

Malik reached out with his index finger and touched her forehead, the contact making her insides revolt and nausea rise. Her sight timed out, replaced with a vision.

"Oh my God," Syd whispered.

*Brie, bound and gagged, in Bryce's loft apartment. Her shoulder bleeding and her eyes fluttering in pain and panic.*

"Sanctuary applies only here, and to you only." Malik removed his finger, the vision receded, and he spread his hands. "Treading in the affairs of demons, you have much to learn, little human."

He bared his razor-sharp teeth. "You will bring me the Archon, and I will grant you and your friend a quick death, instead of taking you and improving upon your frail human bodies through experimentation in Hell."

Then he was gone.

Syd heaved out a breath, the nausea rose again, threatening to overtake her, but she denied it and squeezed her eyes closed. Sinking down into the cold grass, she pounded her fists against the unforgiving ground and let out a scream.

She had no idea where Devon was. She could call him, but then what? Ask for his help and put him directly back in the line of fire? No. She could do this. She had to save them both.

Syd's eyes sprang open, her mouth set in a hard line. Before her thoughts caught up with her actions, she sprinted back to the Goat, peeling away from the cemetery parking lot. Headed downtown. To Bryce's loft. Driving like a born and bred Detroiter, with little to no regard for stop lights, signs, speed limits, or other impediments of the law, Syd flew down the city streets.

Longest ten minutes of her life.

She didn't allow herself thoughts. Things had gone from desperate to horrendously awful. Brie. He had Brie. And she didn't have Devon. She had no one—

Just get Brie safe.

In her panic, her wall slipped, the thoughts and power spewing out with force. *Just get Brie safe*. The echo of assent from all her Guardians resonated in her head. Without knowing exactly how, she knew they had heard her.

She patched up the wall hurriedly. Stop. Thinking.

The gated parking lot to Bryce's lofts was a small deterrent to any would-be burglar, and the disinterested attendant waved her through without a second glance—not that she slowed down. The Goat tore loudly through the parking lot. She revved the engine to get as close to loft 109 as possible.

Pulling her Glock from the center console, she slammed the door and ran to the steel entry of Bryce's loft. Rounding the corner, she picked up the creepy garden-gnome and huffed out a relieved breath. She grabbed the key and jammed it in the deadbolt. The steel door swung open.

She gripped the gun tight in both hands and stepped inside. She let it click closed. Pressed against the frame, she was in shadow.

It was silent. She looked around, searching for Brie. A bachelor pad, the space maintained the barren impression of a warehouse, all concrete floors and huge windows sectioned into smaller squares. The kitchen was central and all black granite. Two worn leather couches off to her right sat like supplicants beneath a massive flat screen. It was cold enough for her to wonder whether the furnace was on at all. The gun was an unfamiliar weight in her hand. Would it even work against Malik?

Panning back, Syd heard the muffled cry.

Dimly, she was aware Malik could be here and wouldn't just let her take Brie to safety, but her concerned panic trumped everything else. Syd ran toward the sound of the cry.

Brie huddled against the rope and duct tape at the stone kitchen table. Her mouth was bloodied, and her head lolled. The shoulder of her cream-colored silk blouse was soaked crimson.

Syd rushed over, cringing at the sight. She set down the gun and worked with shaking hands to remove the duct tape from Brie's mouth.

Halfway off now, Brie was free to speak, her normally forceful tone tumbled out slurred and subdued. "You shouldn't've come, baby..."

No point in answering. Syd continued to pull the tape free with limited success.

Brie coughed and grimaced, struggling against the binds on her hands.

Syd looked around the kitchen. Second drawer from the wall— a pair of kitchen shears. She grabbed the scissors and Bryce's largest knife, then rushed back to Brie. She dropped the knife next to her gun. With shaking hands, she raised the scissors to the duct tape and nearly caught Brie's thumbs instead.

She stopped.

Her wall slipped a touch, and psychic vertigo caused the room to spin. *Calm down.* A wash of serenity rushed through her, and her hands steadied. The shears cut through the rope and tape easily. Syd holstered the shears in her back pocket.

"Are you okay?" Syd pressed a thumb against Brie's bleeding mouth.

Brie shook her head and pushed Syd's hand away. "Just roughed me up some. Nothing serious. He was all mumbling about you, and the demon comin'."

"He?" Syd was confused. Brie seemed to be talking about two people, demon and someone else.

"Bryce," Brie whispered. "He ain't the way he was, baby. He... something else."

Free now, Brie stood, but wavered, her weight carrying her

back down into the seat. She looked down, as if surprised to find herself sitting again.

"You're not okay. What happened to your shoulder?" Syd moved the soaked fabric back, and the room reeled around her. "He bit you," she hissed. The wounds seeped blood and green-tinted puss.

Brie's voice shook. "We got to bounce before he comes back."

Syd nodded and stooped to brace under one of Brie's arms.

Brie tried to lift herself with Syd's help, but she was nearly dead weight. "Too weak." She placed a hand to her head. "Somethin' he did..." Her eyes darted around the room. "You just...you just go on." Brie's untracking gaze traveled upward to the darkening industrial windows, and her voice got shaky. "You got to go. Bryce said the de...demon would come at dusk."

With more force, Syd tried to pull Brie up. "I'm not leaving you." But moving her injured friend was so not happening.

Brie's eyes drifted closed, and her head slumped forward. Syd's hope drained like a colander trying to hold onto liquid. *No, no...*

The air shifted, inverted, making the air too thick to breathe.

Throughout the loft, a deep bass note like a movie theater surround-sound boom reverberated. Wind whistled through the loft, twisting and moving with terrible speed and bellowing a howling sound.

Syd grabbed the gun in one hand, the knife in the other and whirled around, eyes searching for the threat. She pointed the gun with her, hoping like hell she could hit the target—

"Sydney?" The wispy voice sounded exactly as it had in life.

Joanna Hoven's tall, lithe frame dressed in the dress they had chosen for her funeral. The jeweled cross hung at her neck.

Syd blinked, her weapons clattered to the concrete floor. "Mom?"

The wind stopped, but the silence was worse.

Joanna took a step forward, and a smile tugged at her lips. She reached, arms outstretched, waiting.

From behind Syd, a moan sounded, but Syd had a hard time identifying the sound. She turned her head to look, but Joanna reached out and gripped her face. "Don't worry about anything else, now, Sydney. Be here, with me. I have so little time to help you."

Syd's skin itched from the contact and a confusing smattering of images flickered across her vision. *A castle under a lake, hundreds of tubes of blood, a beautiful woman, a crone.*

"I forgive you, Sydney, for killing me." Her mother released her face, her lips tipped up.

The words cracked along the interior of Syd's skull. "I didn't—"

"I always told you to keep your abilities to yourself, to shield them away from the world. The Devil's work. I *told* you."

"Mom," Syd whispered. "I did. I did what you wanted. I locked them away."

"Not enough, though. Not enough. I'm still dead, aren't I?" Her mom held out a hand, her expression patient. "You must come with me."

Syd's chest constricted and squeezed tight. "Where?"

Joanna Hoven smiled. "Where you belong."

Syd's lungs were still tight, but on a whisper, she pushed out the words. "What do you mean?"

Her mother's face came into view, inches away. Her eyes weren't the warm brown of life, but dark, so dark now. "You can be forgiven. Just tell me where the Archon is."

Syd swallowed, and heartbeats ticked by, rapid fire. Her lungs still weren't working.

Something wasn't right.

Finally, a burst of air as her thoughts came back on line, in time with Jack's words in her head. 'Shapeshifting isn't out of the question. You may think it's Brie, but we'll know for sure.'

*This isn't my mother.*

The unnatural quiet cracked wide open, and Syd heard Brie's screams clearly.

Sheer force of will kept her stock still, and her wall in place.

Keep her, *it*, talking. This is your opportunity.

Syd reached out, with shaking hands. "Mom." She embraced the demon, choking back a gag and smelling the sulphur on the beautiful funeral dress, the mirage exposed for the lie.

Startled, the thing wearing her mother's body obeyed. Enveloped her. Welcomed her.

Syd gripped tighter.

Tighter.

"Give me your hand." Syd whispered.

Her mother's body obeyed, and Syd took the offered hand, pressing the demon's manicured nails into her own palm. She kept her head tucked into her mother's shoulder, not trusting her eyes to keep her intentions quiet.

Syd squeezed, a steadily increasing pressure.

Her mother's body pulled away.

Syd's breathing sped, but she had no option. She held fast.

"Please, mother. I'm so sorry I let you die."

Four half-moon impressions pressed deep, not breaking the skin, not yet. Not deep enough.

Her mother's voice tickled against her hair. "You wish me to hurt you, my daughter?"

Syd's wall vibrated, pulsed with the need to strike back. She pushed out a hissing breath. "I deserve it, don't I? I killed you. It's my fault. Please—"

Her *actual* mother would've reassured her. Pulled away. This mother's body did none of that.

The force in her palm increased, turning to a scratching, sharp pain.

Syd winced, but did not fight the building pressure.

Her skin gave, clear as the snap of bone.

A boom like thunder at close distance shuddered through the warehouse loft, and her left shoulder burned like acid.

Her mother's mouth opened on a loud scream, large, sharp

teeth protruding from her jaw. Syd staggered back, falling against the concrete, stunned as the demon took form before her.

"It is not possible," Malik hissed. "What have you done?"

"*First blood drawn*." Syd scrambled up, showing her palm, slick with four half-moons of blood. Now, to kill him.

Unfortunately, her blade and gun lay useless, on the far side of the demon.

# CHAPTER FORTY-ONE

D evon thrummed the greasy diner counter in front of him, in beat to the vintage hip-hop the crackling speakers belted. He drained the dredges of the coffee, thick and black. The diner was empty, save him and the kid working the counter.

How many times had Devon wished for Rainbow Bright to leave him to his own devices? Countless. Never figured his wish would be granted, and he'd be wishing it was Rafael he still took orders from. Irony, you vicious bitch.

"Yo, you want a warm up?" The teenager working the counter raised a freshly brewed pot.

Devon nodded curtly in answer, pushing his cup toward him.

Syd had told him to go away, stay out of the demon's line of sight, and all he wanted to do was jump in the middle of the damn fray.

Question was, did she have the balls to take him out of service when he disobeyed? Yep, that was a *when*. Not if. And she can't say he hadn't warned her.

"You don't have any whiskey back there do you?" Devon rubbed his temple.

The kid creased his forehead. "Nah, man, we don't sell hooch."

He pointed out the window. "Al's down the street would do you solid, though."

"Caffeine will do the trick for now."

The kid had no sooner filled the cup then Devon drained it, liking the steaming burn, needing the pain to center him. He offered another refill, but Devon held up a hand to decline.

The kid sauntered away, half-heartedly wiping at a stain that had probably been on the counter longer than the kid had been alive.

Devon was back to beating his fingers against the counter. Like he was about to leave Syd and the Guardian Army to fight off Malik alone, regardless of what she said?

Fuck. That.

He wasn't stupid. Reckless, egocentric, brazen to the core. Check, check, and check. But never stupid. The demon had gutted him the last time they'd met, and Jack wasn't around to play Operation on him this go around. He needed to be smart. This wasn't about playing around. This was about surprise and going immediately for a kill.

He needed a blade.

He stood, shrugging his leather back into place.

Where to find a blade? It had been a long time since his mind or his bullets hadn't taken care of his problem demon children.

Clapping a hand on the counter, Devon called, "Hey kid, where can a guy get a sword in this town?"

Drying a plate, the kid looked up with a lifted eyebrow. "Yo, man, whiskey and swords don't mix."

Devon's lips twisted into a wry grin. "I'm foregoing the whiskey for swordplay. Ideas?"

The kid scratched at his tightly curled hair. "I could hook you up with a gun, maybe."

"Won't do for the job—"

The kid laughed. "My kid brother was crazy hyped about the Samurai exhibit at the DIA his class just went to see..."

A Katana would do nicely.

He tossed a fifty on the counter and waited until the kid turned his back.

Twisting toward the door, Devon was about to move through space and visit the Detroit Institute of Arts to borrow a Samurai sword when then the bell above the diner door tinkled, indicating a new player.

The newcomer passed over the threshold, and Devon forgot entirely about the blade.

Devon stood rigidly while his instinct to fight and kill was a beast in his chest, clawing to be let out.

Demon-stink burned Devon's nostrils.

The blond-haired, date-raping, ex-human Devon should've killed three nights ago leaned lazily against the diner booth nearest the door. "Been looking for you, pretty boy. My new boss wants a sit-down." Then he smiled, and it was cruel. "You lose track of Syd? 'Cause I happen to know where she is."

The threat destroyed Devon's control. He moved through space directly in front of Bryce and grasped him by the throat. Rematerializing behind the diner, Devon released the chokehold on his captive and pushed Bryce face first into the litter-encrusted chain-link fence of the alley.

Devon bared his teeth. "Should've killed you days ago."

Bryce spun, hands fisted, and grinned. "Won't be so easy now."

"Because you've been touched by a demon?" Devon sneered. "Bet you liked it, too."

Bryce roared and launched himself off the chain-link.

"You're gonna need stronger cologne to cover the stench," Devon goaded, leaning his body backward. He wanted Bryce thinking he stood a chance. He wanted Bryce thinking he wasn't taking this seriously.

He wanted Bryce in pieces, scattered like trash.

Bryce took two steps toward Devon and produced a switch-blade from his back pocket.

Devon continued, keeping his face relaxed. "That smell's not so appealing to the ladies."

Blade-first, Bryce threw himself forward, crazy fast. Dev pivoted sideways and struck Bryce's forearm, pitching Bryce face-first into the ground. Jesus Christ, these guys were slow learners. The heel of Bryce's hand hit pavement, and the blade skimmed across the concrete.

Bryce rolled onto his back and threw his body in a reverse wave, the momentum helping him gain his feet. Didn't look like it slowed him down a bit. He stalked forward, grinning.

Damn, those formerly human brown eyes were starting to look like pots of ink. The blackness spread, bled over into what should've been white.

Bryce growled.

Not a human sound. Not waiting to witness any more of Malik's upgrades, Devon telekinetically drew the dropped switchblade to himself. He flipped the blade in his hand and advanced on Bryce. Yeah, he had a gun in his belt, but the blade was so much more *personal*. Malik should've considered improving Bryce's hand-to-hand skills. Devon dodged a punch to the face, countered with an uppercut that made real nice contact, snapping Bryce's chin upward, exposing his vulnerable throat.

The next second—the blade. Syd's face flashed through his mind. *Don't do it.*

Sorry, Lioness, you kick me out, and you lose your vote.

He shoved Bryce against the wall. The blade at his throat didn't deter Bryce from opening his mouth.

Bryce sneered. "Thought you were supposed to be protecting her."

Increasing the pressure, Devon spat out, "What the fuck does that mean?"

Bryce snarled. "Malik's with Syd now."

Breath left his lungs, and he couldn't seem to draw in another.

"*Where is she?*" Straight to hardcore compulsion. Bryce's mind warped and twisted around him, the demon upgrades only a mild impediment to Devon's fury and power.

Bryce cackled, blackened spit flying to hit Devon's cheek.

Bryce's Adam's apple pushed against the blade, but his throat worked, choking out the words. "My loft. Unless. Malik. Has ripped her apart already."

Shit. Syd was with Malik? Now? Fuck, *fuck*—

Bryce cracked him a good one, right to the temple. Followed it up with two shots to the kidney and then came the tackle. Disgusted with himself, Devon centered himself on the fight, his focus rubber-banding back into place. This was the problem with emotional attachment. It landed you on your ass in a dirty Detroit alley.

Bryce leaned over his body, both hands coming in. Forming the shape, as if Devon's throat were already in the middle. On his back, Devon threw his head forward, knocked Bryce in the nose, added a little telekinetic push to his punch, flashed himself a few feet back and onto his feet.

Sick of his conscience, which always spoke in Syd's voice, sick of his hesitation, and sick of this *ass*hole, Devon sent his power through the thick barrier of Bryce's demon-altered skull. Disorienting him.

He added a kick to the telekinetic punch of force, and Bryce stumbled backward until he hit the crumbling brick. The air pushed out of Bryce's lungs with a whoosh. Dazed, Bryce stood still, but his arms and legs were quivering, and his lips had ripped upward in a vicious snarl, baring teeth.

Syd needed him, provided she was still alive. Devon flashed over to Bryce. Grasping the back of his head and staring deep, Devon laced compulsion into his next words. "*Where do you live?*"

Body wobbling with the residue of the fight and the compulsion, Bryce clenched his teeth, but slurred, "Lafayette Lofts. 109." He pulled a visual from Bryce's head, so he could move through space directly there.

One more piece of unfinished business.

Devon drew the switchblade telekinetically back to his hand, put it flush to Bryce's neck. "Pity I don't have more time to enjoy this." No hesitation this time. He cut deeply, ripping through the flesh, connective tissue, and muscle. The skin parted, but no blood trickled out. Instead, the same blackness flooding his eyes shone beneath the dissected skin.

"And for good measure, *don't ever come near Syd again.*"

Roughly, Devon shoved the man-no-more away, and the wound sprayed black in its wake. Like a stone, Bryce dropped.

Devon let the blade fall and flashed out of the alley.

# CHAPTER FORTY-TWO

Her mother was gone, and the massive demon stood towering above her. The air felt thick and dirty, as if she had trudged through miles of muck and mud. Syd's lungs constricted, and she eyed the knife, her only option. Guns hadn't worked before. What was it Devon had said, decap or burn? She had no matches, no fire. Too bad she didn't have Devon's telekinesis.

Brie sat directly behind her, unbound but unable to move, mumbling *Hail Mary*'s.

Malik snarled. "Have you any idea what you've done?"

Syd swallowed. "I did nothing. *You* violated the Pledge."

Malik roared, his claws clenching into fists.

"Guessing Lucifer's not gonna be too happy about that."

Malik pulled a massive serrated blade from inside his robe. "It means I also have nothing to lose, and no reason not to kill you."

Syd's adrenaline spiked, raining fear all over her courage.

Malik advanced two more steps, placing him less than ten feet from Syd. "But first, you will tell me where the Archon is."

Syd fisted her hands. Give him Devon? "Not happening."

Faster than Syd could track, the demon tackled her. Her head bounced off the concrete floor, and constellations of pain speckled her vision. His clawed hand pawed her body, made her gorge rise.

She bucked and screamed. The gun and knife lay on the floor near Brie, who was still incapacitated. She grabbed for the shears in her back pocket.

Malik batted the shears away, and his other hand gripped both of hers and pinned them above her head. He tore at her clothes. Malik laughed, enjoying himself and her terror.

"Summon the Archon here. It's him I need. You are nothing more than a weak human, Pledge or no."

*Weak human?* A human would cry. A human would scream as a demon tore them apart. A normal human would succumb.

"Perhaps he will respond to your terror, your pain. You are his master now, after all."

Malik flipped her over onto her back, claws breaking the protective boundary of her skin again. He pushed down on her left shoulder to pin her. The marking on her shoulder flared to life, and Malik hissed like it burned.

She was *not* weak. And right this second? She was damn thankful. Rafael's words echoed around her brain. *Extraordinary.*

She crumbled her psychic wall, and her power flooded the room, finding new depths as she reached into her angelic tattoo. Everything the demon's nasty, dirty energy coated, hers incinerated with its white heat.

Pushing all her righteous pain and fear into her power, Syd screamed, "Hurt him."

Surging forth, the power whipped through the room, energy pouring forth to obey her command.

Deep slash marks appeared on the demon's stunned face. But still he held her hands tight. Her strength was no match for his— outclassed, pure and simple.

He howled a growl, and black blood coagulated in the cuts, steam rising from the wounds.

Shit, her power could do that? Slash and...burn? Could she—

Syd fought harder, her shoulder popping painfully loudly in her struggle. His hand twisted both her wrists harder, and she heard the crunch of a snapping bone. The pain followed a moment later, squeezing like a vise around her wrist. She screamed.

Gravity was doing its dependable work, and, from the cuts she had demanded, demon blood burned her pale skin wherever it touched. Her broken arm. Her face. Her chest.

It hurt, hurt so bad—

Ragged screams tore out of her throat, and she attempted to kick, brawl, buck him off. Anything. She may as well have tried to move Everest off her chest. She screamed again, hoping to direct her power's violence at him, but it was ill-timed. A single drop of demon blood found its way into her mouth.

Foul. Profane. *Get it out, get it out, getitoutgetitout....*

She choked, but was unable to spit, the blood blazing a trail of agony down her throat. Her vision blurred and blinked out like a TV ripped of power.

*Oh God, not now.*

Held in the thrall of a vision, the struggle left her body.

*A castle beneath the lake. An army of monsters, sleeping in an induced state, waiting. Waiting for war. Blue. Everything was blue. Cold...it was so cold. Hell's heat was a myth. Here there was only the chill of death.*

*A magnificently beautiful woman, draped in white, paced in a large dank chamber. As if Syd were having a conversation with her, the woman whispered, "Keep the secret of my children, Guardian. Everything depends upon it."*

Then she was gone, and Syd's vision fast-forwarded her through the halls and dungeons of Hell.

*An immense throne, upon which sat a huge and starkly beautiful Archangel, black-eyed, blond hair. The Dawnbringer, her mind whispered.*

The crack of her skull upon the concrete brought the vision's tenure to a premature and abrupt end. Her throat had spent too much time on a hot barbeque; her head pounded jackhammer-loud.

But the demon had released his hold of her hands.

Fighting her swimming vision and her muscles' weakness, she reared up and grabbed onto the demon's robe, her broken wrist crying out.

"I want you to *burn*," she croaked. She held on with strength born of desperation, drawing into her mind the Packard Plant fire, but she magnified it, her mind wide open and raw. Power crashed out of her in waves, saturating the air. The painful sensations of her body blurred and blended. *Just let go.*

No. *Fuck* no. Panic rose in Syd, and a remnant of the moment her body had kicked her spirit out reared up. She locked herself down, centering herself in the pain of her body.

Her. Body. She wasn't going to lose it now.

The fire in her mind spewed heat like the sun's core. She saw Malik in the middle of it, deep inside the heated, angry inferno. No escape.

Malik's eye went wide in speculation but quickly turned to panic. Flames erupted all around him. From *within* him.

His cry was agony, and Malik dropped the full length of his massive, burning body onto hers.

"Burn," she screamed. Her power filled her to bursting. The wall fully down, it flowed through the room like wildfire.

Her grip on her body slipped. Without thought, she pulled back on the power and clenched her hands so tight into fists her chipped polished nails cut into her skin, puncturing the wounds already there.

Malik's black eyes reflected the flames that licked up his robes. He opened his mouth, to shout, to curse, to scream—but all that came rushing forth was fire, straight from his throat. He pushed his body off her, trying to retreat.

Syd sat up, stars flashing in her vision from her injuries and the quickness of her movement. She tried to grab onto Malik's robe with both hands, found her broken wrist not complying. She put everything she had into focusing the power, through her hand and into him, increasing the heat that ripped through Malik.

Her gaze held the blackness in his, hypnotized by the flames.

*Burn, burn, burn.*

The black face drew closer, closer. His burning body gave up the fight and began to melt.

# CHAPTER FORTY-THREE

Taking form in the courtyard of the Lafayette Lofts, Devon scanned the repurposed warehouse. He searched for 109. Didn't take much of his deductive skills, however. Most likely the one on fire. That, and he could hear Syd's screams from here.

A hand on his arm had him swinging around, fist at the ready.

"Easy, killer." Dutch's good-natured voice raised in surrender, as were his hands.

Devon pulled the punch, and his mind processed what he was seeing. Didn't make sense. Three people. Dutch, Free, and the chick he didn't know. All Guardians. All standing around with their thumbs up their asses.

"Aren't you going to help her?" Devon moved forward, not looking back and not waiting for a response to the clearly frigging rhetorical. Getting inside 109 consumed his entire thought process. They followed.

"We felt her call," Dutch spoke.

"Just got here." Free unholstered one of his guns. "What's your excuse, dick?"

"How could she call us?" Dutch asked uneasily.

No time, not even for the short version. Devon spared a quick glance back to give Free the bird and then flashed himself into the burning loft, though he had no idea what would happen.

Bad. Move.

Smoke had replaced the air in the loft, and he immediately coughed. The dryness burned wherever it hit his skin, but this was no ordinary smoke. It was far too acrid, far too nasty. What the hell was burning? He pushed through the wall of noxious gas by sheer force of will.

"Syd!" he yelled, hoping like hell he would get a response. He automatically dragged air into his lungs and gagged as the foul smoke hit his throat.

"Over here." A faint reply.

He shuffled his feet as quickly as he could. No flashing over to her, not when he had no idea what was waiting there.

He made his way deeper into the building. As if he had entered an alternate dimension, the smoke cleared, and his vision restored itself fully.

Syd knelt next to Brie, who was unconscious and bleeding. She raised those green gems to meet his gaze, and her fierce determination rocked him.

Then he looked behind him.

The fire raged, bright orange flames licking up the wall, the smoke thick. But here, he was in a bubble of protection, extending only far enough to include Syd, Brie and himself.

"What is this?" he whispered.

Syd swayed back and forth, cradling her friend, and murmuring, "It can't burn us. It can't burn us..."

He hated to ask, he really did, but... "What's burning?"

Syd's eyes met his again, but this time the green was glow-in-the-dark bright. She whispered, "Malik."

Devon stepped back, the air leaving his lungs sure as if he had taken a full gulp of the nasty smoke. "You killed him?"

Her dazed expression told him everything he needed to know. "He drew first blood..."

Which meant she was injured. He scanned her, her clothes

torn with bloody wounds peeking through, her hands shaking, her wrist hanging limply—

He needed reinforcements.

He flashed out to the street. Except, when he opened his eyes he was still in the loft, still in the safety of Syd's bubble.

He swallowed thickly, the intensity of her damn near flooring him. She had prevented him from leaving. How the hell—

No time, figure it out later.

He gestured slowly to Brie. "Will you let me take her to safety?"

Syd nodded once, expression glassy with impending shock.

He approached cautiously, really not wanting to spook her. She was too on edge. He picked Brie up as gently as he could and flashed, hoping Syd could control herself enough to let him out. Otherwise, the safety of this bubble was gonna get tested hardcore real soon.

He let out a relieved breath when he appeared outside, Brie's bulk carried easily in his arms. He laid her down in the weedy courtyard and was about to flash back inside for Syd, when Dutch's hand on his shoulder had him reversing direction.

The loft blazed hotter than ever, some of the flames bright blue. Windows shattered. The door swung inward, and Syd appeared in the threshold. Her clothes were torn, and she walked gingerly, as if injured. She supported her left hand with her right, and her head was bowed. But there was no evidence of burns on her body.

"Hot damn," Dutch said reverently from behind him.

Devon cleared his throat. "There's something you should know."

Time to rock the world of the Guardian soldiers.

# CHAPTER FORTY-FOUR

Syd staggered out of the burning loft, and her eyes weren't tracking. They clouded over, making her stumble. All she could see was Malik, on top of her, flames engulfing him from inside. Her insides twisted around.

She shook her head, and the vision came loose. Devon stood with several other people, Brie on the ground, unconscious.

He was safe. Devon's secret was safe.

At her approach, the people began to drop to their knees one by one. Confused, she sought Devon. More gently than she had ever seen him, he lowered himself down on one knee and bowed his head.

"I don't understand." Her voice cracked from all the recent screaming and acidic demon blood.

"We are yours to command, Captain." Freelander—it was Freelander from Byrne's house. She stared harder, willing her mind to make the connection. The rope of connection tugged like a cable against her battered spirit. She was connected to him. He was—hers.

And yet—

Syd pulled back at the title. "I'm not...."

"Leader?" Dutch called out tentatively.

She shook her head. "No."

The sole woman, Valentina, spoke gently, mocha-dark eyes masking none of her intelligence. "Sister?"

Syd's knees began to buckle. A facet of family through all her longing she had never hoped to have. Tears welled, the internal barrier of sorrow cleaving and breaking.

Before she hit the ground, hands supported her weight, taking her burden. Strong hands gripped each arm, braced her back. Through her tears, Syd nodded. "Sister."

They released her when she seemed able to stand, and Devon hugged her hard. He planted a kiss on the top of her head that sent happy chills all the way to her toes. "You are our...*my*...lioness."

# EPILOGUE

Syd stared at the cast on her left arm. She rapped it with the fork in her hand.

Yep, it was real. Solid.

Basically, the opposite of the previous evening. Evening being way too polite to describe the sequence of hours when a demon took her best friend hostage, she had incinerated him, and she had saved Devon's terrible secret.

Syd took a deep breath, trying like hell to refocus her attention on the meal in front of her. Her stomach hadn't gotten with the program, though. She wasn't hungry, couldn't imagine ever being able to stomach a meal again.

"Syd?" Dutch's voice was soft as he called from the kitchen doorway. "You might need to intervene out here."

Grateful for the interruption, she let the fork clatter to the plate and followed him into the great room. Devon and Free stood face-to-face, the anger radiating like UV rays off the sun.

"You disobeyed orders," Free spat.

Devon's lips lifted into a sneer. "No worries. Syd, your new Captain, already kicked me out."

Disbelief on his face, Dutch whipped his head back to face Syd. "Is that true?"

"Well, yeah, I suppose for a minute—" she stammered, gingerly holding her casted arm.

Devon raised his hands. "Told you." Then he faced her, his whole body stiff. "Can I speak with you a minute?" He glanced pointedly at Free and then Dutch. "Alone."

Dutch turned to look at her, and Free did the same.

All the scrutiny had her confused. "What?"

Dutch cleared his throat. "Do you want us to leave?"

Permission. Holy shit. They were asking her *permission* to leave. This leadership gig was something she was definitely going to have to get used to.

"Yeah, of course," Syd murmured.

Devon pointed a finger toward the foyer and began walking. He reached the front door, opened it and gestured her outside. She stepped outside, breathing in the October brisk air.

His face was serious, hiding something deeper she could only guess at. The fact the mask was back was bad enough. "Bryce won't be an issue. I gave a serious attempt to separate his head from his body, compelled him for good measure to never think of you again."

Devon stood still, tall body and long arms hanging idly at his side, the cold not seeming to affect him.

She tried to approach him then. She wanted the distance that had wedged between them since she'd dismissed him to dissolve. Reaching, she tried to stroke his face.

He stepped back but kept her eyes captive with his. His expression hardened further.

"Thank you," she whispered, frozen in place by his rejection, but needing him to know she could never repay him, all the same.

He snorted. "I should be thanking you, Syd."

"What do you mean?"

Ignoring her, he continued. "I wanted you to know about Bryce. Also, you were right to kick me out. I'm not a good soldier."

"Devon, wait—" His reasoning was messed up on so many levels. His secret was on the verge of spilling out of her. He was nearly gone, she could feel it, and only something drastic would keep him.

"I won't get in your way, but don't think I'm some puppy you can call to heel whenever you feel like it. That won't end well for either of us."

"Dev, it doesn't have to be like this. There are things you don't understand—Rafael told me—"

He paused, his masked expression cracking. "I can't hear it, Syd. Not from you."

Then he disappeared.

"Damn it," she whispered.

———

AWAKENING, Syd stretched, and dull pain traveled through the cast on her arm. The sunlight floated in through the bay window of her bedroom, but not due to the lateness of the hour. October was nearly over, and winter's tide rolled in, washing away more and more of the daylight hours.

A week had passed since Syd had immolated Malik.

"Knock, knock." The soft female voice that carried over to her had become familiar. Valentina.

"C'mon in." Syd yawned.

Any pretense of privacy had been erased after the Malik show-down. Her powers were too spastic and new for any of her 'army' to concede she could truly handle herself—by herself. Dead demon wasn't evidence enough, apparently. They didn't trust that the demon-melting thing hadn't been a fluke. Maybe it had.

But on the plus side, things had calmed tremendously. Whole days had passed without her heart rate rising at all, or her feeling like she might be ripped right from her body. Progress. Well, progress in some departments. The dealership had called after two days of no-call, no-show. She was jobless. Unless she went back to work at the House of Cards. Captain of an angelic army she might be, but she still had bills to pay.

Valentina studied her. "You okay, Capt—I mean, Syd?"

The Guardian Army was trudging through a serious adjustment period.

She smiled at Valentina. The woman was all reserve, and she blended into the background perfectly. A perfect spy, which Syd had learned, had been exactly what she'd been. Before she'd become a Guardian soldier.

"Yeah, I'm good."

Valentina nodded and glided out of the room.

Syd's smile faded, and she looked anxiously toward the window.

She had fought Malik. She had killed him, keeping Devon's secret. But Hell was in violation of the Pledge. If she chose to take issue with the violation, which of course she wouldn't.

Still, she had spent the past week waiting for a deluge of disgusting creatures to overrun Earth. Maybe Rafael had kept his word and not told Hell the Guardian Army had been through a regime change.

Nothing had happened. Yet.

She turned her thoughts away from the problem and tried to ground herself in the present. She had invited the Guardians to stay at her house if they wanted. Dutch and Free had looked uncomfortable until she figured out they weren't used to making their own decisions. She was supposed to tell them what to do, which made *everyone* uncomfortable.

News of Jack's release from service had spread, the soldiers all seemed to feel it a greater loss than Rafael's...um, retirement. There was no man she had met who hadn't respected Jack, no woman who hadn't adored him.

And Devon hadn't come back. She swallowed down her hurt. She had no clue what he was thinking, but then, she never really had.

Other random people—her soldiers—kept showing up. Her substantial digs would need to be upgraded to a hotel soon if they kept up this pace. The trend had become routine. The doorbell would ring, she would answer, they would kneel and say something to the effect of 'reporting for duty.' Then it would get silent and a little weird.

Her psychic call had touched a number of her soldiers, and she seemed unable to replicate the action to tell them to stand down. So they kept showing up. After awkward introductions, they usually went back to whatever they'd been doing before.

Syd threw back the covers. Her only plans for the day included visiting Brie at the hospital. The doctors weren't sure exactly what ailed her, or what had attacked her, but supportive care seemed to be slowly doing its job. Prognosis was good.

An hour later, Syd had showered, dressed, and twisted her long locks into a messy bun. The cast on her arm made everything take ten times as long. She hopped down the main stairs.

The doorbell rang.

All righty, here we go. Again.

"Got it!" she yelled, seeing a massive form on the other side of the frosted glass.

The power hummed behind her wall, a happy little camper, so the new arrival was a friendly.

The door swung inward, and Syd gaped.

"Syd?" The voice was deep and kind, as usual, in utter opposition to his Mr. Universe physique.

"Jack—" A complicated mix of feelings swelled up in her gut. Jack had left her with Rafael. Yeah, he'd been acting under Rafael's orders, but that hadn't changed the outcome, had it? Then there was the whole 'he was supposed to be dead' angle to consider. In reality, he wasn't a Guardian soldier. He was a hybrid. So maybe the rules didn't apply? She couldn't think about Jack without thinking about Devon, too. Her thoughts could be poster children for chaos theory.

"Syd, I am...so sorry. I didn't know." Jack's shades shielded whatever emotion was in his eyes, but his stance was hunched, and his white tee and ripped jeans were rumpled. He dropped onto one knee, his head on his knee. "I am at your mercy."

An angel, offering her his service. Humbled. She was so humbled.

"Look at me, Jack." Syd let her hands hang loosely at her sides, the door now wide open against the elements.

He dropped the duffle bag he carried, and he took off his sunglasses. His expression was earnest. Open. Raw.

The secret would have to come out. She would be the one to deconstruct his entire life, and with only one sentence. *You're an angel.* She couldn't lie to him for years on end like Rafael had. But there was so much she didn't know, and Rafael's way had kept them safe for so long.

"Syd?"

She held her arms out, an invitation and an apology in advance.

His heavy arms wrapped around her, lifting, and holding her weight easily.

"Looks like we both put our trust in the wrong people." He clutched her, his grip bordering on *ouch*, and his mouth moved against her shoulder. "I understand if you can't forgive me."

"Do you know what happened?"

He shook his head, still pressed into the tight embrace. "Nothing after Rafael...but you feel different."

She stayed there, hanging off his body, a tiny ornament on a massive Christmas tree, and he walked into the house.

"LT?" Syd recognized Dutch's voice from behind her, but the tremor running through it was new.

She dislodged herself from Jack's embrace, hopped down and turned around. Tears ran a trail down Dutch's face, but he seemed cemented in place.

"How is this possible?" Dutch breathed.

Jack shook his head. "I don't know. Other than Rafael lied to me."

Dutch dragged in a stuttering breath. "I've never been more grateful for a lie."

"Jesus, boys. Hug already." Syd added a few choice words to hurry the process.

Jack smiled wide.

Soon, both men were laughing and clapping each other on the back. Everyone in the house had come to see what the commotion was about. Damn near a crowd, actually.

Jack turned his attention to her. "What happened?"

Syd grabbed his hand and led him further into the house. After guiding him to the loveseat, she pulled him down next to her.

Next, the detail deluge. And yeah, there were a lot of blank spaces to be filled in. When she got to the part about her leading the army, Jack's jaw dropped slowly. She ended the catch-up and shrugged. "What about you?"

It took him a minute.

"I healed Devon so much, I think I was as close to death as I can get. Rafael... He sent me back to my house up north. Not... Not to—" Jack cleared his throat. "I was basically comatose." He stared at her, and she could see the truth in his words. "I came as soon as I possibly could."

She looked away. Rafael didn't have the power to take Jack from Earth because the Archangel had never had any real power over him. No one held that knowledge but her. And Jack and Devon's safety depended upon it.

The memory of burning demon blood on her tongue surged up. Now Malik was dead. Devon being an Archon remained a secret only she knew. Jack's secret, too. A hybrid human-angel. Yeah, that knowledge was under firm lock and key in the Fort Knox of Sydney.

Jack dropped his head and apologized again.

"It's okay. It's *so* okay. I'm just glad you're here." She forced a smile.

Seeming to remember, Jack searched the room, and not seeing what he was looking for, he addressed Syd. "Dev?"

Not trusting her voice, she could only shake her head. She

stared at her lap for a heartbeat longer, and Jack lifted her casted left wrist.

"Let's see what we can do about this."

A small saw from the garage and about five minutes later, Syd stared at her left hand, flexing easily and without pain. "Thank you."

Jack smiled and squeezed her hand. "He'll be back, Syd. I've never seen him care for and protect anyone the way he did you. Not anyone, ever. His pride may be hurt, but he's too contrary not to come back."

Syd smiled weakly. "I'm just not sure it will make a difference."

Jack shrugged. "With your new position, you could always make him come back."

Her reply was immediate and vehement. "Never gonna happen. I wouldn't do that to him. Not to any of you." Shaking off the thought, Syd rose from the chair and held out her hand. "In the meantime, I have a few things on my plate."

"Oh?" Jack gripped her hand and pulled himself up to towering above her.

She looked up into his warm blue eyes, wondering what the future would hold.

"I have an army to lead."

# ACKNOWLEDGMENTS

They say writing a book is a solitary endeavor. It can be, and it was for the first couple years of my journey with this book. But since then I've learned that it's so much sweeter when you share the ride.

Sometimes you need someone in the trenches alongside you, sometimes you need someone to crack the whip, and sometimes you need a cheerleader to just believe in your story. Sometimes you get special people who will do all three and then some. It's overwhelming and breathtaking, that type of support. It's the type that holds you up against the tide when you're convinced this thing will never work, is the dumbest idea ever put to paper, and you need to find the nearest incinerator for your contaminated hard drive. To C.C. Dowling, Nikki Goodwin, Kara Leigh Miller, and my incomparable agent, Sarah Younger. Without each of you, I sincerely doubt I'd be holding this debut in my hands. I'm more thankful than you'll ever know.

To my first editor, Teresa Crumpton, at AuthorSpark.org. Thank you for offering just the right mixture of compassion and common sense and for giving me the courage to allow someone else to read my words. Without that gentle but firm push, I'm not sure I ever would have.

And then there's the larger writing community. It would be impossible to list everyone. To all groups I've been fortunate to be a part, The #Pitchwars community, the Table of Trust, Greater Detroit RWA, Detroit Working Writers, and all the people I've connected with at conference or retreats. The writing community is like no other. Thank you.

And to my husband who has yet to read a word I've written and still believes in me.

## ABOUT THE AUTHOR

Amy Sevan is a lifelong Metro Detroit resident, has too many dogs, and loves fast cars in obnoxious colors.
Find her on the newfangled internet:

Facebook.com/AmySevanBooks

Twitter.com/AmySevanBooks

Or, better yet, sign up for her newsletter to get freebies and more at her web home here: AmySevan.com

If you enjoyed PLEDGE OF ASHES, please consider leaving a review. It would really help an author out.

Look for Book Two of the Rise urban fantasy series, CURSE OF ASHES, coming mid 2019.

CPSIA information can be obtained
at www.ICGtesting.com
Printed in the USA
LVHW011558130519
617637LV00001B/187/P